OTHER GODS

OTHER GODS

GODS

by Pearl S. Buck

New York

P. F. COLLIER & SON
CORPORATION

THIS BOOK is dedicated in true humility to all those hapless human beings whom their fellow creatures, by one accident or another, for a moment or for eternity, have made into gods. A few have been great enough to endure godhead; most of them have not. It has not mattered whether they could endure it because they themselves have been of no importance to those who chose them for worship. They were made symbols and when they were compelled to this unearthly shape by that most powerful force on earth, the desire of men for a god, they were lost. No one will ever know such a one as he was meant to be, any more than anyone will ever know as a human being the Dalai Lama in Tibet, yesterday an old man, today a child. What he might have been as a man, a husband, a father, the citizen of a state, he will never be. His life as an ordinary man among men has been taken from him and the loss to him, as to all other gods, is irreparable.

In the pages to come he is called, for convenience, Bert Holm. The name does as well as any. Readers may say he is like this one or that one of those they know. He is none. In so far as he is like one he is like all, as the woman who tries to be his wife is the type of all sensitive, true women who marry gods unaware. For such gods are alike. If they had differences in the beginning the differences are soon obliterated, as in some countries the faces of stone images, which people set up for worship, are worn smooth and similar by the touch upon them of millions of adoring, pleading hands. And this resemblance is not only in the faces of gods. In their hearts is a common bitterness, whether the hour of their godhead was long or short and whether they loved or despised it.

Although the theme of this novel is a part of American life as it is today, none of the characters represents any actual individual and the story is entirely imaginary.

OTHER GODS

I

AMONG the ranges of the Himalayan mountains there stands a certain lofty peak well known to mountain climbers but long unexplored. As lofty as others more famous, it presented a repellent face to those men who are urged, by what they do not know, to leave the lower surfaces of earth where people live, to ascend to peaks where people cannot live because they pierce too high a heaven. Therat, though not as high as Everest, yet was far too high for pleasure climbing. Mountain climbers looked at its high shouldered shape, fortressed with cliffs, and then said, "If we are going to climb Therat we might as well try for Everest," and because Therat thus fell between Everest and other peaks a little lower, it remained unconquered until a certain afternoon in July, in a year now well remembered, when Bert Holm, a young American, climbed the icy crag which was Therat's crest and reached its top alone.

That this feat might have anything to do with glory did not occur to him, partly because his imagination never carried him beyond the moment and partly because once he had reached the top and was coming down again, he grew alarmed at what Sir Alfred Fessaday, the head of the British Meteorological Expedition to Therat, might say about it.

This alarm grew acute toward the end of what had in the morning promised to be one of those Himalayan days which seem to have no end, so early is the sunrise, so late the sunset. It was that promise which had given him the impulse to desert the others and climb alone when it appeared that the expedition could not go on.

Bert Holm had no business to be on the mountain at all. He was nothing but the mechanic whom Sir Alfred had brought along to manage the two specially built American caterpillar trucks and he ought properly to have stayed with those trucks when they stopped in the foothills. But he had known since the beginning that when the time came he was not going to stay with them. When the expedition started up the mountain he appeared before Sir Alfred, his greasy cap in his hand, and upon his young and extremely handsome face a grin which Sir Alfred found, in the kindness of his secretly soft English heart, an argument not to be easily denied.

"Ah, Bert Holm," he remarked with reserve. Whenever he felt this softening under his ribs he guarded himself.

"Could I speak to you, Sir Alfred?" Bert inquired.

"You may," Sir Alfred returned.

"Please, sir, could I go up the mountain with you?"

Sir Alfred was amazed. A mechanic, a youth who had never climbed, jeopardize the success of this venture, whose important members, except the meteorologist, Nevil Lane, were all trained Himalayan climbers and officers of the British Himalayan Club?

"Certainly not," he said, looking away from the young man's face and over the bleakly beautiful Tibetan countryside beyond his tent door.

"I've climbed a lot at home," Bert said earnestly. "I climbed everything in New York State that was higher than a hill and then one summer I ran away from home and climbed in the Rockies. Another year I climbed Pike's Peak and Rainier."

"This is a scientific expedition and not merely a climbing party," Sir Alfred returned. "Besides, you were brought along to look after machinery."

"I know what you brought me for, but it ain't exactly what I come for," Bert retorted with a trace of stubbornness.

Sir Alfred looked at the young man again. So far as he knew

4

he had not heard Bert say anything on the whole journey. He gave way to a slight curiosity.

"Why did you come?" he inquired.

"To climb," Bert replied simply.

Sir Alfred was silent. He was something more than a scientist and he knew it. A mere scientist would not at this moment be in a tent pitched outside a filthy Tibetan village. He would have been in a comfortable laboratory in England. Sir Alfred was first of all a lover of mountains, and because he thoroughly distrusted love in any form he justified its indulgence only by something as practical as science. That was why he had brought Nevil Lane, although his better judgment had told him that Lane was not fit for mountains. "You like climbing, do you?" he asked, pulling the lobe of his right ear as he always did when in doubt.

"I'd rather climb than eat," Bert replied, and added with a fresh grin, "And I'd rather eat than anything else."

There was an extraordinary charm in this chap, it occurred to Sir Alfred. He had not noticed it before except to approve the tirelessness of Bert's tall square-shouldered frame. But now the charm could not escape notice. It poured from him, a compound of youth, extreme and obvious beauty, health and simplicity, all totally uneducated, of course, and yet somehow needing no education in its unconscious self-sufficiency. "The chap seems at home anywhere," Sir Alfred thought, and liked him. He coughed and blew his nose tremendously. Two dirty little Tibetan children who had been peeping from the door fled.

"You won't ask any special favors?" he said sternly to Bert.

"No, sir," Bert replied promptly. So the old man was going to let him go!

Sir Alfred gave up to his heart. It was a fortunate thing he had no sons, he told himself; he'd have spoiled them.

"Very well," he said shortly, turning to his papers. "Only mind you, I don't want to hear anything from you—don't want to know you're on the mountain."

"No, sir," Bert said joyfully and disappeared.

He had known so little that Bert was along that when a week later, eight hundred feet from the top of Therat, Nevil Lane developed pneumonia, so that the expedition had to turn back, he had not missed Bert Holm until they set up camp that night. It had been a wretched camping place, but Lane had been too ill to make the further one. The Tibetan porters had fumbled over the tents and wept with the cold and moaned about the danger from the Mirka, the fantastic Snowmen who they believed inhabited the mountains.

"Where's Holm?" Sir Alfred shouted.

It appeared that Holm was nowhere. No one had seen him all day. And Sir Alfred himself, exhausted with anxiety over the responsibilities of the moment, lost his temper and shouted:

"Trust the Americans not to be there when you want them——"

But Holm did not appear even to deny this, and there was nothing for Sir Alfred except to go out himself and threaten the porters into obedience, while secretly he pitied their terrors. Therat was more terrifying by night than ever, and the enormous solemn moon, rising over the snowy ranges, only added the terror of pale cold light. He went into the sick man's hut and between his attentions worried himself to nausea about Bert Holm, lost undoubtedly upon some slope of Therat's icy breast. That he was also irritated did not lessen his worry.

At a little after midnight he heard someone at the flap of the tent and he went out. There in the unearthly brilliance of the sinking moon he saw Bert Holm. He could have wept with relief, for Lane was certainly worse, and so he grew intensely angry.

"Where have you been, sir?" he roared at Bert.

"To the top," Bert replied.

"Nonsense!" Sir Alfred cried.

"Yes, I was there," Bert said.

6

Sir Alfred stared at him. The chap was shaking with exhaustion. His face, even in the moonlight, looked burnt to a crust with snowlight. But he knew the look in the eyes. It was the right look, and his heart quivered.

"You may consider yourself dismissed for insubordination the moment you get back to the machines," he said. "You will be responsible for yourself and not return with me to England."

"All right, if you say so, Sir Alfred." Bert returned Sir Alfred's haughty stare with peaceable mildness. Nothing could happen now to make him care one way or the other.

"I guess I'll go home by myself then, Sir Alfred," he remarked, "now that I've done what I wanted to do."

That was how Bert Holm came to go back by way of China.

Everybody in America knew, in a few weeks, what Bert Holm had done. People drank the story of it into their thirsty souls. For what he had done in that peculiarly dispiriting year took on a passionate symbolism for them far beyond its actual meaning. People were disillusioned, and frightened because they were disillusioned. Something had been lost, they said, out of life, something good and young and full of hope. The world was terrifying in its confusion. At least nothing was clearly right or wrong in the good old simple way.

Then across the miasma of general hopelessness had come the story of Bert Holm. Thousands of people lifted up their heads. A hero? There was a short hesitation over this. Some asked could one be a hero at mountain climbing? Others answered why not? The poles were discovered, the oceans were flown, and man had not yet devised the means of exploring the stars. The great peaks of the Himalayas were all that was left unattained upon the earth, and Bert Holm had climbed one of the greatest, for only Everest and Pangbat were higher than Therat, and Bert was a hero. He had defied glacier and crevasse and the dangers of avalanche, and alone in his own way he had done what

7

a seasoned expedition had not been able to do. Even if pneumonia had been the cause for its failure, that did not change the fact of Bert Holm's success. To succeed was proof. He was an American. The old spirit was not dead after all, though it had been too long since there had been a hero in a nation that must have heroes. They had made many heroes—heroes in pioneering, heroes in war, heroes in exploring and in aviation. Here was the latest hero—a new sort, a hero of the mountains. In the old days he would have planted the American flag upon the top of Therat. In their imagination Americans saw it there now.

Who was he? With quickened millions of people clamoring to know, Bert Holm, taken by surprise by reporters at Singapore and Hong Kong, Shanghai, and Peking, said shyly that he wasn't anybody.

How did they know about him, he asked himself suspiciously. "Say, what's your game?" he demanded. They roared with laughter, not believing in his innocence. When they perceived he was not pretending they explained that Sir Alfred Fessaday had mentioned something in Calcutta, and an American reporter, catching it up, had cabled a story to New York immediately; and newspapers, quick to feel the popular pulse, had demanded by cable full details of Bert Holm's past, that they might know what were the materials from which this hero was to be made.

The materials were good. His father was a farmer, he said, near the town of Misty Falls in upstate New York, but he himself didn't like the farm much. After he finished high school, he found a job in a garage for a while. But he never liked it. More than anything else he liked climbing. He had planned if he had not come on this trip to climb down Niagara Falls some day, underneath the falls somehow, maybe in winter when the water was frozen. Misty Falls itself was near deep gorges and he used to climb around the cliffs a lot.

Over and over he had told the same quiet story, never adding to it or changing it. He hadn't, he said, really done anything any-

8

way to make a fuss over—it was only that having come so far to climb a mountain, he didn't like to go home without doing it.

But a fire, long prepared and ready for any flame, caught this, and America began to worship Bert Holm. When Sir Alfred said it was extremely dangerous to go alone like that to the top of Therat, Americans reading their newspapers snorted and said of course it was dangerous, but so had the American Revolution been dangerous! Besides, Bert Holm had done it, hadn't he, and come down safely again. It was crazy, but that was American too.

And Bert Holm said yes, it was crazy, he guessed, but then he had always done what he wanted to do without asking if it were crazy, or not, if it was what he wanted to do.

And millions of people cried out that this was American, this youth, this simplicity and courage and modesty. He gave them back their hope in themselves and they began to believe all they wished to believe about him. There was always someone to tell a new story about Bert Holm and the story flew from mouth to mouth, and there was no one to ask whether it were true or not, because no one in his heart wanted to know the truth. Truth was sad and without romance; truth made them face the fact that theirs was not a good world or a perfect country and that they themselves were therefore insecure. They thrust truth aside and did not want to know it. Instead they clamored to know what he believed, and out of what he said they made their new commandments.

"Bert Holm Says Japs Want To Fight U.S.A.," the newspaper headlines told them; "Bert Holm Declares National Defenses Weak," "Bert Holm Considers Airplanes Dangerous," "Bert Holm Believes World Needs Religion." Whatever he did, whatever he said, people took it and wove it upon the loom that made magic garments for Bert Holm.

Thus every small thing about Bert Holm was their material. He was not married. The first thing the reporters had asked him was, "Are you married, Mr. Holm?" To which Bert Holm had answered shortly, after a scarcely noticed pause, "No, I'm not." And then he had gone on to say he hadn't had time for girls— much. And this added to the people's worship. He was pure, in a time when people were beginning to sicken of their own impurity and to be afraid of their own wickedness, having still some buried remembrance in them that once they had been taught that there were those things, now outworn, called sin and hell.

They clamored for Bert Holm to come home where they could see him, though the papers were full of his photographs. He was tall and blond and good-looking in the way they loved best. His blue eyes looked out of a face naturally grave until a child's smile changed it completely, and his fair hair was always tumbled. His picture was taken in Shanghai in his climbing outfit, against an artificial background, and out of such Himalayan snows he looked at the millions who looked at him at breakfast tables and on subways and in offices and trains and homes. And in the rooms of many lonely women, old and young, he looked at them out of cheap frames they bought for the pictures they cut out of newspapers. "He's sweet!" they murmured, each to her own heart, dreaming.

He was due home in September. He wasn't going to hurry, he said. Everybody told him he ought to see Peking as long as he was in China. And people, reading, restrained themselves, and smiled. He was not going to be spoiled, then, as sometimes their heroes had been. They could safely pour out their worship and they gloried in the way he went on being simply the honest mechanic. Their warmth overflowed into organizing Bert Holm clubs everywhere to collect money for the hero, to welcome him home, until the president of the American Alpine Club, alarmed at the possibilities of Bert Holm's not getting all that was given, organized a central bureau for collection and announced that when Bert came home he would find himself a rich man.

And of course no one cared anything more about what Sir Alfred Fessaday had to say. It remained for Sir Alfred only to declare the expedition officially closed. Later, he announced, he would attack the mountain again with his properly accredited scientists, since the purpose of the trip was purely scientific. Sometimes in a small group Sir Alfred went further to say that it had been of no scientific value that young Holm had rushed to the top alone, and that there was no definite proof that the chap had ever really reached the top, though he did not doubt he had. There was no reason to believe he was dishonest. And except for the cold and the altitude, the roughest climbing was over where they had encamped when Lane was taken so ill. From there on the climb was gradual, at least until the last hundred feet. Weather conditions were, of course, frightful, and in mountain climbing he had never felt he could take responsibility when it was obviously dangerous for his men to go on. He preferred to stop and do it more safely and slowly, since his were scientific expeditions and not stunt trips. Besides, when so valuable a man as Nevil Lane was threatened with pneumonia it was his duty to bring him down. Undoubtedly his life had been saved by the decision.

But publicly Sir Alfred said nothing like this. He merely smiled and agreed when he was called upon for enthusiasm about Bert Holm. Bert was a good mechanic, and one had to say he put on no side whatever about what he had done—had run like a hare, in fact, from the reporters and photographers in Calcutta, at least. Undoubtedly the chap had had no idea what was waiting for him in America. When they asked Bert Holm what he was going to do when he got home, he said he didn't know.

The day was hot in Peking. Over the city there hung a vague moist cloud, unusual to that city even in August, and as noon drew on it sank slowly of its own weight into courtyards and alleyways. It penetrated even the foreign quarter where the hotels were, and carried its faint stench into the large comfortable room where Mr. and Mrs. Tallant and their daughter Kit sat in silence, dressed in the thinnest possible garb. The silence was partly exhaustion after a morning of sight-seeing, but partly, too, it was a family understanding that when one was absorbed, one was not interrupted.

Mr. Tallant, however, was restless. He rose and roamed about the room, smoking a cigar and glancing now and then at his wife. She had the newspaper he wanted to read and he was impatiently waiting for her to get through with the society news in order that he might examine the really important financial columns. He had somehow to make up his mind how to cable his bank directors in New York on the matter of a Chinese loan, when silver was dropping every day like a weighted parachute under the threat of Japanese invasion. He pulled at his already open collar.

"I do believe even the climate is worse here in Peking than it used to be!" he said.

Mrs. Tallant did not hear, but Kit looked at him with her slow slight smile that seemed always to come from such a depth in her that when it reached the surface of her dark eyes and soft full lips, it brimmed but scarcely stirred them. Kit was sitting at the small Chinese table which served as a desk, writing in her book. She looked cool in her lounging pajamas of clear yellow silk, but then she always looked cool on the outside. Her father knew her well enough to know it was merely external, though he pretended to no great knowledge of women, being fixed in the common conviction of men that women were not to be understood by rational beings. Nevertheless, though he disliked women in general, he was fond of his own wife and his daughters without feeling any necessity or indeed desire to understand them. He was too busy a man for that sort of thing.

"Aren't you about through with that paper, Dot?" he asked Mrs. Tallant in a voice that was mild by habit.

Mrs. Tallant apparently did not hear this, but she suddenly looked over the top of the paper at her daughter.

"Bert Holm is in Peking, Kit!" she exclaimed.

Kit Tallant did not answer. She was listening to something that neither of her parents heard. Out of the confusion of street noises beneath the open window her ear had plucked a wiry thread of tantalizing melody played upon a two-stringed Chinese violin. She stopped writing and drew a few hasty lines and bars and jotted down notes. Then the unseen musician turned a corner or entered a door and took his melody with him. She listened, thinking, "Now I'll never know the end!"

"Kit, did you hear me say Bert Holm is here?" her mother inquired.

"Yes, I did, Mother," she said. She put down her pen and lit a cigarette. Listless as she felt, it was no use pretending she had not heard the name of Bert Holm. She was gently interested to find that now, though she was too modern to believe in eternities, even a slight curiosity stirred in her. Not for a long time, months at least, had she felt that small curiosity about any man's name. She was still in love with Norman and saw no hope of not being in love with him except that she knew anything ended, of course, if one could only weather it to that point of its conclusion.

"Did you know Bert Holm was coming to Peking?" Mrs. Tallant inquired now.

"No, I didn't, Mother," she replied.

Mrs. Tallant yawned and tapped her mouth with her hand. No one could possibly have mistaken her nationality. Her fresh good looks, though she was not really pretty, the energetic lines of her body even in repose, and her pleasant but slightly domineering air announced her American by birth and long breeding. "I'm crazy to see him after all the fuss he's made," she said laughing a little at herself. She yawned again and handed the newspaper to her husband, smiling with wifely tolerance. "Al-

13

ways the good old business man," she said cheerfully. She reached to a small table near her for a cigarette and an old magazine. "Well, don't let me bother anybody, but it's awfully hot, isn't it!"

"Broiling," Kit agreed, and turned back to her book. In the silence she tried to finish what she was doing, a "silly poem" she would have called it, careful never to take herself seriously any more. But she could not go on. The melody had driven her own lines out of her head, as though the blind musician, walking away, had drawn all melody with him. She felt hot and a little fretful and restlessly she began drawing heads of nobody on the page. She was so empty that in her idleness she began actually to wonder about Bert Holm and mountain climbing and all the remoteness of his adventures. Everybody knew about him even a month ago when they had left home. Blind and deaf and dumb as she had been then in her own first sorrow, still she could not keep from hearing his name and seeing headlines and knowing a little of what he had done.

So now, though with her own heart mocking her, she listened to what her mother said. There was so little to do when the heart refused its interest in anything. Even Peking could then become sad, and palaces merely the ruins of dreams unfulfilled. Mrs. Tallant had taken the paper back again in a moment when Mr. Tallant laid it down to put together some figures, and she began to read aloud in her quick crisp way what it said to the last detail about Bert Holm.

"Mr. Holm is no longer with the Fessaday expedition. Sir Alfred was called back to England, but Mr. Holm is returning homeward by way of China. The American Consul will entertain Mr. Holm at luncheon today at the consulate——"

Mrs. Tallant broke off. "Why, Kit, we'll meet him today then!"

There was mild excitement but no triumph in Mrs. Tallant's voice. She came of an old American family and so did Mr. Tallant and she had met too many important people to show excitement over anyone like Bert Holm, who after all, came of what she tolerantly called "very plain people." Mr. Tallant had represented his own New York banking firm in most of the capitals of the world and everybody was glad to meet him and his wife. Mrs. Tallant when she was younger had been presented at the Court of St. James. But it had not seemed worthwhile to go on with that sort of thing. She was robustly democratic in spite of a healthy and human amount of snobbery, and there had been something about European society even then which she did not like.

"Not that I care, of course," she said, now. "It's funny, though, isn't it, Robert? A young mechanic the nation's hero over night! It may be romantic and silly, but I like it." Her rather too bright blue eyes grew soft.

But Kit thought, now drawing vague circles and squares, there must be more than a farmer's son, more than a mechanic, inside Bert Holm's tall body. There must be imagination to have led him alone through the dark and snowy dawn. How desperately lonely were the tops of mountains! She herself was greatly afraid of loneliness—not of being alone, but of the present deep intense solitariness which kept her alone in any company. There could be nothing in the world so solitary except a mountain crest where no human being had ever been. Think of breathing for the first time air that had never been breathed, of seeing what human eye had never seen and knowing that the snow upon which one stood, and beneath it the ageless rock, were all untouched by human presence!

"I will ask him when I have the chance," she thought, "what he felt at that moment."

"I believe," Mrs. Tallant said out of deep reflection, "I'll wear that striped silk of mine. After all, it will be a formal occasion. I suppose, Robert, you will have to sit on the left, for once, because naturally today they'll give the place of honor to Bert Holm."

Mr. Tallant did not answer for a moment. He had taken the paper away from her again and was reading it, rubbing one side of his large nose slowly with his forefinger as he did so. He and the consul were going to talk over those Chinese loans after the luncheon today. It was the main reason why he had come to China, though he would not have told either his wife or daughter this, and so far as they knew it was a vacation. He never believed in talking business with the women of one's family. Business was not women's affair. Besides, he took pride in sparing his women all that sort of thing. They had a good time and bought their pretty dresses and went to Europe or Florida when they liked. He had no son, and his other daughter, Gail, had married his junior partner, who was a decent fellow as men went. As for his daughter Kit, she was a cute little thing, though with that occasional flare-up of temper over incomprehensible matters, and he had sent her to the best schools and she had made Phi Beta Kappa in college, which was something to be proud of even if there were no need of it for a woman. Since she was fairly pretty, of course she would marry, though so far she had not had the boys around her the way Gail had at her age. Dottie had said something about that play-writing fellow Linlay, but it had not come to anything. He looked at Kit. She was writing again in her book—a pretty thing she was, in her quiet dark-eyed way. He was proud of the looks of all his women, especially of his wife. When he looked at the women some men had to cart around he pitied them.

"I don't care where I sit," he answered. . . . If the Chinese government could give any sort of security, he hated the Japanese enough to take up those loans. Though why should he feel that way about the Japs? The president of the Osaka Specie Bank had given him an enormous dinner and he had seen the best of Japan when he was there. Reasonless dislike, maybe, but there it was. One could not help it any more than one could help falling in love.

But James Carleton, the American consul, did not put Bert

16

Holm at his wife's right, nor indeed at her left. Bert Holm was half-way down the long table and, young and pretty white women being rare in Peking, beside him was Kit Tallant, as temporarily the youngest and prettiest woman. She had come in late, having gone first to a curio shop where she had seen ivory seals a few days before. There had been one she liked, a tiny mountain peak carved delicately out of ivory, with the figure of an old man clinging to its side. But today she was not sure she wanted it, after all. What would she do with it, she thought, turning it over and over in her hands? Then seeing how late it was she put it down and went away, telling the old dealer she would decide and might come back after luncheon. People were just going into the dining room when she reached the reception room of the consulate and she had time only for a moment's clasp of her hostess's hand and to hear her murmur, "I've put you next to the young man, my dear."

When she reached her seat he was already there, standing very tall and silent. He was only a boy, she saw at once with her quick upward look, and her flickering interest fell. Then they all sat down and for a moment she thought she would not talk—just wait. Besides, everybody was looking at Bert Holm. Mrs. Carleton leaned toward him, the ruffle of her lacy gown falling across her plate.

"I can't tell you how excited we all are about you, Mr. Holm!" she called.

Around the table faces turned toward Bert Holm. It was difficult for him, Kit thought. How could anyone avoid looking silly! But he only said in a hearty young voice, "It's good to be back." He laughed a little. "I guess you know what I mean, Mrs. Carleton? I mean among Americans again."

A warm little glow went over the table. What he had said was pleasant and plain and without conceit. People looked at him kindly and then turned to their food.

Kit took up her spoon. What did a hero say to a girl? Better

17

to let him begin! He must be already growing used to chattering, too enthusiastic women. Besides, she thought willfully, for herself she would rather have had him Sir Alfred. She liked men older than this one. She hated all young men just now. Asserting her hatred, she turned to the old French consul on her right and began to talk to him in her rather conventional French. She was not very good at languages though she so loved poetry, both to read and to write. That is, if what she wrote was poetry? If it was not now, some day it would be. She lived in a confusion of cynicism and romance. Nothing would ever happen to her again —this was her chosen mood. Actually she knew anything might happen. But that was not to say she was good at languages. She was not, even in English. When feeling was clear in her, she had to let it distill before she could find the way to speak it. And then all the rush of her feelings came to nothing but a few words, a verse or two, which she always thought good at first and later despised.

"Have you, Mademoiselle Tallant, seen the Temple of Heaven?" the French consul asked her carefully. He was staring down into his cold jellied soup as though he did not understand it and feared it as a new American dish.

"Yes, Monsieur," she said, and then went on a little recklessly, "I did not care for it. This is reprehensible, I know, since it is so much praised. But it seemed to me formal and cold. Yet perhaps one should so worship a just God, who sends rain and sun on all alike."

"Ah!" he murmured and cast a startled look at her. He tasted his cold soup and put his spoon down at once, discouraged, and then painstakingly he inclined his ear to the lady on his own right, and she was alone again. "I frightened him, talking about God," she thought with pleasure.

That is, to all practical purposes she was alone. Bert Holm continued to eat heartily although the day was so hot. She could feel his silence encasing him like an armor. He might be shy or

18

he might be conceited, she thought. If she had done what he had just done, which would she be? Doubtless shy enough, though she hated her shyness which came over her like a spasm when she least wanted it. But it was of no importance to her whether he spoke or was silent.

Meanwhile, Bert Holm glanced secretly at her downward drooping lashes.

. . . He was as hungry as hell and at first he had not noticed her much. She was not the sort you would. And then this dame on his left kept warming up to him the way women did. He had turned to his right to get away from her, and then he saw the girl's eyelashes. He had never seen such lashes. *Kit Tallant,* her card said. He did not often listen to people's names, but he had heard of the Tallants—read in the Sunday papers about them. They were high class—now he remembered. He had seen pictures of a Tallant girl, but not this one. This one was kind of cute and he had not talked to a girl since—oh well, not in a coon's age! You couldn't count these Chinese sing-songs, or whatever you called them, that he had seen last night at that feast the Chinese guy had given him.

Gosh, she was quiet! He made it a rule to let the woman speak first. Then he knew where he was at without giving himself away. But she did not say a word. He would have to begin. . . .

"Do you like mountain climbing?" he asked suddenly.

She looked up surprised, and there were his blue eyes looking down at her with self-possession.

"Why, I believe he's conceited after all!" she thought, and widened her own dark eyes to perverse innocence.

"No, do you?" she asked.

His look did not waver. "Yes, I do," he answered. He turned away from her and she was not sure whether he was angry with

19

her or only unaware of her mischievous intent. A Chinese man-servant brought fish and set it before him and he began to eat it. How absurd she had been, she thought, to think she could ever ask him what he felt when he stood on the top of that lonely peak! What would this boy feel indeed? She was going to dis-like him after all, and she was glad of it. Dislike was easy to her these days and on the whole pleasant. It confirmed the darkness of her mood.

"You have to know how to do it, like anything else," he said abruptly. "Most people don't know how." He looked at her. "I don't know why you shouldn't do some mountains well enough, for a girl. Did you ever climb?"

She shook her head. He was quite serious and not making fun of her at all, nor had he grasped her malice. She stopped smiling and listened to him, incredulous of such simplicity.

"Most people eat just before they start. I've found that was a mistake. It's much better to start a couple of hours after a meal, or else after eating just a little something——"

"Tell me," she interrupted, making up her mind suddenly to ask, after all, "what was it like on the mountain top when you reached it?"

He looked at her again, and she saw for the first time the full blueness of his eyes. They were the brightest, clearest, most wil-low porcelain blue she had ever seen, and as he looked at her she seemed to perceive him as he had looked out over that stretch of the globe which only his blue eyes had seen. What had they seen? One could not be sure what he was, but at least these eyes were totally different from the dark ones she remembered with such pain. That, at any rate, was relief.

The woman at his other side was saying something in a clear, imperative voice. He turned toward her.

"Yes, ma'am?" he asked.

"Did you have any idea," the woman demanded brightly, "just

what you were doing, Mr. Bert Holm, when you started up Mount Therat?"

"No, ma'am," he answered.

He turned to Kit again.

"It was awful cold for one thing, you can bet on that," he said to her. "I don't remember thinking about much except how cold my feet were." He paused and lowered his voice a little. "The truth is—I hadn't really planned anything. But that morning when we had our orders not to go any further and the men were packing to go down, I looked up and I saw the top of the mountain, as quiet as a hill at home. 'Heck!' I said to myself, 'I've gone through a lot to get here. I guess I'll just keep a-going.' I could go a lot faster alone—take short cuts and all and I guessed it wouldn't take me more than a day to do it. By night I'd be back at the camp."

"It was dangerous," she said. "Suppose you had slipped?" Not that she would have cared but she was curious about the way people behaved in extremity. If, for instance, she found herself in danger of death would it seem worth while to save herself?

He gave his first laugh, a short dry laugh. "Yeah, but I didn't!" And after chewing a moment, he added, "I don't know how it is, but I always seem to have luck."

He turned to a new dish set before him, and she saw his profile, clear and boyishly handsome. At her right the French consul, reassured by familiar roast duck and rice, was asking, "Have you seen the Forbidden City also, Mademoiselle Tallant?"

She turned to reply, and then remembered that Bert Holm had not really told her how he felt upon the mountaintop. She must remember to ask him again before the dessert. But the French consul kept his hold, and when she glanced at Bert Holm the woman beyond was talking again and she saw only the nape of his sunburned neck, where his fair hair grew smoothly down into tow as soft and white as a blonde child's. Then suddenly a moment later, she thought, or imagined, that his shoulder touched hers more than accidentally. She was repelled by the touch, accidental or not. It came again—his shoulder was against hers. She withdrew a little. No, she could not be sure, though it would not be surprising. He would be the sort of man who would begin like that, she thought scornfully. But the table was crowded and the Chinese boys pressed in between the guests as they served them. And his shoulders were broad. Perhaps she was wrong. Perhaps she imagined easily in her too sensitive state. The American consul was asking Bert something; no, he was teasing him a little. She turned her head to listen.

"I suppose we shall see your face upon the silver screen and all that, Mr. Holm? With a cardboard mountain behind you?"

"No, you won't, Mr. Carleton," the young man answered instantly. "I won't fall for anything like that. When I go to the movies I want to see something else except my own mug."

Everyone laughed at his earnestness, but she could feel them liking him too. He was likable—she felt it herself in spite of her will to dislike him.

"All I want now," Bert Holm was saying, "is to be home for a while and get some of my mother's home cooking."

"Surely the mountains will lure you again," the woman beyond exclaimed, rattling her long Chinese gold earrings.

"I'll want to climb some more mountains, sure," Bert answered, "but not right away."

Everyone laughed again and Mrs. Carleton rose. "Coffee on the veranda," she said, and they all rose with her.

On the big veranda Kit stood a little apart, sipping her coffee. She felt dull and sad once more. It had begun to rain out of the morning's heavy gray sky, and the thickly planted garden of the old consulate sent up a hot steam, too earthy for fragrance. The rain held the heat of the August day and the high brick walls shut off all hope of a breeze. People stood about in momentary silence, oppressed by too much food and the damp midday heat. Most of them were too fat. They had the soft and effete look of those who live in a foreign country and concern themselves with nothing except their own welfare there.

Among them Bert Holm stood fresh from the Himalayas, alert and lean and hard. He was quite beautiful, Kit thought restlessly, if one cared for his type. But then it was nonsense to pretend that anyone, any woman at least, did not care for it. Cold as she was where young men were concerned and never like Gail, she too could see the beauty in his broad shoulders and fleshless hips and in the high coloring of his blond hair and blue eyes and brown skin. Or was it only that she had had enough suffering from a man who did not look at all like Bert Holm?

When this came into her mind, she put it away again. She had left America to escape Norman Linlay—no, let her be honest. She had left America because he had first left her. If she had told her father that she had been secretly engaged to a man who deliberately broke the engagement, he would have been ridiculous and old-fashioned enough to want to demand honorable amends. But what were honorable amends in her generation when the man one loved said simply that he had ceased to love in return? One smiled and quite understood—and said good-by and good luck and all the short casual things people say when they are going to be nothing to each other after having been everything. She wished that she had had the courage to destroy even his picture. Some day she would do it, of course. To be faithful in the old silly vaporish sense was absurd. She had no wish to pine for lost love, and she earnestly desired to be healed and rid of it. But she had not yet been able to destroy Norman's picture. It was still in her trunk, under her things. The question each morning was whether she could get through the day without looking at it, though to look at it, she knew, was as empty of joy as to awaken again from the dream. She despised herself as she wept, and yet she always wept.

Especially she could not tell her mother. She would have been sick with shame to tell her mother. Her mother would have in-

23

sisted, "But, Kit, you simply didn't manage things properly! Men don't know themselves what they want—or did another kind of woman get hold of him?"

If there had been another kind of woman, it would have been easier to tell and easier to bear. But there was not. He said so, and she believed him. No, she had not been able to keep alive the love she had awakened in him, that was all. He was clever and full of a talent that might be more; his play had been a great success last year in New York. It was about a farm family, a hard-driving, brutal play which externally she admired and yet which her instincts hated.

Nor had it been possible for her to tell her sister Gail, so well married and so complacent over her two children and equally complacent over having no more. Gail would have been ironical about it. She would have said decidedly. "You shouldn't have let it come to such a pass. One can always tell when a man is growing cool—there are ways. Why didn't you come to me? Men aren't very clever, bless them! If you wanted him, Kit, you should have been careful."

It would have been impossible to explain that though she had wanted Norman with all her heart, she did not want to be careful, because she did not want him unless he wanted her. That was her foolish romanticism, but then there it was. She could not help it any more than the curl in her hair. Gail would have said that was nonsense, that you had to make men think they wanted you or else how would they know it? Look how she had managed Harvey! He was a determined bachelor and man about town until she had made up her mind, after getting over a young love luckily, that she wanted Harvey Crane, old enough to be depended upon no matter what she did—and was he not perfectly happy? "No one could deny it, Gail," Kit murmured in her imagination, "but then I wouldn't be happy married to Harvey—or to anyone I had to manage to get."

She demanded, of course, far too much of marriage. What was

24

at fault was her foolish childish expectancy of life—romance, again! A party, a trip, a friendship—she was always expecting too much of even quite small things although actually she knew better. Then how absurd was her expectation of marriage, so huge that it demanded comprehension and complete relaxation between two human beings! The truth was that the more two were in love, the less they comprehended each other and the less relaxed they could be with each other. Merely the presence of one passionately loved made the heart tense and unnatural in its beat. And she had a curious theory that if the rhythm of one's being were thus disturbed then everything was wrong. Norman always disturbed her out of herself. They would have been miserable.

She leaned against the wooden railing of the veranda a little wearily. No, the fault was in herself. That was the hardest thing to face. It was not Norman—it was that there was nothing in her to hold his love. She feared secretly that she was not very interesting or exciting; she never talked a great deal. She wanted to, but could not somehow begin straight off the way Gail did, so easily——

"Take care, dear!" Mrs. Carleton's voice called. "I wouldn't trust that railing, if I were you."

She moved away. "It looks quite strong," she murmured.

"Yes, but you wouldn't believe how the white ants eat away the insides of things, especially in rainy weather," Mrs. Carleton answered. "They look all right until you lean on them; then they let you down."

Kit smiled vaguely for thanks, moved away, and then saw her mother talking to Bert Holm. Her mother had gone straight to him after luncheon in her bright, self-possessed fashion. Her father was nowhere to be seen, nor was Mr. Carleton. The others were talking together languidly. She could hear the French consul asking his questions of Mrs. Carleton in his careful English. She went toward her mother diffidently, not knowing quite what to do with herself. She was at once repelled and comforted by her mother's arm that reached out as she drew near and enfolded her. Mrs. Tallant was at her brightest with Bert Holm.

"I was just saying to Mr. Holm, dear, that he must come to see us when we get home to Glen Barry. We have some very nice hills of our own, Mr. Holm. I think you'd enjoy climbing them. Of course they aren't the Himalayas—but we've had fun on them, haven't we, Kit?"

"More fun than we'd have on the Himalayas, I suspect," she answered, trying to smile.

"Gosh, I'd love to come!" Bert Holm answered instantly. He grinned cheerfully to show startlingly strong white teeth. His hand holding the small Chinese porcelain coffee cup was big and clean—a good hand, except for blunt fingers.

Kit, Mrs. Tallant observed, was looking yellow again. What was the matter with the child? So difficult—so much more difficult than Gail had ever been! She smiled beamingly at Kit and said with determined cheer:

"And now, dear, what about the afternoon? Since it's raining, I suppose you can't ride to the Western Hills, can you? She's a great horseback rider, Mr. Holm! Besides, Kit, I don't know when your father . . . he said we weren't to wait. Do you know, dear, I think I shall go back to that silk shop and see if there is any more of that green silk. Don't you want to come with me? I'm afraid I have just a few yards short of what I want if we are going to use it for the library curtains—and it would be effective with the new Chinese furniture I'm getting—in spite of your father!" She laughed and looked at Bert Holm with the habitual coquetry of a well-preserved middle age. "Mr. Tallant says he won't sit on Chinese chairs if I do get them! But he'll get used to them—he'll have to!"

Kit Tallant felt Bert Holm staring at her and she felt him thinking slowly that maybe he might ask her——

"No, thank you, Mother," she said quickly. "I'm going back to the ivory shop. I've made up my mind about that seal. I want it."

26

Now he was going to ask her. How simple he was, she thought scornfully, and still let him go on.

"Could I come with you?" he asked. He flung his head boyishly to toss back his hair. "I haven't been anywhere yet in Peking or seen anything since I came, except a big dinner last night in some Chinese hotel."

"Why, of course you can," Mrs. Tallant said comfortably. "I don't really like your going about alone anyway, Kit, when you can't speak a word of Chinese. It seems perfectly safe, of course, but one never knows, now with those Japs around, especially. But I shall feel perfectly easy if you are with Mr. Holm."

"Fine!" Bert Holm exclaimed. "I'll take care of her, you bet, Mrs. Tallant!"

Mrs. Tallant squeezed her daughter a second and then let her go.

"And you'd be interested in that seal, Mr. Holm," Mrs. Tallant went on, "the quaintest seal of a mountain top, Kit was telling me; she says you can't imagine how they've managed to catch the suggestion of great height in a thing tiny enough to hold in your hand. The Chinese are so clever."

"It is the man," Kit murmured vaguely, drawing on her glove; "they've made him so small."

Let him come, she thought. She did not care what became of her. She detected and instantly despised a faint pleasure in herself as she walked away with Bert Holm.

His idea of taking care of her, she discovered, was to stand between her and any Chinese who was near. But she was not in the least afraid of the people on the streets and after three weeks she was used to the crowds that collected when she stopped to look at anything. Now and then a child put out a tentative finger to touch the material of her dress or to feel the silk or leather of her bag, but no one ever hurt her. When she moved they fell back a little, waiting to see which way she would turn, and then followed

27

her again. Each time she had gone into the ivory shop they had come after her and had stood, patiently curious, while she examined one piece after another. When she held the little ivory mountain in her hand this morning, they had murmured to each other appreciatively.

"What do they say?" she asked the old ivory dealer.

"They talkee Missee like this piece very good," he answered.

She turned and smiled at them, and instantly a score of smiles shone back at her. She liked these cheerful, idle people as much as she disliked the earnest little Japanese whom she avoided.

But now at the shop Bert Holm stood between her and the crowd.

"Hey, get back, will you?" he shouted.

"They won't hurt me—" she interposed, "I'm used to them."

"I don't want them pressing up against you," he answered vigorously.

"But I like them!" she protested.

"You're kidding!" he said.

She did not answer. It was not necessary. With the persistence of an ocean tide the people closed around both of them. She laughed and told him, "They'll do exactly what they like."

But to her amazement she saw that he was really angry. His face set in a scowl and he squared his elbows.

"Don't!" she cried. "Stop, I tell you!"

She had the ivory mountain in her hand, but now she put it down. The dealer was standing, alarmed. The temper of the crowd had suddenly changed. They were muttering and staring at Bert Holm with angry eyes. A boy of fifteen or sixteen jostled him.

"More better you go inside," the old man murmured.

"Come!" she cried.

She took him by the arm and pulled him unwillingly into the little inner room of the shop, where the old man shut the door upon them. Through the lattice they could hear him talking quietly to the crowd, expostulating and explaining, doubtless.

"You were silly," she said sharply to Bert Holm.

But his blue eyes were as stubborn as a boy's eyes. "I wasn't going to take anything from them," he said.

"You didn't have to take anything from them," she said impatiently. "They weren't doing anything to you."

"I didn't like the way they pressed against you," he insisted. "I wouldn't like it for any American girl, but especially for you."

His eyes grew luminous and translucent in their melting blue.

"I guess I may as well tell you," he said simply. "I've fallen for you—hard."

"How—how—ridiculous!" she whispered.

... Maybe it *was* ridiculous, he thought, when a few hours ago they had not met. He had better be careful. That was the way he got mixed up with Lily—before he knew it almost. He had been caught with her alone all of a sudden—they had run into a barn out of the rain and he felt—the way he felt now here in this stuffy Chinese room. He had not known Lily then either, any better than he knew this girl. He must not get into a fix like that again —he'd had to marry Lily and then it hadn't worked and it had cost enough to get the divorce and all. And he'd promised his folks afterwards he wouldn't get caught like that again in a hurry. He held back for a minute, until he saw how cute her mouth was. Gosh, but you wanted a thing when you wanted it, even if it was crazy ... !

"I guess it is," he admitted, "but that's the way I am. I guess everything I ever do seems kind of crazy maybe. I've always done things right off—as soon as I see what I want to do I've got to do it."

It was ridiculous, she thought, but in its very suddenness and foolishness there was something sweet and salving to her wounded pride. Since Norman had told her that day in a corner café in New York that he had made a mistake about loving her, nothing had meant anything until now, when Bert Holm's gay blue eyes . . .

"And when I fall, I fall hard," he was saying.

"You don't know me," she said in a low voice.

"I'm crazy," he admitted readily. "I've always been told I was."

"You are," she said, biting her lip.

"Well?" he demanded. "How do you feel about me?"

"I'm not so crazy," she said, laughing a little. "No—no—" she cried, fending him off, for he was actually putting out his arms for her.

Then they both saw that the door was open and there was the old curio dealer staring at them, amazed. He said gravely, "Missee, more better you come outside now."

"There!" she said lightly, "now you've shocked him. He'll think all Americans are bad."

"I don't care what an old heathen thinks," Bert returned. He followed her into the shop, though rebellious.

The crowd was gone and the door to the street was closed. The dealer took his place with dignity behind the counter and picked up the ivory mountain.

"Now, Missee," he began, "I talkee true plice—fifteen dollah."

"Oh, but I don't want to pay much for a man on a mountain!" she said gaily. She had not in weeks felt so gay—no, not in months. She felt willful and pretty and reckless—wonderful to feel so again even for a moment!

Bert Holm took out his wallet and threw a handful of bills on the counter.

"Here," he said, pushing them across to the old man, "I'll buy him myself."

He took up the ivory toy and put it in his pocket while the old man stared.

30

"Now he's mine!" Bert Holm declared to her. "If you want him it'll have to be a present from me. Do you want him?"

"I don't know," she considered. Her heart was dancing. It was all silly, but she had not been silly for so long. The old dealer was counting the money. Now he handed back four bills.

"Too much," he said gently. "Plice fifteen dollah—no more."

"Keep the change!" Bert Holm commanded him. "You don't know what it's going to be worth to me."

She saw the old man's face grow frightened. Obviously he thought these white people were insane.

"Please, Mastah—" he began.

"Come," she said to Bert Holm, "we are only scaring him."

He seized her arm and they ran out of the shop.

"Now you must stop!" she insisted. "We'll have the whole city at our heels. They'll think we are going to quarrel."

"We are," he declared. "We're beginning the godalmightiest fight in the world! Say, will you have this, or won't you?" He snatched the ivory seal from his pocket. "Say!" he repeated, examining it. "It's kind of cute, isn't it?"

He stared down at the man, the size of a pin prick upon the mountain's crest, and turned it over. "You know, it's queer, but at the top of that old mountain I climbed there was a spur like this, sheer rock for a couple of hundred feet. I thought I was licked, but I found a place where it was split on the inside, and the slope there was just enough so I could get my feet into steps I cut in the ice. That's the way I went to the top, just about like this old fellow. I guess I looked just about as much like a fly, too!"

She stood, catching the memory from his eyes. "And when you got to the top," she asked quickly, "what was it like?"

He looked at her helplessly. "I don't know how to tell you," he said. "I wouldn't know how to say it!" He paused and then went on, hunting for his words. "There had been a terrible wind all the time," he said slowly. "But when I got to the top, there wasn't any. I remember thinking how quiet it was. I'd been fighting my

31

way every step and then when I got there it was calm and quieter than any quiet I ever felt before."

"How did you feel?" she persisted.

He struggled for the words with which to answer her. "I felt like a king," he said at last.

She listened, her eyes on his. Around them the crowd was gathering silently, staring at these inexplicable foreigners. But she saw no one. She put out her hand for the seal. "Give it to me," she said. "I do want it."

"You're sure it's not just the climate?" Mrs. Tallant said anxiously.

"I don't know what it is," Kit answered, laughing. It was fun to laugh again. She had laughed a great deal at Bert lately. He was such a boy he made her laugh. Sometimes, though, her laughter made him angry—yesterday, for instance, when he took her left hand and measured her third finger with a grass blade.

"I'm going to have to have this size some day soon," he said.

She was sitting on a grassy slope between two fields outside the city, and he lay beside her. Near them the tethered ponies were jerking at the short grass.

"It's been measured before," she said wickedly.

Either he did not perceive her malice or he chose not to do so.

"No others count," he said.

An old peasant in a patched blue coat came up to them to protest their ponies upon his bit of grass. They threw him a coin, mounted, and went on.

"I got one blade away from the old miser, anyway," Bert said. "It's going to mean a lot to me, that blade of grass," he added with heavy meaning.

She had refused to answer this. Instead she had laughed and then, seeing his face grow sullen, she had whipped up her pony and galloped away. But behind her she heard the dull clop-clop of his steady pursuit. So directly, within a few quick weeks, had he pursued his single desire.

"It isn't like you," her mother went on. "You've always been so level-headed. Gail, now, I might have expected it of her. It was really astonishing to me that after all we went through with her imagining she was in love with her riding master and then that foolish chauffeur we had—that what's his name—George something or other—and then one boy after another—that she settled down and decided she was in love with a solid man like Harvey. A shock to him it was too!" Mrs. Tallant paused to laugh. "Well, it was a relief, of course. But you never were like that."

"I don't know that I am like that now," she said willfully. "Maybe it's only that I want a good time."

"You're making a good deal of talk around Peking if that's all it is," her mother said severely. "Of course, any girl Bert Holm looked at now would make talk. I said to your father this morning that maybe we'd better go on with our trip. After all, we have you to consider. I wouldn't like it said that he took you up and dropped you."

Her heart could still wince. How well it had been that she had told no one about Norman!

"Even if you refused Bert Holm, nobody would believe you had," her mother went on, polishing the nail of her forefinger diligently.

She was in her mother's room in the hotel. In ten minutes Bert Holm was coming for her and they were going to ride to the Western Hills as they had done almost every morning now for the weeks since they had met. America was clamoring for Bert Holm to come home, but three times he had canceled his steamer passage, and today a letter had come from Gail saying excitedly that the newspapers were full of a story—was it true that Kit and Bert Holm were going around together?

"I do feel you have to decide something," her mother said gravely. She put down her buffer and looked up at her daughter,

33

suddenly troubled. "After all, Kit, I don't know about this Bert Holm. What is he? His people are very plain and he hasn't much education. He'll have money now, of course, and contracts and jobs and all that offered him. But I don't know."

"What?" she asked.

"He's not a bit like you," her mother said, evading her. She took up her buffer again and stared at her fingernails. "You know last spring I thought maybe you were interested in that young playwright—what's his name—Norman Linlay."

"Oh, no," Kit burst out. "He didn't care anything about me."

"Well," her mother said pacifically, "I just wondered. Now, he——"

"I wouldn't want to marry a man like Norman," Kit said bitterly. "His plays meant more to him than any woman could. He talked about nothing else. It got very boring."

"What I was going to say," her mother broke in, "is that he was interested in the same things——"

"He didn't think so," Kit said quickly. "We were hateful capitalists to him."

"I mean plays and poetry and such things," her mother retorted.

"Oh, Norman despised my poetry," she cried. She denied angrily the bitterness that sprang at her out of her own heart when her mother talked about Norman and went on. "He's only interested in writing about social problems." She wanted to punish Norman, to pursue him and hurt him before her mother and herself. "I wish you could have heard the way he talked about Father," she said. "He called him a menace——"

"Oh, well," Mrs. Tallant said comfortably, "your father's used to it. Young men often talk like that before they get themselves established in life. I rather liked Norman, myself. He'll get steadier once he is really beginning to make money on Broadway."

"It's time for me to go," Kit said abruptly, looking at her watch. "Bert will be waiting in the lobby."

"Well," Mrs. Tallant sighed, "do be careful. This is the most gossiping place I ever saw. And, you couldn't have picked a more public character than Bert Holm. I'm sure I don't know. I suppose I ought to be flattered—the national hero—" She looked up at Kit with doubting pride.

Kit stooped to kiss her mother's softly rouged cheek.

"Don't marry me off," she said. "I haven't made up my mind."

But on the way down to the lobby she acknowledged that already in a few weeks it had come to the point between herself and Bert where she knew she must make up her mind. It was not only that the gossip of bridge parties and legation teas was beginning to creep around the world. It was that between the two of them had come the necessity to decide. She saw for herself that this man's whole nature was now concentrated into a determination, simple and almost sullen, that he would have her. He made no pretense at anything else. Wherever they met, and they met everywhere in the crowded small circle of exile society, he came straight to her side and refused to be diverted. She could feel other women's doubt of her. "Is she or is she not engaged to him?" people's eyes were demanding. Either she must be engaged to him or she must go away—it had come to that. For he belonged to them all, and she must not keep him tied to her by this uncertainty. That was what people were feeling. If she were engaged to him, they would accept her as warmly as they would the heroine of any romance. She was Kit Tallant, daughter of the wealthy old Tallant family, sound American stock. Some of the romance might be gone if Bert Holm were to marry, but a new romance would be there, the romance of young love and of happy family life, beloved ideals of the American people. She would be raised up beside Bert for worship, not quite equal, but almost.

But she hated such worship, she thought with impatience, and she knew now that Bert did not want to be public property any more than she did. He had said over and over again that he wanted to marry her and settle down. Once every year or so they would go on an expedition somewhere to mountains, that was

35

all. She must go with him and he would teach her to climb mountains and they would have a lot of fun together. She had listened, not sure that the loneliness of a mountain would be the less for his presence.

She saw him now in the remotest chair of the lobby, lounging with his back to the main door. He rose when he saw her and stood waiting, not seeing that people in the lobby were staring at him, or if he saw it, determined not to see it. One could never tell about him.

"Hello," she said, trying to be casual, and acutely conscious of the eyes upon them.

"Been waiting a hell of a time," he said.

"But it is only just eleven," she rejoined.

He did not answer as they moved together to the door. Outside, where the Chinese ponies were saddled and waiting under a big tree, he swore under his breath as he tightened the girths.

"What's the matter?" she asked.

But he only answered, "Let's get going."

They trotted in silence down the wide street and turned to the west through the suburbs of earthen houses and small shops.

Against a sky of piercing blue his profile under his white sun helmet looked Indian in its carven gravity. He was in one of his moods when he was angry and yet would not give his anger a reason. She would not say one word to him, but she knew from his sullenness that today she must decide something. Neither could bear any longer the tension of her indecision.

She sat her horse listlessly in the still hot sun of early September. The trouble was she did not know what she wanted now, having once been refused all she had wanted. Had the shock that Norman had given her been really mortal? She did not know, and yet there was no love left in her for him. She could summon the picture of that dark sturdy figure and she could tell herself, believing it, "I don't care any more—I wouldn't care if he were here." It was no longer Norman. After Norman

36

had come emptiness, and in the space of that emptiness she had met Bert Holm. She looked at the silent young man at her side. She liked him, of that she was sure. Sometimes she loved him, not in the foolish sickening way she had loved Norman—no more of that! She wondered, with the cynicism left like a scar from healed despair, whether she and Bert had no more than the union of race in a country foreign to them both, so that had they been at home they could not have come so quickly, or at all, to this moment. In the Chinese crowds they two, speaking a language not to be understood by any except themselves, were alone together and their speech intelligible to each other beyond reality. What would he be at Glen Barry or in New York? She could only see him as he was now, very handsome, very sullen, demanding her. In the surrounding brown of people and of hills he was as spectacular as a statue in marble of heroic size.

But then just now she liked his immense silence. He was nearly always silent. Norman had been talkative and eager and vivid. Ideas had poured out of him in jets and sparkling fountains of words—there was never a moment's pause. Sometimes she had grown tired, madly in love as she had been with him. There were times when she had felt dazed with weariness, as though she had been stretched, mind and soul, this way and that. Fundamentally, she told herself now, she liked quietness. In quietness one could ponder and grow and see. If she were married to Bert, his silence would leave her time and space for her own being. Besides, was it not always said that silence in a man went with strength? Physically he was enormously strong. When she stepped into his hand to mount her pony, he lifted her as though she were nothing. "I'm as bad as Gail," she thought with disgust. Gail in love always exclaimed, "My dear, he made me feel so *little*—and *helpless!* He's *wonderful!*" Women! There was a fatality in merely being a woman, perhaps. One succumbed, sooner or later, to femaleness.

They had come beyond the suburbs and now they were in the

level fields and headed toward the sharp-edged hills. They had been there often, always on horseback, and they had come to know one spot and another familiarly. The hills were bare against the sky, but in their valleys one came upon deep groves hiding temples and cool streams, and in the temples the Chinese priests served them tea and little sweet cakes made with vegetable oils and scattered with sesame seeds. They had spent some very pleasant hours there. Bert was not curious as she was about what the priests said as they stared at them, but he could take an amiable interest in what interested her, when he was in the mood. An amiable interest was perhaps enough, if she knew love for her were behind it. After all, did she not expect absurdities? Who would not call this romance? To be riding with Bert Holm across a Chinese landscape, under this sharp blue sky, headed toward those fantastic hills—there was not a girl in America, perhaps not in the world, who would not envy her. Her heart softened suddenly. She smiled and with her whip touched softly the back of his hand clenched about the bridle reins.

"Speak to me, please," she begged him.

He turned to her instantly, his eyes charming.

"I've only got the same old thing to say," he said. "You want to hear it?"

She did not answer. Now that he put it to her like this she felt a little frightened again. If she did not stop him now he would go on. He went on, before she had decided. "Because I'm all through waiting, I guess," he said. "I've been thinking a lot the last two days. And I've decided I'll ask you one more time to marry me. You'll have to make up your mind on that or I'll go home alone."

"Can't I choose the time and place?" she begged him. Underneath her pretended playfulness she was thinking breathlessly, "Now I have to decide something, because he means what he says."

"Any time today," he answered steadily, "and any place on that first hill." He pointed with his whip to the approaching mountain.

She gave up her playfulness.

"Very well, Bert," she said. "Let it be at the bamboo grove. There's a stone seat there—remember? And we can tie our ponies."

He looked at her sharply.

"All right," he said.

She had less than an hour in which to make up her mind.

. . . He knew now that he was crazy about her as he had never been about Lily even at first. This girl was different from any girl he had ever known. She would not let him touch her, not even put his arm around her. He had just to think about how soft a little thing she would be to hold. He kept thinking about that night and day. But you could not just reach out for her. Little as she was—you could snap her in two like a match— there was something about her. It was not just wanting to hold her or kiss her, either, the way it had been with Lily. There was something more to it. He wanted just to be with her, to be around where she was, in the room with her even if there were a lot of other people there, too. When she came into the room, everything was okay. That meant just one thing—that he had to marry her. . . .

In silence they dismounted, and in silence he took the horses and tied their reins to a bamboo. She sat on the stone seat and took off her hat and let the wind blow through her hair. It came fresh and cool from over the lotus-filled lake in the distance. She had a feeling of curious solemnity as she laid her hat and whip upon the ground and drew off her riding gloves. Thus she sat waiting for him, her hands clasped lightly about her crossed knees. She wanted to be cool and detached, but she could feel her heart swell, hot and beating, against her ribs, as he came near. When she accepted him, a sword would cleave her in two and the past would be gone. Would that part of her thus wounded grow whole again, or did one go crippled? She did not know. But at least she was ready for the cleavage.

But he did not sit down beside her. Instead he stood, his hands in his pockets, looking down at her as he spoke.

"I guess you know what I want to say, Kit. I've said it every way I know how, in fun and serious, according to how you were. But it all comes to the same thing. I want you to marry me."

She nodded. "I know, Bert."

He was thinking out his words. "I believe in hunches," he said slowly. "I've always gone by my hunches. And I had a hunch the first day I saw you that you were the girl I wanted. There was something about the way you smiled at me when we sat down at that dinner table. Maybe my hunch was wrong this time. But I don't believe it is."

He looked away from her and stared across the landscape with clear and steady eyes. She had never seen him like this. He had been overbearing and arbitrary and sometimes boyish and complaining, but never so quiet, so nearly reasoning and reasonable, so much a man and so little a boy.

"You seem real to me," he said at last.

"You seem real to me too," she answered, borrowing the simplicity of his language.

He brought his eyes back to her.

"Do I?" he replied. "That's swell. I'm glad of that. That means yes, don't it, Kit?"

He sat down beside her, and she waited. Now he would take her in his arms. She was always having to fend him off—his wanting immediately to kiss her. She had never yet let him kiss her for the simple reason that no one had kissed her since Norman had—and until she was sure——

But he did not move toward her. Instead with the tip of his

40

riding whip he traced the outline of her high leather boot and her foot. Then he threw the whip on the ground and leaned toward her.

"Well?" he said impatiently.

It was absurd still, at this last moment, not to know what she really wanted. There must be some test, some pressure that would bring down that waiting sword of decision.

"Kiss me," she said unsteadily.

The red flew into his face.

"Sure you want me to?" he demanded.

She nodded, and instantly she felt his arms about her, hard as thongs. Then his lips touched hers and pressed down firmly upon hers. They were fresh and young and unexpectedly sweet. She felt cleavage, sure and clean, inside her heart.

When she had been in love with Norman Linlay she had wanted no one to know. If no one knew then it was as though there were no one in the world except herself and Norman. But nothing about this love was like that one. She wanted to tell— to tell everyone. When Bert left her in the hotel lobby she flew up the wide old-fashioned stairs to her mother's room. It was the hour before dinner when she would find them both there together, her father and mother. As long as she could remember, it had been the time when she and Gail had chosen to tell them things and ask for what they wanted. They were there now, her mother in an old blue silk dressing gown, her face carefully cold-creamed while she rested on the chaise longue, and her father in his shirt sleeves, his collar off, smoking his pipe.

They looked up at her as she came in, and she stood, her back to the door, smiling.

"I'm engaged to Bert Holm," she said.

"Why, Kit!" her mother cried.

"Well, I'll be—" Mr. Tallant said.

"Come here and be kissed!" her mother said briskly, sitting

41

up. Kit went to her and felt two hearty kisses on her cheeks. "I'm glad you've made up your mind, one way or the other."

"Well—" Mr. Tallant said again. And then feeling it was not enough, he added with ponderous mischief, "Isn't he coming in to ask my consent?"

"Tomorrow," Kit said. She had not wanted Bert to come tonight, though why she did not know. Yes, she did. She wanted first to go to her own room and write to Norman and tell him. When she told him she would be free of him forever. A woman should not dream of one man when she was engaged to another. Norman must know that she would not dream of him any more.

"You aren't planning any hasty wedding, I hope," her mother said. "I hate a hurried, patched-up wedding."

"We thought we might be married quietly, here, quite soon. Bert doesn't want to wait," she said.

"No," her mother said firmly, "no daughter of mine is going to be married in a foreign country. Gail had a nice home wedding. Besides, Kit, you aren't marrying just an ordinary person. You're marrying a conspicuous figure. It's all the more reason why we should have everything as nice and conservative as possible." She frowned, planning quickly, "We'll go on home the way we planned, and he had better go by another boat. As soon as we get home your father and I will announce your engagement, and then we'll have a dignified small church wedding at Glen Barry."

"There won't be much dignity to it," Mr. Tallant said suddenly. Things were beginning to come over him. He was going to have to be Bert Holm's father-in-law! "You don't realize, Dottie, what it is going to be like when that boy gets home. There won't be any peace. Remember how it was when that fellow—that what's his name—came home from the South Pole? The whole country turned into a lunatic asylum overnight. My advice is that you let them get married here, where at least

42

there won't be as many reporters to the square inch as there will be in America wherever Bert Holm is."

"But I want Kit protected from gossip," Mrs. Tallant protested.

"Then she had better be married right away," Mr. Tallant replied. This marriage was not going to be simple. Indeed, his rapid mind told him, it looked as though nothing could be simple for a long time ahead. He felt slightly ashamed, hearing the jeers of his solid partners when they heard he was Bert Holm's father-in-law. Who would have thought that Gail would marry Harvey Crane, a man as sound as a square-rigged ship, and his steady Kit take to this skyrocket of a fellow?

Kit looked from one to the other of her parents. At this moment it did not seem to her so urgent when she was to be married as that she get to her own room and write the letter to Norman. All the way back—no, ever since the moment when Bert's lips had touched hers—she had been thinking of what she would say to Norman, how she could make him understand that she was going to be happy—very, very happy.

"When you've decided what to do, my dears, I'll come back and we'll see if I agree with you," she said, and closed the door upon them and went to her own room as swiftly as though it were flight.

Dear Norman, [she wrote] you'll be interested to hear—or will you?—that I am going to marry Bert Holm. Man of the Moment, you once called him, didn't you? Well, you're wrong—he's the man of my whole life. We are going to be married soon and very quietly, and here, because we both hate noise and publicity. And then we are coming back to America to live happily ever after. Where, we don't know. But somewhere near mountains for him, and somewhere near a lake for me. I've had a glorious trip and now it's had this unbelievable, fairy-tale ending. I am the luckiest woman! Thank you, thank you, Norman, for seeing what I did

43

not see as soon as you, that we were never meant for each other. How wise you were!

KIT

She did not read it over. Why read it when she had every word by heart before she wrote it? She stamped the envelope and rang the bell and when the Chinese room boy came to the door she gave it to him with a tip.

"I want this letter to catch the first mail to America," she told him.

"Yes, missee," he said, clutching the silver coins.

She watched him go off in a dogtrot and then she shut the door. Now she was free.

She stood a minute, grasping her freedom. . . . But if she were really free she could take out his picture from her trunk and destroy it at last. She had not looked at it in weeks. That meant something, didn't it? Even though she had thought of it again and again, she had not looked at it. She thought now, counting the pulse of her heart, that it did not even quicken as she went to the trunk, opened it and drew out the picture.

Once even to look at this picture had been enough to compel her to wildest weeping. Now she need not weep. And then his dark eyes claimed her. She felt them fastened upon her, but she did not move.

"You didn't want me, you remember," she murmured. She could bear this pull upon her heart as one learns to bear, at last scarcely knowing it, an old accustomed pain grown no longer acute. Already the cleavage was healing. "Now," she thought, "I can do it."

She tore the picture slowly across the thick white mat. She stopped—yet only for a second, perhaps two. Then she tore the face quickly into small pieces and flung them into the wastebasket.

It was done. She went to the window and stood, her hands to

44

her cheeks, and gazed across the crowded Chinese roofs. Nothing of him was left—no, nothing, except now only the remembered look of those dark eyes. How did one tear memory to pieces and fling it all away?

"Oh, Bert," she whispered, "please——"

She stopped herself. Silly! What she was about to say was, "save me!"—whatever that meant!

II

How right she had been, she thought, watching the approaching docks at San Francisco, to decide that they must be married at once! It had been bad enough at every port, but nothing like this. Letters and telegrams were piled unread upon their berths, and people had come aboard to follow Bert like admiring, infatuated dogs until he had rushed downstairs to their cabin and locked himself in, furious because he was being followed.

"Gosh, they're waiting for me at the door of the john, even!" he shouted. "Kit, I swear when I——"

"Hush!" she said with rueful laughter. "Don't—if you are as angry as this now, what will you do when we get home? It's only the beginning."

He sat down on the couch and looked at her desperately. "Kit, I swear if I'd known when I went up that damned mountain——"

"It will be all right after the first few days," she comforted him. She was glad that her parents had decided not to come back with them. Bert as a famous man was none too easy to manage. She evaded the word; she would never manage anybody. It was only that Bert was impetuous and people did not understand. Without meaning it she found herself standing between Bert and reporters, Bert and autograph hunters, Bert and anybody who made him angry. But it would be different once they reached home and could live by themselves. She had taken her leap into the dark and she would go on until there was light from somewhere. It had not come yet. Ever since their wedding in the small mission church in Peking she had felt as though she walked in

46

a fog, seeing Bert dimly, touching him and being touched by him intermittently as they moved through a hurry of travel overcrowded with other people. She had not yet had time to see him whole and as he really was. For surely he was not this angry, swearing, scowling boy who was looking at her now!

"Stay here," she said quietly, "and let me go out. I'll answer questions for a while." She was used to reporters, for the Tallants were news too, in their own stable way.

"Give me a drink," he demanded.

She poured a little whisky into a glass from the bottle on the table and gave it to him and then opened the door and went out into the hallway. Instantly a young man in a dark blue suit came forward.

"Are you Mrs. Bert Holm?" he inquired.

"Yes," she answered calmly. "What can I do for you?"

His notepaper was in his hand and his pencil was poised.

"I'm from the San Francisco *Time and Tide*," he said. "Would you mind telling me where Bert Holm is?"

"He is not here," she said firmly. "But if you will come up into the lounge and gather up every other reporter you can find, I will tell you anything I can for him. I'm sure you will understand that it is impossible to repeat the same answers over and over to the same questions from different people."

"Yes, ma'am," he said docilely. He followed her as though he were afraid that she would disappear, but somehow as he went he managed to collect four other young men, a young girl, and an elderly woman.

Kit sat down near a window where, when she lifted her eyes, she could see the mountains on the other side of the Golden Gate. Beyond them, beyond the further plains, lay what she had always called home. But she felt now as though she were coming to a strange country.

"Mrs. Holm," an eager, respectful voice began, "would you mind telling us just when you met Mr. Holm?"

"On August the third," she said obediently, "at the house of the American consul in Peking."

"And you were married—?" another voice demanded.

"Eighteen days ago, at high noon, in the Community Church there," she answered.

Over and over again she had answered these questions, in Shanghai, in Kobe and Yokohama, in Honolulu.

"Then you only knew each other about a month?"

"Before we were married? Yes."

"Do you believe in short engagements, Mrs. Holm?"

She smiled slightly. "When people want them short, yes."

"Excuse me,"—this was the girl—"but will you tell me the name of that material in your suit?" She was sketching rapidly as she spoke.

"It's an English tweed," Kit replied. She glanced at a sketch of herself that was a fashion chart with colors and styles annotated by arrows.

"Have you any plans, Mrs. Holm?" The young men were beginning again.

"Only to go home."

"Where is home?"

"We don't know yet—but for the present with my parents in Glen Barry."

"That's near New York City, isn't it?"

"Yes."

"Can we see Mr. Holm?"

"He isn't feeling very well," she answered.

"Then could you tell us what Bert Holm's opinions are on some of the questions of the day? For instance, the American people are awfully confused about why the Japanese want to fight——"

She broke in: "Because my husband climbed a mountain doesn't make him an expert in politics."

"No, but people would like to know what he thinks."

"I have never heard him say what he thinks—" she replied, and added, "about that."

"Well, then, could he make a statement on the neutrality act as it ought to be applied in the next war?"

The young girl cut in sharply: "What is his opinion on women in business——?"

"I don't know," Kit replied coldly. "I don't know."

On and on the stream of questions went. She answered automatically, her mind busy with herself and Bert and that life between them with which all this had nothing to do. That life had not yet begun. Where was the real Bert? She gazed out at the gaily decorated dock. The ship was near enough now for her to see the crowd except where it was hidden by waving handkerchiefs and flying flags. She looked quickly at the hills again. She had always disliked crowds of people. Why, she wondered? She was too insignificant, she thought relentlessly scornful of hurt— she was afraid of being lost, perhaps. No, it was not that. It was because they intensified the sort of loneliness of which she really was afraid and now more than ever because being married to Bert had not saved her from it after all, though that day on the Western Hills she had been sure, or nearly sure, that it would.

The elder woman reporter spoke. She had been watching Kit's face quietly, writing as the others asked questions but saying nothing herself.

"Mrs. Holm, you don't realize, I'm sure, just what you and your husband mean to us all."

Kit turned, a little startled, to look into a middle-aged, tired face.

"Hardly any of us have had much fun—or what we think is romance," the woman went on. "I guess we're hungry for it. We're the most romantic people in the world, everybody says, and I guess it's true. But it's kind of pathetic, too."

The woman saw they were all listening to her and she turned pink with shyness, but she went on again, looking from one to

49

the other of the young men. "I guess young men like you just see the romance of courage and daring, but older folks see the romance of being clean and young and good in a world like ours, and we remember ourselves as we once were and we wish we could have stayed so. And young women see the romance of your wonderful love story, Mrs. Holm—the way you fell in love at first sight—you did, didn't you? Anyway, that's what the papers said. And old women like me—well, I see the romance of marriage and a lovely home and maybe children after a while——"

Her plain face quivered a little and she smiled and her eyes filled with tears. "I'm just as silly as any of them," she murmured, searching in her bag for her handkerchief. "It's funny where handkerchiefs get to!"

Kit snatched her own handkerchief from her bag. "Here, please, take this——" she begged. She was so sorry for the woman that she felt cold with shyness. How could older people pour out such sentimental stuff? The young might be cruel, but cruelty was clean. Sentiment was muck; she hated it the more because she felt moved by it against her will. She turned away from them all. . . . "You must please excuse me now," she said, hurriedly.

She flew down the long corridor to her room and burst into the door. Bert had curled himself into the lower berth and was asleep.

"Bert!" she cried, "wake up—we're home—we're home!" At least the woman had suddenly helped her to understand how people would feel about him—silly people, but touching, like this old tired newspaper woman, still able somehow to feel romance! She began to see something she had not thought of before.

He opened his eyes drowsily. "What's the rush?" he murmured.

"Come on, darling," she coaxed, tugging at his shoulder. "I want you to get up and take off your sweater. I want you to put on your new gray suit and your blue tie."

"Aw, Kit, I'm dressed——"

50

"No, please! There are thousands of people out there waiting to see you."

He looked at her a little sheepishly, and she laughed at him, though without too much malice as she discerned the pleasure which he pretended he did not have. "Come on!"

He rose and began pulling off his sweater.

"That's my good boy," she said.

She was quietly changing her own plain gray costume for one of white wool. Over her dark, straightly dressed hair she pulled a white wool beret, and she wound a scarlet-striped scarf about her throat. There, now she looked like a bride! She hated rouge because old women used it to hide themselves behind, but now she put it on her cheeks and brightened her lips. She looked at herself in the mirror and saw scornfully a dark-eyed pretty girl, a girl almost pretty enough to be Bert Holm's bride.

"You aren't going to get me to stay dressed up like this, Kit!" he declared, and looked so handsome that something gave way in her. She was as silly as any of them!

"Oh, no," she said, laughing. "I wouldn't want you to. But all those people are out there waiting to see the wonderful Bert Holm, and I want them to see how blue your eyes are and how nice and tall you are and how broad-shouldered you are—and everything that you are!"

He was smiling too now, though his eyes were still shy and he was reluctant to be pleased. She thought, "I haven't been managing him properly," and then thought again with a stab, "Oh, but that sounds like Gail and Mother—" She wasn't *managing*—not already!

But there was no more time to think. They had already felt the easing of the ship against the dock and now someone knocked at the door. When they opened it there crowded into the narrow corridor three men and two women, all smiling and holding flowers. One of the men put out to her a great armful of red roses.

"Mrs. Holm, ma'am?" he inquired.

"Yes," she said. She wanted to laugh with some secret inner wry mischief. This was so ridiculous! But she kept her lips grave while her eyes danced. Then she drew to her aid the hundreds of pictures of motion picture stars that had passed before her amused gaze in newspapers and magazines and news reels, and smiled as brilliantly and falsely in the midst of her self-scorn. The faces before her responded with warm earnest answering smiles.

"These flowers are from the Chamber of Commerce," the man said. "We welcome you and your distinguished husband."

"Here he is," she interrupted gaily and pulled Bert to her side and stood, holding his arm. "And oh, what lovely flowers!" She took them into the curve of her other arm and buried her face in them. "Oh, thank you all a thousand times! It is so good to be home!" Home! Where was it? Never here!

They were all smiling at her and she smiled back at them steadily and one of the women, encouraged, cried out, "Oh, Mrs. Holm, please come out on deck! Why, there are people who have been waiting here five and six hours for you!"

"They would appreciate it, ma'am," a tall, thin, grave-faced man said.

"Yes, of course we will," she said. Why refuse anything now when there was nothing yet worth privacy between Bert and herself?

She felt Bert pulling back as she followed them, and looking up she caught his questioning blue glance.

"We must—" she whispered, "just at first."

So they stood side by side on the deck at the railing, she with her arms full of red roses, smiling and smiling. Bert would not smile. He stood there, looking over their heads, his face grave and his mouth sullen with shyness.

But it did not matter. Nature had given him that profile and that blond brush of hair, and his eyes were steady and wide and blue. Indeed, it was rather becoming to him to look sullen—

52

and certainly natural, she thought, still hovering on the edge of strange laughter.

She clung to his arm while the crowd shouted with happiness and thousands of eyes fastened themselves hungrily upon them. She could feel the warmth of thousands of dreams soaring about them like white birds, the dreams of all these people which somehow Bert was fulfilling. She looked down into their yearning faces and suddenly, to her own surprise, she felt a sob thick in her throat, and scorn drained away from her heart. How sad people were when they were crowded together like this! She had not seen it before, and now she saw it so clearly she would never forget it.

"We mustn't disappoint them," she told herself and, thus melted, she quivered again with new understanding. Dreams! Nothing was any use after a dream broke.

She sank into a chair and closed her eyes for a moment. Now, long after midnight, they were in their hotel room at last.

"Oh!" she whispered.

Bert sat down on the bed and began pulling off his shoes.

"I don't know what you're doing tomorrow, my girl," he said, rubbing his stockinged feet, "but I am going to take a train out of here before sunup."

"Where?" she asked.

"Misty Falls," he said firmly. "There isn't a newspaper in the town, and anyway my dad's farm is ten miles out. Nobody is going to walk ten miles to find anybody."

"It's a beautiful idea," she said, "but tomorrow they are having a banquet for you and giving you the keys of the city."

"I don't want 'em," he replied. He threw himself back on the bed and yawned loudly. Whatever pleasure there had been in the morning was gone. He was tired. "I'm not even going to be here," he said.

53

"Yes, you are, Bert," she said quietly. She rose and began taking off her things.

"Now, Kit——"

"You're not going to disappoint them," she said. "They've spent thousands of dollars for you."

"Who asked them to?" he demanded.

"It's already done," she said, "so it doesn't matter. Oh, Bert, please let's not wrangle tonight! I'm just as tired as you are!"

"That's why I say let's get out."

"We can't!"

"What's keeping us?"

"Bert, don't you see you can't just think of yourself now? You've done something that makes you seem wonderful in the eyes of millions of people."

"They're goddamned fools——"

"You've become a sort of symbol to them."

"I don't know what you're talking about."

"I know you don't," she answered sharply, and then stopped herself because of the look of hurt astonishment in his eyes.

"See here, Kit, you haven't stopped loving me?"

She flew to him. "No, Bert!"

"You're lecturing me already!" he complained.

She did not answer except to curl herself under his arm. If things would only stop long enough for her to find out how much she loved him!

"I know I'm a grouch," he said, after a moment.

"Yes, you are," she agreed in a small voice.

"See here," he said, "it don't sound so good from you."

She lifted her head to look at him and laughed.

"Then you mustn't say things you don't want me to agree with. Besides, you are a grouch, you know," she went on playfully. "You fight with waiters and you won't give enough tips and you snap at me—" She was lightly enumerating small grievances

54

about which she had kept silent when they happened, surprised that she had not forgotten them as she thought she had.

"When do I?" he demanded, astonished, and went on without waiting for her answer. "You wouldn't want me to be the kind of fellow everybody thinks they can cheat, would you? Besides, I'm darned nice to you!"

She traced the outline of his mouth and chin with her forefinger.

"You wouldn't shave tonight before dinner," she murmured.

"Nobody's going to get me to shave more than once a day," he declared. "And not that often when we get home." Suddenly he seized her in his arms and rubbed his stubbled chin roughly into her soft throat.

"You haven't got a sissy for a husband," he said thickly, "you've got a man!"

It was over at last. Across a mass of flowers she was waving to the crowd upon the platform and Bert was beside her. The train was moving slowly out and now it was gathering speed. The faces grew into blurred blanks as all faces did at last and then disappeared. She sat down. Bert was already ringing the bell. When the porter appeared he said loudly,

"Take all the flowers and chuck them out."

"Yassir," the porter said, shocked. He gathered them up with a grave face and went away.

"Now we have room to spread out," Bert said.

She did not protest. A little woman had pressed out of the crowd to give her a bunch of home-grown roses. "They're out of my own garden, dearie," she had said. "Just roses I raise myself. But I'd like to think they were in your room somewhere, helping to make it gay. Oh dearie, he's so wonderful—I hope you'll be happy ever after!"

"Thank you—thank you," she had said. But now she let the porter take them away with the others. Tomorrow there would be another crowd and more little women with home-grown flowers to give to her while they looked wistfully at Bert.

Oh, the blessed quiet of nothing but the wheels rolling over vacant countryside, the lovely impersonality of nothing but a machine about them! And yet after last night, Bert had tried hard today. He had gone through the hours in a stolid silence of endurance. They were growing used to his silence; reporters were making much of it, building it up into a dignity. Perhaps it was best that he was silent. Silence seemed strength, she repeated to herself. Perhaps he was strong. She did not know, for they had not had time to know each other. The days had been full and at night they were too exhausted for more than the simplest passion and then sleep. Sometime when they were alone and not tired perhaps they could really explore each other's minds, and then she could lead him into speech and feeling. He had talked very little even to her. She thought, "I don't even know what he likes to eat or to read or to do. I don't know him."

Now nothing mattered so much as to get her clothes off and to put on a robe and then rest. She had listened to so many voices all day that she wanted nothing but silence.

Bert had not spoken again. He sat in his shirt-sleeves, so quietly that it was almost as good as being alone. She smiled at him and put on her robe and curled up on the seat and closed her eyes. Instantly she saw their faces, the faces of thousands of people, moving, milling, straining, all staring at Bert and at her. She opened her eyes and looked at Bert's face. His eyes were fixed on a point above her, and upon his crossed knees was his right hand. Her eyes fell to his hand. There was always something fascinating and repelling about his hands. They were rough and direct in their touch, but they were strong, though the fingers were too blunt and one of them was badly bent. "Got that caught in a thrashing machine when I was a kid," he had told her. "Lucky I didn't lose it. But then, I'm always lucky."

Now as she studied his face a curious thing happened. She

lost its outer familiarity and he looked intolerably strange to her, so that she had the momentary illusion that she had never seen him before. It was so strong that she had to hear his voice to bring him back.

"What are you thinking about?" she demanded.

He brought his gaze to bear upon her blankly and did not answer.

"Something you don't want to tell me?" she asked.

"I wasn't thinking about anything," he said.

He shut the door against her like this again and again. "Bert, do you know—" she burst out, and then stopped. "What, Kit?" he asked. She shook her head and closed her eyes. No, she could not begin tonight a discussion that might go on forever. She heard in her ears, between the grinding of the wheels, the echoes of hundreds of voices. "I wish I could tell you how wonderful we think he is—" "It's the greatest moment of my life just to touch his hand—" "He's going to put it all into a book for us, isn't he?" "Of course nobody's quite good enough for him, but you're just lovely, my dear—" "Ever so much prettier than your pictures—" "Oh, we're so excited—" "Mrs. Holm, what is Bert's opinion on the question of—" Against the purplish-black of her eyelids the faces stared out at her again, envious, curious, greedy, wistful, confused. Foolish, foolish faces! Then why was she afraid when she thought of them . . . ?

Perhaps he really was thinking of nothing at all.

Denver was long past, and so was Chicago. They were near New York. They had had scores of telegrams from New York, and a representative of the mayor had come on board the train and told them how New York would feel if Bert Holm did not come there.

He was a pert, talkative, cynical young man, whose name was Horace Finberg, and he made them see in a few minutes that it was better to come and get it over with.

"People will be awfully sore if you don't," he said brightly. "In fact, it might do you a lot of damage, Mr. Holm, in many ways. For instance, I know one organization that is going to issue an invitation to you to become an honorary president at a salary—well, I wouldn't care to name you the salary—they'll do that—but it runs into five figures. And the people are all pepped up to give you a parade up Broadway with all the fixings. It's good for 'em—gives 'em a chance to work off steam. Those sort of impulses, if you don't let 'em out, turn sour in people. The crowd hates you as easy as they love you, you know, if you don't give 'em what they want!"

He laughed loudly, but Kit did not join in that laughter. She had already had an intimation of that hate in a town in the midwest. The train had stopped for five minutes and they had gone out to the platform to breathe the cool fresh air of the countryside. A boy of twelve or thirteen had come up and recognized Bert Holm.

"Hello, Bert!" he sang.

But Bert was tired and had only glared at him.

"Fresh kid," he muttered. And then the few people on the platform looked at Bert angrily.

"It wouldn't hurt anybody to be decent," a man said loudly enough to be heard.

"He's only a child, Bert!" Kit had said gently.

"Fresh kid, though," Bert reiterated. And had added, staring at the man, "I'm gettin' pretty sick of everybody thinkin' they can do what they want to me."

The boy had gone away and found a ripe tomato somewhere, and just as they climbed the steps into the train he had thrown it with so exact an aim that it splashed a dripping scarlet across the back of Bert's light gray suit. People laughed and Kit had not liked the sound of their laughter. And the porter had been too good-humored as he wiped off the stains.

"Sho' did know how to th'ow, dat kid," he chuckled.

58

And in Chicago there had been a draught of acid in one of the reporters' comments.

"Mr. Holm upholds the American theory of rugged individualism to the last extremity," he wrote . . .

"We had better go to New York, Bert," she said soberly. She was not afraid but she comprehended something which could be terrible enough to fear if one admitted it.

Horace Finberg leaped to his feet.

"I'll telegraph," he said, and rushed for the door.

She had known the city of New York all her life, but not this city. Quiet handsome streets shining in clear sunshine, quiet well-dressed people, opera and theater, the inside of large quiet houses, soft smooth voices—these were what she had known and taken for granted. And Norman for all his preaching against the rich, had not really showed her any other city, certainly not this city which she and Bert found waiting for them.

They were in a big black open automobile going up Broadway in the midst of shouting delirious people, and it seemed to Kit that she realized for the first time fully their predicament as human beings. She had from childhood feared all those forces which seemed to have no center of control. Wind she hated, not so much for its noise as for its reasonless fury. The ocean had the same potential and foolish power, and beneath her deliberately acquired and fostered joy in swimming and sailing there was always horror ready to spring out if the water grew wild. And as a child she had been taken to see Niagara Falls, and then, though she was nearly six years old, she had fallen into such terror that she could not keep from shivering and crying, though she could tell no one why, for she did not herself know, except that she was afraid of the power running uncontrolled so near, as she stood where the water turned, smooth and strong, over the ledge.

Now, sitting beside Bert, she felt the old horror deep and blind, creep over her. Madness was about her—something mad and uncontrolled. Her knees began to shake, and she crossed them. She wet her lips. She tried to think: "These are people. This is only a crowd of ordinary people. They like us. They don't want to hurt us. They're glad we've come home." She tried to separate them into human beings, even into separate faces, but she could not. They made only a great furious whole as remorseless and as wild in their mass as any ocean.

She knew that they were standing still and that her feeling of their swirling about the car was an illusion. She and Bert in the car were moving. But though she knew this she could only feel that they were the motionless ones, caught and held in the midst of a rushing, howling, senseless force. Her body felt caught and stiff in spite of its silly trembling. She could not move to brush away the bits of torn paper that fluttered down upon her. The air was thick with flying paper, sheets torn from telephone books and shredded newspapers and ticker tape. A bit of newspaper drifted down and she saw a few big black letters, "Bert Ho——"

Her ears gathered together all the shouts and yells and welded them into an enormous primitive beat. She saw the little mayor sitting opposite her move his lips, but she could not hear what he said. She forced herself to smile and shake her head. Then she saw he was motioning to Bert to get up—get up!

She felt stupidly obedient from terror.

"Bert!" she cried, shrieking into his ear, "get up!"

He got up, bewildered, and stood as the car crept through the crowds. She knew he was bewildered and yet his simple gravity seemed only a suitable dignity. Immediately the noise rose into a high wild howling. Women's voices lifted it and sharpened it and sent it off into a crazed new key. The brass band beat on, loud, steady, drumlike.

Once she had taken a winter cruise with her parents to South Africa, a tamed and docile South Africa which had seemed as safe as any spot in the world except that on still nights when an inland wind blew toward the sea, it carried upon its waves a thick, deep beat like this. Having heard it one night, she could never forget it. Whatever the day, she never again in Africa lay down to sleep on any night without dreading that she might awake to hear that dull and solemn thunder from behind the forests they could not see. She fled from Africa at last before her parents had wanted to leave and could not tell them why.

But there was no flight possible here. This was home. She clasped her gloved hands together and sat staring at the huge silver figure upon the hood of the mayor's car. It was a shape, undefined, of fine and upward lines. It seemed to strain to spring, but it was held there, and staring at it thus fixedly she felt the strain in her own body. What was she, Kit Tallant, who hated crowds and hated being conspicuous even among a few friends in a closed room, doing here in the midst of streets full of people she had never seen before, from whom there was no escape?

Then reason flowed back into her like quiet. She would not be held forever. Time would free her from this one predicament, at least. This day must end because all days end. Night would scatter the people and she would discover herself again, alone, though now she was lost. As soon as she was alone again she would be safe.

. . . Bert woke in the early dawn with that queer feeling that he had all the time now. It kept him from talking, or even from feeling anything else. Where was he? What was he doing here in this fine hotel, in all this noise? When he hit the bed every night he was so tired he thought he would sleep till noon, but every morning he woke up with a bang, before dawn, to lie awake in the noise. He was dizzy with noise.

He lifted himself on one elbow to look at Kit. She was his wife, but he had hardly found it out. At this hour she was always asleep, so still she was like dead. She always lay the same way, flat on her back, stretched out, her head turned a little to the right. At this time of day she was only part of all the queer stuff that had suddenly happened to him. He—married to a Tallant!

"Wonder what it would be if I just walked out?" he asked himself, looking at her quiet face. She never seemed even to move when she was asleep, or even to breathe. He did not know her. She was not half as real to him now, lying there, at this moment, though he was crazy about her, as Lily was. But maybe that was because he hated Lily. Hating people always made them real. "What if I just walked out and never showed up?" he thought. The Explorers' League was giving him a big dinner today. Suppose he just wasn't there?

He lay, listening to the rumbling of New York waking up to the day. He hated noise. Maybe that was what had started him on his mountain climbing, wanting quiet. That was why he had liked Kit right off. She was quiet, and he had not known any quiet women. His mother was a talker, and so had Lily been a talker. Lily would keep on jabbering all night—nothing sensible —but Kit was quiet even in her sleep. People made a lot of noise when they talked, and half the time he didn't understand what they said. All this noise could not go on forever. Sooner or later, Kit had promised him, it would all be over, except of course, the good jobs. What was an honorary president, anyway? Why did people want to pay him for doing nothing? But it was their business, not his. It was an easy way to make a living the rest of your life, just to climb to the top of a mountain. Why were people crazy—about that? The hardest thing was their wanting to know what he thought about things he never thought about at all. When it was all over, he and Kit would go somewhere and he would build Kit a house to live in, full of all the latest fixings. House and garage, they would be as good as money could buy. And even if he had to take a shotgun to them, there would be no more reporters hanging around to make their livings off him. That was what one of them had had the nerve to say to him when he did not want to talk.

62

"Don't think we care," the fellow had said. "We got to make our livings, that's all."

"What business is that of mine?" he had said. Give him as good as he sent!

He looked down again, this time to find Kit's brown eyes on him. She was awake. She waked quietly as she did everything else, with none of the yawning and stretching and grunts that told Lily was awake. Funny how when Kit looked at him, he always knew it! Sometimes he wondered if he oughtn't to tell her about Lily. He kind of hated to because he had told reporters over and over again that he wasn't married. He had said so the first time without thinking because it was none of their business and then it was easier than not to go on with it. Besides, he wasn't married any more—a Reno divorce had fixed him up while he was away. He bet Lily had had a swell time there, too—probably she had stayed right on because it would be her kind of a town. It was lucky it had been done anyway before he climbed Therat. Well, it didn't any of it matter now except it was kind of hard to tell Kit after everybody thought different. If it ever came out he could tell her how it was. Anyway, he hadn't asked Kit anything. But there hadn't been anybody before him probably, with Kit. She was one of the quiet ones that fellows didn't look at much. It just happened it had taken Lily to show him he really liked quiet ones, maybe because he hadn't had any kids to play with when he was little, only himself, and he was used to being the only one. And Lily wanted to be the only one herself. . . .

"What are you thinking about, Bert, when you look at me like that?" Kit asked suddenly.

"Nothing," he answered, and turned away from her and she did not ask again.

She had once answered Norman with that very word, and he had said angrily, "No one can think of nothing. Simply say, 'I don't want to tell you.'" She remembered prefectly what she had

63

been thinking of—that his mouth was too beautiful. He was actually not half as good-looking as Bert, but when she remembered it now, his mouth was still too beautiful. And it had not been true then that she had not wanted to tell him so. But he had not asked her again, and at that time she could not yet insist on telling him. Later she could and did, until he told her he did not love her any more. Well, it was over. . . .

She looked at her watch—half-past five—far too early to get up.

Bert turned over suddenly.

"Let's get up, Kit," he said restlessly.

"But what would we do?" she protested.

"It's morning at home," he answered.

"It's barely dawn here," she said.

He turned away from her again and buried his head in his pillow. She lay tense and still. Did he feel and she not know? But if he would not speak, how could she know? Inarticulate, her mother had called him! "He's very inarticulate, Kit—you'll have to use your own dynamite." It had not seemed a fault in Bert when her mother said that. It was not a fault now. Only, what did one do when a man locked himself up so that nothing came out except through the eyes and the shape of lips and movements of head and hands? She was accustomed to people who spoke and used words as a means to make themselves known. But to Bert words were obstacles to be avoided, and speech a trap into which he must not fall. She sighed and lay rigidly awake, feeling his silence as cold and heavy as darkness between them.

She saw him most clearly when they were not alone. This she realized at a great dinner the next night. People, eager to praise and to welcome, gave him perspective. These upturned faces, the intense, devoted, curious eyes, were a mirror in which was reflected for her Bert Holm. She looked at him as one of them might look and saw him beside her at the center of the head table, straight, aloof, a little cold, exactly as a man should be who had done what no other man had done. He was learning to behave better. He was not nearly so rude to people as he had been before she told him that his rudeness gave him away as much as talking might.

"How do you mean?" he had asked, instantly disturbed. She had shrewdly discovered that more than anything he feared what he called giving himself away.

"I mean people will think you have not been educated or taught ordinary ways of behavior," she said plainly. She wondered at her own plainness with him, she who was too soft even to catch a fish! But she had learned that he would not understand her if she did not speak plainly.

He had looked at her without answer as usual, but afterwards he had been less rude and she did not wince as often as she had before and did not need so eagerly to make amends for him as best she could. And his first strange embarrassed jocularity was gone, too. That was because she had been able to see fairly soon that his rough joking was really only shyness. Inside he was a shy awkward boy, who, being noticed, does not know what to do with himself and tries absurdity in self-protection. She had helped him out of that by praise, plainly spoken.

"I'm so proud of the way you take all the silly things they say," she told him.

"How do you mean?" he had asked with instant interest in himself.

"Oh, you just say—'thank you,' in that quiet way as though it didn't matter to you. I'm glad you don't try to wisecrack, Bert."

"Oh, I don't know," he said, looking uncomfortable. "People kind of like wisecracks."

"Sometimes, of course," she conceded. "Only in you it sounds just a little cheap. You're a great hero to them all, you know."

"Shucks," he said smiling and ashamed.

"Yes, you are," she said, half-laughing, "it's true."

65

It seemed touching to her now that he tried to do what she wanted, even though it meant that in public he sat in this stiff silence. But she had learned she need not be afraid of his silence among people because his good looks were enough to satisfy them as they dreamed.

Tonight he was at his best. The ballroom of New York's greatest hotel was decorated with flags and flowers and crowded with tables. Photographers flashed their lights, and took pictures of Bert in every possible pose. But they would all be good, for he took a perfect picture always. She sat beside him, looking quietly down upon the hundreds of well-dressed people. Nothing to fear here! This was a crowd among whom she knew many. She had spent almost every winter of her life in New York. Here and there over the room as her eyes gazed, a hand was lifted to wave to her. After it was over, a rush of women she knew well or little would come up to her, to surround her, to congratulate her, but especially to stare and stare at Bert.

"Oh, I do think it's just too romantic!" they would cry. "You sly little Kit, walking off with Bert Holm!" They would whisper, "My dear, he's handsome as a god!" That was what they always said, unless they said, "He looks like a movie star, doesn't he!" And when she introduced Bert, which was what they were really waiting for, they clung to his hand. "I've known Kit since she was this high," they declared, even when she could not remember having seen them but once or twice before, or even at all.

Gail had been heartbroken because Harvey had not let her come in from Glen Barry for this dinner. Gail would have loved all of it. But if she had come, by now people would have thought she was Bert's bride rather than Kit, and Harvey knew it. Gail could never help getting into the center of things, and Harvey had said very firmly that he was not going to have his wife mixed up in all of that. So she had only written beseeching letters, begging Kit to bring Bert to see them. It was so amusing, she said, to think their little Kit had married Bert Holm!

66

But they were going to Bert's home first. Tomorrow they were to be at Misty Falls and only when they had seen Bert's parents were they going to Glen Barry to stay as long as they liked—at least, until they knew where they wanted to live. Then, she summoned from somewhere the faith still to believe, her marriage to Bert Holm would really begin—a honeymoon postponed.

"We're getting a good meal out of this, anyway, Kit," Bert said in a low voice. He had not spoken once during the dinner. It had not been necessary. On the other side of him the master of ceremonies had been in a state of distraction because so many more people were there than had been expected. Across Bert's silence he had panted to Kit, "Please excuse the confusion, Mrs. Holm. I do assure you—if we had had any idea—I do assure you I don't think there is another figure in the world who could have drawn New York out like this. Your husband has been a tremendously stimulating——"

An agitated headwaiter whispered into his ear.

"By all means—" he agreed excitedly. "Certainly!" He turned to Kit. "They're putting tables into the gallery," he explained proudly. "The resources of the hotel are taxed to the utmost." He picked up the program before him and studied it hurriedly, wondering how long the people's patience would hold.

She had a strange sense that she was in an atmosphere about to burst, an iridescent, shining, fragile bubble that might instantly shatter into a rainbow mist, leaving her still quite alone. It was all too huge, too bright, wholly unreal. Indeed Bert, eating young lamb with stolid enjoyment, was the only stability. She yearned toward him unexpectedly.

"Don't eat so much you can't make your speech," she whispered playfully.

He grinned and winked at her.

But she was learning already that she need not fear the moment when he rose. At first she had suffered miseries of apprehension, afraid lest—what did she fear? She was afraid lest they would not appreciate him, these New York people she knew so well, lest they who were always ready to laugh would mock him for his simplicity. She knew better now. They were like every other crowd.

The dinner lengthened and the waiters were overworked and perspiring. Around them people were growing restive.

"We'll have to begin," the master of ceremonies whispered, alarmed. He rose before the dessert was finished and began his long introduction. Embarrassed by his fulsomeness she looked down so that she could not see people's eyes. No human being deserved or could deserve all that was being said. It really was not fair to Bert, it made him ridiculous. She glanced at Bert and she could tell by the look on his face that he was not listening. She looked at the people but to her wonder there was no amusement on their faces, only wholehearted appreciation and excitement. They believed, at least for the moment, because they were so eager to believe.

"And now," the dramatic voice declared, "I present to you our American Sir Galahad, Bert Holm!"

And now she found again that she need not suffer for his simplicity in their presence. They liked him the more because he offered them no rivalry. The plainer, the more stammering he was, the more shy and halting, the better they liked him and the more "real" he seemed to them, nostalgic still, in the midst of a sophistication pretentious and acquired in a generation, for the simplicities of pioneers and what they called "the soil." He rose and stood a moment looking straight ahead of him. She knew he was deliberately trying to put them all out of his mind so that he could remember his speech—the same speech he made everywhere.

"Well, folks," he began slowly, "I don't know what to tell you exactly except to say that was as good a dinner as I ever ate, outside of what my mother cooks. I don't know even if she could come up to it, though she is a good cook. You sure have treated

68

me to one swell time and I will always remember this town as a place where I had one swell time. I guess though you want to hear something about my trip up the mountain. There isn't much to tell. When Sir Alfred Fessaday gave the order to give up and go down on account of one of the men having the pneumonia he was, of course, right in what he did. But I says to myself, 'Hell,' I says, 'I've come a long, long way to climb this mountain——' "

In the hot and stagnant city air people leaned forward to stare at him, to catch his every word, to see him climbing slowly up those frozen perilous slopes, to feel the terror of the moment when he slipped twenty feet into a crevasse and had to work his way out again, to face the impassable wall of rock at the top about which he had to creep until he found the great crack where he could slip in and find foothold. They breathed the icy air, clean with the cleanliness of ages, they looked out over the heaped mountain tops, snowy as far as eye could reach toward the borders of Tibet. She had helped him to tell more and more of what they wanted to know, so that now he could talk almost an hour in his halting, simple fashion that won their hearts because it was so different from that to which they were accustomed, their own smooth wit with its undertones of secret malice. They were afraid of each other in the private incessant rivalry of their life, but no one need be afraid of this lad. They could not have forgiven him if he had been like themselves, but they could love him because he was not.

The room was full of the rush of hand-clapping when he sat down.

"They liked it," she whispered, keeping irony to herself.

"I'm getting the hang of it," he boasted under his breath.

... He was terribly thirsty always after he talked. Talking such a lot dried the very spit out of his mouth. But he really was getting better at it. He didn't mind it hardly at all. The fact was, there were times like this when he was getting even to kind of like it, to have all these dressed-up guys and women looking up to him, thinking he was pretty swell. Well, it had been no easy thing, climbing that mountain. When he was doing it he hadn't thought much about it. But now the more he told about it, the more he could see that it was a big thing he had done, climbing a mountain in the Himalayas that nobody had ever climbed before, that Fessaday himself had given up. He could see he had done a pretty fine brave thing. He didn't mind anything except these goddamned photographers' lights flashing in his eyes. It always took him by surprise, and when he was taken by surprise, he felt hot and mad. . . .

"Cut it out, will you?" he shouted impetuously at a cameraman. "I've had enough of it for one night." People around him laughed. He turned to the master of ceremonies. "Say, I don't think——."

Kit pressed his arm steadily and gently, and he stopped.

"It's almost over, Bert," she whispered.

Just at this moment, a small fastidious-looking man came up, holding his eyeglasses in his hand. He said to Bert in a quiet thin little voice, "I merely wish to say that when you want to organize an expedition of your own, Mr. Holm, I should like you to know that I will give a hundred thousand dollars toward it. I will put this in writing. My name is Albert Canty."

He bowed so quickly they could not answer him, and disappeared.

Kit knew him by sight and by hearsay from her childhood —Albert Canty, the multi-millionaire American son of Scotch peasants, who had given a fortune for Biblical archæology to prove old truths now questioned, Albert Canty, whose beautiful Irish wife had deserted him for a young French captain, whose son had killed himself at college, whose daughter, though still with her father, was a recluse and little different from a nun! His thin figure, appearing suddenly out of this glittering mob, had all

70

the asserting effect of the melody motif of a symphony, restored after orchestral roar and dissonance. Even Albert Canty and with such an offer! Was there some hidden wonder in this man she had married? But in the instant in which she paused for this question and before the crowd caught them again, Bert said to her:

"An expedition of my own, Kit! I never thought of it." He looked dazed by this new idea.

That night he talked of it a little to her before they slept.

"Those mountains," he murmured doubtfully. "Well, I don't know, Kit. What would I go for again?"

"Why did you go in the first place?" she asked.

In the darkness he paused a moment, then laughed.

"I dunno now," he said. "One of my hunches, I guess. I wanted to do it all of a sudden and so I did. Maybe I will, again. But now I'm here I don't know as I want to go again. Oh heck!" He yawned raucously. "I want to go home. Kit, we're going home tomorrow!"

She did not answer. She must remember to tell her father what Albert Canty had said, and then she could not sleep for thinking of that thin drawn figure in whose desperately weary and cynical eyes she had seen a moment's self-forgetful light.

It was symbolic of all that was unexpressed between them that she had never told Bert she dreaded this homegoing to his parents. She wished she could be as Gail had been when she first went to Harvey Crane's family as the new daughter-in-law.

"Aren't you afraid?" she had asked Gail then.

"Of what?" Gail had demanded. Then she had added, her eyes full of mischief, "I'm sure they're much more likely to be afraid of me—after the first day, at least!"

If only she had some of Gail's insouciant self-confidence! But she had none. She dreaded beyond daring to think of it the arrival at that strange house which perforce she must call home,

71

and of meeting those strangers whom she must by the accident of marriage to Bert call father and mother. The very thought of this outraged some inner secret loyalty to her own. It was a loyalty beyond that to her family. It was to those whom she called "my kind"—that is, a few persons, not people, to whom thought was more active and more valuable than any other exercise, whose thought was fed by new ideas and whose emotions were the quicker because they were informed and stimulated by new perceptions. "Rich, would-be intellectuals!" Norman had scoffed. To which she had returned with a quiet shrewdness that always confounded him, "At least not unsuccessful intellectuals who despise their own brains, Norman. You glorify farmers and bricklayers because at least they are successful. And so you think brawn, which you haven't, is better than brains, which you have." She had said such things sharply to Norman, loving him to the core, while to Bert she was always patient. So to Norman, in such a situation, she would have said, "I don't want to go to Misty Falls. They won't be my kind."

To Bert she said instead, "What shall I wear to go to Misty Falls?"

It was early morning and she was packing, having been too weary for it the night before.

Bert, still in bed, yawned. "Something fancy, Kit," he said. "Mom loves fancy dresses."

She paused, horrorstruck. Fancy! She had nothing fancy. Her garments were always plain. She hesitated, then went on packing quietly the things she would have worn at Glen Barry, tweed skirts and jackets and jerseys, a simple evening dress or two, a plain frock.

She saw Bert's mother very clearly in that one word he had used—as clearly indeed as she was to see her on the morrow— and then she remembered practically that she had always been reluctant before anything new. Her first days at boarding school, the whole first term at college, the evening of her debut had been miserable with varying sorts of dread. She must just get used to Bert's people, she told herself. When she grew used to things she nearly always could like them. It occurred to her at this moment that the only sudden thing she had ever done in her life had been to marry Bert Holm.

"I wonder why I did?" she thought, and added quickly, "so suddenly." But she allowed the question to go unanswered.

At the station in Misty Falls they were met by a fat excited woman in a large flowered print dress and a new mustard-colored cloth coat too tight for her. Beside her stood a stooped, heavy-shouldered man in a rusty black suit. But behind these two were scores of other people.

"Gosh!" Bert shouted, joyfully, "the whole town's here!"

"I thought you said we'd be quiet!" Kit exclaimed.

He grinned at her. "I was wrong, I guess," he admitted. "Well, they're here, all right. Hell, if there isn't that old son-of-a-gun, Jackie Rexall, even. I used to work with him in the garage! Hello, you old son-of-a-gun! Hello, Mom! Hello, Pop! This is Kit!"

The train had stopped and she felt herself taken into Mrs. Holm's fat, soft embrace, and in her ear she heard an excited voice babbling, half weeping.

"Dearie, dearie, it's too good to be true that Bert's brought home such a lovely bride! Jake, isn't she a nice little bride?"

She looked up into Mr. Holm's solemn blue eyes and put out her hand which he took into his own hand, at once huge and lifeless. "Pleased to meet you," he said. He looked about him, dazed, smiling aimlessly as the crowd yelled at Bert. Bert was yelling back, wild with joy. Men were roaring at him and clapping him on the back.

"Well, you old tinker, you had to get to the top, did yuh?" "Well, the bad penny's home again!" "What d'ye think you are, Bert, a goddamned mountain goat?" "He's the goat, all right, all

73

right—I been readin' about you, Bert!" "Naw, he's got 'em all fooled—we know he's no great shakes—the town good-for-nothin', he is!"

They were all worshiping him, the same adoring worship, the greater because they could appropriate for themselves some of his fame. "I come from Misty Falls—place where Bert Holm was born," they said casually, carefully, when they were away from home. "Yeah, known him all my life—a swell fella!" they said.

A burst of wavering music sprang up from a drum and two horns.

"Hey, shut up, you!" Bert yelled. "I ain't the president yet!"

"Any time you want to be, let us know!" they yelled back.

Then suddenly he remembered Kit. She had stood quietly and a little to one side, waiting for she did not know what. He swept her into his arms and held her high over his head.

"Folks, meet my wife, Kit!"

From the height she looked down on them, smiling painfully. "Put me down, Bert," she muttered through set teeth. But he did not hear her, and they stared up at her, subsiding as they stared into shy silence. Everybody knew who she was because they read the Sunday papers. She was Katherine Tallant, Robert Tallant's daughter. They had seen her picture. It was only a year or so ago she had made her debut, whatever that was. They were all shy of her—society folks her people were, rich society folks.

"Put me down, Bert," she begged.

But they did not get over their shyness, even when Bert put her down at last and introduced them one by one. She shook scores of hands and smiled over and over again. But they were still shy, and Bert's father moved rather soberly toward an old car into which she climbed after Bert's mother.

It was as though a party which had been merry and at its height were suddenly over and finished.

This was quiet. The square white farmhouse stood on a hill-side, half hidden by trees. It had no special beauty, except that of fields and trees among which it stood and of the immense surrounding silence. But after the incessant noise of the last weeks, after the treadmill of public functions, silence, bare and free, was enough. She stepped out of the old car and into the soft uncut grass of the shady front yard and stood a moment, feeling the silence.

"I like it," she said.

"Gosh, it's swell to be home!" Bert yelled, and hugged her.

"I'm glad you like our little old farm, dearie," his mother said.

But what she really loved was this safe enwrapping silence, where even the winds brought no other voices than their own.

For in a very few days she knew she could not love Bert's mother and father. It was her own fault, at least much was her own fault, she recognized honestly. She had too finicking a sense of smell, for one thing. There was no use pretending she liked the smell of cows in which Mr. Holm walked enveloped. He could not help it, of course, on a dairy farm. He washed himself patiently at the kitchen sink whenever he came in from the barn, and that, too, she had not to see—that washing at the sink. Bert reverted to it at the first meal, though there was a bathroom upstairs of which his mother was proud.

"Bert, why don't you use the bathroom?" Kit had asked astonished.

Mrs. Holm spoke up positively, though cheerfully. "I ain't goin' to have all that dirt in my nice bathroom," she said.

Bert winked at Kit. "I know that, Mom," he said.

"And you use them back stairs, young man," Mrs. Holm added with authority. "You kin climb all the mountains you want to but you can't dirty my front stairs for me to clean."

"All right, Mom," he said gaily. "I haven't forgot. Come on, Kit, let's eat."

No, but these were honest, good people who adored their only son and were proud of him to pathos, and ready to love her if she would let them. She hated herself because she could not let them. It was Mr. Holm's hands that she dreaded most—those great horrible ham-shaped hands, with the black dirt hopelessly and eternally in the creases. "How can he help that, when he has to work?" she asked herself fiercely, forcing herself to eat. "He's decent and good, and it doesn't matter if he can barely read and write."

And then she recognized that these were arguments which Norman had once used against her when she had said half-playfully at a rehearsal of his play that winter, "Let's stay to windward of the carpenter." She had nothing against that carpenter except that he smelled of unwashed sweat. But Norman had flown at her, Norman the son of generations of quiet well-to-do New York living.

"I hate you, Kit," he said calmly though his dark eyes were angry. "You're so damned fastidious. What's wrong with the smell of sweat?"

"Nothing, if you like it," she said as calmly. "I don't, though."

Their quarrels had always begun in such calm fashion, each determined to yield nothing, but to remain reasonable.

"Berger's a good chap," Norman said a trifle more warmly. "I've drunk beer with him several times across the street. He has a wife and four kids. And he was out on strike three months last winter."

"I don't doubt it," she replied very cool. "But he needs washing just the same."

"Kit, you're loathsome," he said furiously. "He's honest and good. He's the stuff America is made of—he's——"

Then she threw away pretense.

"I happen to be American—and so do you, Norman Linlay— and so are our families generations back, in spite of not smelling like this man."

"You're so damned narrow," Norman began.

76

"You're damned narrow," she broke in. "All I say is—let's sit to windward. But you insist that all good Americans must smell of old sweat to be honest. Well, most Americans don't! Most Americans are just ordinary, clean, fairly comfortable people who move to windward as a matter of course when the few like this—this Berger are around. But you aren't satisfied unless you're smelling sweat. Clean commonplace people aren't real to you. What you mean is they're not easy to write plays about. It's much easier to write about starvation and sweat and unemployment and flood and violence than it is about what really goes on in most people's lives. But most Americans don't starve and don't smell of sweat and most of us are employed and have never seen anything that you'd call violent!"

He had been so angry that he had got up and left her, his loud footsteps echoing down the empty theater aisle. She had resisted the impulse to run after him, to cry, "Oh, darling, how stupid to quarrel! What do I care about smells?"

She had not run after him because she knew what she had said was true, and because it was true Norman had been angry.

Afterwards she was not so sure that truth was the most important thing in the world. But then it had seemed necessary that between them truth could be spoken. She waited but he did not come back, and after a while she got up and went home. It was the first bad quarrel they had had, but more were to follow, because neither of them ever said he was sorry. They simply took up again over the gulf the quarrel had made.

And all through that afternoon Berger, the harmless subject of their quarrel, had gone on working at the set he was putting up. It was a farm kitchen, where the farm people Norman had made out of his brain were to sit about a deal table and eat their plain and hard-earned fare.

But that was a play and this was the reality. The difference was very great!

"Father," she made herself say it, though her blood rebelled, "will you have some more stew?"

He shook his head. "Nope—had 'nough," he replied. He sat eating steadily in great gulps while Mrs. Holm talked.

At first Kit had listened to Bert's mother talk and had even tried to answer and make a conversation. Then she discovered that this only upset her. For years Mrs. Holm had talked without interruption from her husband and son, and she was not used to it. Kit sat in silence after a few days and Mrs. Holm resumed her wandering monologue.

"I don't know I'm sure, Jake, what I'm goin' to do if you don't get at my garden. The dahlias are a mess of weeds. I'd get at it myself if I could bend my back anymore. Bert, why don't you do it? You ain't done a thing since you come home. You mustn't spoil him, Kitty. I raised him to work."

Bert laughed. "Yeah, and I ran away from home, Mom!"

"Shut up, you," she ordered him good-humoredly. "Well, I guess you're such a big bug now you'll never lift a hand for your old Mom any more. I'm sure, Kitty, if you knew what a good little boy Bert was and how he used to help his old Mom—I never missed a daughter around, he was as good as a girl until he grew up, and then the devil began to come out in him. Well, I guess all young fellers are so, and we'll let what's gone be gone, Bert. You've done noble and made us all proud of you." She leaned over to Bert and patted his hand.

But beyond the house the quiet was perfect. It was in the woods where she could wander and on the meadows where she could lie on the slope of a hillside. The quiet gave perspective to everything. For she was too American not to know that it was also true that many a great American had come out of houses such as this one where Bert had been born. This small wooden structure, cold in winter and hot in summer, flimsy in storm and wind, and yet somehow indestructible, was essentially American and it was all part of what went to make up Bert. Long before she had seen it actually as it stood now in the hollow beneath her as she lay on the hillside, she had studied it on a front page in California. Pictures of this house had been on the pages of newspapers everywhere and people felt it appropriate. American heroes ought to come out of houses like that because it could have been anybody's house. What they forgot was that the heroes had not stayed in such houses. They had refused to stay in them as Bert himself had.

"Tell me about the rooms, Bert," she had begged.

But he could never tell her much. "Aw, I don't know," he had said. "It's just a house, I guess."

"Can't you remember it, your own home, Bert?" she had urged.

He had remembered the strangest thing in the house, the thing with which surely he had had the least to do. He said, wrinkling his forehead, "Mom has a parlor with a cupboard full of queer things she picked up. Somebody sent her some junk from Africa once—a missionary or something. Mom's great on foreign missions."

And indeed on the first Sunday afternoon Mrs. Holm had shown Kit the cupboard. "When we have the dishes washed, Kitty," she had said with dignity at dinner, "I want you should see my things." So they had gone into the parlor and she had drawn up the shades and unlocked the cupboard.

Then she had taken the things out, one by one. "This here," she explained, "is a knife they chop each other up with in Africa. I can't remember what they call it, but it's some special name, the missionary told me. Our church in Misty Falls helps support a missionary in Africa, an awful good man. We support one-quarter of him. This here's a basket. It's wove out of coconut bark, somehow. It's wonderful what those poor heathen people over there know how to do. I declare I feel so sorry for them, so ignorant and all. Reverend Shankey does tell us the saddest

79

things about the things they do because they don't know any better. They're so ignorant, they're real pitiful."

Kit, sitting in a small old-fashioned rocker, handled one thing after another in silence. It was incredible, it was all incredible— she felt nearer at that moment to those Africans whom she had seen living amiably in sunshine than she did to this good woman who was Bert's mother, who was enjoying her pity of them.

Kit, lying in the thick meadow grass one windless afternoon in a sunny October, remembered how she had felt that first Sunday she had come. What made people belong together or apart? She looked at Bert, lying beside her. His eyes were shut.

. . . He was thinking lazily that he needn't have been scared Kit wouldn't like it here. She liked it and the folks liked her well enough. Not that it mattered an awful lot if they didn't because as soon as he got around to settling somewhere they wouldn't be here any more much. He didn't know whether he wanted to stay in Misty Falls or not. Something had to be done about Lily if they stayed here. She was back again working in the soda fountain. Jack had told him that on the quiet, down at the station. She hadn't stayed in Reno, after all. She was back at work exactly as though she had never been away—"takin' no sass about you, neither," Jack had said. "She acts like she never heard of you."

"Hell, I don't care," he had replied. "She's nothing to me."

That was true enough, but of course he had to tell Kit about her sometime or somebody would if they stayed in Misty Falls. It had been decent of Lily not to show up at the station. She could have as well as not. He'd half expected her to show up or want alimony or something now that he was a rich man and everybody was talking about what he had done. When she got the divorce she'd been so mad she said she didn't want anything from him. But then she knew he didn't have anything, though he wouldn't have given it to her if he had. She left him of her own free will.

Now that he was rich—or going to be rich . . . Maybe they'd better not stay in Misty Falls. Kit was saying something. He opened his eyes . . .

"What's that, Kit?" he asked.

"I said," she repeated dreamily, "that I had been looking forward so long to our being alone, Bert. Do you know we've hardly talked together at all since we were married?"

"That's right, Kit," he agreed.

"We've had no quiet until now," she mused. How could she persuade his heart to open, his mind to speak? Now, if ever, they should be able to talk, to tell each what each had never told. Sometimes she had longed to tell him about Norman. Perhaps telling Bert would drive out the last shadows of memory, but it was not a thing to be told between coming back exhausted from a late luncheon to hurry into evening clothes for an early reception before a dinner. This place made her think of Norman, not with love so much as malice left from love still not quite healed. She did not long for him. She thought, "I wish he could see what it is really like when it's not on a stage!" But even this made her think of him more than she had since her marriage. Or was it simply that in the quiet she found him still there?

"How heavenly this day is!" she said, sighing.

Autumn lay like a richer sunlight over the hills around them and the valley below. Upon her lips was trembling that which she wanted to tell Bert. If she told him, then her honesty might be the bridge between them.

"Sure is," he agreed again. He plucked a grass and sat chewing it. Far off on a hillside he saw his father turning the cows into a fresh meadow.

"Pop's goin' to plow up that old meadow before winter," he said.

"Is he?" Kit murmured.

She delayed. The afternoon air was pure and delicious. This

81

was beauty, this sloping meadow, the orchard to the right, the house below, and beyond it the low interlacing hills. The earth felt warm beneath her. She put out her hand and took Bert's hand and held it. When the moment came she would seize it, the moment when they were near enough for her to begin.

"Bert, when you were a little boy did you dream of leaving here and going to the other side of the world and climbing mountains nobody had ever climbed before?"

He chewed the grass thoughtfully, his blue gaze concentrated in the effort to remember.

"I don't think I thought about much of anything then," he said after a while. "I can't remember that I did. Say—" he broke off, "what's going on down at the house?"

He pointed and she sat up and looked down the hill.

A car had stopped jerkily upon the stony country road before the house. Out of it came three men, carrying a large camera and a tripod.

"Hell!" Bert whispered. "Let's run!"

She leaped up and they joined hands and ran into the orchard and lost themselves among the apple-laden trees.

"Now they can't see us," Bert declared.

It was suddenly fun running away like this together in the brilliant sunny afternoon. Around them the fragrance of the warm ripe apples was like wine. She felt wild and free and excited. She had been trying to coax a moment to approach as one tempts a timid bird. But it was nearer now as they ran together than speech had been able to bring it.

"Oh Bert, I think I love you!" she cried. She flung herself into his arms, and he seized her and held her.

"I'm crazy about you," he said tensely. "Crazy—crazy—crazy——."

He lifted her against him until her feet were clear of the earth. He was strong and she felt his strength with a quiver of new interest. And then the moment fell into bits. They heard someone tramping up the low hill in the grass, and Mrs. Holm appeared over the stone orchard wall.

"Well, here's where you are!" her surprised voice exclaimed.

Bert let Kit go and she felt her feet hard and suddenly upon the ground. They looked down to meet Mrs. Holm's embarrassed eyes. She was hot and red, and panting from her climb.

"I been looking everywhere for you, Bert," she said sharply. "Didn't you hear me calling you? They're men here from the county newspaper, wantin' to take your picksher."

"Hell!" Bert began. "Can't I——"

"Come on—they're waitin'," Mrs. Holm ordered. "And bad language don't do anybody any good," she added severely.

"Oh, all right," Bert said.

They followed her down the hill, soberly and in silence.

There was no quiet. For, these having found Bert, others followed. Every day cars drove up to the house. Sometimes they brought newspaper men, sometimes only tourists coming to see where Bert was born, and wanting autographs. It was always Mrs. Holm who went out to see them. She was beginning to enjoy being Bert Holm's mother. She kept a clean apron on the kitchen shelf ready to slip on when she saw a car stop. And it was she who went and found Bert wherever he was, and made him come to the parlor which now she dusted every morning.

At first Bert quarreled furiously with her.

"Heck, I can't go on like this, Mom," he protested. "Whadd'ye think? I'm no continuous show—I gotta have some peace!"

"Don't talk like a fool!" she returned. "It ain't nothin' to come and be a little civil to folks that have druv a long way just to see you. I hate folks who think they're too good for other folks. The least you can do, Bert is to stand and let 'em see you."

She ignored Bert's sullenness and herself laughed and talked and told endless stories of Bert as the wonderful baby and the wonderful little boy.

83

"I knew he wasn't no ordinary child," she boasted. "He could chew meat before he was a year old as good as you or me—mouth full of teeth a'ready." Bert, when he heard her, protested, "Aw, Mom! Shut up!"

People listened, stared, took snapshots, and cried, "Oh, Mrs. Holm, would you mind standing beside him?"

In a few days all over America the papers were full of pictures of Bert standing tall and frowning beside a fat, laughing woman who was his mother.

They asked for Kit, too. "Aren't you married, Bert?" men drawled. "Where's your wife?"

"Oh, we'd love to meet her," women said politely.

But Kit had learned to slip out of the side door in the cramped little dining room and to go over a bit of swamp up the hill into the woods. The swamp was her salvation. Mrs. Holm would never risk getting her feet wet. Once she had sent Bert after her when she had chanced to see Kit escaping toward the swamp. He ran after her and caught her midway and there, balanced upon a rock in the midst of the muck, they had argued.

"Kit, Mom says come back just this once. It's somebody she knows. They want our picture all together."

"Bert, I had rather throw myself into the swamp. I can't stand it."

"Well, I have to stand it!"

"But I don't. I'm not you."

He looked at her helplessly. "But what am I going to tell Mom?"

"I don't care what you tell her," she said passionately, "only if I have to—to have my picture taken and talk to people I'll go away."

Deep in her heart she knew her supreme ridiculous fear was that her picture would have to be in the paper beside Mrs. Holm's. She could not bear the thought of what Gail's amusement would be if she saw her beside Mrs. Holm.

84

"All the same, you're my wife, Kit," Bert said.

She looked up. "What has that to do with it?"

"If Mom can be proud of me, it don't look good for you not to be," he said solemnly.

"Bert, you don't want me to play the fool too!" she cried.

Then she saw she had hurt him and she turned and fled across the swamp without once looking back until she reached the trees. From among them she watched Bert walking dejectedly across the field. Poor Bert—but indeed she could not!

For weeks the glorious autumn weather had been an invitation to every tourist. Mrs. Holm was dressed and ready to entertain from morning until night. She had collected all she could find of Bert's baby things and had spread them upon the big table in the parlor, upon a clean sheet. Women exclaimed over yellowed baby dresses of thick white cotton edged with hamburg, over worn little shoes and patched blue overalls. And it had come to be a matter of course that in the morning Kit left the house. She and Mrs. Holm had said nothing after her refusal. Only Bert had said shortly, "I told Mom to leave you alone, Kit."

"Thank you, Bert," she said. It was very good of him to take her side against his mother, but still they must go away as soon as they could. She asked nearly every day, "When do you think, Bert, we can go to Glen Barry? Dad and Mother are back and you haven't even seen Gail and Harvey and the children." She knew now that merely being married to Bert could not make this place her home and she longed to return to her own.

And each time Bert said, "Oh, pretty soon, Kit. Mom's having such a swell time, I kind of hate to spoil her fun. Soon as the good weather's over there won't be so much doin'. Then we'll go, sure." His first anger at being followed to his father's house had passed and he was beginning to feel tolerant. She was not sure that he was not even beginning to enjoy being Bert Holm. His mother had a deeper influence over him than anyone else.

85

As for the moment she had lost that day in the orchard, Kit gave it up. It would never come so long as they were here, that she now knew.

But she would not blame Bert for this. His mother was the sort of woman to whom one must yield or else from whom one must escape. Apparently easy-going and full of amiable talk, she dominated everything within hearing of her loud flat voice and heavy footsteps. Hers was an enormous personality. Without enough intelligence to control or guide it, it overflowed and clutched in its grasp every other personality. Its power was its amiability, which reproached all rebellion. In the emptiness of her days, Kit tore to pieces the woman who was Bert's mother. Norman was totally wrong. If he were here, they would fall again into that old quarrel of theirs, whose issues somehow they could never clearly define, except that she knew he was wrong when he felt that all good was to be found only in the simplest of human beings. Poverty and physical labor and low birth had no magic of their own to create souls in human beings, let democracy preach as it would.

That again he would have denied. He would say, she told herself, remembering against her will his intense, dark face, that it was not people whom he defended but a kind of life, a life of the hands and the body, work that used them and so drove the whole being to simplicity. He was sick of intelligence. There was too much of it spread too thin. The most intelligent mind was the one that recognized its own futility and gave itself back to the body to work and eat and sleep and call it life.

Well, here it was, she thought. She wished he could see it and then call it life, if he could! And then she told herself sharply that she was thinking far too much about Norman these days. She was making excuses to think about him. What did it matter whether he was right or wrong, when she was married to Bert Holm?

At this particular moment of thinking she was wandering

through the woods, now at their fullest height of late October color, and she came unexpectedly upon Bert's father. He was clearing out some young trees when, coming over a low hill, she found him in the hollow beyond. She had never been alone with him before and at once she felt shy; but then, so did he. She saw his face flush a dry red.

"Hello, there," he said.

"Hello," she answered. He chopped with new energy because he was so shy, and she hesitated a moment, not liking to be rude and to go on without further speech, and yet longing to be gone.

"Walking?" he asked perfunctorily, pausing a moment.

"Yes," she answered. Then she smiled. "More than that, I'm running away."

"Don't like tourists, do ye?" he said.

She shook her head.

"No more do I," he said. She saw now for the first time that Bert had his very blue eyes from his father. Mr. Holm was looking at her.

"Say," he said suddenly, leaning on his long-handled ax, "you don't like it here much nohow."

"Oh yes," she said quickly. "I like a great many things, the woods, for instance, and the quiet at night. I am very quiet naturally, though so much of my life has had to be spent in New York, since my father's business is there."

"Banker, ain't he?" Mr. Holm inquired, coughing for politeness.

She nodded.

"Don't know much about banks myself," he said.

She sat down on a log.

"I don't, either," she said.

"No?" he said politely. "Well, I never could get enough ahead to use 'em."

He seemed about to begin chopping again, for he rubbed the edge of his ax with his forefinger as though it were a leather-strop. Impossible to tell what those hands had been when they were young, so misshapen were they now!

"Say," he began abruptly, "why don't you take Bert away from here?"

She stared at him, inquiring.

"Take Bert away from his home?" she asked.

"His Mom," Mr. Holm said curtly. "She's goin' to make a fool out of him. I had to fight against it all my life, her makin' a fool out of him. But now it looks like everything's working together toward it enough without her."

"I don't think he likes this!" she said. "All this publicity——"

"Don't you be too sure he won't get to like it," Mr. Holm said warningly. "I ain't sure myself. It's a self-deceivin' thing. Folks pull somebody up and then he begins to get the notion he is somebody. I seen it before. And he don't have gumption to see that when he gets stuck-up they don't like him and run after somebody else."

"You mean—" she faltered. She remembered how Bert now dressed every morning as though it were Sunday. When he first came he had delighted in old pants and a shirt with no collar, but now each day he shaved carefully and wet his hair and put on a tie.

"We've fought over Bert since he was born," Mr. Holm said, "her and me. Me wantin' him to work like a real man, and her sayin' he was too good to be a dirt farmer like his Pop." Mr. Holm drove his ax into a tree and pulled it out again. "All I know is, now she thinks she was right. She's always tellin' me so. This is what she likes, all this comin' and goin'." Mr. Holm's voice rose to vehemence—"People comin' from everywhere, to where they ain't wanted! Why don't they stay to home where they belong?"

He stopped and spat on the edge of his ax and chopped down a sapling with two strokes. When he spoke again his voice had returned to its usual dejection.

"What I'm tryin' to say is, Bert's a good fair mixture of her and me. He's got good in him, but he's got her in him, too, see? And I don't know how much of which. But I know from past experience Bert ain't above bein' made a fool of." He looked at her with a strange glance.

Why did he look at her like that?

"Well," he went on, "that's not here or there, now. My advice is get him workin' somewhere at anything. Maybe your Pop could get him a job in the bank bein' a doorman or somethin' where he don't have to do much head work, or even runnin' the elevator. Bert wasn't much in school."

Bert a doorman! She looked at him to see if he were joking, but he was not. She rose.

"Thank you," she said. "I do appreciate what you've said. And I think you're right. I see what you mean." She hesitated. "I think myself that perhaps Bert is growing to like all this—better than he did."

"That's it," Mr. Holm said. "You see it for yourself. They'll ruin him if they can, just for their own fun—like runnin' to see a sight."

They looked at each other, and suddenly she realized she could like him. He was even a little like the man in Norman's play.

"I've been very glad to know you," she said.

"Same here," he replied and instantly began to chop at another tree. She hesitated a moment longer, but he went on chopping and she turned into the woods again.

Outwardly the days went on exactly as they had, but she saw that what Mr. Holm said was true. Bert was being changed. No, it was not so much a change as though what was happening to him was developing something in him, some side which had not been apparent before. When he had been with strange people and in strange places he had had no confidence in himself, he had seemed self-effacing and modest. Even his flashes of sullenness had seemed part of his modesty.

But when people came to him here in his own surroundings he greeted them boisterously, made fun of their cars and of them, and enjoyed all the stories his mother told of him. And there were nearly always Jack Rexall and two or three of his old friends from Misty Falls who came in the late afternoons on Saturdays and Sunday afternoons and sat wherever Bert lounged or followed him. "The claque," she called them.

"What's a clack?" Bert inquired.

"The indispensable part of any show," she replied flippantly. She saw he did not understand and that he did not want to show it by asking another question, and, feeling that afternoon contrary with subdued misery, she explained no further. She stayed away from the claque as much as she could. They had a strange look of knowing something that she did not, something more complex, more furtive than their simple brutish staring at her legs and breasts. What it was she disdained even to think about, though after the day she went into the village with Bert she was certain of her instinct. He had wanted to go to the small fly-ridden drugstore for ice cream. When they went in the claque was there, eating. They were distant enough when she and Bert came in—but their eyes were watchful. Watchful of what, she wondered irritably? Bert swaggered to the counter in a careless lordly way and greeted the girl at the soda fountain.

"Hello, Lily," he said loudly, "meet my wife!"

The girl was blonde and her heavy features were accentuated by coarse make-up and she wore a red leather belt she kept pushing down.

"Pleased, I'm sure," she said, and stared at Kit out of unmoving gray eyes. She had kept on staring at her so that each time Kit looked up while she sipped her orange juice, she met those large empty gray eyes. But Bert had paid no more attention to the girl. He was too busy shouting greetings at everybody who came in. And everybody in the town seemed to come to the drugstore as soon as they heard Bert was there. They shouted back at him and stopped to talk with him, but secretly she felt them all staring at her and she had not gone with him again to the village.

The weather held in one beautiful day after another through a long Indian summer into a late November of unprecedented warmth. Her mother, back from India and Europe, wrote her from Glen Barry, "When are you coming, dear child? I don't want to hurry you if you are happy, but we long to see you." And Gail wrote, "I don't believe there is such a person as Bert Holm."

She lingered on in the farmhouse, neither happy nor exactly unhappy, poised in a sort of space where she was nothing but a mind working on the meaning of itself, not as an individual but as one of millions, like and unlike her. She learned to speak so that they could understand her simple speech of things done or to be done. She learned to help with the housework, to gather fruit and to bring in milk, to listen to Bert or his mother, to carry on indeed that life of the body which Norman had so extolled, but still the mind lived, waiting and unsatisfied. She had never thought or felt so deeply as now, and what she thought and felt had nothing whatever to do with what she physically did. If ever she met Norman again she would ask him, "But what does one do with the mind in this return to simplicity? There it is, as much a part of the being as the hands are. While the hands work, it waits. Better, it may be, to be born without mind, but what if one has it as one has the color of the eyes and hair?"

She felt at times the tyranny of her own mind, ruthlessly pushing her on to wonder and to think and to feel, even when her will was to let all thought and wonder pass her by. She was ready now to grant to Norman this, that it might be happier to be born a fool, provided of course one could be enough of a fool not to know it.

Then one day after Thanksgiving she had a letter from her

father. Her father seldom wrote letters. All during her college years she had not heard from him more than three times. When he wrote her, she knew he had something to say.

In his small cramped script, which always looked more like figures than handwriting, he wrote: "Dear Kit. The publicity now coming out about Bert is unfortunate. It won't do him any good. Your mother and I agree it is cheap and undignified. I advise your employing a sound publicity agent and controlling things a little more. I recommend Roger Brame, my own agent. Be glad to see you home. With love, Dad."

She had purposely not been reading the papers for these last weeks of her deep inward living. What were people saying outside about Bert? It was time to go out and see. She folded the letter thoughtfully.

"Bert," she said that night in their room. He was whistling under his breath and he stopped and cocked his eyebrow at her. "Please—I want to go home."

She braced herself for his refusal, or at least for his unwillingness, but there was neither. He sat down on the edge of the bed and pulled off his shoes.

"Okay," he said cheerfully. "I'm ready to go. When do you want to start?"

"Tomorrow?" she asked. Would she ever know him?

"Okay," he agreed calmly, so calmly that she stood staring at him. "What's the matter with you?" he demanded.

"Why—nothing," she replied. "Only—would you have been willing to go before?"

"I don't know," he replied lazily. "Why?"

"Because I thought you didn't want to go! I thought you liked it here."

"Sure, I like it," he said. Then he laughed. "I guess I have it fixed now so I have fun wherever I go."

He fell to whistling again, and she thought, "Now what does that mean?" It meant nothing. She had one of her sudden turns

92

of mood. It was she who was foolish because she was too earnest and too intense. Why not accept what she had? What if he had such parents? Plenty of Americans had them. Her own father boasted that his grandfather had run the bank in a small town and had owned the general store and the mill—a good American. In such beginnings were America. It was only that Bert's were more newly there. She had found him a generation back, that was all.

She put away the memory unexpected at this moment of the one time Norman Linlay had taken her to his childhood home in an old New York house. His mother had been there, a gentle old lady in a soft plain black dress. She had taken Kit's hand between two caressing palms.

"I hope you will come often into this house, my dear," Norman's mother had said.

And she had answered, "I'd like to—I love this house."

But she had never gone back to it. Instead she was here.

"Bert, I want to be proud of you when I get you home!" she said quickly. She went to him and dropped on her knees before him and clasped her arms about his waist. His body was lean and firm in her grasp.

"You'd better be," he said, laughing. "I'm all the husband you've got, my girl!"

She did not answer or move. She simply knelt there, straining him to her, her face pressed against him. Under her eyelids tears began to burn. And he, mistaking agony for passion, quickened to what he imagined and fumbled at her bosom. She leapt to her feet.

"Kit——"

"No—not that—always and eternally."

"But Kit"——

"No, I say!"

"All right!" he shouted.

He stamped out of the room and banged the door until the

93

thin partition shook. "It's as unreal as a stage scene," she thought. Norman used to groan and curse and spend hours over stage partitions.

She walked to the window and saw Bert cross the road to the barn and get his father's car and turn down the road to the village, the dust rolling after him through the darkness like a storm. "He wants his claque," she thought scornfully. "He has to be praised and wondered at and admired." She began to pack her bags feeling so desolate that she was frightened.

When Norman left her, pain had been sharp, a positive actuality which she could combat because she knew where it was. But now she was in a void. About her, in her, ahead of her, there was only—nothing. . . .

After a long time she heard Bert. He was on the stair—he had come back.

He opened the door and stood there looking at her uncertainly, like a big child. "Here I am," he said.

. . . He had been so mad that he had some crazy notion of going back to Lily. He had gone down to the drugstore and met Jack going in. Jack stopped.

"What's a matter, Bert?"

"Kit makes me so goddamned mad. She's stuck-up—always usin' words I don't understand—actin' like I'm some kind of a dumbbell."

"You get to hell back to her," Jack ordered. "If you don't want to be clean ruined."

"I won't."

"We helped you out onct for the sake of the town. We told them reporters there was nothin' to the story. Folks here won't stand for it again—whole country won't stand for it now. You're not just Bert Holm now. You're a whole lot more."

Jack kept edging him along back to the car and he went, because maybe Jack was right. No, hell, he went because he wanted to. . . .

Kit, looking at him sorrowfully, put out her arms. He went to her and bent his head to her shoulder and felt her arms go about him. She was trembling with crying.

"What's matter, Kit?" he asked. He tried to lift his head to see her face but she pressed it hard to her shoulder.

"It's—just—nothing," she whispered.

III

"THE beeches are more beautiful than ever," she said to her father quietly. She was sitting between Bert and her mother in the back of the big touring car which had met them at the station.

"Coddle tells me one of them has a blight," he replied. "I sent for the tree man at once."

They gazed at the long line of copper beeches which were one of the glories of Glen Barry. Coddle was the Scotch gardener and, Mr. Tallant always insisted, his own best friend. Coddle did not believe in banks, nor did Mr. Tallant. He had put his own fortune into investments as remote as possible from banks, and stayed in banks, he said, merely to keep them as honest as he could. He sat now, very stiff, upon the small seat in front of his wife.

. . . He did not, he felt, know his son-in-law in the least. Now he would make it a point to know him. Kit was looking thin in spite of being on a farm so long. But then farms were overrated. One got the poorest food in the world on farms and, more likely than not, even skim milk. The cream and eggs were always sold to city people. He'd speak to Dottie about the way Kit looked. He stole a sidewise glance at his son-in-law. He was robust enough, and so good-looking it was repulsive to any decent man to look at him. One couldn't see another man under such camouflage of beauty. He wondered if Kit had been fooled by it? Catching Bert's eye, he looked away in discomfort. Not much there, maybe? . . .

Mrs. Tallant was talking on and on amiably. "I had Gail stay for a week or two more so that we can all be together after so long. Harvey can go on driving back and forth to town with your father. Personally I think Gail indulges him by living in town all winter with the children, simply because Harvey doesn't like to drive and doesn't like golf, especially when she enjoys riding as much as she does. I've been surprised, really, that Gail has settled down as she has." Her talk flowed on in its pleasant calm discussion of the family.

Bert sat in his usual silence. Kit could not tell what he thought. But it did not matter. It was good to be home. When they drew up at the house she could scarcely wait to see everything, her own room, the library, the swimming pool and the garden.

"When is dinner, Mother?" she asked. "Shall we have time to see everything first?"

"Yes, indeed, dear," her mother said. "You don't have to dress for an hour or more. Only don't, darling, run about in the dark, trying to see things. Remember tomorrow is coming and there is time for everything. It will soon be twilight."

"Only what's near the house," she promised.

So clasping Bert's hand lightly she had taken him to see what she loved, the rose garden beyond the pool—the pool shimmering in the late afterlight of the sunset. He stooped and put his hand in it. "Gosh, it's not even cold!" he exclaimed. "It's warmed," she answered. That was one of the luxuries of the place, an outdoor pool artificially warmed, so that they could swim late into the year and early in the spring, leaping from water of exactly the right temperature into woolly coats and nipping air. He went with her, hand in hand, listening to her excited explanations. Everything was beautiful and lovelier than she remembered. The past weeks were swept out of her mind. She was home. No, she and Bert were home together. In the clothes she had chosen for him he looked handsome and more than passable even here. She drew him toward the house with her. It stood, huge and solid, among the surrounding trees, every window alight. Here was where she belonged, whatever Norman said.

"Come, let's go in," she said. She led him in, saying to Smedley at the door, "Smedley, this is Bert Holm!"

Smedley had been there at the door as long as she could remember, to let her in.

"I'm very glad, 'm sure, Miss," he replied, bowing, but she could feel his excitement. Of course Smedley knew everything about Bert Holm! Among the servants Bert Holm would be a legend.

She led Bert upstairs to her own room. She could scarcely wait to see it again. In what misery of solitary grief she had once lain awake there, night after night! Must there not be, she thought, with her hand on the door, some shadow left? But when she opened the door, the fire was burning brightly on the hearth and the rose-red curtains were drawn and the lights shining. If there were shadows they were hidden by these things. She turned to Bert.

"This is my own room," she said, "where I grew up from a little girl, where everything happened to me. Now you're here!"

She gazed at him in a sort of pleading.

"It kind of looks like you, Kit," he said slowly. She could not be sure that he understood merely because she longed for it, but there was the chance that he did. It was impossible to tell what was under that bright hair, behind the perfect face.

Then before there was time to wonder, the gong rang.

"We'll have to hurry!" she cried. "That's only ten minutes before dinner."

"Think I can tie one of those black strings in ten minutes?" he demanded, and rushed into the room adjoining hers.

. . . Everything was pretty swell around here, he thought. He'd take his time getting to know her folks. They had class, he could see that. A house like this cost plenty. He wouldn't want it

—well, maybe he would. It was the kind of thing you saw in Sunday papers. Maybe it would be fun. Anyway, what he had to remember was that there was nothing to be afraid of. These people were nothing but her family—his in-laws, if they were classy. And he had nothing to be afraid of—not even Lily. Well, Lily could never get at him here. He'd maybe tell Kit all about her some day, after they'd been here awhile. He'd tell her he and Lily were divorced and all that, and so there wasn't a thing to worry about. If he hadn't started out not telling about Lily, it would have been easier. It was nothing, but somehow he couldn't tell it now.

"Kit!" he shouted. "Come and tie this damned thing!"

"Coming!" she answered.

She had a nice voice, Kit had. There were a lot of things he liked about her. She came in, looking awfully pretty in a blue dress he had never seen . . .

"You look swell, Kit!" he cried. "It's a new dress!"

"No, it isn't," she said. "It's an old one."

"It looks new to me," he said.

"You've never seen it," she replied, and then she added, "Many things about me you haven't seen yet, Bert!" It was one of the little tentative feelers she put out toward him. Would he or would he not . . . ?

But he was looking at her uplifted lashes as she stood on tiptoe and tied his tie with her neat little fingers, and he put his arms about her.

"There're a lot of things about you I know I like!" he exclaimed. "Those eyelashes, for one thing—I never saw any before so long and black! I fell for 'em the first minute."

The gong clanged again.

"Hurry," she cried, "we can't be late here!"

They ran down the stairs hand in hand, and into a room walled with books, and there they all were, her dad and mother,

99

and a fattish fellow with a long face, and a very pretty woman in a silver dress who didn't look a bit like Kit.

"This is Bert," Kit said.

And he felt a thin hand take his.

"Bert Holm, at last!" Gail cried. . . .

There in the library before dinner, Kit knew she was afraid of Gail. Gail, sitting on the arm of Harvey's chair, was sipping her sherry and laughing and talking.

"Really, it's been humiliating not to be able to tell anyone what one's own brother-in-law was like," she was saying. "With everyone agog and asking me a million questions, all I could do was to say, 'My dear, you know as much as I do. I believe he is handsome'—as he is"—she flung a little bow at Bert—"'but beyond that you must consult your local papers.'"

They all laughed, except Harvey who merely smiled.

But behind her chatter Kit saw Gail's clear hazel eyes on Bert, measuring and appraising. She rose and went to the chair where Bert was sitting and sat upon its arm and shared Gail's gaze. If she sat beside Bert she could protect him. She could convey to him, by all the little ways she now knew, what he must not say or do. But he did not say anything. He was looking at Gail with his frank pleasant smile, his teeth shining, his hair shining, his eyes at their bluest. Gail's look grew ironically good-humored, because he was so beautiful.

. . . Whatever Kit had done, Gail thought, finishing her sherry, she had married a handsome man. She felt the familiar slight giddiness she always felt when she met a beautiful young man, "temporarily irresponsible," she called it to herself. She herself was, as she knew, irrevocably married to Harvey, irrevocably because he ruled her like a slave and she liked it. It was, she told her friends, so unusual in American husbands. Nevertheless it was pleasant to maintain that being a mere slave she could feel free to rebel in small secret ways, as for instance, to wonder what it would be like to be married to a very handsome young animal such as anyone could see Bert Holm was. Kit, of course, didn't know him—never could. Anyone could see that Kit had married the last man in the world she ought to have married. If she didn't know it yet, it was only a question of time. She had pressed her mother hard about that and her mother veered away from it so instantly that she had suspected the truth at once.

"How do they get along, Mums?" she inquired.

"They're married, my dear," her mother said firmly.

As if that meant anything at all! She felt secretly excited. . . .

"Dinner is served," Smedley said at the door. He looked indirectly at Bert Holm.

In the kitchen the cook and the second man and the maids had asked right away, "How does he look?"

"Exactly like his pictures," he told them. And so he did. . . .

"I shall sit next you, Bert," Gail said. "I won't be put off any longer."

"That's okay with me," Bert answered. Gail's smile grew a shade more ironical. What a pity he needed ever to speak!

Behind their backs, her hand barely touching Harvey's stiff sleeve, Kit saw her sister's pretty profile turned charmingly upward to Bert. It was a profile which had made Gail one of the season's most popular debutantes five years ago, at once lovely and a little too sharp.

But Gail was being very pleasant to everybody in her keen crisp-voiced fashion. She was pleased about something, Kit thought, and felt afraid again, but helpless. And yet between Gail and Mrs. Tallant the evening was kept what their family evenings had always been, good-humored, mildly gay, properly intimate. There was a little talk of everything, the children, the bank situation and foreign loans—the loans vague, since neither Harvey Crane nor Mr. Tallant would for any reason have told anybody anything about any business which was not also in the papers—and a dash of gossip about friends. If Gail edged on malice, her husband or her mother changed the subject, and Gail smiled, perfectly aware of correction. And after dinner, while her mother poured coffee in the drawing room, she drew out of a large striped silk bag a sweater she was knitting for her small son, and looked, as she meant to do, the picture of what a young matron should be. Kit, watching them all, felt her uneasiness almost depart from her, except for Gail.

Gail behind her brightness was dangerous and knew it. Her marriage, now five years old, was solid as rock beneath her feet. But one could dance upon rock—no better floor, indeed, for dancing feet! Upon this knowledge of security her glittering, wayward, mirthful heart flickered and flashed. A wife, a mother, a dignified young matron, and among all these her central self, the girl Gail who as long as she lived would never be any older than she had been when she fell in love with a handsome chauffeur named George.

"I am ashamed of your lack of taste, at any rate," her mother had said severely.

"But George is working to go to college," she had said demurely, while she cared not a whit whether he was or not. She had cared nothing indeed for anything about George and all those for whom George later stood except for a moment, an hour or two, certainly not more than a month or so when she wanted a new companionship, though not necessarily of the body. Since she had married Harvey, she had indeed not wanted an affair. What she really wanted, perhaps, was freedom for the unthinking gayety that was the essential Gail quality. She wanted to forget the children, the home, and even Harvey, forget them without dispensing with them in the least, but forget them with someone and not alone.

This need, assuaged in the first years of her marriage, she had felt spring alive again when now she first saw Bert Holm. She recognized it at once and sitting decorously in the library she thought, "God, I'm going to be bitchy again!"

She let her gaze fall upon Bert boldly. Her cake, she thought —no brains, no conscience, nothing there except beautiful body and reckless impulse. She measured a certain speed in her heart-beat that did not for a moment deceive her. Where had that bitch in her come from? What ancestor in malice had thrust the seed of it into her being to confuse the heritage of a practical puritan-ism which was hers also? Bert was looking at her and she looked down again and knit steadily and in silence for fifteen minutes, her eyes shining under her dropped lids and her red mouth warm. And Kit, feeling something hot and hidden, felt that she was never quite sure of Gail. She must see Gail alone and know the meaning of that bright ironical innocence that Gail knew so well how to assume. But there was no time that night, unless the few moments before they went upstairs could be called time.

Mr. Tallant, looking up just before eleven o'clock, said, "Bert, as the newest member of the family, I had better show you where the liquor is kept."

"I guess you'd better," Bert said heartily, springing to his feet. They went out together, Bert's arm over Mr. Tallant's stiffly slender repelling shoulders. And then Harvey leaned toward Mrs. Tallant to talk about a new issue of one of her stocks, and Kit looked at Gail.

Gail had thrown down her knitting and was yawning gener-ously.

"Oh dear," she murmured, "I hate knitting!"

"But you keep on doing it, silly," Kit said.

Gail nodded. "Harvey likes the picture," she said lightly. "He feels I'm so safe if I knit."

Kit laughed and went over to her elder sister's chair and sat on the arm of it.

"Well?" she asked after a moment in a low voice.

Yes, it was essential that she know what Gail was thinking

under that bright casual air. She looked down into Gail's widely opened eyes and Gail understood.

"Why, he's perfect!" she said in the same light way. "Only I wouldn't be you, my dear, for a cool million in my hand."

"Why?" Kit asked.

"Too, too good-looking," Gail replied. "It's such a responsibility to be married to a beauty."

"He never thinks of how he looks," Kit said.

"He will, after he's been told by a couple of thousand women," Gail replied.

"He isn't like that," Kit persisted.

"Oh my dear," Gail protested, winding up her yarn, "don't be so childish! Why, the only thing that saves even my poor dear old Harvey is that he's so intelligent he wouldn't believe any woman who told him he was good-looking. He'd know she was only trying to get a bank loan or something, because he knows he's ugly. Poor Harvey—he'd have so much better times if he weren't so intelligent!"

Kit did not answer, but looked at her with reproachful eyes. Gail was in her perverse mood when there was no knowing what she really thought.

"Don't look at me like that," she said. "Didn't I say he was perfect, you ungrateful woman?"

"Perfect what?" Kit demanded.

"Perfect Public Hero No. 1," Gail answered.

She stood up. "Damn," she said pleasantly, "my yarn's gone under the chair." She stooped, found it, and stood a moment over Kit. Suddenly she dropped a kiss upon her hair. Kit felt it fall as light as a flower and flavored with Gail's particular French scent. "Don't be silly," Gail said. "Who could help liking him? He's a natural."

The door opened and Bert came in, carrying a tray on one hand.

"Here I am!" he cried. It was what he always said when he entered.

"By the way, Kit," her father said the next morning, "I have asked Roger Brame to come and see you today. The sooner Bert gets his publicity organized, the better."

"Yes, Father, thank you," she murmured.

She had come down to breakfast with him early before he went to the city. All through her childhood, whenever she had been at home she had done this. But she had not been much at home so that they had never got as far as they might have. There were always the long terms away at school, which it took a whole vacation to amend, and then it was time to go again. But he had not forgotten, and when she came into the big square dining room he looked up at her affectionately over his newspaper.

"Good morning, my dear," he said. "Marriage hasn't changed you, then?"

She shook her head. "Bert was sleepy," she answered. "He can't sit up late."

"We weren't very late," Mr. Tallant said mildly. Smedley was pouring his second cup of coffee.

"Bert calls anything after ten o'clock late," she said, smiling.

"Ah," Mr. Tallant said, and then he had told her about Roger Brame.

"You can trust Brame absolutely," he went on.

"With what?" she asked innocently.

. . . Mr. Tallant shot a look at her from under his thick gray eyebrows, a little alarmed at her tone. Did it mean she knew nothing about the things Brame had been telling him? Maybe there was no truth in them, then. It was not likely, when she had come straight from Misty Falls, that she had heard nothing at all, if it were true. Besides, it was the sort of thing a man should tell his wife—probably nothing to it if she didn't mention it. He wouldn't say anything if she didn't. She was a sensitive little piece —shrank up at the slightest touch. She had been so as a child and had never been able to get over it. Anyway, one never knew what was true about these national heroes. People told the most absurd stories. Women, especially, loved to say they'd had love affairs. It might be nothing more than a young man's foolishness. He had appreciated the fact that Brame had come to him. A disgruntled newspaper man might print something they wouldn't dare to sue for as libel. He had said at once to Brame, "Use money in the right way to make the right impression. . . ."

"The car is here, sir," Smedley announced.

"I didn't get here early enough to be of much use," Kit said.

He stooped to kiss her. "I appreciate the gesture, nevertheless," he replied.

He was, he realized, extremely fond of his younger daughter and he would do a good deal to make her happy—always had, as a matter of fact, as soon as he knew what it was she wanted. In Peking she had seemed to want this young man. He hoped she still did, though since they came home it had been a good deal like having a white elephant for a son-in-law. He was tired of having even men at the bank ask him about Holm. Having always been himself, it made him a little angry now to be primarily the father-in-law of Bert Holm. He could stand the men's jokes better than their respectfulness, though. The fellow was all right, but somehow he didn't want to think about him much. He remembered with disgust certain newspaper pictures Brame had showed him.

"Brame will be here at eleven," he said. He hesitated a moment. "Better see him alone, first," he added. "It's very hard for a man like Bert to understand the necessity of proper publicity. He can't realize his own importance—just as well, perhaps, but someone has to manage him. He thinks he is free to do as he likes, but he is not, of course. Only entirely inconspicuous persons are." He paused and added again. "Brame will want to talk to you frankly."

"Yes, Father," she said.

He looked at her sharply.

"You aren't being too sweet about something?" he inquired with supicion. Kit too sweet usually meant a later explosion somewhere!

"Not yet," she said, gravely. He looked at her until suddenly she laughed. He rose, relieved.

"So long as you can laugh, I won't worry," he said and, kissing her good-by, forgot her.

Only, she thought in the library at eleven o'clock, looking at Mr. Brame's gray, smooth-shaven face, frankly about what? Outside on the lawn Bert was playing with Gail's two little boys. She had never seen him with small children before, and she kept looking out of the window. He was down on his hands and knees and they were climbing on his back and Harry, the baby, was screaming with excitement.

"The approach to our problem," Mr. Brame was saying, "is eminently one of choice. What is the picture of our hero which we wish to present to the public? When we have decided that, we can survey our material, eliminate anything which does not conform to the picture, and build up everything which would increase and enhance the impression which we want to make."

He coughed and looked sharply at his client's daughter. He was perfectly prepared to find her what she obviously was, a delicate, rather too sensitive girl, obviously without the slightest experience of life, the typical product of a wealthy and conservative home. A good many things which he had held tentatively in his mind to say to her he could not say. She looked, however, intelligent, and she was Robert Tallant's daughter, which meant that somewhere behind that too quickly responding face there was shrewd hard sense. Once she understood a situation she would know how to behave, however she felt.

"We have here," he said, ruffling a handful of papers, "a confusion of newspaper stories about Mr. Holm. They do not present anything like a consistent picture. The public loves consistency. They want to be able to say, 'We know Bert Holm. He is brave, youthful, courageous, honorable. Though of fairly humble origin, there is no stain on him! In short, the perfect American type!' "

He paused.

"All that would be quite true," Kit said quietly.

"Of course," Roger Brame agreed.

The thing was twice as hard as he thought. She knew nothing at all. He had better deal with Mr. Tallant on this story that was beginning to creep around. It had not broken into the newspapers yet, but he knew newspaper men were toying with it, deciding just how far they could go. They could go a good deal further if they were annoyed. Besides, there were always the gossip columns which were beyond decency. If he could have said to her plainly, "Mrs. Holm, of course we know that the matter of Mr. Holm's previous marriage is of no personal importance any more, but with a man in his position anything can be of importance, however honorably all obligations have been discharged and legalities observed. And unfortunately he has denied this marriage publicly, for some reason of his own."

The affair had doubtless simply been a matter of extreme youth. It would have been better if there had been no marriage. No, if it had to come out, perhaps the public would prefer a marriage, even though a divorce followed, provided of course the grounds were respectable, such, say, as the usual mental cruelty. A woman could get a divorce for mental cruelty if her husband kicked the cat out of the house. But then, anything except adultery would do. Adultery the public would not have, or the disclosure of adultery. It must be avoided at all costs. Whether there had been such a thing actually was of no importance. He had not yet met Holm. But it was probable, he decided, looking at this girl's quiet face, that he was a hero to her as he was to millions of others. Otherwise, why had she married him? If so, then there must be a great deal of good in Bert Holm, except—why had he not told her? For her eyes held no hint of any knowledge about the sort of thing he meant. And if she knew she could not hide it. She had not the kind of face that could hide anything.

The room was suddenly filled with the buzzing roar of an airplane dropping low. Mr. Brame looked out of the window hastily. A small plane was dipping sharply between the trees over Bert and the playing children.

"Photographers," Mr. Brame said coldly. It was in the morning papers that Bert Holm had come to Glen Barry.

"Oh dear," Kit whispered.

"It will not be too unfortunate in this case," Mr. Brame said in a judicial voice. "The public likes to see prominent persons at play with children. But I wish, Mrs. Holm, that you would leave all this sort of thing to me. You see how it is. I suggest, therefore, that I meet Mr. Holm and form an opinion of what would present his best aspects to the public. Then if you will refer to me anything of a publicity character, I could judge whether or not it would contribute to the effect we desire." He smiled and added with complacence, "Publicity is an art now-a-days."

She sat quite still, listening to everything he said. There was something about this which she did not like, though it was as intangible as the vague odor of smoke somewhere. The idea of a figure built into Bert's outlines, and colored to suit popular imagination, made her uncomfortable.

"I think you will find that all you need to do is to present him exactly as he is," she said with quick resentful pride.

"Of course," Mr. Brame replied dryly.

She was about to ring the bell and tell Smedley to ask Bert to come when the door opened and he came in to find her, his hair tossed and his tie askew.

" 'Lo, Kit," he said. "I wondered what had become of you."

"I was just going to send for you." She smiled up at him and put out her hand, very conscious of Mr. Brame's slate-gray gaze. "Bert, this is Mr. Brame."

"Glad to meet you," Bert said heartily and put out his hand.

"Thank you," Mr. Brame said, withdrawing his own quickly.

It would be easy to build up almost anything from this young man, he thought, examining him. He had all the requisites—good figure, blond type, hail-fellow-well-met—everything with which to predispose. The thing was to build up that front. He doubted, now that he saw him, that the man was bad—more likely a simple fool. He wondered if there were a way to tell Robert Tallant that his daughter was likely to have trouble unless Bert Holm were properly managed? Pity she looked so sensitive and idealistic and all that! The other daughter would have been a better wife for a public figure—a better manager.

"I was just saying to Mrs. Holm," Mr. Brame said, "that I feel it scarcely necessary to trouble either of you. I have a fair idea of what the public likes, and with what data I have, I am sure we can build up the sort of publicity you both would approve."

He could see bewilderment in the young man's blue eyes—rather empty eyes, he thought. But Bert laughed as he answered, "Sure. I'm no publicity hound myself. Anything will do as long as it don't bother me."

It would be hard, Kit was thinking, to find a creature more beautiful than Bert was at this moment, the fresh morning air in his eyes and cheeks. She would have to take him as he was. That was what one must do—see a beautiful body and love and enjoy it for its beauty. And so deciding she felt a causeless sadness creep over her like a mist from the sea, cold and dim.

Upstairs in her large old-fashioned bedroom, Mrs. Tallant was getting ready for bed. She sat before her draped dressing table and yawned. She was sleepy, but she had no idea of yielding to it, although the room enticed one to sleep. The fire had smoldered to coals, and the deep soft four-poster bed was made ready. She loved sleep better even than she loved bridge. But she had broken up the family party early this second night especially because she saw there was something on Mr. Tallant's mind. There was a great deal of public pride about what was called Mr. Tallant's poker face, and newspaper reporters whenever he came back from abroad liked to make a little fun of him for talking to them frankly about everything and telling them nothing, as they discovered afterwards when they were working up their sheets of notes. But he never fooled his wife in the slightest. She knew at once when there was something wrong. His face grew so inscrutable that it took on the look of rock, and he talked at length on any subject that came up. When he was happy his conversation was a series of jokes, and not, as she put it, his bank-president style.

Tonight he had been so carefully diffuse on so many subjects that she perceived before half the evening was over that it must end early. Not even Gail and Kit at the piano singing the Gilbert and Sullivan which he adored could move him to give up his lengthy talking and join his slightly off-key bass to their voices.

Now she looked at him as he tied the belt of his gray silk pajamas about his waist. His face was still as solemn as rock. If it were business, she thought, she could do nothing about it in the first place, and in the second place she did not need to worry because he would come out of it all right. If it were anything else, he would tell her, for he could never keep anything away from her.

"What's the matter with you, Rob?" she asked as she brushed out her waved gray hair.

"Nothing at all," Mr. Tallant replied as usual.

"Is it business?" she inquired, paying no attention to the reply.

"What? No, business is as good as can be expected now," he returned.

"The children are all right, aren't they?" she hinted.

He hesitated a moment before saying, "So far as I know——"

The hesitation betrayed him.

"What's Gail done now?" she demanded swiftly. "I should think that Harvey could manage his own family affairs without running to you. After all, Gail is grown up and the mother of two children, and if she isn't going to behave herself now——"

"Don't get so excited," he interrupted. "It has nothing to do with Gail."

"Well, Kit is quite happy," she rejoined.

"Oh, Kit's all right," Mr. Tallant agreed, and then being incurably honest beneath her gaze he felt compelled to add, "so far."

"Robert, what do you mean by 'so far'?" Mrs. Tallant demanded.

He sat down and looked at her uncomfortably.

"I wish we'd looked into that fellow a little more," he said. "We let her marry him right away like that, 'way off in a heathen country, where any white man looks pretty good and better than he is."

"Why, Rob, Bert Holm would be a great catch anywhere!" she exclaimed. "Besides, it seems to me she is perfectly happy."

"He's not like her at all," he said gloomily. "She likes books and poetry—she's a delicate little thing. And he never looks inside a book."

"Things like that don't matter in the least in a marriage," Mrs. Tallant said briskly. She was adjusting over her waves a pink silk net cap which she now tied under her chin as she looked at Mr. Tallant. "As far as that goes, I used to write poetry myself in school, but I haven't since we were married, Rob. I haven't needed to. Personally, I feel Bert may be just the man to bring reality into Kit's life. She has always seemed rather remote, somehow, from reality."

Mr. Tallant stared at his wife, trying to think how to tell her. He craved the support of her brisk common sense, and her principles of family honor would be an instinct to guide him. But his wife was the last person with whom he could discuss without shame matters of men's sexual behavior. He had nothing to do with Bert's conduct with women, and yet he knew very well that if he told her of it, she would at once feel that he did have something to do with it, merely by being a man.

Mrs. Tallant perceived a dilemma in his mind.

"Now, Rob," she said firmly, "you might just as well tell me what is the matter."

"I know it," he acknowledged. "It's—well, damn it, Dottie, the fellow has a past and it's dogging him, as usual. What wouldn't have mattered at all if he hadn't climbed that mountain seems to matter a lot now that everybody thinks he is wonderful."

Mrs. Tallant looked cold.

"Just go on, please, Robert." She folded her hands in the lavender silk lap of her dressing robe.

"Well, he was married before——"

"Married before!" Mrs. Tallant repeated in a whisper. "You mean he's a bigamist?"

"Oh no, not that," Mr. Tallant said hastily. "It's not quite as bad as that. But some fellow went to his home town when he first began to get all this publicity, and they told him there. In fact, he claims he saw the woman—a waitress or something."

"Did she acknowledge it?" Mrs. Tallant demanded.

"No," Mr. Tallant said slowly, staring at his wife. "You'd think being that kind of a woman she would talk. But she didn't. In fact, when he asked her, she said it was none of his business. Seemed to take it as an insult, in fact. There seems to be some—some general talk that—well, that Bert married the woman only because—because he had to."

Mrs. Tallant looked hard at her husband. He was blushing. "You mean there's a *child*?" she demanded.

"No, no," Mr. Tallant said hastily and then added, "That—didn't come to anything."

"You mean there wasn't a child?"

"So it seems."

Mrs. Tallant looked relieved. "Probably the whole thing is a fabrication," she said. "I can't imagine a woman who wouldn't make capital out of it. And even if it's true, if there was a divorce——"

"There was a divorce," Mr. Tallant said gloomily. "But the devil of it is he told all the reporters he was never married, you remember."

Mrs. Tallant sat staring. So much had been made of Bert, the unsullied young man. A waitress—a forced marriage!

"Well, of all things," she said at last, "for our family to get into! A sordid affair——."

"It was a marriage, Dottie," Mr. Tallant interrupted, "and that makes a great difference with most people."

"A sordid marriage," Mrs. Tallant said, "and a sordid divorce."

"It was just an ordinary Reno divorce," Mr. Tallant put in mildly.

"Any divorce is sordid when the public gets hold of it," Mrs. Tallant rejoined tartly. "Besides, it's so awkward now, when, as you say, he's given such a wonderful impression of being—well, young and pure." She broke off. "Has anyone else seen the woman?" she inquired.

"I don't know," Mr. Tallant said shortly.

"It doesn't matter to us, of course," Mrs. Tallant said quickly. "But does Kit know?"

"I don't know," Mr. Tallant said thoughtfully, "but I think not."

"I'm sure she doesn't," Mrs. Tallant said. "She couldn't have hid it. She told me his family was—well, I could see she couldn't bear them. But as she said very sensibly, a great many fine American men come from impossible families. Look at most of our presidents! But if there had been something worse, I should have seen it in her."

"Brame believes she doesn't know," Mr. Tallant said.

Mrs. Tallant thought rapidly for a few moments. "After all," she said at last, "everybody has something to keep silent about. Look at the way we had to shield poor Uncle Harry while he was in the Senate! I believe Aunt Maria never let him out of the house without examining the whites of his eyes to see whether he were drunk or not. But he lived with a respectable name until he died, and no newspaper man ever knew he drank himself to death."

"Well, a few did," Mr. Tallant reminded her. "But they never told."

"Oh well, of course everybody liked Uncle Harry," Mrs. Tallant said reasonably. She added, after a moment, "Everybody likes Bert, too."

"I suppose so," Mr. Tallant said.

They looked at each other in mutual understanding and support. Then Mr. Tallant looked away. In the minds of each was the same thing. Once long ago when they were very young they had gone to see a famous French actress in a play. It had been on their honeymoon in Paris, and Mr. Tallant had felt unusually gay, not only because of his honeymoon, but because of Paris. And he had not known much about women then, especially a woman to whom one was married, and he had talked too much about a certain Rachel who was a dancer they had seen, and especially he had talked about her beautiful legs. The outcome of it had been that the young and very willful and pretty American girl he had married had cried a whole day in the hotel and had insisted on going home at once. They compromised on Germany because, as she had said spitefully, there were no wonderful legs there. Besides, both of them knew they could never explain to their families if they had gone home, and it was characteristic of them both that they could still be practical, though in a honeymoon quarrel.

That had been all there was to it, but even now at the distance of years, they both remembered exactly how it had been, and Mrs. Tallant knew that if she had not done as she did there was no telling what might have happened, and Mr. Tallant knew always angrily that that was how she felt.

"Roger Brame is certainly the man," she said.

"That's what I thought," Mr. Tallant replied.

A high wall surrounded Glen Barry. Coddle locked the gate and if Kit stayed away from it she need see no one. At the gate automobiles stopped and people stared in, but that was all. And there was a quarter of a mile between the house and the gate. The only things that could not be prevented were the airplanes that bore down upon them, skirting the tree tops. There was no way of locking them out, though her mother said there must be something one could do. Still, she could simply imagine they were great birds. Besides, they were gone in a moment and the place returned to quiet and loneliness, the lovely loneliness of her childhood.

She had stayed at Glen Barry as a little girl through long autumn weeks alone with her governess, because in a rather delicate childhood her mother had not wanted her to go to town until winter. Gail had been sent early to boarding school, because she was obviously the sort of child who needed companions of her own age, and no governess could manage her.

"Don't be lonely," her mother used to admonish her, year after year, as she stood on the terrace to say good-by. She stooped and kissed Kit's cheek. It was never necessary to add, as if it were Gail, "And mind you obey Miss Hart." Kit was an obedient child.

She was obedient because that was the way to be rid of people. If she obeyed them they let her alone, and when she was alone she could do what she wanted to do. And Glen Barry was the place where loneliness was the most beautiful occupation in the world. The woods, the streams, the horses to ride, the trails and paths and country roads—no day was long enough for all of these. On rainy days there was the library, where her grandfather's books were, as well as their own, and even years of assiduous reading had not been enough to finish all the books. She had learned how to dream here, over books, and here she had been able to write most easily her secret, closely packed verse.

Only for a while had she fled from loneliness, for a little while after Norman Linlay had told her his need for her was ended. Glen Barry had then been intolerable—then, when to be solitary had seemed her doom and not as it had been before her refuge. So when her father had said he was going to go to China she had eagerly wanted to go, too. If she had not gone, what then might have happened to her? Nothing from Norman. Hope was foolish. She had given up the habit of hope. And now she discovered almost as soon as they came to Glen Barry that what she wanted most was the old loneliness. She woke in the morning with the impulse to leap from her bed and go outdoors by herself.

But a married woman, she found, could not so behave. Bert, waking to an empty room next his, felt aggrieved.

"Why didn't you call me?" he demanded when she came in hours later, fresh with the early morning wind upon the meadows.

"You were asleep," she said.

"I'll bet you didn't look to see," he accused her.

She had not. The truth was she wanted to go alone and his being asleep was her excuse even to herself, but she could not possibly tell him so. She was beginning to find out that if one were married there were a great many things which could not be said. She had once told Norman that people who loved one another ought to be able to be absolutely truthful to one another. He had agreed to that and yet somehow it had not proved true even with him, for he used to be annoyed with her if she spoke too honestly, especially about something he had written. The first scene of a play was, she had once told him, clumsy and indirect in the way the characters entered upon their story. He had not liked it when she said so. She felt his displeasure, even though they had agreed upon honesty, and long afterwards, when she knew she was not to see him again, she realized that the change in him had begun that day. It would have been better if she had told him nothing. No, she could be honest only with herself, and with no one else.

Gail had gone at last, lingering after she had sent the children back to town with their nurse, until Harvey on the third night drove out for her.

"Gail will be going back with me after dinner," he told Mrs. Tallant quietly. Gail twisted a corner of her mouth at him, and turned her back on him.

"Bert, let's have lunch together, you and I, when you come to town," she said perversely.

"Sure thing," Bert said. He still couldn't make Gail out. If she hadn't been his relation, he would have known exactly where she was, but a sister-in-law wasn't a woman.

"The first day," Gail persisted, her eye cornerwise on Harvey.

"Swell," Bert said promptly. Harvey must be a fool, he thought. Harvey sat there sipping his cocktail, his eyes upon his wife as amiable as a watchdog's upon a beloved mistress.

But after dinner Harvey had gone home early and taken Gail with him exactly as he had planned.

"Somebody can fetch your things tomorrow," he had said.

Then the fine November weather broke, and December began in a cold rain. Her mother at the breakfast table this morning shivered and told Smedley the house was too cold. She and her mother and Bert were at a late breakfast. The dark day had made them all oversleep.

"I suppose we must go to town," Mrs. Tallant said briskly. She always put on especial briskness when the weather was dull. "It's time we did; everything has begun there. And this rain ends your father's golf for the season. There is no reason not to go back to town when that happens. Oh dear—perhaps I had better wait until after the week end."

"Is there anything you'd like me to do, Mother?" Kit asked.

"Oh no," Mrs. Tallant replied. "The house in town has been ready for weeks. I've just been putting off going. I'll send Smedley up Monday, and we can go on Tuesday."

They were talking as though Bert were not there. Unconsciously they had all fallen into that habit. Mrs. Tallant, looking at him as he ate pancakes thought, "It's well he is decorative— otherwise what would be his use?" Ever since her talk with her husband she found herself full of small acid thoughts concerning her son-in-law.

"What are you doing today, Bert?" she asked briskly.

Bert looked up. "I'll get along," he answered. "Maybe I'll work some on my stamps."

He had begun collecting stamps. Until Mr. Brame had told him, he had had no idea how valuable stamps could be. Now it seemed foolish not to collect stamps when he had such a lot of mail and letters from all over the world. Mr. Brame attended to the letters but sent the stamps on to him.

"I'll be in my sitting room," Mrs. Tallant said, "in case anyone wants me." She touched her fingers to the water in the bowl Smedley set before her and went away.

Kit, left alone with Bert, leaned on her elbows and smiled at him a little vaguely.

"Where are you going to work on your stamps?" she asked.

Bert's face was almost a blur to her. She saw his blond good looks no more, for the moment, than if she had opened a magazine to a photograph.

"I don't know," he said. But her ears were dulled by her own inwardness and she did not catch the overtone of restlessness in his voice. "I might come in to the library where you are, Kit, if you're only going to read."

She was alarmed and then ashamed. Why should it disturb her if he sat quietly at the table working on his stamps? But she had never been able even to read happily if she were not alone in the library. And Bert, who could be so quiet when there were other people, when he was alone with her was noisy in a score of small restless ways, clamoring, she perceived, for her attention. She had thought it rather touching and at first she had responded instantly to his every demand. It was pleasant to be needed when she had not been much needed in her life as the youngest child in a house busy with servants. There was something dear as well as amusing in having this tall boy stoop to have his hair parted or his shirt collar buttoned. And ordinarily she was not changed in this but today she was alone. The deep grayness of the day lay like a fog between her and every other being. Weather outside had been always the weather, too, of her spirit. She could not be gay on a somber day until night fell and curtains were drawn and she could no longer see the melancholy hills. Even then she must not hear the wind, or else she heard it above every human voice. It was a withdrawal to which she was accustomed and against which she had never struggled. She perceived now with a sort of detached curiosity that Bert's face seemed no nearer to her than any other.

"Why don't you go into my sitting room?" she asked. "I'll put the stamps ready for you there."

"All right," he said docilely, staring out of the window. The rain had begun to fall heavily and the last of the color was draining from the trees in the downward fluttering leaves.

. . . But he didn't feel like sitting down. He felt like doing something. There could be no riding today; he'd go into the gymnasium and bat some balls around.

"Guess I won't do stamps," he said suddenly. "I need exercise."

He rose from the table abruptly. It seemed to him all of a sudden that he could not sit there another moment. He had nothing to do. He felt as though his body were a horse, straining against a bit. He had to work himself hard at something—anything. The house was so quiet. If he were home he'd go downtown and play pool. But he wasn't home. He stooped and kissed her cheek.

"So long," he said, "maybe I'll drop in on you later." . . .

She went to the library and allowed the deep velvet quiet of books to enwrap her. It was a quiet far beyond the mere stillness of the body. It was the meaningful silence of thought and reflection and poetry working itself soundlessly into her own depths. She had often said that this room, built by her grandfather and added to the house which had been his own father's in a simpler age, was the most beautiful room in the world. It was oak-paneled and dim, the lights shaded except where they could fall across a book, the carpets deep and soft and green as moss under forest trees, and a wide window was thrown toward the hills, and books covered the walls from floor to ceiling. Time did not exist for her here. She shut it out when she shut the heavy oak door upon all else. No one, she knew by long habit, came here in the day time, if it were not Sunday. She was safe to be alone.

She curled into the deep window seat and lay gazing out over the rainy hills. At once her mind stripped itself. Everything was gone except this primary struggle with its own thought. She sat in a long fruitful daydream, shaping her own mood, holding fast her own feeling, until at last she began to feel slowly words in a rhythm, two lines, then another and another. And once this process began it went on to a completion, whether final or not she could not tell now, but at least to some sort of end, because she felt released and full of ease. She turned away from the window and closed her eyes and floated downward in the quiet like a bird into a windless valley.

She slept a long time, or thought she must have, when she heard the door open and her mother's voice call to her with a sharpness which snatched her instantly awake.

"Kit, we're going to town immediately. I've changed my mind."

She opened her eyes and sat up. Her mother's face was disturbed in spite of its careful calm and her neck was spotted with red.

"Now?" she asked.

"As soon as we can have luncheon."

"Is something wrong?" she asked.

"No," her mother said quickly. "You had better go and get ready."

The door shut. She knew that her mother was telling a lie. She must find Bert. Something was wrong.

She found him on the couch in her room, lying with his arms under his head, staring out of the window. It was, she now saw, still raining.

"Bert!" she exclaimed.

He turned morose eyes on her.

"I suppose your mother's been making out I'm a—" he began.

"She didn't say anything except that we are going to town at once," Kit said, looking down at him, astonished.

"Not a word?" he demanded.

"Nothing but that," she replied. "What is it, Bert? What's happened?"

"Nothing," he said sullenly, "except we had a fight—sort of——"

"Oh, Bert——"

He sat up and pushed back his hair. "Gosh, I'm getting tired of doing nothing, I guess."

She watched him a moment, scenting a difference in him. "I believe you are," she said quietly. Something had happened, but he was going to tell her nothing. Her pride rose and she said no more.

Mrs. Tallant, in her formal rose taffeta decorated bedroom of the town house was explaining to Mr. Tallant why she had suddenly left Glen Barry.

"I dismissed the girl at once, of course," she said.

The red spots were back on her neck. She could see them in the mirror before which she sat dressing her hair for dinner. That meant her blood pressure would be up, though her doctor had warned her particularly. "Her home is in Parton's Corners, and I had her driven straight to her own door and left there. Her father is the butcher, she says. It was disgusting. I simply couldn't stay at Glen Barry another moment."

"He wasn't really—doing anything, was he?" Mr. Tallant inquired after a delicate pause. He held in his hand a copy of the publicity Mr. Brame planned to release for the morning papers. As soon as Dottie had telephoned she was coming, he had telephoned Brame. When people heard that Bert Holm was here invitations would pour upon them. All hope of quiet would be gone. But if it had to be, it was better to have it properly announced. It was all troublesome enough without this extra fuss about Bert. In his secret heart he felt that his wife made far too much fuss over this sort of thing. Privately he believed that even though a man were happily married, with two beautiful daughters, he could still enjoy looking at a pretty woman, though for himself it would not be worth it, even if he were that sort, because of the fuss Dottie would make if she found out, as of course she would! Women seemed fairly to smell that sort of thing. It was on their minds all the time.

"I don't know what you mean by doing anything," Mrs. Tallant said. "He should not have been doing anything, if that's what you mean. I can only be grateful that I and not Kit came upon them."

"Where were they?"

"In that little dark passageway leading to the gymnasium. I always said it was too dark in there. He was in his shorts. She'd gone down to—to clean, she said. And I'd gone down to see what was the matter with the outlet to the indoor pool. Smedley had reported it wasn't working. They didn't expect me, of course. And I certainly didn't expect them."

123

Mr. Tallant felt he could press no further.

"I wonder if we are being fair to Kit to say nothing?" Mrs. Tallant said thoughtfully. She turned to him. "If I thought he were bad, Rob, I'd tell her in a moment. But he's just a fool. And she's so tender. If she were like Gail, I would simply leave it to her. But how can Kit cope with him? She has no experience with men. I keep feeling if we could only get something for him to do he would be all right. Can't you take him into the bank?"

"No," Mr. Tallant said strongly. "I won't, and that's all there is to be said on that, Dottie. I'm not going in for nepotism. He's a perfectly ignorant young man, and I wouldn't think of such a thing as taking him into the bank. Just because for the moment he's America's greatest hero doesn't make him fit for anything else."

Mrs. Tallant looked at her husband with a despairing sigh.

"What are we going to do with him?" she asked.

"Keep the publicity right," Mr. Tallant said grimly.

"But Kit?"

"Keep up the publicity with her, too," he repeated. "Don't tell her anything."

He took a pen from his pocket and wrote a large O.K. upon the copy in his hand. Then he rang the bell. When an elderly maid appeared, he gave her the envelope.

"Get that to Mr. Roger Brame at once by special messenger," he told her.

"Well," Mrs. Tallant said, "we'll never fool Gail. She's too much like me."

Gail looked at her husband across their own breakfast table. Her light hazel eyes were dancing. There were times, Harvey Crane thought to himself, when Gail's eyes were full of splinters of light. He admired them, but he knew his Gail.

"What are you doing for lunch?" he had asked.

She lifted her eyelashes at him above her cup. "Don't you

remember? It's Bert's first day in town," she replied. "We have a luncheon engagement."

"On guard, Gail," Harvey said quietly.

She put her cup down and looked at him with a too perfect surprise.

"You're a strong drink for a man who can't hold his liquor any better than Bert," he said. His face changed no minutia of expression. Harvey Crane's exterior was unalterable and even Gail could not penetrate it. "Someday," she had declared, "I shall take to cutting little wedges out of him, as one does out of a watermelon, to see what's inside."

"Me?" she now inquired, too innocently.

"You," he replied.

. . . He was not in the least afraid of her indiscretion. Before he had proposed to Gail Tallant he had made up his mind how to manage her—plenty of head but a hard hand on the bridle at the last, and no change from that. She must know that whatever she did he knew it, but he was inexorable only at a certain point. She could lunch with any man she liked, but she must be home for dinner with her husband. She could sit out a dozen dances, but he brought her and took her home himself. All of the liveliness which he recognized as essential to her was only to play over the solid earth of his home and of his marriage. He had gauged her well enough before he married her to realize that she wanted the contrast of that stability. He knew that of the two sisters Gail was the one to be trusted for the final conventions. She was wild enough, but the final part of her was docile and wanted to be held. Whereas Kit—Kit was the sort who would sell her soul to please and to obey and then go completely crazy when her self-control broke. What was that story he used to hear the old Episcopal rector in St. Mary's read when he himself was a dogged little choir boy there? Something about a man with two sons and one said when his father told him to go to the field that he wouldn't go, and then he did. That was Gail. But the other said he would, and then didn't. That was Kit. Only Kit would mean to go and want to go. But there was something essentially unstable in her—the instability of the soul too sensitive to endure even its own decisions. . . .

"Why?" Gail was asking michievously. Her elbows were on the table and her pretty chin rested on her interlaced hands. She looked up at him from under the long gold-brown lashes which she wielded as women wield an ostrich-feather fan. "You don't think I'm too——."

"Of course I don't," he replied. "I see you sparkling your eyes at all my friends, don't I? But they're used to it. Bert isn't. He begins to melt in the heat."

She burst into bright laughter and rose and went over to her husband and ruffled his smooth dun-colored hair.

"I like you," she declared. "I don't know why—you're not half as good-looking as Bert."

"I see through you, that's why," he answered. He took her hand and kissed it with apparent calmness. But Gail, used as she was, felt a faint admiring quiver of the flesh. He could see through her—and he never let her see through him. And she was used to seeing through men and women, too. She had always been cleverer than anybody around her until she married Harvey. He had not told her anything about himself before they were married, and never would, though to her own surprise she always told him everything—sooner or later.

Now, perched on the arm of his chair, she said mock-mournfully, "It's a pity Bert is married to Kit. It would have been rather fun too—to——"

"Make a fool of a public hero," he finished. He folded his napkin and pushed her gently away, and rose. "But it would be short-sighted of you, my dear, to make a fool of your own brother-in-law—too close home—the Tallant home, not to mention your own."

She sighed and put up her mouth to be kissed.

"How is Dickie's cold?" he inquired.

"I haven't been in," she confessed, "but the nurse hasn't——."

"Run up and see before I go—there's a good girl," he commanded her imperturbably. She was not the best of mothers—but he wanted her for a wife, first. He saw to the children himself when he felt it necessary.

She obeyed, pausing at the door to make a little face at him.

"I don't know why I get up to breakfast every day with you," she remarked. "No woman I know does as much for her husband."

He smiled slightly, without answering. Between them was a bond of absolutely mutual passion. He had made sure of that. He knew, and he knew Gail knew, that no man in the world could more perfectly fulfill her needs than he. He understood her to the last drop of her blood. He watched her, proud of her and of himself.

When she turned into the nursery door he lit a cigarette and went to the hall closet for his topcoat. He prided himself on being practical. And certainly the only practical basis of marriage was complete mutuality. He had Gail by the inward tether and she knew it.

"Gail!" he called.

"He's much better," she answered, coming out to the stairs. He looked up at her. She was absolutely beautiful to him. Every line of her spare graceful body suited him. He hated fat women—fat being his own enemy. He waited while she came near. The atmosphere between them quickened. He was aware of it and so was she, he knew. When she was face to face with him, he seized her in his arms and kissed her, a long deep kiss. She said nothing, but she was limp in his arms. He let her go quickly.

"I don't know another woman in the world who could induce

her husband to make love to her immediately after breakfast," he remarked.

She stood, smiling at him. "It is sickening, isn't it!" she agreed.

He went no further with it. She was capable of teasing him into anything.

"I must get to the office," he said and kissing her lightly on the lips, he went away.

She stood a moment after he was gone. She gave Bert up easily enough. There were plenty of men like Bert. He had his importance for her, not because he was important, but because he had showed her that the girl Gail was still alive, waiting impatient for some of the old fun! Wildness danced in her brain and in her blood. She knew what would happen. Wildness could come out of her and make her feel like a werewolf, or like the fox woman in an old Chinese fairy tale she had once read in a collection of fairy tales that Kit had. Bert had waked her again and she would go prowling out into the world, in search of someone to play with, a beautiful young man who would agree that no foundations must be shaken, no rock beneath their dancing feet touched by any dynamite. She was young and graceful, light and pretty and brimming with gayety, mischief, and malice. When she went out today men catching her scent and glitter would turn to look at her. She felt grateful to Bert and only a little regretful for him, as she went to the telephone and rang up her mother's house.

"Mr. Holm, please," she said to the answering maid. And when Bert's eager voice shouted in her ear, she said quickly, "Bert, I can't have lunch with you, my dear. I forgot and made a bridge date."

She listened, smiling and pleased with his protestation. "Aw, Gail——"

How pitifully easy it would be to be first a pretty sister-in-law, and then—just a pretty woman—a too pretty woman!

"No, I can't tomorrow, either. Let's make a foursome—you and Kit, and Harvey and I—some night next week."

She hung up. Poor Kit! She dallied about her sunlit rooms, her eyes as golden as a tiger's.

. . . Bert, hearing that definite click, put up the receiver dolefully. This day was spoiled for him, empty, just as it used to be when he was a kid and his pop had promised to take him to town and didn't. Queer how Gail's being so lively made Kit seem too quiet, though no time ago he had been saying he liked her because she was quiet! Kit was probably in the library now—stuck in a book. He might go and find her. But she'd look up with those faraway eyes. She always said, "Of course I will," when he wanted her to go somewhere or do something, but you knew she didn't really want to. He wanted to do something off on his own, with somebody who wanted what he did. Gail, he'd bet, would have been game for anything. There was play in her. . . .

He wandered toward the dining room, and opening the buffet, found an empty decanter. He rang the bell, long and hard, and Smedley appeared as suddenly as if he had been shot out of a box, struggling into his coat as he came. He stared at Bert.

"What the heck makes you look like that?" Bert demanded.

"Nothing, sir—I'm sorry, I'm sure," Smedley replied, hastily. "It's only that nobody rings long like that, except Mr. Tallant, and him I know to be at the bank at this hour."

"Get me some of that stuff we had last night," Bert commanded him.

"It don't belong in this decanter, sir," Smedley replied anxiously. "It was Scotch, sir."

"Well, get it," Bert answered. And then as an afterthought he added, grinning, "Scotch or Irish, I don't care. I can drink 'em both."

"Yes, sir," Smedley said, without smiling.

He waited until Smedley brought back a gold-labeled bottle and poured him a small glass.

"That's why they call it Scotch—stingy, eh?" he complained.

"It's very strong, sir," Smedley replied, cautiously.

"Give me another," Bert demanded. "I'll see for myself. That's my motto. That's what I said when I went up the old mountain. Say, Smedley, I kinda wish I hadn't gone."

"Yes, sir," Smedley's voice was altogether colorless.

"Yeah, I do," Bert repeated. "For instance, here I am, all dressed up and nowhere to go. For I don't call these soup and fish joints any place to go—do you, Smedley?"

Smedley coughed behind his hand. He was pondering what he would do if Mr. Holm should ask for a third glass of Mr. Tallant's best whisky. It was a pity such a young man couldn't stand up better under it. Mr. Tallant now was a wonder. Nothing threw him off his feet, but then he was used to it.

"Smedley," Bert began, "if you was me—in my shoes, you know—and you'd counted on going out with a lady and got turned down, what would you do with your time?"

Smedley coughed again. Extremely difficult, he decided; yet no one could help liking the young fellow.

"Pity it isn't tonight, sir," he remarked. "There's a very good fight over on First Avenue, at a little place I know."

"Is there?" Bert said eagerly. "Let's go together, old boy— what say? There ain't a goddamned fellow I know to go places with in this whole city. You know what I mean—a real man——"

"You mean go incog, so to speak, sir?" Smedley said, thoughtfully. Why not, he asked himself? Hadn't he boasted to various friends of his that he knew Bert Holm? After all, it was a free country. The only person he feared was the madam and what she didn't know wouldn't hurt her.

"You have a stag dinner, sir," he reminded Bert. "The Alpine Club, sir."

"I'll leave early," Bert said excitedly. "Come on! I haven't had a bust since—since I broke loose from that old Englishman!"

He must break loose—go off on his own, among people of his own kind. He'd often thought, as he sat at the table and Smedley served him, that the fellow looked a good old boy—knew his way around probably, too.

"Very well, sir," Smedley said, after a moment's further thought. "I'll just write the address." He pulled out a small pad and pencil and wrote on it and tore out the leaf and handed it to Bert. "I'll be there myself at a quarter to ten, sir."

"Swell!" Bert shouted, and clapped him on the back fit to burst the bottle from his hand. He winced and bore it. It would be something, wouldn't it, if he showed Bert Holm off? After all, the men there had as much right to see him as anyone else. It was a democracy, wasn't it?

He made up for this by being all the rest of the day as formal as though Bert were the Prince of Wales, ignoring his wink over the salad at luncheon. For Bert lunched at home, between Kit and Mrs. Tallant.

"Bert!" Kit cried softly, "where have you been?"

She sat up in bed, astonished. He stood in the door between their rooms, smiling at her. She scrambled out of bed and went over to him. "Why, you're feverish!" she exclaimed.

"Full of f-fever," he agreed dolefully. He stared at her as she came to him. "I want to lie down," he said. He turned and fell upon his bed. Then suddenly he sat up. "Go away, Kit," he said. "I want to be sick—all by myself."

She fled out of the room to call her mother. But outside in the hall she found Smedley standing as though he were waiting for her.

"You're not calling madam, are you, miss?" he inquired.

"Yes, I was!" she answered, again astonished. "How did you know?"

"Don't, miss," Smedley urged. "He'll be all right. He—over-et —something extraordinary. He'll be all right, as soon as—if you'll excuse me, miss—it's all up——"

They listened to Bert in the bathroom being very ill.

"I'd better go in, miss," Smedley said gently.

She went back to her room full of doubts. After a while, hearing only silence, she peered into Bert's room. He lay in his bed as though asleep and Smedley stood looking down at him.

"Is he all right?" she whispered, stealing in.

"Perfectly, miss," he replied. "All he needs now is sleep." He coughed slightly and added, "A real enthusiastic young man, miss—the disposition that never knows when to stop."

They stood looking down at Bert. When he slept his face went back to its childhood, even to the shape of his babyhood. His cheeks grew smooth and his lips pouted. It was impossible not to feel him touching and young.

"Wonderful likable chap, miss," Smedley said, and smiled at her. . . . After all, he'd known her since she was in socks and little dresses. But she didn't answer, only smiled back the same little half-sad smile she'd always had. Getting married hadn't changed her much, he thought—not like Miss Gail, who settled down nicely. But then, Miss Kit was always serious—too serious . . . "Wonderful," he repeated. "Good night, miss," he added.

"Good night, Smedley—and thank you," she replied.

He left her and tip-toed away. In the crowded hall where the fight had been, it had got around of course who Bert was, and the men had gone wild. The fight was nothing compared to it. And Bert had shouted with the best of them, telling them what they wanted to know—one of them, he was. He'd had a fine good time out of it and he hadn't wanted to come home at all.

Smedley, in his own small private part of the Tallant house, shut the door.

"He don't belong here," he thought, "not half as much as I do myself, in a way. It's a good thing, probably, to let him get loose once in a while on the sly. He'll keep in line the better for it."

Thus he justified himself for the night's adventure.

"What they don't know won't hurt 'em," he added. But he was thinking again especially of Mrs. Tallant. . . .

Kit bent over Bert and put her hand on his forehead. His face which had been so flushed when he came in, was now almost pallid, and it was wet to her touch. There was no fever in him any more, at least. He felt cold. She pulled the gold-colored eiderdown closer about him, gently, lest he wake, but he slept as though nothing could ever wake him.

So she sat on the edge of the bed and looked at him. All this evening she had longed for him vaguely. That was because of the music. She had gone with her father and mother to hear *Tristan and Isolde,* and the familiar opera had swept her along its river of feeling. She had wished Bert could hear it, yet knowing, too, that he did not care for music. But there was so much more than mere music to this. Who could keep from feeling that this music was only a symbol? She held him fast in her mind while he had gone off to his stag dinner, looking wonderfully handsome. He had learned how to wear his evening clothes and they became him as they did all tall blond men. And he would enjoy himself—men nearly always liked him. She had sat, quite at rest about him, and let herself be carried deeper and deeper into the music. And when it was over, they had come home in the silence which must follow such music and she had kissed her parents good night and come upstairs. Sometimes, she thought, she was sure her parents were more than usually kind to her these days. It was almost as it used to be when she was a child and something had gone wrong with her. But nothing was wrong now. She had undressed and bathed and gone to bed and then waited for Bert to come home. That was all.

She sat now, curled at his feet, thinking of the music she had heard. Those lovers had found in each other the end and meaning of life. That was what they always taught you about love—that it was the end for which everyone sought. When it came all problems ceased and life took its pattern forever. You knew where you were after that.

But the strange thing was you never knew. Less than before she now knew where she was. What no one ever told was that after marriage people were really more confused than ever. For simply going on as she and Bert were now doing was no use at all. He knew no more than she what they should do—less than she, for he did not even feel her lack. If they had been poor and had had to work to live, that would have been one necessity to guide them. Without this necessity what had they? Love was no end to anything. In itself it was only a state of being and it could be even meaningless. Bert loved her but his love provided him with no guide even for himself.

She sat in the silence, hearing Bert's sleeping breath, and hearing Tristan's voice, retreating into echoes.

Gail, dancing with her own husband at the party they were giving for Kit, watched over Harvey's solid shoulder the spectacle of Bert Holm growing moment by moment more thoroughly drunk. Now that Harvey had put his taboo upon Bert, she watched him with nothing but a fairly mild curiosity. It was a pity that Kit never saw him getting drunk in time to stop it. This was the third time it had happened in a month, the first time at the Whitfields and the second at the Van der Meers. Both times it had been embarrassing. Bert did not hold his liquor well, and he had no knowledge of how or what to drink.

She watched the inevitable effect upon him. It made him not boisterous or noisy, but full of a teasing childish mischief, a desire to snatch at women's hair and shoulder straps and to pretend he was pulling zippers up and down their backs. If the women were a little drunk, too, there would be loud laughter. But more often even quite young women, if they were still sober, simply moved away or parried him a little too gaily. After all, whatever he did, he was still Bert Holm.

"If he were in a night club," she murmured into Harvey's ear, "I wouldn't lift a finger. But this is our own house. Don't you think you'd better just—guide him away somewhere?"

Bert was dancing with Rita Blakeslee, a debutante newly out of finishing school. They were romping along, beautiful to look at, both of them mad, but there was nobody here who would mind very much, for she had purposely invited a rather small crowd of smart people. And yet, of course, Bert could not do what other men could, for somehow or other stories crept out. In spite of Roger Brame there had been a story last week in the tabloids about the cocktail party where he had poured a glass of ice water down his hostess's back, and one heard queer tales of his appearing in strange, vulgar places, late at night, drunk.

"He doesn't remember anything about it," Kit had said in distress the morning after the cocktail party. But by then it was too late. Of course some people only laughed, but the people who mattered did not laugh. In spite of her own mocking fun of conservatism and what she called the "old guard," Gail knew very well that all her mockery was safe only so long as she was securely married to Harvey. A married woman, never divorced, and the mother of two sturdy and carefully cared-for little boys who looked beautiful in photographs with her, could be as free as she liked in what she said. Men rather liked a young matron with an edgy tongue, especially if they knew there was nothing loose about her except her talk. There was something sharp in the contrast. When she made willful argument they laughed and she simply built up her reputation for wit. Poor Irene Cavanaugh, her roommate at finishing school who had married twice, so unluckily each time, and was now divorced again, had to be as careful as an old-fashioned Sunday school teacher.

"Where is Kit?" Harvey demanded a little irritably. "Why isn't she looking after him?"

"She is dancing with somebody," Gail said. "Besides, Kit's the last person to see unless she is told. She's always like someone in a dream, that girl!"

Even as she spoke she saw Kit and their eyes met. She nodded slightly toward Bert.

"She sees him now," she murmured. "Poor Kit!"

Kit saw Bert instantly. She must not, of course, make any sign that she saw. But the sense of dismaying helplessness which was her inner state most of the time, fell upon her again. What should she do if Bert really began to make a habit of this, as Uncle Henry had? But it wasn't the same. Uncle Henry had been so clever and determined about it, and made up his mind deliberately to get drunk twice a month. Bert could never be so determined or so clever. He slipped into it, not realizing what was happening to him. What did one do with someone who never realized what was happening to him?

As soon as the dance was over she moved through the crowd toward Bert. He was standing alone and a little uncertainly, by the window.

"Bert, will you take me out on the terrace?" she begged. "I feel dizzy."

He stared at her gravely through eyes that did not quite focus. "You haven't been taking too much, Kit?" he inquired.

She smiled, put her hand in his arm, and guided him toward the door. When she got him into the cold clear wintry air he would know what he was doing. She opened the glass door and stepped out and walked across the tiles, and he followed her to the balustrade. Behind them were Gail's beautiful rooms, full of flowers and light and warmth. Against a background of Harvey's inherited mid-Victorian furniture, Gail wore her ultra-modern evening gowns and her fantastic new coiffures, as though she were a woman stepping out of the nineties, in a perpetual symbolism. Everything in Gail's house was planned to show off Gail by contrast.

They stood side by side, looking down on Central Park and the inverted sky of the city lights. The windless air was edged with frost. It was one of New York's matchless nights.

"Gosh," Bert whispered, sobering for a moment in the cold, "there's something about this that makes me think of that old mountain top."

"Oh, Bert, what?" she asked.

There was no use in telling him how silly it was for him to keep on drinking. She shrank indeed from thinking how foolishly he behaved when he was drunk. In a time when most of her generation accepted getting drunk as an inevitable occasional accident, it seemed useless even to tell him that she hated it. Besides, she knew that the trouble was that he had not enough to do. But whenever she talked to her mother about their own house and finding a place where they could live more quietly than they could in New York, her mother said, "Not yet, Kit darling, not just when Mr. Brame is getting his publicity so nicely organized. This winter you and Bert must give yourselves to his public. Public interest won't last—nothing does, you know, darling. It's so important to have it all end in a dignified way—important to us, darling. . . ."

"I guess it's the sky," he said, looking up. "It's a big piece of sky. Maybe it's the buildings. They look sort of like mountain tops, don't they?"

"Yes, they do," she murmured. It was easy to imagine, looking at the tops of the towers around them, that they were the precipitous cliffs of lonely mountain ranges. High up like this, on the thirtieth floor, the earth sank away into valleys. She stood for a moment transported. If she and Bert could get away into mountains!

"That's strong stuff Gail serves," Bert said uneasily. "I hope it don't make me sick. I feel kind of funny."

She came back to him. "Why do you drink so much of it?" she asked helplessly.

"I don't know," he said as helplessly.

They stood gazing in silence over the city.

"I kind of wish," he said at last slowly, "that I could go away from here—get right out of here."

"Oh, Bert, yes!" she agreed.

"I'd like to go back where I was, before all this began."

"I'd love to go with you, Bert," she said.

And why not? Perhaps there upon the mountains he loved she would find Bert, the man she had married. She had not found him elsewhere. Why not go away from this? The earth was full of freedom in which they had no share.

For they lived their days now in a rush of people and parties and interviews and dinners and photographers, all, it was true, judiciously and quietly managed by Roger Brame. They did nothing without Roger Brame; the Lion Tamer, Gail called him, laughing at him. But what he really tamed was the crowd. Kit felt his little dry practical figure standing between them and that crowd she never once forgot. She and Bert were safe as long as Roger Brame kept them at bay. Each invitation was subjected to his careful appraisal before it was accepted or rejected.

And yet it was slavery. The days were planned from breakfast until midnight. In the midst of luxury and ease they lived in slavery to Roger Brame. No, not to Roger Brame. What they were enslaved by was that super-hero, Bert Holm. Shaped by Roger Brame, Bert Holm was beginning to take on the immense potentialities of the popular hero who by his sterling personal worth was proving to be more than the figure of a moment. She knew that figure, according to the newspapers. He was a family man. His devotion to his rather fragile quiet little wife was beautiful. They were never seen apart. Whenever his tall person was set upon a page, there looked out from beside him her own shy face. Kit, gazing at the two faces, thought with a sort of surprise, "They look quite happy together."

And so they might be quite happy, she thought with resolu-

138

tion for happiness, if they could ever be alone. But they were never alone—they had never been alone. And if it were not for Mr. Brame, they would have been overwhelmed. The public was always beside them waiting at the door with autograph books, with scraps of paper and stubby pencils. Boys climbed on the running boards of their car when a stoplight held them and begged hoarsely through the windows.

"Oh come on, Bert, give us your name—it don't cost you nothin', does it?"

But Mr. Brame had told them he must not put his name to bits of paper. One never knew what could be written above a signature.

It had grown intolerably tiresome. What had once been amusing and even touching, she thought, remembering the pathos of the upturned, straining, wistful faces of crowds, was now unbearable effrontery, the too ardent attentions of strangers to whom yet somehow they belonged.

And then, suddenly, to her amazement Bert was crying upon her shoulder.

"Why, Bert!" she cried. "Why, darling!"

"You look so sad," he sobbed. "It's because I'm no good. I know I'm rotten."

"Bert, you're not!" she cried, her arms tight about him. "Think of all the people who say you are wonderful!"

"They don't know anything about me," he sobbed. "You're the only one who really knows about me—or cares a damn about me——"

"But I think you're wonderful, too, Bert——"

"No, you don't, Kit!" He was actually clinging to her. "Why, you couldn't! You're so sweet and good—and I'm just stinking! You don't know half how bad I am, Kit. Why, I——"

In the midst of his sobbing he was about to stammer out something when the glass door opened. It was Gail in her scarlet dress.

"What on earth are you two doing?" she demanded. "A Romeo

and Juliet out here on the edge of the terrace? Or are you trying to throw yourself over, Bert?"

Her voice came cutting across Bert's emotion like a cold wind.

"Bert is—isn't feeling well," Kit answered hotly.

Gail drew three steps nearer and stared.

"He's just drunk, Kit," she said and laughed.

And against her shoulder Kit felt Bert's body begin to tremble. He pressed his face into her shoulder—sobbing? No, he was laughing! She drew away from him quickly and he lifted his face and looked at Gail.

"You're right again. . . ." he stuttered. "I'm just too—d-damned drunk!"

He broke into helpless rocking laughter.

Gail had been very kind in spite of laughter. Kit, sitting beside Bert's bed the next morning, poured him a glass of ice water from the carafe. Gail had let them in by another door and they had taken the elevator down and had come home. And Smedley had said nothing when he opened the door. He had simply helped Bert upstairs to his room.

"Is there anything more, Miss?" he had asked when he had taken off Bert's clothes and put him to bed.

"Nothing more, thanks," she had said. Smedley could be trusted to remember nothing in the morning.

Now the telephone rang.

"Oh, gosh!" Bert groaned.

"Just lie still, darling," she begged him, and took up the receiver. It was Gail.

"How is he?" Gail's voice came over the telephone with all its warmth extracted, until only the thin essence of it remained, but she was used to Gail's voice like that on the telephone.

"He has a fearful headache, of course," she answered.

"Of course," Gail agreed. She hesitated, and then went on briskly. "Kit, I don't know if I should say anything, but after you

140

had gone last night Rita told everybody Bert had proposed elope-
ment to her."

"What—oh, Gail—that's silly!"

"Of course it is, but the only thing I could say to excuse him
was the truth—that he was stewed and didn't know what he was
saying."

She waited for Kit to answer, but when Kit did not answer
she went on. "Nothing will come of it this time, except Rita went
on to a night club. I called her up this morning and told her she
mustn't talk any more. She was very decent, I must say—said she
was half stewed herself and couldn't remember what she said.
But she says Bert really did. And I told her that she had to understand even great men went on the loose a little sometimes." Gail
laughed over the telephone and listened. "Kit, darling, are you
there?" she inquired when she heard nothing.

"Yes, I'm here," Kit replied.

"Don't sound so mournful, Kit! It's not his fault—mostly—it's
just that nobody can stand what he's getting."

"Yes, Gail, thank you."

She hung up the receiver and turned to Bert. He was lying
crumpled against his pillows, his eyes shut.

"Bert," she demanded, "what did you say last night to Rita
Blakeslee?"

"Rita Blakeslee?" he groaned. "Never heard of the woman."

"But Bert—" she began, when there was a knock on the door.
"Come in," she called.

It was Sarah, the elder housemaid. "It's Mr. Brame, Miss," she
said. "And please, Miss, he says it's urgent."

"I'll be down at once," she answered.

She rose and went into the bathroom and found an ice bag and
filled it with crushed ice from a bowl full upon the table. Smedley
had brought it up a few moments before without explanations.
She put the cap upon Bert's hot head and then drew down the

shades against the too bright morning sun and went downstairs to Mr. Brame.

As soon as she entered the library she knew something was wrong. Her father and mother were already there. It must be something very wrong if her father were not now on his way to Wall Street. They sat in the dark handsome room, looking a part of it indeed, three elderly people deciding, as she knew, upon Bert. She came in a little timidly.

"Good morning, Mr. Brame," she said. Her voice sounded so faint that she cleared her throat to excuse it.

"Good morning," he said gravely. "I am sorry to have to call you to business so early, but there has been an unfortunate bit of publicity this morning, not, I am glad to say, in the important papers, which we have well in hand, but in a woman's gossip column. Of course she is known to be catty and all that, but her column is read because of a supposed wit. And anything that makes people laugh at Bert Holm just now is most unfortunate. There have been too many stories lately, from unexpected quarters. And I might say, Mrs. Holm, that his remarks on birth control last Tuesday were most unfortunate. Many people have strong prejudices on the subject. It is always wise for a public figure to avoid a definite statement on a controversial matter."

She stopped the flow of Mr. Brame.

"Bert doesn't care anything about birth control."

She had said last Tuesday, over the newspaper, "Bert, did you say you believe the government ought to enforce birth control among the lower classes?"

He had blushed and looked sheepish. "Hell, no," he said. "Some female or other kept pesterin' me last night at that dinner, and I said I guessed she was right."

"Then it is a pity he said so," Mr. Brame retorted. His dignified gray face turned a strange red.

Her mother broke in swiftly. "Mr. Brame thinks, dear, that

142

we should plan something for Bert—an expedition or something, just to get him out of the public eye for the moment——"

"Rather, if I may explain, Mrs. Tallant," Mr. Brame interposed, "to get him in the public eye again in the proper light. You may be interested, Mrs. Holm, in some detailed studies which I have made of important public characters in recent years, with the graphs of the rise and fall of their popularity."

He took from a leather briefcase on the floor beside him some mimeographed pamphlets and looked them over rapidly. "I have handled a number of personages. Let me see—hm, let me see, perhaps—here's one, although almost any one I might choose out of the hundred odd that I have would be about the same. In this case as in Mr. Holm's, the popularity begins at a high point immediately following some single act which fires the ready imagination of the public. It rises rapidly until after the public ovation. After that there is a slight decline, natural because the public has somewhat overspent itself. They are ashamed of their own warmth, so to speak, and their curiosity is satisfied since they have seen their hero. There is, however, a slight rise again, or a continued level high for a short time, during which they have opportunities to hear their hero make public speeches and new crowds are seeing him at closer range in different places. When this secondary public is satisfied there is a rapid decline in interest, unless a spectacle of some sort again presents itself, and it is likely to waver away entirely while the public begins looking about for a new object to worship."

She reached for the pamphlet Mr. Brame held. It was a biographical sketch of Charley Bigge. She remembered the name. When she was at boarding school the girls clipped his picture from newspapers, and one of the older girls had seen him. Over and over again they had begged the girl, "What was he like, Sally?"

And Sally would begin dreaming, "He's not very tall but he's dark and his eyes just make you *squirm*——"

"What's become of Charley Bigge?" she asked. She had not heard his name or thought of him for years.

"He's still alive," Mr. Brame said gently, "a sad example, Mrs. Holm, of what I mean. He was unable to stand his own popularity. He began to feel self-important. He began to expect constant attention. The public grew disgusted." Mr. Brame coughed behind his hand. "Even I did, in fact. I remember our last interview was very distressing. I pointed out that after all he had only performed a single noble act. If you remember, Mrs. Holm, he saved an entire audience at a matinée in which he was performing in vaudeville. Let me see—it was fifteen years ago. The theater caught on fire. He leaped to the front of the stage and by singing and dancing held the crowd. The papers were full of it and he received many medals. I handled him at the time. A weak character, Mrs. Tallant. He was unable to capitalize himself. Adulation went to his head. The public soon forgot him—very properly."

Kit gazed at the face in her hands. It was a weak face, a little too pretty for a man. But surely the eyes were innocent and even bewildered.

"Richmond Pearson Hobson," Mrs. Tallant said suddenly. She had been sitting, looking thoughtfully at Mr. Brame.

"Ah," Mr. Brame murmured, "he was another."

"I remember when I was about twelve," Mrs. Tallant said, "my mother took me to a meeting. I do believe every woman in the room except my mother kissed him. He leaned down and said, 'Ah, here's a dear little girl,' when he saw me and kissed me. I remember I thought he smelled of lilac. But maybe it was only all the women."

"He was the hero of Santiago," Mr. Brame said. "He sank the ship which closed the harbor to the enemy."

"I never heard of him," Kit said.

"He was too early for you," Mr. Brame explained gently.

"Then it needn't last long?" she inquired.

"It is my business to help it to last," Mr. Brame said with a bow.

"We would be glad, Bert and I, if there were no more public attention," Kit replied.

Mr. Brame coughed. "Unfortunately," he said dryly, "there is another phase to this public interest. It not only declines, it takes on a sort of reverse action. That is, in proportion to the adulation which has been lavished upon an individual, reaction sets in and the public is not satisfied then with ignoring what hitherto it worshiped. When this phase sets in, nothing will satisfy people unless they can blacken and vilify the beloved object. Small peccadilloes, unnoticed in the average person, or merely laughed at, will assume large proportions. Personal habits and individual behavior or too free speech are resented. At this point it becomes impossible to escape public notice of a most unfavorable sort and the only resort is either to withdraw entirely and hope that a new love object will make the mob forget, or else to perform some new feat which will for a time restore public interest."

"But Bert hasn't done anything really wrong!" Kit exclaimed.

Here in her parents' house where at least she had felt safe and sheltered, they were beginning to intrude. Even Mr. Brame could not hold them back. Once as children she and Gail had been taken to Coney Island for a treat, because they had begged for it. The chauffeur had driven them there and the governess had gone with them, disapproving it all. They had ridden on everything and done everything, and Gail had laughed and laughed. But all Kit could remember was the crowd of people staring and sweating and eating and yelling. These were the people!

"I don't think they should count little things," she said aloud. "Everybody—nearly—drinks too much now, Mother—not people like you and Father, of course, but plenty of people do, and nobody thinks anything of it."

"Quite true," Mr. Brame said.

She saw them look at each other, and like an odor, she smelled something she did not know.

145

"It isn't only the drinking," her mother agreed. "After all, your Uncle Harry was quite a drunkard and we all knew it, but no one thought the less of him, because he was a gentleman even when he was drunk."

"But Bert's not used to it," she said pleadingly, looking from one to the other of the three grave faces. "He'll get better. He's ever so much better now than he was at first. Most of the time he's quite—sensible. And it wasn't any time ago that everybody was saying how dignified he was and how well he carried everything off."

"If they were saying that some months ago," Mr. Brame said in a melancholy voice, "it is sufficient reason why they do not want to say it now. The period of revulsion has begun. Any slight accident now will be turned into scandal."

Mr. Tallant had not spoken. He had sat, staring across the room and out into the sunny morning air as they talked.

"Besides, Kit," her mother went on, "it's a matter of importance to our family. Your father has a very high position to maintain, what with these new international loans and the whole banking situation so uncertain. People look to him, and it doesn't sound well for his son-in-law to—to—and anyway we're in for a period of conservatism from people, now that the government's radical. Everybody says so."

"The boy hasn't anything to do," Mr. Tallant said suddenly, "except to play the fool."

Kit's lip quivered. They were all hard on Bert, and probably they were blaming her because she had not been able to manage him better. How could she tell them that Bert was as changeful and difficult as a child, how tell them that she herself did not know from one hour to the next what to expect from him, that he had no real interests of his own, that he never read a book, that she did not know how to interest him in anything? He was as restless as the lions at the zoo.

146

Mr. Tallant looked at Kit and rose with gusty impatience for his wife and Mr. Brame.

"Oh, hell," he exclaimed. "I don't have any use for this. We're treating it all too seriously."

"Robert, it can't be too serious," Mrs. Tallant said sharply.

"I agree—under the circumstances," Mr. Brame said. "If yours were an ordinary family, Mr. Tallant, we could allow Bert Holm simply to take his course and disappear as other popular heroes disappear. But the Tallants are too well known. It is more important to the Tallants to maintain the figure of Bert Holm than it is to Bert Holm himself. Should all the facts become public, it is the Tallants who would appear as the—the dupes."

They were looking at each other as if she were not here. She turned from one to the other, trying to catch what this was that they were throwing between themselves and that they were keeping from her.

"You are hiding something," she said. "Father, Mother—there's something you know that I don't. Why does he say—dupes?"

"Dupes is perhaps too strong a word," Mr. Brame said hastily. He realized that he might have gone too far with a valuable client, but he was an honest man and, indeed, would have considered it bad business not to be honest. Besides, he was beginning to doubt the wisdom of hiding anything from this slight dark-eyed young woman. After all, she alone was the one to handle Bert Holm. Everything depended on her private management.

"Personally," Mr. Tallant said, "I think we should come out into the open with everything and beat the public at its own game. If we let them know we know everything, they can't do anything to us."

"But do we know everything?" Mrs. Tallant whispered.

"Mother!" Kit cried. "What do you mean?"

Mr. Tallant looked at his watch. "I have to go," he said. "The directors are waiting for me and I've put them off half an hour already. And we promised the President a report in Washington by noon today. Settle this yourself, Dottie. But my advice is take Kit into your room and tell her everything and let her see what she is up against. She's his wife, and she's no child any more. Brame, we'll call you up. But I think your idea of an expedition is a good one. There won't be any difficulty about financing it, I'm sure."

"I hope not," Mr. Brame replied. He was gathering up his papers. "But be prepared, Mr. Tallant, to find that funds promised readily a few months ago will not be there now. That's the public."

"Damn the public!" Mr. Tallant said quietly. He stooped to kiss his wife's cheek and then Kit's, and went to the door.

"It is of you I think," Mr. Brame said with emphasis, following him. "Good-by, madam—good-by, Mrs. Holm—I am at your service." He bowed and followed Mr. Tallant into the hall.

Left alone, Mrs. Tallant said at once to her daughter, "Let's go into my sitting room, child, where we can be comfortable and undisturbed." By that she meant, where Bert would not come in. She put her arm around Kit, and feeling that firm support Kit grew very still within herself. It must be something worse than drinking, she thought, because she could feel her mother's will to keep calm. Her mouth went dry and her heart began to beat in thick hard thumps.

"Yes, Mother," she said quietly.

It was nearly noon when at last she came out of her mother's room. She must go and see how Bert was, but not quite yet. Just for a few moments she must be alone and think how she would approach him and what she would say. If she were like Gail it would be much better, because then she could shut up her own heart, she could harden her voice and her eyes and go upon a breeze of caustic laughter to demand of Bert, "Why didn't you tell me, silly? Mother's had to do it—it's been as bad as if she were confessing she'd done it herself." If she were Gail she could talk like that to Bert, and to herself she could say with Gail's hard brightness, "What a fuss about nothing! As if everybody didn't have silly things to hide!" There were plenty of women who had rather not be told what their husbands had done before they met them. At school the girls used to talk about that, and they said, many of them, they'd rather not know, because after all, every man had experiences, and why not? It made them more exciting.

She sat down on the edge of her window seat and looked out over the East River. No, but Bert was a country boy who had grown up in the plainest and simplest of ways and what had happened to him would have been important to him—too important, so that he had wanted to hide it even from her.

Deep inside she heard her heart inquiring in a daze of queer pain, "But why didn't he tell me?"

But his mother had not told her either, or mentioned it. There had been no sign. The deceit seemed suddenly intolerable and absurd. Then she remembered Mr. Holm's shrewd sudden upward look at her when he said, that day when she had come upon him in the clearing, something about Bert's having been made a fool of once. That was why he had hidden it, poor boy, she saw in a flash, because he didn't want people to think him a fool. It was the naive fear of country louts, she thought in a sudden hard relentless judgment. His parents had taught him to be like that lest he reveal himself ignorant.

She felt she could not breathe unless it were told and the air about her clear again of hidden things. She had asked her mother straight out, "Why do we care? Why don't we tell it ourselves?"

And her mother had said quickly, "Oh no, Kit—it would be so absurd—his saying it hadn't been, and now we saying it had—the newspapers would go and find the woman and all that. It would be horrible for us."

She had not answered her mother because she suddenly thought

149

of the people who believed in him, the millions of people, and she put aside herself. She did not feel at all hysterical or emotional, only sad and not a little bewildered about how to tell Bert what she now knew. It was Kit's duty, her mother went on to say, to manage so that what was merely a youthful mistake might not become an ugly story which could open the whole family to its exaggeration, or even to blackmail. There was no knowing what sort of woman this Lily Roos was, and whether or not she would make demands. Up to now she had made none and probably would make none if there was no commotion. If she did appear, they would tell her quietly that they knew the whole story and that it had no significance. But she might say that she could sell it to the newspapers. That was what Mr. Brame wanted to guard against by keeping up Bert's public standing.

To all this Kit listened with intense silent attention.

"We could just go away, Bert and I," she told her mother. "If we built a house somewhere far away from everybody, in some quiet place like—like Glen Barry."

Her mother had looked at her strangely, and then after a moment had told her about the maid. She had broken down—just a little—and her mother had been kind again. Men had such queer seizures, she said, and then the red spots came out on her neck, and she said, "I never told a soul, Kit, and I wouldn't now, except to help you understand—but your own father—" And then she had gone on to tell her something about a French actress in Paris years ago, and Kit had wanted to laugh and cry because it was so funny and old-fashioned like something in Henry James, only she could see how her mother really thought it was exactly the same thing as the maid at Glen Barry. . . .

"Try to take it in your stride," her mother had ended. Her voice was brisk and energetic again. "Why don't you talk to Gail, dear? She has such a sane wholesome outlook, I think, especially about men. After all, it's not the marriage and divorce that amount to anything, really. It's the ridiculous situation into which it has brought us."

She had not answered this. There was the private ache in her breast because Bert had not told her, not even when they were alone together, when she had been trying to find him.

But what, she asked herself, was the use of talking to Gail . . . ? She was not Gail, and she could not be like Gail. She sighed now, a long quivering sigh. On the next building a man was crawling out of the window. He was a window washer, and he adjusted his heavy leather belt carefully and began to work. She watched him, without thinking of him. . . . If she couldn't think and feel as Gail did, then what was the use of talking to her? Her own mind could tell her all the things that Gail would say, the sane, wholesome, sharp, common-sense things that everybody she knew said, things stripped of all idealism and dream and romance. But why was it of any help to know that most men would have behaved exactly as Bert did, and wouldn't have thought they had to tell anybody, and that what their wives didn't know wouldn't hurt them? That was wrong, anyway— because it did hurt. Even when she had known nothing it had hurt her, because not telling her had made Bert a certain sort of person and that had hurt her though she did not know it, and it hurt her doubly now that she did know. . . . The man was leaning out over the precipice and she looked away. How horrible to get up every morning knowing you had to spend your day hanging on the edge of a precipice!

And then, just as she was about to go into Bert's room, he came stumbling in, still in his blue pajamas that she had given him because his eyes were the same blue. His fair hair was tumbled and his face flushed and his eyes full of bewilderment.

"Kit, where have you been all day?" he demanded. His voice was thick. "I called you and you never answered. I've been sick as a dog."

He dropped on his knees before her and buried his face in her lap, and clutched her around the waist. "Oh, I'm so hot I'm in hell!" he muttered. She laid her cheek against his forehead.

"Why, you are full of fever!" she cried. "Bert, come back to bed at once!" She stood up, half lifting him, and led him back to bed. From the pillow he looked up at her with bright, empty eyes.

"I called and called," he said drowsily.

"But why didn't you ring?" she asked, tucking him in. "They'd have told you where I was."

"I didn't think of it," he said, and smiled a little at himself. "Gosh, I'm not used to bells, Kit."

"Silly," she said, smiling back at him sadly. "Lie still—I'm going to call the doctor."

She took up the telephone.

"Don't leave me," he begged her.

She shook her head, smiling steadfastly. "I won't," she said.

Pneumonia, the doctor said, lifting his bald head from Bert's chest. . . . Not serious yet, he added.

He rose and scribbled a prescription. "I'll have a nurse in half an hour. Meanwhile, if you and Mrs. Tallant can manage——"

"Of course we can," her mother said.

It was less than an hour ago that they had been talking about what they would do with Bert. Now he had settled it himself by getting pneumonia and having to be taken care of. It was wicked to be glad he was ill, Kit thought, but it made her know what she had to do. He had to be taken care of and not disturbed, and she could ask him nothing. She must sit by his bed and do the things the doctor said must be done until the nurse came. That was infinitely better than anything else. So much was a clarity in her confusion. He was too feverish to know any change in her. But perhaps there was no change. She would not know until this was over.

And her mother was always wonderful when anyone was ill. When they were children she minded no naughtiness if she thought they were a little ill. Now, in the same way, she seemed to have forgotten that an hour ago they were talking about something Bert had done.

"I'll just go and get things organized," she told Kit in a brisk whisper. "I know what trained nurses can do to servants, if you don't get them prepared; it was so awful when your father came down here alone that summer with the intestinal flu and we were in Europe. I thought I'd never get things straight again. Even Smedley was upset." She tip-toed to the door. "Don't worry!" she hissed across the room. "Everything's going to be all right." She nodded brightly and shut the door with elaborate softness.

Kit, left alone, leaned over Bert. He seemed asleep, though she was not sure of it except that he was beginning to breathe very heavily. His hair was over his flushed forehead and she pushed it back gently.

"Bert?" she said softly. But he did not seem to hear her.

Then suddenly the telephone rang. She took the receiver off instantly lest he be disturbed.

"Yes?" she said.

It was Roger Brame. "Mrs. Holm? In regard to the proposed expedition, I have one more point to offer——"

She interrupted him.

"It is no use, Mr. Brame. Bert is very ill—with pneumonia."

"What?" she heard his surprise breathed into the telephone. "Oh, I beg your pardon, Mrs. Holm, but this is such a surprise— a shock, I might say—I'm sorry, I'm sure——"

"We have only just found out. The doctor has been here. So there'll be no plans—" she said rapidly.

Mr. Brame's voice came over the wire, full of relief.

"I don't mean to wish any evil, I'm sure"—he was almost laughing—"but really, speaking purely from the point of view of publicity, it's the most fortunate thing! An illness is very appealing to the public. Let us hope it is not serious. Now if you will keep me in constant touch, please, Mrs. Holm; and when Mr. Holm is

himself again, let me recommend that we take advantage immediately of public sympathy and organize the expedition——"

"Kit—Kit—" Bert was murmuring heavily.

"Excuse me, Mr. Brame," she said swiftly, and hung up the
receiver.

"Oh damn, damn, damn the crowd!" she thought. Poor Bert—
his lips were dry with fever. She poured some water. "Here, my
poor boy," she said, and held the glass to his mouth. Whatever he
was he was hers, and no one else had anything to do with him.
He had no one but her in all this foolish world. She would try to
be a better wife to him—when she could think how to do it. She
knelt down beside the bed and put her arms about him.

The door opened and she looked up to the stiff uniformed
figure of a nurse, a stout woman of middle age, whose iron gray
eyes looked coldly upon her.

"I am the day nurse—Miss Prynne," she announced. "Is this the
patient?"

"Yes, my husband," Kit murmured and stood up, hesitating.

"Very well, Mrs. Holm," Miss Prynne replied. "Now if you
will just leave the patient to me, I have the doctor's instructions."

She waited while Kit stood, undecided. "Is there something—
anything—I can do for him?" she faltered.

"No, thanks," Miss Prynne replied. "I much prefer being alone
with my patients. I'm trained for pneumonia."

There was nothing left but to go. Kit tip-toed away. At the
door she looked back. The nurse was already busy about Bert and
did not know she was gone. Outside his door she stood a moment,
remembering the morning, while repulsion and longing and loneliness confused her. And yet, simplest and most clearly, she was
conscious of this—that Bert was somehow taken away from her
again by strangers. It would be a long time before she could ask
him anything, or indeed speak to him.

Nor, it appeared as the day went on, was he to be returned to
her. When night came Miss Prynne's place was taken by a blonde

and pretty young woman whose warmth and instant devotion were scarcely to be better borne than Miss Prynne's efficiency. When Kit went to Bert's room before she went to bed, she found the night nurse here beside him, watching him. He was delirious now with fever. The doctor had gone before dinner and would be back again. The delirium, he had said, meant nothing in itself, for Bert was obviously one of those who went easily delirious.

"Believe me, Mrs. Holm," Dr. Leavett said, his large protruding brown eyes solemn, "I feel the responsibility. People would think I was a murderer if anything happened to Bert Holm. Both Prynne and Weathers are thoroughly competent."

This was Weathers, she supposed, this young woman whose gold hair stood out in feathery fluffs around her nurse's cap. She rose instantly.

"Mrs. Bert Holm?" she breathed. "Oh!"

Kit did not smile. "How is he?" she asked.

"Oh, he has such a wonderful constitution," the young nurse said gladly; "I'm sure he's all right. He's just got to be, hasn't he? He's so important!"

"Yes," Kit agreed. And after a moment, because it was intolerable to hear that thick scraping breath panting from Bert's chest, she said, "Isn't there anything I can do?"

"Not a thing, dear," Miss Weathers said promptly. "That's what I'm here for—to do everything. It takes a person trained for pneumonia. Don't you worry, dear."

As surely as Miss Prynne had compelled her, she felt Miss Weathers' bright smile forcing her out of the room because there was nothing she could do for Bert.

She went to her room, undressed and put out the light and soberly climbed into her bed and drew the covers beneath her chin. Then she lay listening but she could not hear Bert's breathing through the heavy oak door between their rooms. She sighed, and suddenly, because she was young and tired, she escaped herself and fell into dreamless sleep.

IV

Even the Tallant house became now nothing but a background for Bert, and at his side the two nurses stood sentinels. Within a week they bitterly hated one another, each convinced that his slightest setback was because of some fault in the other's care. To Mrs. Tallant Miss Prynne complained that if she could alone take care of Mr. Holm——

"Nonsense!" Mrs. Tallant exclaimed curtly. "You couldn't possibly do it. Besides, Weathers feels the same way about you." She did not believe in any foolishness with trained nurses. They took the upper hand the moment you let them. Things were badly enough upset as it was. The house was jammed with flowers, with telegrams pouring in and letters. In all the confusion she had had no time to talk any more to Kit. It was just as well, perhaps, that Bert had been taken so ill. It put off everything else, and if things could be put off long enough, usually nothing happened.

Kit, leaving her mother at Bert's door this morning, had gone downstairs to find Mr. Roger Brame announced and in the library. When she came in he rose, in his neutral grayness exactly the right shade of decent awareness of her situation. He kept in hourly touch with Bert Holm's condition through the nurses in order that the newspapers could be reliably informed of how he was, and he asked no questions now, therefore. But he drew from the inner pocket of his gray suit a cheap crumpled envelope, addressed in a large pencil scrawl to Mrs. Bert Holm.

"This, I regret to say, was opened by mistake at the office," he said apologetically.

She took it and opening it saw at once that it was from Bert's father. She had, she thought in sudden guilt, forgotten all about his parents. They had had to see from the papers——

They had seen. Reading the big illegible scrawl, she saw that they were piteously afraid of Bert's dying and they were coming to him.

"I couldn't help noticing what it was about," Mr. Brame said. He coughed a little behind his very clean linen handkerchief.

"They're coming," she said. "They'll be here tomorrow."

"They mustn't," Mr. Brame said quickly. "It must be prevented."

"I scarcely see—," she began.

"Oh, but believe me, it must," he repeated firmly. "It would be disastrous. It is all very well to have an agricultural ancestry, Mrs. Holm. In fact, it is quite the thing in our democracy. But it would never do to have them here in New York. They would be played up—very disastrously——"

"Nobody need know," she said.

"Just look out of the window, if you please," Mr. Brame said.

She obeyed. There against the opposite house a young man lounged carelessly. He had a camera in his hand.

"He's taken at least one snapshot of everyone who enters the house," Mr. Brame declared. "Why, he even took me!"

He took his handkerchief and wiped his forehead. "I really cannot undertake the elder Mr. and Mrs. Holm," he declared. "That type is very difficult—impossible to fit into any dignified publicity except as background. But background is background; it must stay there," he added.

Yes, she saw that. They would never do here in this house. Her father might understand them, but her mother would not, and they would be acutely unhappy. And it might be many more days, the doctor said, before it could be known how Bert would be.

"But they have a right," she murmured.

"All private rights," Mr. Brame broke in with impatience, "but none public."

Then when he saw her continuing look of doubt he began with double vigor. "Believe me, Mrs. Holm, it is only what any public character must do, in all kindness, too. There is no one whose relatives are entirely desirable. It would be cruel to subject the elder Mr. and Mrs. Holm to the sort of merciless ridicule——"

Behind his opaque gray eyes he was watching her. Ah, now he was getting at her! He was learning how to appeal to her fear of hurting anyone. It was the key to her, he decided. Each one of his clients had a key—to Mr. Tallant it was business expediency —always honest and fair, of course. To Mrs. Tallant it was family pride. To Bert Holm—there was perhaps no key to his oversimplified nature. One could count on him no more than on a child. But there was a good deal of fundamental stability in this young woman's apparently soft and gentle nature and it had always to do with other people—not herself.

"You can see for yourself," he went on. "They would not even know they were being made the butt of cruel jokes. It could scarcely add to Bert Holm's prestige to have his parents appear in such a light. In their proper place they have their dignity, but they must stay there."

"I see what you mean," she said unwillingly. This monstrous public, whose vagaries governed their lives!

"Is there no escape for us?" she asked Mr. Brame.

"Escape?" he repeated, puzzled.

"Can't we get away from the public and go back to being people?"

He shook his head. "Impossible," he answered. "It has never been done. Sooner or later, of course, you will have some relief. That is, a new sensation will appear. I have been rather expecting it. There was a flurry, you know, last month over the young man who sailed around the world in a motor boat. But he didn't catch on in the way Bert Holm did. No, it is doubtful if the public will ever completely forget Bert Holm. He came at exactly the right moment and he touched off something more than mere adventure. There was the fact of outwitting an Englishman; that, of course, is always successful with the crowd—has been since 1776. But there was considerably more than that. I don't quite understand it myself, but of course reason has nothing to do with it."

He was rambling and he caught himself, checked by the look in her eyes of not listening to him.

"I might go and see them myself," she said, thinking aloud. "I could do that. I'm not needed here," she added.

"Excellent!" Mr. Brame said heartily. "It would be a real solution. Only, I beg you, go quietly. And avoid the young man at the door by going at night, I advise."

He rose and shook her hand limply and went away.

In the car she curled herself into the back seat warmly under the rug. Her father and mother had bade her good-by behind the closed front door, and she had run out alone and walked two blocks and met the waiting car and jumped in. "All right, Curry," she said to the chauffeur. It would be an all-night drive, but better than the train. Arriving at dawn she would avoid the village entirely and drive by country roads straight to the farmhouse. She had sent no telegram, knowing the operator at Misty Falls would spread the news of her coming. The little village would be eager for any news of Bert.

She slept in bits, curled upon the seat. Bert was the same—not better, but no nearer the crisis. She would only be away a day and the two nights and he would not know that she was gone. He lay in stertorous stupor under the hovering care of the nurses and the doctor. Strangely enough she was sleeping better here in the car than she had at home in her bed, where the dreadful sense of uselessness had kept her restless. The moment she knew she ought to come she felt eased merely by something to do.

159

Two hours before dawn she was wide awake. She did not move but lay thinking of what she had resolutely not thought of all these days since Bert was ill. It had become almost unfair to think while he was so helpless, to allow blame to grow in her mind when he could not speak in his own defense. But just now she had thought of something. If she were going to be there all day at the farm, why not—find out for herself? Why ask Bert for that which he had not himself wanted to tell her? There might be no truth in the story. She could ask his parents, casually, "There is an odd story—something about Bert's having been married and divorced." No, she would say it more straitly, "Was Bert married and divorced before he knew me?" Her heart was thumping foolishly. What did it matter whether she knew or not? Why did she care? It was over long ago.

Gail had once said laughingly that she wished Harvey had been married a couple of times before, so that he would not expect so much of her. "Two or three marriages," Gail had said, her eyes dancing at Harvey, "one before he was twenty to disillusion him, and a few more to make him realize that women are fools, and all my life would be different. He would expect me to be a fool, too. It's best to be a fool! Why don't all intelligent women see it? It saves so much explaining!"

But Gail's gayety was because her marriage to Harvey was, in its own queer way, a successful one. If she had not admired Harvey, would she have loved him? There was nothing maternal in Gail. Her own children she held away from her, surveying them as shrewdly as though they did not belong to her. And if Harvey had been dependent and clinging instead of being her master, she would have been ruthless and intolerable. It was lucky for the family that Harvey had her well in hand. She loved to say she managed him, but everyone knew that Gail's management of Harvey was only in accommodating herself to him. What a maze marriage was! The old dream she once had of straightforward love was only a dream. But she could not give it up.

For she did care about the thing Bert had done. Yet not so much about the thing itself—only, why had he lied about it and kept up the lie to her? That was the core of her pain. He had been secretive to her when she would have said his one strength was his childlike frankness. That frank smile of his, the clear blue of his eyes, and all his seeming simplicity—did these mean nothing? For, she kept telling herself again and again, he might so easily have said, "Kit, I'm in a silly mess—" and so have told her. But he never told anything, he never said anything; he was silent—silent—silent! What could she do with silence? How could she break it down and find out whether there was anything beneath or not? Here was the crux of it. Was there anything? Somewhere out of the floating foolish echoes of all that women had said to her about Bert Holm, women who passed in an endless procession of yearning white faces and longing eyes, there was the echo of a girl's voice crying to another girl, careless of her hearing, "He's so strong and silent, ain't he! I love big strong silent men!"

But what if silence were not even duplicity, but merely stupidity? What if behind silence there was—nothing? That was the question upon which her marriage hung. She must find the answer and face it. A little glimpse of the hardness of Robert Tallant's jaw line crept into her soft oval face. She must discover the man she had married. She sat up suddenly and straightened her clothing and, pushing back her hair, put on her hat and examined her face in the mirror. She was pale but it did not matter.

The dawn was near. A moonstone glow was creeping over the sky and soon on the horizon light began to ray out of the east. She felt invigorated and clarified with sudden decision. She would find out the truth of Bert for herself and then make up her mind. The hours of solitude had been good for her. She had been freed from the crowd that dominated her life. Foolish to endure that domination! Her mother, Roger Brame, the nurses, she let them depress her. They were all wrong.

Fundamentally she belonged to herself. She didn't have to stay married to Bert if she didn't want to, that is, if the answer to her question was nothing. Life was too valuable and everything was only a step to something else. Perhaps this marriage, too, was only that, if she could see it in its perspective. But then she always lost her perspective too easily. Eternity was always comprehended for her in each moment. When she was a child at Glen Barry, in the midst of a gloriously happy day it had been impossible to think that a time might come when she would grow up and go away. And at college, once she had grown used to it, the thought of leaving it had been dread. And then loving Norman had seemed essential to eternity. When that was gone, eternity had changed again to endless despair. Yet each one of those eternities had not been eternal. They had gone, leaving her still intact. For the first time in her life she perceived her own intactness.

"Turn right, Curry," she directed the old chauffeur.

"Yes, miss," he replied. He had not spoken a word all night. She thought with a glimmer of stray humor that silence was a comfort at least in a chauffeur.

All this time she had been staring at the sky and at this moment the sun darted up just as it used to do. Often as a child she had seen the sun come up and it had always seemed to leap upon the horizon when it appeared, and so it did now. Instantly the landscape was filled with a pale and liquid sunlight. There had been a heavy frost and it shone a sharp silver upon every edge.

"We'll soon be there," she told Curry.

"Yes, miss," he answered.

"You'd better go to the village for breakfast after you drop me," she went on.

"Yes, miss."

There, she could see the house now. It looked pleasant enough,

162

standing whitely among the bare maples, but the thought of its interior filled her with revolt.

"But come back immediately after your breakfast," she said. "I might want to go away."

He nodded. Yes, she must at least have the means of getting away whenever she wanted to go.

Without Bert the place was completely strange to her. She walked across the frosty grass and knocked at the door. She did not feel free even to open the door without knocking when she stood outside alone. It was Bert's home, now less than ever hers.

The door opened and Mrs. Holm stood there in a gray wool dress and a black and white checked apron.

"Well, of all—" she began, and then threw her arms around Kit. "Come in," she cried. "If I ain't glad—how is he? We're just fixin' to go today."

"I know—that's why I came."

It had not occurred to her until this moment how it would be to have to tell them not to come. She hurried on, "He isn't allowed to see—anybody. The nurses scarcely let me——"

Mrs. Holm pulled her inside and shut the door. The house was full of the smell of warm soapsuds.

"I was just gettin' the wash out before I went so it could freeze dry while we're gone a couple of days," Mrs. Holm explained. "Come in the kitchen. We're havin' breakfast. Now tell me everything. Land, who's that man standin' out there?"

"That's only Curry, our driver," Kit said hastily.

"Will he want breakfast, too?" Mrs. Holm inquired.

"Oh, no—he'll go to the village," Kit replied. "Don't bother about him."

"It wouldn't be bother just to put on a couple of extra eggs," Mrs. Holm declared.

They went on into the kitchen, where at the oilcloth-covered table by the stove Mr. Holm sat eating.

"Look who's here," Mrs. Holm cried.

He looked up at Kit with his vague blue eyes. "Hello," he said.

"Hello," she replied.

"Sit down and eat," he bade her.

"Thank you," she said, and took off her gloves and hat and coat and sat down.

"Now tell me," Mrs. Holm said.

In a zinc tub the washed clothes were heaped ready to hang outdoors. The kitchen was heavy with the smell of clothes and food.

"I'll tell you about Bert and then go on and tidy myself," she replied. Perhaps if she felt fresh and clean herself she could endure this air.

So she told them about Bert's illness, and then she said, hesitating, "I hardly know how to say it, but they—seem to think—Bert had better not have any visitors at all. They scarcely let me come into his room."

They looked at her unwinkingly.

"We couldn't hardly hurt him," Mr. Holm said. The muscles in his lank cheeks stood out as he chewed a piece of bread.

She could feel them blaming her for what they could not understand. "I know how you feel," she said. "I feel it, too. Sometimes it seems as though Bert were someone else—someone who doesn't belong to us at all. He seems to belong to everybody else."

"We wouldn't stay," Mr. Holm said. "I couldn't. I've got the cows on my mind. I can't get but a couple of days help and I'd have to get back."

"It's the photographers—the public—" she murmured. "Ever since he's been ill, it's been worse than ever."

"I wouldn't mind them," Mrs. Holm said brightly. "I guess I'm used to——"

"The nurses wouldn't let you stay with him—" she began.

"I guess I'd take care of my own child!" Mrs. Holm cried.

"You couldn't," she said plainly. Better to make them under-

164

stand. "He has to have trained care. He can't be allowed to run any risk. The doctor wouldn't allow it. It's all public news: the trained nurses, how he is every morning and night, all that's being done——"

"My own mother died of pneumonia," Mrs. Holm said with spirit. "There's nothing I don't know about it, for I took care of her until the very end. Flannel on the chest and a red-pepper poultice—have they got the windows sealed?"

"They sent me to ask you not to come," she said distinctly.

"Well, I never!" Mrs. Holm whispered.

"Everything is being done," Kit pleaded.

"I guess they don't want us around," Mr. Holm said suddenly.

She did not deny it. They sat in silence a moment. Then Mr. Holm said, "I guess I won't need Tad to see to the cows."

"You ain't goin'?" Mrs. Holm demanded.

He shook his head. "Not where I ain't wanted," he said simply.

Kit wished she had not obeyed Mr. Brame. They should have been allowed to come if they liked. What did it matter if what they wanted most was to be with Bert? She flung Mr. Brame away.

"They're all wrong," she said. "You must come. We'll all go back together in the car. Bert won't know you; you won't mind that, will you? And the nurses—they're difficult—they won't let you stay. But you have the right to come to him."

Mr. Holm shook his head again. He got to his feet a little stiffly.

"No, I ain't going'," he decided. "I see what you mean. It ain't —he don't hardly belong to us now. It's like you said."

"I'm goin'," Mrs. Holm declared.

"No, you ain't," Mr. Holm told her. "Like he is now we won't do him any good. Leave him alone."

"I——"

"Leave him alone!" Mr. Holm roared out at her suddenly. He

snatched an old cap from a nail on the wall and went out. Mrs. Holm sat down.

"I'm sorry," Kit said.

"Sometimes I wish he'd never climbed up that mountain," Mrs. Holm said heavily. "He's always scared me so—climbin' things. He'd get a notion to climb the Falls or somethin'—go and do it and never tell me till he done it. I didn't want him to go off to that heathen country anyway; a minister of God at home is what I always wanted him to be. I always prayed he'd be a preacher, and we could go and live with him. Then I had to give that up. He went and—" she stopped herself. "I'll go and get the wash out," she said dully.

"What did he do?" Kit asked sharply. "What did he do before he went away?"

Mrs. Holm was taking away the dishes and she clattered them in the sink.

"Now, Kitty," she said. "You go and get yourself washed and I'll boil you an egg the way you like it."

She might have been a child, so firm a dismissal was in Mrs. Holm's voice and manner. She was suddenly intensely angry.

"I know already," she said very quietly. Yes, she was going to find out exactly what Bert was, and then she would know what to do with him.

But Mrs. Holm replied, "Anything that happened to him didn't make him any different from what he is."

She turned her back but Kit went out of the room upstairs. She had made up her mind. After she had eaten she would go and find that girl at the drugstore—Lily, Bert had called her. Lily Roos, Mr. Brame had said, was the woman's name. It occurred to her for the first time why people had kept coming into the drugstore the day Bert had taken her there. They wanted to see them together, Bert's wife and Lily Roos. How had he dared to put her in such a place? People had gone home, doubtless, to laugh. She felt entangled in the cheap senseless secrecy, and it was intolerable

166

to her. It came to her suddenly that it had been wonderful of Norman to tell her baldly that he did not love her. It was kind of him, brave of him—kind to *her*. She could trust a man like that, whether he loved her or not.

She went back downstairs, her hair brushed and her body bathed. The kitchen was empty. She sat down and ate her egg and some bread and butter and milk. Through the window she could see Mrs. Holm standing firmly against the wind as she pinned clothes to the line. Curry was already back.

She opened the door and called, "I'm going down to the village!"

The wind carried her voice and Mrs. Holm turned and nodded, and Kit, her heart beating hard, went out to the car.

"Take me to the drugstore," she told Curry.

"Where I've just et, miss?" Curry inquired.

"Yes, there's only one," she answered.

The car gathered speed silently over the hilly road and she fought against a faint sickness crawling in her flesh. It was disgusting to think of this other woman who had been Bert's wife. The whole fastidiousness of her own life and upbringing rose up to draw clean of it. But she would have to cleanse herself, for Bert would never tell her even if he were well again. If he could be silent on their marriage day, silent when he brought her back to his home, silent when he went to Glen Barry, then he would never tell her. And she would not stoop to drag it from him, question by question.

When the car stopped at the drugstore she went in quickly lest she fail in courage after all. The store was quite empty except for the girl behind the counter, who had her back turned as she washed dishes busily in the sink. She was singing in a loud cheerful voice, but at the sound of the door she looked up and burst into talk.

"Well, hello—I didn't hear a soul! But I don't hardly expect anybody now for an hour or so, unless it's on the drug side. Say,

I knew you was here. Your shofer come in here for coffee and doughnuts. 'Who're you?' I says. I didn't know his rig, see? So he told me. Now, what'll it be?" She mopped the counter as she talked, her light gray eyes never quite meeting Kit's gaze.

"Please, just to talk a little while," Kit said.

"Sure thing," the girl agreed smoothly. If she were surprised, her powdered pink face showed none of it. She wiped her hands and came from behind the counter. "Want we should go in a booth?" she asked.

"Yes, perhaps that's best," Kit agreed.

They sat down and Kit gazed into this full, coarsely pretty face. The girl had been chewing gum but now she held her jaws still.

"You'll think me strange," Kit stammered. "I hardly know how to begin. But we—I—have heard something about you—and Bert." She wanted to say "my husband," but the words would not be spoken.

"Bert tell you?" the girl demanded. There was a mirror set in the back of the booth behind Kit's head, and the girl gazed at herself there as she talked.

Kit shook her head.

"I just bet he wouldn't!" the girl exclaimed. "I said to Rexie that you wouldn't of come here to the store that day and act like nothing had happened." She paused and patted her hair again and laughed, admiring herself in the mirror. "Ain't it just like Bert!" she cried. "Not to say nothin'!"

"Will you tell me—just what happened?"

"Sure," the girl replied. "Call me Lily, will you, Kit? Everybody does. There ain't any reason why you and me should hate each other at that. You maybe see something in Bert I didn't see. Hell, that's no harm; I told 'em right off when anybody asts me how I feel about Bert Holm's marryin' again.

" 'It's nothin' to me,' I says. I went out to Reno, and got myself as good a divorce as any Mrs. Van-what's-her-name's. Had

168

one swell time out of it, too, and I might have fell for a cowboy if I'd wanted to, only I didn't because I fell once for a good-lookin' feller, and it didn't do me no good. Next time I'm goin' to fall for a real man and a good provider. I ain't lettin' my soft side get in any dirty work on me, I says, not again!"

"Were you and Bert married a long time?" Kit asked in a low voice.

"It seemed long!" Lily laughed loudly at her own reflection in the mirror. "Actually I guess it wasn't hardly a year. We didn't hit it off. It happened kind of too quick. You know how them things happen, donchah? You're kind of—well, you know what I mean—kinda ready to fall, and Bert's awful good-lookin', and when he wants to, he knows how to get a girl all right." She looked away from Kit. "But I won't have no funny business. I'm wise to men. I says no, not unless you mean marriage. So, he says —we was at the Sunday School picnic—Say, ain't that a joke? 'Hell,' he says, 'I mean whatever you mean.' So I says, 'All right, lead me to the preacher.' I didn't think he would. But you know how he is—just like a kid takin' a dare—so he says all right, and we jumped in his car and first thing I knew, I was standin' before a minister, sayin' 'I do.'" She laughed aloud. "Yeah, I believe in keepin' your virtue," she exclaimed. "It's all a girl's got—that's what I say. I don't care if the fellers do say I'm old-fashioned. I gotta take care of myself, see?"

The girl was clearly not going to tell the whole story of herself and Bert. She looked solemnly for a moment into the mirror.

"And then?" Kit asked.

"Oh, there wasn't much to it," Lily replied, carelessly. She twisted a stiff blonde curl around her finger and arranged it against the others. "I gave up my job here and moved out to that farm of his. Say, how do you stand it there? I fought with his ole woman the first day. And Bert stuck by her, and kept stickin' by her, so I says, 'This ain't my kind of life,' I says. So I come back here and got my job back." She paused, considering herself. "At that, I don't know if Bert would have let me divorce him if I had really set myself to beat the ole woman."

"Why, then—why—" Kit murmured.

"Oh, I got sick of Bert," Lily said frankly. She began to chew her gum with little clicks of energy. "I don't know why. Don't ast me; those kind of things just happen, don't they? One day a fellow sends chills up and down you when you look at him, and the next you don't care if he's french-kissin' you. I guess the truth is Bert's too much of a kid for me. I like 'em maturer than what he is. He's the kind that's goin' to be a kid 'til he dies, and I don't want a man I gotta be a mother to. Understand, there's no harm in him. He's just dumb, that's all."

She spoke with large tolerance. The door opened and a man came in, his overalls splotched with grease. It was Jack Rexall.

"Lily!" he sang.

"Excuse me," Lily whispered. "It's my boy-friend come in for his beer!" she rose. Then she leaned toward Kit, so close that Kit could smell her fresh breath, minted with the chewing gum. "Don't you worry, Kit," she whispered. "It's all over with me. I I ain't goin' to bother you. I ain't *low*."

She straightened, showed perfect white teeth in a great smile, and sauntered toward the counter, pushing her red leather belt down as she went.

"Well, what's this the cat drug in so early?" she inquired amiably of Rexall.

"Two cokes," he replied briskly, "one for me and one for you."

"I kin buy my own," she retorted. "I don't need no dirty overalls buyin' me drinks!"

"Aw, Lily!" He leaned across the counter and snatched at her and was stopped by Lily's nod toward Kit.

"Ain't you ashamed before a lady?" she said gayly. Rexall turned.

"H'lo," he said. "Say, how's Bert?"

"Very ill," she replied.

"Say, that's too bad. Give him my best, will ya?"

"Yes," she replied. She rose, wanting to be out of this, and nodding good-by went away. Curry held the door open, correct and severe. She was passionately glad to get into the car and have him tuck the robe about her—glad to roll noiselessly down the street and out of Misty Falls.

"Take me home," she directed.

"Not back to—?" he began.

"No, home!" she repeated distinctly.

"Yes, miss," he replied.

Hour upon hour passed and she sat rigid and intense, thinking about the poor sordid foolish little story that Bert had kept his secret. "He's the kind that'll be a kid until he dies," the woman had said, that woman who did not want him any more.

It was late dusk, and out of the wintry darkness she came into the warm, lighted hall. She had never been so acutely conscious of the value of beauty and luxury and ordered formal living as she was when Smedley opened the door of the house. The drawing-room doors were thrown back and across the deeply carpeted floors she saw the fire burning and the lamps lighted and the glow of flowers.

"Is there any change in Mr. Holm?" she asked.

"I believe he is exactly the same, miss," Smedley said mournfully. "Dinner will be served in about half an hour, miss."

Her impulse was to say she would not be down. And then she decided she wanted to bathe in scented water and brush her hair until it shone and wear her dark blue velvet dinner gown. She felt fastidious to the last drop of her blood.

There were letters on the table and she went to them. They had been sorted, a great pile of fifty or so for Bert, and two for her. She picked them up and glanced at them carelessly and then felt the blood stop in her veins. There was a letter from Norman Linlay; she knew his writing instantly. Why need it still stop her blood to see his close fine writing of her name? No, not her name —this was the first time he had written Mrs. Bert Holm. It made her another woman.

She went upstairs, the letter clutched in her hand, and could not imagine why Norman should write, though probably it was nothing—tickets for a play, perhaps. She did not even know whether he had a new play or not. She went into her room and shut the door and stood with her back against it and tore open the envelope and saw upon his usual sheet of plain white paper a few lines of writing.

"Kit"—her name was there just as it used to be, direct and without address or delay of indentation—"I have been hellishly busy on a play or I'd have written before to say I'm sorry your young man is ill. And my play is the best I've ever done. You must see it and mind you tell me so—none of your free speech, if you please. I want to hear it's the most wonderful play of our generation— nothing less. Matter of fact, it is. It's not farm stuff this time. I've finished with that and maybe you are right about it. Remember the fight we had? Here's hoping the young man is soon well. As ever, Norman."

She folded the letter again and stood trembling. All the careful detachment of these months was swept away. She wanted to hear his voice. She had somehow to know simply that he was. It was not a matter of love; no, it was simply a necessity to know he was himself as he always had been. If she could look at him and hear him speak of anything at all, it would restore some balance in herself.

She went swiftly to the telephone and dialed the old number. She had not even thought of it, day upon day, but it was there in her memory habitual as ever. Someone answered, but it was only a servant.

"Is Mr. Norman Linlay at home?" she inquired.

"I think so, madame—just a minute—" the voice came back.

It was impossible that he could be there so casually as this and so completely within her grasp. She had forced herself so long to think of him as gone, as dead, as infinitely away from her, and all the time he had been as close as this. Why had it ever seemed important to her that he did not love her? The important thing was simply that he was alive.

Then his voice came, exactly his voice. "Hello?"

"This is Kit," she answered, trying not to weep. There was nothing to weep about if he were alive, and yet she felt all unstrung and loose in her bones. She sat down, straining to hear his voice again.

"Well, Kit!"

"I have your letter."

"That's good. How is he?"

"About the same."

"Tough luck, but he'll pull through—has to, with everybody pulling for him. It makes a compelling atmosphere."

"Yes." She hadn't anything to say to him; the necessity was only to hear his voice.

"I suppose you're very busy, Kit?"

If he asked her, she would——

"No, the trained nurses don't let me near him. It's frightfully tedious waiting about—nothing to do, really."

"Dinner tomorrow? I don't lunch, you know."

"I know. Yes, Norman, I'd like it."

"Same place?"

"Yes."

"Good-by, Kit."

"Good-by," she breathed. She heard the telephone click. He was gone, but he had given her tomorrow.

In a luxury of sudden ease she began to undress. In the same ease she poured the bath salts lavishly into the hot bath and bathed slowly and dressed herself to the last fastidious detail. Then slowly she went down the great staircase to the drawing-room. Her parents were there sipping their sherry, and Smedley, hearing her steps, came in with the tray.

"Well, dear!" her mother said. "You look very pretty, I think. Kiss me."

"With pleasure," she said gayly.

"Trip did you good," her father said. "You might kiss me, too, by the way."

She kissed them both.

"Did you accomplish—everything?"

"Yes, thanks," she said, "everything."

She sat down by the fire, drank her sherry slowly, and ate a canapé. It was all delicious—her fragrant, clean body, the fire and the wine—and tomorrow!

She looked at her parents and smiled. They were admirable, the two of them, her mother in a silvery lace and her father's white hair brushed smoothly back from his face now warmly pink with firelight and the comfort of his sherry.

"I am sure everything is going to be all right," her mother said.

"Everything is all right," she replied.

They rose and went out together, she between them, a hand clasping each of theirs. She felt her mother's soft ringed fingers holding hers lightly and the grasp of her father's thin strong hand. And there before them was the dining room, the table shining under soft lights. None of these things, she thought passionately, would she ever take for granted again, though she had always had them . . . Had what? She thought, looking about her, that it was not luxury that was necessary to her, nor ease. The necessity was for something far more fundamental. Feeling and intelligence, these were the essentials. What the necessity might produce, let it produce. But it was at least her right to know she could turn and at her side find a mind that could grasp her mind, a glance that understood her glance, speech which spoke because first there had been the ear to hear.

She sat quietly through the evening. Her mother knitted something for one of Gail's children and talked, and she and her father listened. Smedley brought whisky and soda and left it there, and they heard him locking the great front door and going away for the night. At last Mrs. Tallant rolled up her knitting.

"I'm going up to bed, my dears," she announced. "Kit, I suppose you'll go in to see Bert again before you sleep?"

"Yes, Mother," she said. She did not say she had not yet seen him. She felt with her incorruptible instinct for honesty that perhaps she should—and still did not. She went upstairs to her own room and tried to read and an hour later went to Bert's room and opened the door. Miss Weathers rose, her finger on her lips.

"He's just dropped asleep," she said voicelessly.

Kit nodded and went to the bed. He looked very ill indeed. There was little there to remind her of Bert, and yet she felt nothing.

"Better?" she asked the nurse in a whisper.

The nurse shook her head gravely. "The same," she mouthed back.

She went away as she came. No use thinking ahead—at least not ahead of tomorrow. There was no harm in thinking of tomorrow, for it was not as though Norman loved her any more. If he had, of course she would not go. But if he had, none of this could have happened; she would not have been Kit Holm, but someone else. It was quite safe to think of tomorrow.

The old habits were there as though they had never been broken. She might have been coming here every day as once she had, instead of not at all since that last day. She had forgotten nothing. Beneath the surface of other time and other activity her true habits held. Thus her feet had not forgotten the shallow step of the door into the small restaurant, nor her hand how the door swung; and when she went in her eyes turned straight to the table in the far corner under the doubtful mural of Paul Revere dashing through a cold countryside. They had laughed a good deal of warm desultory laughter over Paul Revere who Norman always said looked like a red fighting cock.

She had waited there often enough alone for Norman, who was late or who never came at all if a rehearsal went on. They had agreed that such a thing might happen to him, but knowing it might had never made it easier when it did.

But today he was there. She saw him instantly. The habit of her heart held, too. It leaped in the old accustomed way. She held it firm—no letting it shine now out of her eyes or sing in her voice! Habit was only blind accustomed instinct of the body, she reminded herself and nothing in her was really the same. She wound her way among the closely placed tables to their own table and he looked up and rose to his feet and they clasped hands quickly.

"I don't remember such a lot of tables as this," she said. He looked as he always had—nothing changed. His same forthright face and his dark straightly gazing eyes were before her.

"Pete is much more prosperous than he was," he answered. They sat down and he took the menu.

"Same as usual?" he inquired, lifting dark brows.

She nodded. "Exactly."

But there was a new waiter—a small lively Italian instead of English Tom, the old ex-butler who used to wait upon them and urge them to try the mutton today.

"Where's Tom?" Norman demanded.

The Italian shrugged himself tragically. "Dead," he said. "Two months ago—he fall dead lika house fall down, here in da shop."

"Oh, poor Tom!" she murmured. He never knew what had happened to them, perhaps, the young couple who had come here every day to eat so voraciously and quarrel so prodigiously.

"Your order?" the new waiter asked. He scribbled down as fast as Norman could speak: "beefsteak for two, a salad, and cheese and black coffee."

"And make the beefsteak bloody rare," Norman commanded him.

They had eaten that meal invariably. He would never experiment with food, though with anything else. The waiter hurried away. She saw Norman frowning after him.

"Wait," he ordered her when she was about to speak, "I can't think what he looks like—that long nose and the round little jowls and his bulging eyes, and his sharp elbows—yes, a grasshopper, in a white apron. Did you ever look a grasshopper in the face, Kit?"

"No," she said and laughed because he had not changed. Tom, he used to say, looked like a superannuated Great Dane.

"Do it next summer," he told her. "You'll see a dessicated wisdom there—wonderfully self-satisfied. A crab, now, yearns. He's always wanting something beyond himself. He struggles against his shell, he's restless and nervous and scuttling away from himself. But a grasshopper is a contented being."

"What's your play?" she asked. "You'll go on and on with grasshoppers if I let you."

He looked at her, immediately vacant and without interest. "Oh, it's a play," he said reluctantly. "Nobody likes it much except me, so I know it's a good play; you wouldn't like it."

"How do you know?" she retorted.

"Not a chance of your liking it, Kit," he declared. "It's all about a roughshod chap who cuts away one thing after another."

"What for?" she inquired.

"Just to be free," he replied.

They had used to quarrel endlessly about freedom. She had said, "Freedom isn't an end in itself. There is no use in chopping down a tradition like a tree, just to chop it down." And he had said, "Yes, there is—because until it's down you can't see for the shadow it throws."

"But what does he do?" she persisted.

"Nothing," he said, shrugging.

"It doesn't sound like a play," she said.

"It is, though," he declared, "a damn good play."

"But what's the end?"

"He gets free!"

"Norman, that's no end—if nothing happens!"

"Silly! It's the only happy ending in the world!"

But this was happy enough for her, she thought, looking at him, watching the old flashing changes of his face. His mouth was still beautiful, still too beautiful. And why more beautiful than Bert's always handsomely curved lips? This mouth was never quiet. There was no telling what its shape was. It changed with every change of his face, a hard mouth, a cruel mouth, a warm mouth. But she had a few times seen it grown miraculously tender, and because of that she kept watching it.

The little grasshopper waiter brought the beefsteak hissing on a metal plate and heaped with mushrooms and red peppers and cut it with quick strokes and placed portions before them.

"Look at his hands," Norman breathed.

She looked and saw little hairy tentacles of hands. When he was finished he stood rubbing them together and they grated dryly one against the other. Norman lifted an eyebrow.

"What did I tell you?" he demanded.

And when the fellow was gone he went on, as though it had come into his head as the next thing, not thought of before. "And Bert Holm is a white cockatoo, isn't he? I've seen them in zoos, wonderfully handsome. They don't need to be alive, they're so handsome. Stuff them and they do as well."

She laughed. "He is one of your favorite characters! His father is a farmer; you should see his hands—they make me think of roots of trees turned up out of the soil. His mother is like the mother in your first play. I said there weren't such people; do you remember? But there are. You could put them all in one of your plays—father, mother, and son. You were partly right, but so was I, too."

He did not answer this. Instead he asked, "What do you do with all that beauty, Kit? Is he really like his pictures?"

"He is," she answered.

"So what?" he inquired calmly.

He was eating with zest as he talked. He was always so, eating hugely of what he chose, and capable of touching nothing of a thing he had not chosen for himself.

"So everything," she replied, on guard.

"Like living with a famous portrait," he went on.

"A favorite portrait," she amended, "one you wanted, chose, and will always keep."

"For decoration?" he inquired innocently.

"Don't!" she said, breaking in upon him. "I won't go on with this. He's lying desperately ill. I shouldn't be here at all."

"All right," he said. "If you want it straight, here goes. I knew the moment I heard your voice that you were unhappy."

"I'm not unhappy."

"Yes, you are, or you wouldn't have called me. A happy woman wouldn't call me up on the telephone."

"Perhaps I didn't want to write you."

"If you'd been happy you wouldn't have cared whether you wrote or not. It would have meant nothing."

"I might be happy, and still not have forgotten—everything."

"Not you, Kit. That's Gail, maybe, tasting the leftovers of an old love out of cold curiosity. Not you, though."

"You mustn't—humiliate me again," she whispered. She pushed aside her plate.

He shook his head. "I never humiliated you. I honored you. I might have married you out of pity, thinking I could neglect you afterwards. But I knew I couldn't neglect you. Any stupid woman can be neglected—God, that's most of them!"

He frowned, and lit a cigarette restlessly. "Kit, I'm not going to stir into your affairs. Why did I want you to come here? I don't know, and that's truth. I wanted to, that's all. And you wanted to come, or you wouldn't have. All I say is, don't think you have to stick anything on earth. You don't, for nobody does. I didn't, did I? And don't wait until you see the next step over the precipice. Go on and cut the rope and get free."

He leaned over to her suddenly and put out his hand across the table to her.

"A white cockatoo!" he said. "I've looked at hundreds of pictures of him! Kit! There's been a woman beside him over and over—somebody with a faint resemblance to you—not you, though!"

She did not answer or put out her hand.

"What made you do it?" he asked so simply that she was overwhelmed with sudden rage.

"You haven't the right to ask me that—you, of all people!" she cried.

"Why of all people?" he demanded.

"Why? Because—you didn't love me." The words tore themselves out of her and immediately she wished them back.

"What has that to do with it?" he asked.

"Instead of suicide," she heard herself murmur and was terrified. The words were like a flow of blood fresh from a wound reopened. It must be staunched or she would die. If he were flippant now, it would be a caustic for her aid. If he would only be flippant—as he so often was! But he was not flippant. Instead he said with a puzzling sort of sadness, "Don't think I am nothing but ruthless. The thing was—I wouldn't go on with less than you wanted. You want a great deal, Kit—more than a man has, perhaps, to give a woman. You'd have been unhappy with me."

She sat quivering under his gentleness. If he had been sharp and smart she could have held him off, but now she was defenseless. She picked up her gloves and began putting them on slowly, watching him with an avarice of love as he sat looking gravely, not at her, but downward. At least, she had seen him, at least heard him speak. "I must go," she said indistinctly.

He went on quickly, "Perhaps I ought to have given you the choice of unhappiness, though, Kit. Perhaps that's where I haven't been fair to you. Granted you'll never be happy, which unhappiness do you prefer, the one you have now or the one you'd have had with me?"

She stood up and belted her brown tweed coat.

"The point is that you told me you didn't love me enough," she said bluntly.

"I didn't," he said honestly, "not for what you wanted. I can't love anybody as much as that. But you haven't what you want now—have you?" He flung the question at her so directly that she felt as though she must physically dodge it.

"I have what I chose," she said.

"What you'd choose again?"

"I—think so."

He put a bill under his glass and rose to his feet.

"You've made me see I was wrong," he said. "I thought—better to make you be free."

"You're a fool for freedom," she said indistinctly.

He took her arm abruptly and piloted her through the tables.

"I see I am," he said. "If you were doomed for misery you might as well have stayed with me."

"I'm not miserable!" she said hotly.

"You are," he retorted. "I tell you, I've looked at you hundreds of times, beside him. You're perfectly miserable."

"If I am, I don't know it!"

They were standing in the street now, arguing. So they had argued in the past, under this very lamppost, again and again, over everything. He stood before her, hatless, the wind blowing his black hair, his eyes blazing and furious.

"God damn you—I say you are!" he shouted suddenly. "I wish I'd gone on and married you. Then I could have beaten some sense into you!"

He jammed his hat on his head and flung himself away into

the dusk. He did not once look back, and she stood there watching him, as she had done so many times before. But he never used to look back, either. Nothing between them could ever change. This was the knowledge she had to carry about with her now. Whether it was a thing she wanted or not, as long as they lived they would be like this toward one another. She could feel him as though his very bones had been made from the same substance as hers, and of the same clay their flesh. Whether or not it was love between them made no difference. It was truth.

She let herself into the house with her own key. When she opened the door, no one was about.

She was halfway upstairs before she heard a step hurrying across the hall below her and looking back, she saw Smedley rushing forward with a tray. "Mr. Holm is took very bad, miss," he said.

In her room she found her mother and father, waiting.

"Crisis," her father said. "It came all of a sudden about an hour ago. We couldn't find you."

"Fortunately both nurses were here," her mother took it up. "We were able to reach Dr. Leavett and he brought another specialist. Everything is being done. They don't want us there."

"Do they expect him to—die?" she asked. Her heart began its thick beating. Bert to die!

"Oh, don't, Kit," Mrs. Tallant said hurriedly. "While there's life, you know. Besides, he's so young." But Kit was gone.

She had gone to the door of Bert's room and opened it softly. They were all there about him. Smedley stood with the tray, his face an agony. She could not see Bert for the heads bent above him. Dr. Leavett straightened.

"I think we can work better if you are not here, Mrs. Holm," he said. "Just wait in the next room, please. If there is any instant danger, we will tell you."

She turned and went back to her own room. Gail and Harvey

were already there. The telephone rang and her father went to it. It was Roger Brame. She heard her father's curt voice.

"No, no news, very low, that's all. They're getting ready for more oxygen—no one knows."

He hung up the telephone. "Those damned ghoulish newspapers," he said simply.

"Let me attend to the telephone," Harvey said. He moved to the telephone as he spoke, a solid firm figure. Kit saw Gail's eyes follow him. Gail in a gray suit fitted to her slenderness, and a dark wine blouse, sat poised and as intense as an exclamation mark.

She felt them all about her, these who were her own and solidly about the Kit whom they knew and who belonged to them. But there was a being in her which did not belong to them and whom they did not know, a being who had somehow to decide for her own life or death.

And yet how curious a gift it was which Bert possessed, so that he was able by some means, when a crisis came, innocently to avert final decision! He was not to be blamed for his illness, nor if he died for his death, but if he died, then in that death would be her solution. She would grieve, but it would be scarcely an intenser grief than she had been feeling all these days, a grief for something that was not and that had never been. Death would mean only that it could never be. Bert would end for her as he was, that was all. Perhaps that was what death was, anyway, the end of a dream and its fulfillment, or perhaps, only freedom. But Norman was wrong about freedom. Simply taking it did not make one free. If it were given to one, if life turned, so that without any lessening of one's duty all ended and freedom began, then of course one took it, as a gift, as one took sorrow also. Life gave or did not give, that was all. There was no such thing as choosing anything. Life gave her Norman and withheld him. Life gave her Bert, but only as he was. If he died now, there would only be return to another emptiness. Or would there?

Her vague sad eyes, wandering, caught Gail's sharp gaze fastened upon her and saw Gail's fingers, lifted to her lips, blow her a kiss. She smiled quickly and defensively.

The telephone rang and instantly Harvey was saying in a low steady voice, "I am sorry—no, no information. We appreciate the sympathy. Meanwhile, if you will call Mr. Roger Brame, Mr. Holm's representative——"

"It's been unbearable all day," her mother said in a loud whisper. "The news about him seems simply to spread in the air."

"It does, of course," Gail said. "When we came, the taxi man wanted to know how he was."

"Strange the hold he has," Mr. Tallant murmured.

"He has a charm," Gail replied. "Everybody feels it. It's a sort of directness out of himself to you."

Kit looked up. "Directness!" she repeated.

"I don't mean truthfulness, necessarily," Gail said, "nothing so complex, Kit! I mean, he simply comes to you from where he happens to be at the moment he sees you. He has forgotten yesterday, or this morning, or five minutes ago; none of that matters, because it's past, and he can't see as far as tomorrow. But all that he is now, he gives you, whoever you happen to be."

"Heavens, that's too complex for me," Mrs. Tallant complained. There was a knock on the door and Smedley came in.

"What is it now?" Mrs. Tallant demanded.

"Oh, madam," he panted, his voice going into a squeak. "I feel I've got to tell you, madam, and you, sir, and miss, ma'am——."

They stared at him. No one had ever seen Smedley like this.

"Smedley! Don't be ridiculous!" Mrs. Tallant said severely.

"No, madam," he whispered. If anyone would have told him that he'd be telling the old lady of his own accord—"If Mr. Bert is going to—die—" he said. He drew his hand quickly across his nose and sniffed. "I don't forgive myself, madam. But I've been afraid something mortal that he took his death that night—one night he went out with me——"

184

"Went out with you, Smedley?" Mrs. Tallant's amazed voice was like ice down his collar.

He gulped and went on, faintly. "Yes, madam, to a prize fight on First Avenue. He got very warm and then he wouldn't put on his coat—said he was hot—" to his own horror he sobbed.

Mrs. Tallant looked quickly at Gail and bit her lip. It was like Bert, her look said, to be dying, so that he could not be blamed or even spoken to—going out with the butler, of all things!

"It is unfortunate you waited so long to speak, Smedley," she said sharply.

"He told me I wasn't to," Smedley faltered, "though it's been on my mind something fearful."

"That'll do," Mr. Tallant said suddenly, and Smedley was so glad it was over he muttered, "Yes, sir," and hurried out.

"I could laugh, if it were the time for it," Gail remarked.

"I don't see anything funny in it," Mrs. Tallant said. "It's just —low."

"Hush!" Mr. Tallant said. "Don't talk about it anymore."

He was looking at Kit. She had not said one word, and now she sat white and stiff, and her mouth strained as though she were trying not to cry.

"Kit, relax!" her mother called to her sharply. "It doesn't help Bert a bit to be so intense. You only wear yourself out, and he's just what he would be anyway."

Kit quivered at her mother's voice. No, but what silly new deception was this of Bert's? Why hide it from her, if he wanted to go with Smedley to a prize fight? Before she could answer herself, the doctor came to the door. He took off his spectacles and smiled.

"I am most happy to tell you," he announced, "he is going to get well."

V

BERT, coming up out of unconsciousness, saw his first glimmer of returning light in a soft spreading gold set about a blur of a face.

"Not Kit," he decided with difficulty. He could not think. There was no strength in him to think. But he was nagged by the question of what gold hair this was. Lily maybe? The effort of thought made him feel sick and he retched. A soft voice cried out, alarmed, "Oh, no, now you mustn't do that!"

The voice brought the face a little nearer and he stared at it, trying to focus his eyes out of his weakness.

"Not Kit." He gathered tremendous energy together to produce these two words aloud. But they were not understood. At least the voice said, "Now rest—no talking—" A hand touched his head for a moment.

"Feel—smashed—" he said more distinctly. Someone turned him over and he cried a little, not wanting to be turned. . . . Why didn't he get fed? Beefsteak—to put guts in him! Someone leaned over him again—not the same. He could see dark eyes— Kit's. Her voice said distinctly, "Bert, why are you crying? What do you want?"

"Beefsteak," he gasped, "—no guts."

Someone laughed—not Kit. Gail! Gail said, "He's alive, all right. Why don't you get the beefsteak?"

His face was wiped and he stopped crying. And after a long time someone brought him soup that tasted of beefsteak.

Then the room was quiet except for someone feeding him. He opened his eyes—not Kit again. It was the blonde.

"Not Lil?" he inquired.

She shook that mass of gold. "I'm your nurse," she said, "Constance Weathers."

He knew something ought to be said to that. But for a long time he could not think what. It was only after she stopped feeding him and had tucked the covers around him that he thought of it.

"Pleased—to meet you," he whispered.

"Go to sleep, now," she told him.

He wanted to argue about that, but before he could begin he was asleep. . . .

In the library they all stood, ready to part again after the crisis which had drawn them together.

"Beefsteak!" Gail cried with laughter. "That's the first word he said."

Mr. Brame smiled reservedly. "I advise that it be kept private, however," he said. He had come over immediately when Harvey Crane telephoned that the crisis had been successfully passed. His plans for publicity were of course already made, either way. He had dictated to his secretary two distinct outlines, the other to be used if Bert Holm died—fortunately not now necessary. But it was his business to be prepared. "If you approve, Mr. Tallant, I shall simply give out a dignified statement for the morning papers to the effect that Mr. Holm has passed the crisis of his serious illness and is out of danger."

"Sounds sensible," Mr. Tallant said cautiously.

Mr. Brame went on with his usual dry smoothness.

"Within the next day or two I should like to submit my plans for taking the utmost advantage of the great wave of renewed interest in Mr. Holm. I assure you," he looked around at them all, "never in all the course of my career—and I have handled some of the most important public figures of our time—have so many letters and telegrams poured in expressing sympathy and grief. The number could have been equalled only"—he coughed —"by Mr. Holm's death, so happily averted. The question now is——"

"If you'll excuse us," Gail said, her eyes glittering with laughter, "we must go home. Harvey——"

"Yes, certainly, my dear," Harvey said.

. . . Harvey was mildly interested in this fellow Brame's theories, but he gave up quickly to Gail in all small matters, presenting a docile front which kept her from embarrassment among her friends, and yet creating no precedent in important matters which he decided alone. Gail, like most women, preferred this, and he knew it. He was eternally grateful that Gail was a sane woman, though clever, and not like her sister Kit. There was something very queer now about that small dark creature. When the doctor told them Bert was going to get well, Gail had clapped her hands and leaped to her feet. But Kit had simply sat, as white as a stone, her eyes wider and more black than he had ever seen them. It was almost as though she had been counting on something else and now did not know what to do. But it would be like her to have prepared herself for the worst; so it might be that she did not know what to do with the shock of good news. He glanced at her. She had said nothing at all since coming out of Bert's room. She sat there now on the large sofa, looking more remote and withdrawn than ever. There was no making her out. He put his arm thankfully about his own Gail. Her complexities were at least of the standard female variety he preferred.

"Ready?" he asked, drawing her gently along with him. "Count on me if you need me," he told his father-in-law in passing. "Good night, Kit—congratulations—good night, good night——"

He released Gail to let her kiss her family. He liked this close family feeling. It was normal and right. His own family had it, though one of his sisters, Mary, had broken away and was rather strange. That was because she had never married. Women always went queer if they didn't marry.

They stepped into the taxi and for a few moments said nothing. Then Gail said, yawning behind her hand, "I knew Bert would get well." She patted her lips. "After more or less upsetting the nation," she added, and laughed.

"Exactly," Harvey said, a trifle grimly. He took out his flat platinum-cased watch. It was nearly two o'clock and he hated to miss his sleep. It upset the next day's routine.

"Shall we say tomorrow, then, at three?" Mr. Brame said in the library after they had gone. "I don't want to seem precipitate, but I can scarcely urge too much the importance of taking advantage of the present public enthusiasm. The papers, as you know" —his sweeping declamatory glance included Kit, her father, her mother—"have played up his brave daily fight for his life, because, as the *Morning News* had it today, he has everything for which to live. The general expectation is that Bert Holm will do something even greater than he has yet done."

Kit was frightened at the stillness which fell upon her when she knew that everything was going to be as it had been. Surely she did not want Bert to die? She stood up, unable to bear her own feelings. "I must go to bed," she said.

Mrs. Tallant rose at once. "Yes, we must, all of us," she declared. "It's been a day! You'll understand, Mr. Brame."

"Oh, certainly," Mr. Brame replied, backing away a little.

"Tomorrow, then, Brame," Mr. Tallant said. He had said almost nothing since he saw Kit's face when the doctor came in. She didn't hate the fellow, did she?

Kit, in her own bed, lay motionless. Her father had kissed her good night without a further word, and her mother had come in to fuss over her covers a little—the night had turned very cold—

and had kissed her warmly and gone away without mentioning Bert. The day spread itself before her immediately.

Bert was going to get well. She had been sure of it herself when she saw his blue eyes looking up at her out of his white face. They had not been able to cut his hair and it lay tossed and fair as a child's upon the pillow. But they had kept him shaven, so that his face looked younger than ever. He would keep that youthfulness as long as he lived because it was from within him. Nothing could happen to him. And anything that happened, happened to her and left its mark. She could forget nothing. The hour with Norman had brought it all back. Did she wish she had not gone? But if it were still all hidden there in her, it was better to know it and reckon with it.

She lay breathing in the icy air from the open window. How did other people go about their lives? Blundering as she did? Yet her wants were very few. She had nearly everything for which people strove and longed—money, place, education, whatever it was. And yet, having always had these things she could not value them because she lacked the one essential, fundamental necessary companionship, the sort of thing that had nothing to with being rich or poor. She had met no one in her life who could give it to her except Norman, and he did not love her enough to give it to her. He had all but said so again this evening.

And yet there was now no agony in it for her as there had been. He had cast her so low before that now, because she knew he felt, however unwillingly, somehow companioned with her, the unwilling certainty seemed very near love. He had said something about the choice of unhappiness. There was that choice. It faced her now. When Bert was strong enough, she might choose at least her own unhappiness, if she could. If she only knew how to be ruthless! But there was no ruthlessness in her and this was her weakness. Lily and Norman, those two opposites, had yet the one serviceable trait of ruthlessness. But to her nothing could become intolerable when she took everything into consideration.

Her life was cluttered with considerations. She sighed, and turned away from herself. . . . At least she would go to see Norman's play. It would be fun to go to rehearsals again. She had sat hour upon hour in darkened empty theaters, watching rehearsals, watching the madness of people trying to put the universe into a single speech, a gesture, a movement. . . .

But Bert was going to get well. She fell asleep with fatigue, though her mind kept waking and remembering in fragments. Bert would get well, and yet there was Norman, never forgotten. Immense considerations lay ahead of her. She saw her own small figure toiling along a path between two great cliffs. Bert's mountains!

The telephone rang suddenly beside her bed and she leaped clear of approaching sleep. Norman's voice sounded in her ear.

"Kit?"

"Yes?" she answered.

"I don't know why in hell I'm calling you."

"I was nearly asleep," she said.

"I can't sleep," he told her. "Been working at rehearsal all evening. What have you been doing?"

She must tell him quickly. "Bert's better," she said. "When I came home, he was very ill. They didn't know—but he's safely past the crisis."

He did not answer for a moment. Then he said, very quietly. "Perhaps that's why I called—to know just that." And he put up the receiver.

"Science," Mr. Brame kept saying, "science may be the right thing for him, as something serious."

She had not slept until dawn and then she had slept all morning, and even now felt half crushed with the weight of unfinished sleep. They were sitting in the library with Mr. Brame again, her father, her mother, herself, surrounded with flowers.

The maids had been struggling with flowers all day. Ever since the papers announced Bert's recovery the flowers had been pouring in. Mrs. Tallant had said grimly, "There could scarcely have been more if it had been his funeral." Now that Bert was really going to get well there were several things she must attend to as soon as she could. The trained nurses, for one thing—the kitchen was in an uproar with conflicting orders from the nurses. Prynne and Weathers were at daggers' points. She had simply refused to discuss the matter as long as it looked as though Bert were about to die, but since he was going to get well, things had to be faced. Science, Mr. Brame was saying? She fastened her fretful attention upon him.

"It is necessary," Mr. Brame went on from his seat by the large mahogany table, "to consolidate Mr. Holm's position. In this country, science is the thing. Nothing is so dignified or so calculated to hold public respect as a study into some scientific question. The public always respects what it cannot understand. To engage Mr. Holm, therefore, in a scientific pursuit along his own line, something rather abstract, which need not be too clearly defined and which could occupy the rest of his life, would be quite suitable. It would make his position with the public at once static and dignified."

"What do you suggest?" Mr. Tallant asked mildly. All this talk of Brame's was, he knew, simply to lead up to a concrete notion. That was why he hired Brame, because there was always something concrete at the bottom of him, if one had the time to wait.

"The second expedition," Mr. Brame said promptly, "not at all like the first, of course. Not an adventure, in other words, but an expedition scientifically planned." He turned to Kit. "Has he said anything about another expedition?" Mr. Brame asked.

She remembered the night upon Gail's terrace when he had looked out over the city.

"He did say once he would like to get back to his mountains," she replied.

"The very best possible thing," Mr. Brame said quickly. "The public likes repetition of the original act with a slight further adventure along the familiar lines. They resent a new departure. Should Mr. Holm now take up a scientific or academic pursuit alone, this would be of no advantage in maintaining his position. The public would have no chart to follow. Mr. Holm is ticketed in their minds as an explorer. He must go on exploring. All we want is a new angle to something already familiar. Science——"

"Bert doesn't know anything about science!" Mrs. Tallant exclaimed. She was sitting in a large dark upholstered chair, looking regal with inner irritation.

"Ah, madam, wait!" Mr. Brame cried. He drew his white handkerchief from his breast pocket and polished his glasses. "It isn't necessary. We can hire innumerable scientists at almost no cost. There is nothing more plentiful unless it be mathematicians. No, the real problem is, what can we find to study in high altitudes? Merely an academic question would be too lacking in appeal to the always hotly sentimental public heart. There might be a humanitarian twist to it or something scientific. The public likes its heroes to be serious—when they are young, that is."

Kit said, smiling wryly, "How old must he be before he needn't be?"

"Be what?" Mr. Brame inquired.

"Anything," Kit said.

"I don't follow," Mr. Brame said with blank gravity.

"I was only joking," Kit said quickly.

Mr. Tallant, catching her eye, smiled suddenly. She smiled back, and then sighed. No, but poor Bert, who in one careless act of heroism had ruined his life!

. . . "This is the life," Bert said, laughing into the pretty face bent above him. Getting well was wonderful. He'd never been sick before. Now everybody was working for him. He didn't feel like reading, but then Connie did that. He slept most of the day when old Prynne was around, and then at night Connie would read to him. She was getting ready to read to him now. Everybody was gone. Kit had come in and told him good night. Kit was sweet these days. He'd wake up and she'd be there by his bed, looking at him. When you were still not strong you could just lie back and not worry about anything—as for instance, when she looked sort of down in the mouth. "Don't worry about anything," the doctor told him. "Eat, sleep, get well—that's your whole duty, young man!" So he didn't worry. But he was glad when they'd all gone and the house was quiet and the shades drawn, and only him and Connie here. She'd get him all ready for the night—he hadn't dreamed there were so many ways of being made comfortable! Then she settled in her chair under the light.

"Take off your cap so I can see your hair!" he begged her every night.

But she shook her head.

"Aw, come on, Connie!" he coaxed. "I like to look at the light shining on it."

"I couldn't, Mr. Holm," she said. That was something else, too. She'd never call him Bert, however much he told her to. "Why, even the newspapers call me Bert!" he told her. But she wouldn't; she was a stubborn little thing; all blondes were.

It was curious how he felt about her. He wasn't sure if he was crazy about her or not. But anyway it was nice coming to after you'd been knocked out and finding a pretty girl taking care of you.

"You remember where we left off, Mr. Holm?" she asked, settling her stiff white skirt.

"Bert says, 'Wherever you stopped readin','" he answered mischievously.

She smiled at him shyly and began in her light pretty voice, "'He took her in his arms'—wasn't that the place?"

"Sounds okay to me," he replied. "I like that notion."

It was fun making her smile and blush. He yawned and

stretched himself. The water was going out of his bones! A few more days and he'd be a man again. Every night he felt better than he had the night before. Another week and he'd be rarin' to go—only, go where? He had forgotten everything for so long. When he was up he'd climb again maybe. He hadn't thought about mountains somehow for a long time. Why hadn't he? It was queer, because now when he thought about it he wanted to climb again.

She began to read:

"He took her in his arms and pressed his mouth upon her red lips. It was the first time in all his mad life that true love had ever swept him clean. It made him pure and good."

He watched her nice little profile against the light and heard her even gentle voice, carrying the hot words like a cool little stream. Wonder if he could ever get her going? No, there wasn't to be any more of that; he'd made up his mind about it after that woman—what was her name?—had tried to devil him into divorcing Kit that evening at Gail's when she was tight. As if he'd divorce Kit, the best little wife a fellow ever had! No, no more of that. He was glad Connie wasn't as easy as other dames. He listened to her contentedly, half asleep, feeling warm and cared for in the center of this great house. Being sick had made him feel at home here. He hadn't felt so when he was well. But in this one big room and everybody waiting on him he felt at home. He hadn't made any mistake in marrying Kit Tallant. . . .

. . . So how in the heck could he be ready for the way Connie was after he had made up his mind really to leave her alone? He hadn't done a thing—took her hand, that's all, the next morning when she was going off duty. He wouldn't be such a fool as to start something then, anyway, with old Prynne coming in at any moment. No, he'd taken Connie's hand when she was brushing his hair, and held it a minute, and when she'd tried to pull away, he'd held on—no more than that. He'd done the same thing lots of times and every time she'd said, "Now, Mr. Holm!" This time she didn't. She looked at him, her face all pinched, and without one word she'd just crumpled up on the bed and put her face in his neck. And old Prynne would choose that minute to walk in!

"Connie," he whispered, "get up!" And she had.

Well, he hoped he'd never see anything hotter than that minute between those two dames.

"Miss Weathers!" Prynne said, like she was biting into a sour apple.

And Connie had jumped at her. "What, Miss Prynne?" she yelled.

"I could report you!" Prynne yelled back.

"Sure you could," Connie said. "Go on and do it!"

"All right, I will, but I'll resign first!"

"No, you won't, because I'm resigning!"

That scared him.

"Connie!" he begged. "Don't go!"

It would have been better if he hadn't spoken, because the minute Prynne heard him say that she gave him an awful look and turned right around and went out. And Connie put her face in her hands and began to cry. Women! They always took everything so serious. He turned over and shut his eyes. Let 'em all go to hell! As far as he was concerned that's where they all belonged. . . .

Mrs. Tallant, dressed early to be ready for a day's shopping with Gail, who was coming in with Harvey after breakfast, stopped outside her door to hear the shouting of women's voices in Bert's room.

"What in the world!" she exclaimed. But before there was time to discover, Miss Prynne rushed into the hall and slammed the door and held it.

"Miss Prynne!" Mrs. Tallant said severely.

Miss Prynne turned, her square face red and furious.

"I'm resigning, Mrs. Tallant," she said, loudly. "I'm not accustomed to this sort of a house."

"What do you mean?" Mrs. Tallant's indignation rose into stateliness.

"Where the night nurse on the case behaves disgraceful," Miss Prynne said in the same loud voice. "I'm a professional, Mrs. Tallant, and I've been trained up that a decent nurse don't allow compromising situations with the patients, like I found just now in Mr. Holm's room, Mrs. Tallant, when I went in to report for day duty."

"Please come into the library and explain yourself." Mrs. Tallant swept past the woman and went on downstairs.

Gail, she saw, was already in the hall. She had just come in and was standing there very slender and pretty in her smooth dark fur coat and close red hat. She waved her hand at her mother. Mrs. Tallant was suddenly unaccountably glad to see her elder daughter.

"Come into the library," she murmured. "There's been some sort of nonsense between those wretched nurses and Bert." She could be as plain as she liked with Gail, and Gail, lifting her delicate eyebrows, followed her mother.

But Mrs. Tallant was not prepared to find, when she opened the library door, that Kit was there. She was curled into the big sofa, a book she had been reading fallen on the floor. When they came in she sat up and looked at them vaguely.

"Have you been asleep so early, Kit?" Mrs. Tallant asked briskly.

"No. I just came here after I had breakfast with Dad. There was a book I wanted to look up."

Mrs. Tallant was thinking quickly. Kit might as well know. It was time to stop shielding her from anything. Some day she would have to cope with things alone.

"Hello, Kit," Gail said casually. She sat down and lit a cigarette, her eyes bright. This might be fun. She could see herself describing it all to Harvey tonight. He enjoyed gossip as much as she did and part of their companionship came from enjoying it together.

"Kit, there's been some sort of trouble between the nurses," Mrs. Tallant said.

And just then there was a knock on the door and Miss Prynne came in, her cap set straight and her face at its usual sallowness. She looked about at the three women, her mouth pursed.

"Say what you have to say quickly, please, Miss Prynne," Mrs. Tallant ordered her. "I am very busy today."

"I just wish to go off the case, Mrs. Tallant, that's all," Miss Prynne said coldly. "I'm a respectable woman."

"Just tell me what is the matter," Mrs. Tallant broke in with firm patience in her voice.

"When I came in this morning the night nurse was in the patient's arms," Miss Prynne said flatly. "I'm not used to anything like that."

"Well!" Mrs. Tallant breathed. She rather wished she had not encouraged the woman. Kit looked suddenly sick.

But Gail laughed, crisp bright laughter. "Oh dear," she cried, "Bert's so irresistible! What do you bet, Miss Prynne, that it was the night nurse's fault? Poor Bert—they all do it! I'm surprised at you, Miss Prynne. Haven't you felt the fatal charm? Why, all women fall in love with Bert!"

Miss Prynne's face was turning its dark thick red again. "I don't allow myself—" she began, and was stopped by Gail's fresh laughter.

"Oh, you too! I think it's simply funny," Gail cried in little bright peals. "Kit, what did I tell you? I told you they'd both be in love with Bert before he was well!"

"You and Miss Weathers had better both go," Mrs. Tallant said sharply. "I'll ask Dr. Leavett for other nurses. Now, Gail, are you ready?"

198

They rose together, and somehow Miss Prynne found herself outside in the hall alone, and the door shut. That was all.

. . . She did not go back upstairs. Instead she went to the service hall and found her coat and hat and soberly plodded away. They were wicked, light-minded women. All rich women were, who didn't have to work. What had really hurt her more than anything was their saying that—that every woman was silly about him. It wasn't easy for a woman of her age. She'd tried to imagine him like her son, that was all, the son she might have had if she had ever married. That was why she was so disgusted when she came in this morning. She'd felt all along that girl wasn't the kind he ought to have about him—poor fellow, you could see he was innocent and young. But it was better not to see him any more. Sometime when he was well she'd maybe write him a little letter just to tell him what a privilege it had been to take care of him. Well, she'd better call up the doctor and explain her side of it, and turn in her name for another case. Poor boy, whatever happened, she would always know it wasn't his fault, not with those women. . . .

Behind the shut door Mrs. Tallant and Gail both looked first at Kit. She was very calm.

"Thanks, Gail," Kit said. "You were very neat."

"It's always best to laugh at that sort of thing," Gail said. "Besides, you can't blame Bert, Kit. It's going to happen over and over again."

"I know it is," Kit said. She looked from her sister to her mother, and went on in the same calm little voice. "So"—her lips betrayed her by the slightest quiver—"I've about made up my mind I won't go on with it."

"Kit!" her mother cried.

"It isn't good enough," Kit said. But she had not made up her mind until this instant, when suddenly she was ready to cut off everything, only to be free. Norman was right, always right. To be free was enough; it was the only happy ending. It was all she wanted, mere freedom. She had given up the hope of love or the right to happiness, so surely she could have freedom.

Gail sat down. There was no hurrying away from this, for she knew the look in Kit's eyes. The first time she had seen it was years ago when Kit, who was afraid of water, had suddenly made up her mind to dive.

"Kit!" she had screamed then, laughing, "you aren't going to drown!"

"I don't care whether I drown or not," that small Kit had said, and had jumped. . . .

Gail looked at her mother meaningfully, and Mrs. Tallant sat down, too.

"Kit, you're not talking about divorce?" she demanded. She glanced at Kit and felt Gail solidly with her. Gail stood up and took off her coat and hat and sat down again.

"What else?" Kit said simply.

"Now, Kit," Mrs. Tallant began. She must think very quickly before Kit became set in one of her rare stubborn moods when she was beyond all reason. "Bert isn't as bad as that. He's annoying, I know, but, my dear, you'll find all men have something. You know, you said yourself once that young writer, that what's-his-name, used to bore you by always talking about his work."

"This has nothing to do with him," Kit broke in. And instantly she knew she lied. It did have something to do with Norman; it might have everything to do with him, though until she denied it aloud just now, she had not faced it in herself. Surely she had been thinking only that Bert was impossible for her and she for him, that they could never be near each other and so she must be free of him. But if she were accusing Bert really only because of Norman—she felt shaken now by her own duplicity. She wanted to go on and say aloud, "All I want is freedom from

200

Bert." But she could not say it out of self-distrust. She said nothing therefore.

Mrs. Tallant went on very gravely. "There isn't such a thing as a perfectly happy marriage in the story-book sense. But there are successful marriages, and they're the ones where the woman has made up her mind to adapt herself, to ignore much, and make the most of little. I dare say even Gail puts up with some things in Harvey, don't you, Gail?"

"Oh, yes, indeed," Gail murmured. Her long lashes drooped over her eyes. "Sometimes I loathe him."

"Exactly," Mrs. Tallant agreed. "It's the same with any woman you'd ask. It isn't that we ourselves would be so silly as to mind divorce. Sometimes it's the only sensible thing to do. But people still don't like it here in America—the people who think so much of Bert, I mean."

"It really never works awfully well," Gail murmured. "You know poor Irene Cavanaugh—she's always struggling to get back again. You say divorce doesn't matter any more, Mother, but actually it does, Kit, even when it comes to our set. There's been a sort of reaction—not moral, but just for convenience. An odd woman is so difficult to invite when there're plenty of pretty young girls always coming out. She isn't placed, if you know what I mean. I know Irene has not been any happier."

"I simply won't have it," Mrs. Tallant interrupted her, "not suddenly, anyway, Kit. It's too much to ask of your family. Think of the publicity! It couldn't be just an ordinary divorce. All sorts of stories would come out. Everybody would ask *why*, when you were married to Bert Holm. All those silly women would never believe it was his fault. You'd lose by it—we'd all lose——"

"Kit, of course if you don't love him—" Gail broke in.

Kit looked at Gail, and bit her lips. She must not let them into herself too far, not yet when she did not know what she wanted.

Gail leaned toward her persuasively. If she could only talk to

Kit as female to female! But so much she had never revealed to her sister, not knowing how Kit's delicacy could be trusted to endure a revelation of the bitch. So now she spoke only from her wisely married self. "He's really sweet, Kit, if you take him as he is. And nowadays you can do as you like if you only keep quiet about it. Look at Nora Brand! All her friends know she loathes Dan, but it pays them to keep on. He directs her plays and all that, and besides it's such good publicity to say you've been married to the same man for twelve years. Divorce really isn't as fashionable as it was before the depression. And that girl this morning—it's nothing. Most men do little silly things that mean nothing, really."

"Kit, promise me this at least," Mrs. Tallant demanded, "that you won't make up your mind until you've taken everything into consideration. You owe it to us all."

"I'll promise that," she said. She stooped for her book and laid it open upon her knee. It was William Blake. She had wanted to read something that would take her straight away from reality. There was far too much reality in her life these days. Reality pressed her more closely hour by hour.

"That's right," Mrs. Tallant said eagerly, and then sighed. "Oh dear, I feel worn out! I don't know if I had better go or not, Gail."

Gail was putting on her coat again.

"Come on," she said firmly. "There's nothing like shopping for restoring your perspective."

"Well—" her mother said reluctantly. She went over and kissed Kit's cheek. "I can always trust your sense of fairness, Kit," she murmured.

"I do want to do what is right," Kit said. Her voice was suddenly thick.

"I know you do, dear," her mother replied. "Oh, I must telephone the doctor about nurses," she added.

They went away and left her alone. What she wanted, she

thought, was someone quite cold and hard—only not Gail—to put down before her the lines of this tangled pattern. If someone could disentangle them and arrange them as they really were, she could see more clearly. Feelings were so little to be trusted. Had she not trusted to Norman's feeling and had it not shifted away from her, and had not a wayward impulse of feeling given her to Bert? If long inward brooding could clarify nothing, perhaps something external and cold could do it. She wanted clear coldness to guide her. She thought a moment. Why not Roger Brame? There was no one in the world so clear and cold as he. She decided to go and see him.

The walk alone had done her good. The sharp pure air of a late winter's day had clarified her blood and brain. She stepped into the elevator.

"Thirty-three, please," she murmured, and was whirled upward through space to the thirty-third floor. There opposite she saw in small gold letters, "Roger Brame, Public Relations Counsel," and she went into a tiny reception hall where a plainly dressed, middle-aged woman sat at a typewriter. Just beyond in a small inner office, she saw Mr. Brame's baldish head. It lifted, and he leaped to his feet, trying not to look surprised.

"Mrs. Holm!" he said, "I'm honored." He came out, and she felt the dry quick touch of his hand on hers. "Come in, please. What can I do for you?"

She went into the musty office, hung with innumerable large autographed photographs. It held nothing else but a desk and several file cases.

"My clients," Mr. Brame said of the photographs. They looked down on her, the smiling faces of actresses, the self-conscious faces of famous writers and lecturers and explorers. Here in this small dingy room Roger Brame had sat and planned brilliant personalities for them to present to the world. Some she knew, but many she did not. Only a few had lived on, and even

203

they were changed. For they had chosen, or Mr. Brame had chosen, to put upon this wall the impermanent moment of their greatest success. Her eye was caught by the face of Charley Bigge.

"Which reminds me," Mr. Brame went on, "that I have long wanted to ask if I might include a portrait of Mr. Holm."

"Yes, of course," she murmured. Yes, Bert belonged there. Mr. Brame had made him, too.

He opened a drawer in the file case and drew out a large photograph.

"This one, if you don't mind."

He handed it to her.

"I remember it," she said and sat gazing at Bert. It was one of his best. He stood, his hands in his pockets, his square shoulders back, his hair tossed, looking at her out of clear and smiling eyes. They seemed to grow blue as she looked at them.

"It personifies, I think, our build-up," Mr. Brame said judicially.

"Yes, it does," she said and put the picture quietly aside. Would this be the right picture for Mr. Brame's wall, or would there come another, to be taken at a higher moment than Bert had yet achieved, a moment without her?

Mr. Brame sat down at his desk and waited for her. She looked at him and plunged in. Once when she was very small, she now remembered, she had made up her mind to plunge into the pool for the first time and it had seemed as though it were death when the water closed over her head. But she had come up again.

"Mr. Brame, I want to ask you directly what would be the effect on Bert, and on my family, publicly, if I divorced him?"

She kept her eyes on him. Mr. Brame did not answer for a moment. Nothing like this, he thought quickly, had entered his plans. He would have to make an entirely new approach. It would be extremely embarrassing, since Mr. Tallant was also a client, and it would be wise, as well as of course only just, to be fair to both. But distressing, confusing, difficult——

"Quite disastrous, I fear," he said quietly.

She waited, grateful that he asked no questions.

"The public," Mr. Brame went on, "expects far more of its heroes than it does of its own individuals. Divorce, we may say, it is true, is so common now as to cause no comment unless it occurs in a case like Mr. Holm's. There, unfortunately, little liberty would be allowed, simply because the public longs to believe in its hero as one"—he fumbled for a phrase, and then smiled—"*sans peur et sans reproche*, you know. They don't want to think he even feels temptation as they do, much less yields to it." He coughed, and glanced obliquely at the young figure opposite him, and decided to go on. "I don't know whether or not you are aware, Mrs. Holm, of any previous—occurrence in Mr. Holm's history——"

"You mean his former marriage? Yes, I know," she interrupted. He was relieved. She knew, then! And as far as he could see she was calm. But one never could tell with these slender composed dark-eyed women.

"A second occurrence," Mr. Brame went on, "would be the more unfortunate. Inevitably the first one, now happily unknown to the public, would reappear in a sinister light. Now, should it become known, I have planned an instant publicity on the grounds of youthfulness and all that. But to be divorced again, and by Robert Tallant's daughter"—he shook his head—"it would undermine him very seriously. In fact, I should feel myself quite impotent."

"I see," she said steadily.

"As to the consideration of your own family," Mr. Brame proceeded, encouraged by her steady comprehending look, "it would also be—difficult. Mental cruelty, of course. But it means anything the public chooses. In your case, Mrs. Holm, you must remember you have not the usual freedom accorded to individuals by law in our country. There is no law to prevent your doing as you like. But, you see, public sentiment, or perhaps I should say, a sentimental public, would condemn either you or Mr. Holm, as the case might be presented to the public, and might very probably condemn you both."

She did not answer him now when he paused. She simply gave him that dark unvarying gaze. There was no telling what she thought. He went on hastily to the concrete idea he had been preparing.

"I should like to suggest, at least, the postponement of any decision until after the expedition, which I am now planning in detail. It may be"—he paused and pursed his lips—"that the expedition will so establish Bert Holm that the build-up could stand the shock of personal disaster. I don't know; we should have to see. And, if I may presume upon a personal reflection, it seems only just to all parties and things considered to postpone definite action for say, six or eight months. You could do that, Mrs. Holm?"

"Yes, I could do that," she agreed.

Still no telling what she was feeling, he thought. She rose and put out her hand. It was small and hot against his cool palm.

"Good-by," she said. "Thank you, Mr. Brame."

She looked so pale about the lips that he felt afraid to let her go alone.

"By the bye," he said, to detain her a moment until he could think what he should do, "have you any ideas about financing the expedition?"

She looked at him, gathering her mind together.

"There was a little man who told Bert once that he would give him a hundred thousand dollars. Would that be enough? It was at the Explorers' League dinner when we first came here. His name was Albert Canty."

"Albert Canty!" Mr. Brame repeated.

She nodded.

"He is one of the wealthiest men in the city," Mr. Brame said solemnly, "a hermit and erratic, but—excuse me, Mrs. Holm, if I just make a note of it. This is very important."

"Is it?" she said. "But, please, I won't wait."

She was gone. He sat down again and drew in his breath deeply. It was a narrow escape from misfortune. He had had the entire expedition planned and ready to move as soon as Bert Holm was well, and now here, too, was money at his hand. He must see Canty at once. If divorce had intervened, weeks of work would have been wasted. But she was a reasonable young woman, Bert Holm's wife, because she was also Robert Tallant's daughter.

And Kit, walking home slowly through glittering sunshine and hurrying people, accepted for herself Mr. Brame's clear coldness. Delay was right. She was so made, she knew, that whatever she did must be right in the doing, so that let the end be what it might, it was inevitable and then the only possible end. Every step to that end must be clean, she thought proudly. She would go straight ahead as she was and play fair, until Bert had had his chance. At least for a while there need be no more deciding.

In this mood she reached home and found her father had called her.

"Mr. Tallant said you were to call at once, please, miss," Smedley said, opening the door.

That meant her mother and Gail had told him. She went to the telephone and dialed and waited for him.

"Kit?"

"Yes, Dad?"

"What's all this? Your mother and Gail——"

"Don't bother, Dad. I won't—anyway, not now, until after the expedition."

"But your mother said—" she could hear how anxious he was.

"I know. I felt so this morning. Then I went to see Mr. Brame, and I saw it would be—disastrous."

"Yes, of course, and I'm very glad you see it."

"Yes, I do, Dad."

He hesitated. "If you're really unhappy, Kit, of course we must look into it."

"We'll wait and see, Dad. Only, don't let's talk about it—eh, Dad?"

"No, certainly not at all," he agreed, "unless you want to——"

"I've made up my mind," she answered.

"Good girl," he said heartily, and hung up.

Then her father thought she was doing right, too. It was the seal upon her decision.

"Gosh, it's good to have that bunch of females gone," Bert said to Kit that night. Then she told him about the expedition, and instantly the world was glory for him.

"Sa-a-y!" he whistled. "That sounds just about all right! I've been lying here wondering what I was going to do with myself. I was just waiting for a hunch. I can feel my legs gettin' ready to go somewhere. They aren't going to want to lay here much longer."

"Lie, Bert," she smiled at him.

"Lie or lay," he said gaily, "they don't want to do either one."

. . . And then because he thought she looked a little down, he had hastened to say again that he was glad the bunch of females was gone, because maybe old Prynne had tattled this morning. Something had happened. He hadn't seen Prynne again and before noon a little middle-aged man with a face like a bird's had come into his room and said he was the new nurse. He had grinned at the man and said, "Bet the old lady found you." The man had not answered beyond saying dryly that his name was Brown. It had felt damned queer to have a man's hands around him. Then night came and no Connie. There wasn't to be a night nurse any more, Brown said. He was going to sleep in the little dressing room on a cot. And Bert had been lying mournfully all

208

day thinking he wouldn't see Connie any more, not unless he could find her address when he got well, and then here was Kit come in and saying there was going to be a new expedition and that he was going to be head of it. Now he knew he'd never look up Connie or anybody. Let 'em all go! He was crazy to be off and on his way. He wanted mountains under his feet and mountains miles ahead and sky on top of him. He wanted to feel himself going up and up and up. If Kit felt bad about Connie she'd show it now and he'd tell her it didn't mean a thing, because he loved her and he had been absolutely faithful to her. He believed in being faithful to his wife and his conscience wouldn't let him sleep with another woman as long as he was married. As long as he didn't really sleep with anyone else, she ought to be satisfied; plenty of women didn't have husbands like him. He was ready to defend himself, but she said nothing to show she was sore or even that she knew anything. Instead she went on about the expedition, and pretty soon she asked him a queer question. . . .

"Bert," she asked, "can you think of any good scientific reason for an expedition like this?"

He laughed at her. "I don't climb mountains for anything but fun," he said.

"No, but what can people find out on high mountains?" she insisted.

He saw she was serious and so he defended himself, a little afraid of her as he always was when she was serious.

"They can't find out much of anything," he insisted. "Old Fessaday was always talking about something or other that would help him tell what the weather would be next year, but I never took any stock in that."

"Meteorology?" she inquired.

"Something like that," he said carelessly. Then his eyes sparkled. "No, Kit, that's not what you go for. It's the excitement

209

—you get to gambling with yourself whether you can make it or not. The wind drags at you to pull you down and the cold eats into you and you can't trust the snow. It may let you down into a hole a hundred feet deep—or maybe a thousand. There's holes under the snow on mountains that haven't any bottom. The sides are solid ice, as blue as the sky. What makes ice blue like that, I don't know. "

His eyes held a boy's wonder. "I suppose because pure water is always faintly blue," she answered. Yes, she knew what Gail meant when she said his charm came from his eagerly meeting you exactly where he was.

"Is it?" he asked. Then he moved his legs in a mighty lunge. "Gosh, can I go tomorrow, Kit?"

"Not quite," she answered, "but just as soon as you're well and everything is ready."

He lay suddenly still. "Say, that's right. Get me a pencil and some paper, Kit. I'll begin putting things down. You have to do careful planning for a trip like this."

It would take more planning than Bert could do, she thought. Still he must think of it as his expedition. She went away to fetch the pencil and paper.

But Bert showed himself unexpectedly good at planning. He was getting stronger daily and the zest of planning was like a tonic. Instead of lounging against his pillows waiting for someone to put a glass of orange juice to his lips or to smooth his bed, he began making secret efforts to get on his feet. Brown, with the agitation of a sparrow, had reported to the doctor that the patient was unruly.

"Hey, you," Dr. Leavett scolded Bert affectionately, "you stay in bed. You don't want a damaged heart, do you?"

Everybody knew now that Bert Holm was going on a great expedition of his own into the unexplored region of the Himalayas. Roger Brame had sent out publicity notes about it that flew out over the country and settled everywhere in newspapers. These were what he called "teasers." His solid information was to be sent out later.

"My heart's my toughest point, ain't it, Kit?" Bert roared out a laugh.

"Wait till you get up that mountain!" Dr. Leavett replied. He took entire credit for Bert Holm's recovery. When he heard a girl in a drugstore say to another, "Gee, ain't it swell about Bert Holm? Say, I saw him once," he felt that he had saved Bert Holm alive for her and for everyone. He felt exalted by his profession and was in fine spirits. He went on gaily, "That's the way with hearts—they wait until a crucial moment and then let you down. And your pulse is just a little bit too slow, you know. I don't know what that means. We must watch you."

"Oh yeah?" Bert scoffed. But he put his legs back under the cover. . . . Damned little sneak of a man nurse to come in just when he'd managed to get across the room! He'd have got back all right if he hadn't been interrupted. . . .

"Work your brains as hard as you like," Dr. Leavett said laughing. "Brains are naturally lazy enough to protect themselves."

Bert, from his bed, then, had really begun to plan. Kit was surprised. They were all, she felt, secretly surprised, though of course no one said anything. They had been so long used to a helpless Bert who had only to be tended. Now he sat up and studied maps and made lists. He would, he decided, take Jack Rexall along as his mechanic. Kit listened, remembering the moment she had last seen him. Only what of it? It mattered less than nothing in a world where nothing mattered much.

"He isn't any mountain climber," Bert told Kit, chuckling. "I'll never get old Rexie higher'n a couple thousand feet. He won't get ahead of me the way I did Fessaday; Rexie gets sick if he really gets high. But he's a great mechanic and he likes me. That's important on a trip like this, Kit. Everybody's got to like the leader."

He interviewed one man after another as he grew stronger,

sitting wrapped in a gorgeous blue brocaded lounging robe. His closet was full of lounging robes people had sent him. He had kept only eight of the ones he liked best. The others Mr. Brame thought he'd better send to a veterans' hospital because it sounded good to do that and he didn't want them and they couldn't be sent back unless people put in their names, which they usually didn't. They just said, "From an ardent admirer," or something like that. He liked best of all this blue one.

And wearing it, he was soon able to saunter into Kit's room, turned now into a sitting room for him, and talk with all the fellows who wanted to go with him. Of course he couldn't take them all. There were hundreds of them. The "hired girl," as he called his new secretary, didn't let any over thirty-five come in to bother him. He didn't want any old fellows getting sick and holding things up the way that that fellow had on Fessaday.

Kit had said, "How will you find men to go with you, Bert?"

And Bert had answered carelessly, "How did old Fessaday find me? I heard he was going and I was crazy to go along. That's how it'll be."

Secretly Kit was surprised at this shrewdness, for indeed that was how it had been. As soon as it had been published that Bert Holm was out again for adventure, men were ready to follow him into it. They wrote letters and sent telegrams and arrived, unannounced, with suitcases or with nothing. Bert's secretary sorted them out—no one over thirty-five, no one who had not climbed, no one who could not show a perfect physical record. Then those that were left came one by one into Bert's presence. One after another he saw them, eager boys, eager men, wanting only to go along as cook, as helper, as anything—only to be with Bert Holm on adventure. He was ruthless with most of them, trusting entirely to his "hunches."

"I get a hunch when I look at a fellow," he told Kit. "I like him or I don't like him. The ones I like I keep their names; the others I forget, that's all. Then I'll look 'em over again and choose. I don't want more than a dozen men in the bunch, and they've all got to be for me, see?"

But Brame was firm on one man. John Baker must be the scientist. Mr. Canty said it must be so if he gave the money, because he knew and liked John Baker, and besides Baker was going mainly for new rhododendrons and orchids, and had promised duplicates of all he could find for Mr. Canty's own private orchid collection.

What purpose could be found for Bert? Only Everest among mountains would be exciting enough to stir public imagination again, and Bert was not experienced enough for Everest. They all searched for a good purpose to put behind Mr. Brame's daily bursts of publicity. Mr. Brame, in distraction at last, telephoned to ask Kit if he and John Baker might discuss the matter with her, since Bert, while undoubtedly a born leader, Mr. Brame said, was not inclined toward science. "A perfectly natural thing," Mr. Brame's wiry voice hastened to declare at her ear, "my clients, I find, are nearly always unable—" he tapered off without finishing.

Kit found herself, therefore, one morning in March face to face with John Baker and Mr. Brame in the drawing room, where Smedley had conducted them. As soon as she saw that square rugged ugly face and tall knobby frame, she said impulsively, "Oh, do come into the library—it's so hard to talk in this barn."

So they had gone into the library and there sat down, and John Baker had folded himself into a large chair and said nothing while Mr. Brame explained why he had been brought here. Then he said in a precise but pleasant voice, "There isn't much use in mountain climbing, if that's what you mean, Brame. It's some sort of psychosis, of course, which drives men to climbing mountains, some instinct of escape from the humdrum or perhaps from themselves. But it's an instinct and partly blind, at that."

Mr. Brame looked slightly disconcerted.

"You mean," Kit said, "that science is not served by such expeditions into high altitudes?"

"Not much," John Baker said, "that is, after the plant life disappears. Fessaday professes to have ready to publish his data on long-range weather forecasting. But I haven't seen them. My own interest is plants, as you know."

"It is rather essential in this case," Mr. Brame repeated anxiously, "that we have a good reason for the expedition. Albert Canty is ready to put up the money."

John Baker chuckled suddenly, a hard dry chuckle. "How did you get Canty? I've been working on him for years, and he always told me he wasn't going to finance any more expeditions because his last one was with some archæological chap who used up about fifty thousand dollars and came back with an early Roman bathtub that looked like an ordinary American one. It's in the museum at this moment."

They laughed, and Mr. Brame said modestly, "It was not I who did it, I must confess. Mr. Canty saw Mr. Holm on his return from China and at that time promised to finance him. Mrs. Holm told me about him the other day. I went to see him and we had a very satisfactory talk."

"I'll have to see Holm," John Baker declared, turning to Kit. His eyes were a clear rock gray.

This was an honest man, she decided. "He'll want to see you, certainly," she said quietly.

Mr. Brame was pinching his thin underlip in profound thought.

"I suppose," he said slowly, "we could say that Bert Holm was going in search of rare plants." He looked up with a moment's hope at John Baker. "They're not medicinal, by any chance, are they? That would make a good story."

But John Baker shook his head grimly. "They're not worth a darned cent to humanity," he said.

Kit laughed, but Mr. Brame declared with sober energy, "I'm not going to give up on this. There must be some use in this expedition, and I'll find it and publish it."

In the end he scribbled a paragraph of notes.

"How's this?" he inquired. "The Holm Expedition, due to leave for the Himalayas on June 3 of this year, is planned to include various scientific objectives, one of the most important being the discovery by John Baker of rare Himalayan plant life. Mr. Holm will devote his own time to broader aspects of life at high altitudes."

Kit, staring in wonder at Mr. Brame, saw him look away hastily as he went on:

"The great thing in a case like this, is to get the central idea of science before the public and then work out the details." He rose and shook hands with Kit. "I'll leave Mr. Baker with you, Mrs. Holm. If Mr. Holm feels well enough——"

"He feels quite well today," Kit said.

"Ah, splendid!" Mr. Brame replied. "I'll make a note of that." Left with John Baker, she said, "Shall we go up?"

"I am quite at your service," he said.

She led the way upstairs and opened the door of her old room where a big desk stood in place of her bed. Upon it was a heap of letters which Mr. Brame had culled and sent to Bert now that he was nearly well. But he had not opened them. He was lying upon the couch, tapping the end of a pencil against his beautiful white teeth and frowning over a list of equipment he had written in his sprawling unformed writing.

"Bert," she said, "this is John Baker."

He looked up. "Hello," he said, turning his bright blue gaze upon them. John Baker bowed slackly and sat down.

"I'll leave you to talk," she said, and went to the door. And then, happening to glance at Bert, she saw his look and instantly knew its meaning. He was having one of his hunches.

"Why, he's going to hate John Baker!" she thought, amazed.

"I have a hunch against the fellow, I tell you," Bert was saying stubbornly. "I don't want him. He's one of those wise guys and I told him I wouldn't need him."

They had all hurried to Bert's room because Mr. Brame had telephoned Mr. Tallant in agitation that he wanted to be allowed to resign from Bert Holm.

"You can't resign, Brame!" Mr. Tallant had roared over the telephone. "Damn it, man, what'll we do with him?"

"I don't mind telling you, Mr. Tallant," Mr. Brame's thin voice seemed to crackle over the wires, "what I didn't dare tell Baker this morning, that I only got Canty to back the expedition after he heard Baker was going. Canty isn't as enthusiastic about Mr. Holm as he was when he made that offer. He's not a climbing man himself, and he's heard some stories he doesn't like. He's a very religious man and a teetotaler. One never knows where one will find fundamentalism these days. It goes to show we must get some positive publicity going at once, because a popular reaction against immorality has set in. But Canty knows Baker is straight; and finally he said he'd stick by his promise if Baker was going, for he knew Baker wouldn't go in for what he called a hoopety-hoop publicity stunt. I'm afraid his interest in Bert Holm has cooled. I've tried to get another good scientific name—Benton Ayres—but he won't go. Says he doesn't want to get into the Holm limelight."

"You go right on with the plans, Brame," Mr. Tallant shouted, and clapping down the receiver he had gone straight home in a taxi and found Kit and her mother and they had all gone up to Bert's room. They talked for an hour.

"See here," Mr. Tallant said finally to Bert's stubbornness, "it's this way. Baker goes and you all go. He doesn't go and nobody goes—that's the gist of it."

"Bert, don't be silly," Mrs. Tallant said briskly. She could scarcely wait for the expedition to start. The house wouldn't be itself until Bert was out of it. She was so sick of flowers that if another box of roses was opened in her presence she would scream. "You're the leader, aren't you? You can do what you like, surely, once you are on the way."

216

"I rather liked John Baker," Kit said quietly. So she had, though his gravity had been so immense when he came downstairs from Bert's room this morning that she had felt a premonitory shadow.

"Good-by, Mrs. Holm," he had said formally, and had given her hand one abrupt shake and had said not a word about being glad to meet Bert.

"Make up your mind, Bert," Mr. Tallant insisted.

Bert looked suddenly exhausted.

"Oh hell," he said peevishly, "let him go, then. I don't care."

He was in bed and he turned away from them and put his face to the wall. Kit felt suddenly sorry for him, and when her parents were gone she went to him and put her hand on his shoulder.

"Bert?" she whispered.

But he shook her hand off with a shrug of his shoulder. She waited a moment more, and then when he did not move she, too, went quietly away.

VI

THE decision that Kit was to go with Bert upon the expedition to Pangbat was never made at one particular moment that she could ever look back upon. Like all other large imperious necessities it seemed to shape itself as a visible mist gathers out of an empty valley, and, like the mist, the question was first tentative and nebulous. Someone must help Bert to gather together the hundreds of parts necessary to the expedition and she began to do it. He could think of the disconnected parts. "Kit, we must have some sort of shoes to climb in that are light and warm. Those things Fessaday called boots weighed eight pounds. I weighed 'em! And lugged 'em to the top of Therat and came down with frostbite. I'd better have worn sneakers."

"Light warm shoes," she wrote down on the little pad she had learned to carry.

"Sleeping bags," Bert said suddenly one day at breakfast, "I haven't done a thing about them. They oughtn't to be heavy, Kit, but warm. And wide enough to move in. Fessaday's were so narrow when you got 'em zipped up you couldn't cough for fear you'd bust out again. And when the zippers wouldn't work, you were out of luck for good."

"Light warm sleeping bags—no zippers," she wrote.

The list grew by accumulation. She discussed it with her mother and Gail and John Baker and wrote down what they said. Gail's imagination was strong on matters of comfort.

"I'd want something like an eider down," she said. "Two bags, an eider down and then a close outside covering, canvas or denim, and laced with big brass eyelets over a flap."

In the big softly carpeted living room of the New York house Mrs. Tallant and Gail, who had never in their lives known cold or hunger or fatigue, sat imagining and planning what men would need upon the snowy slopes of the Himalayas: lightness because everything must be carried upon men's backs over rocks and frozen tracks beaten out of the ice and snow; warmth because the cold was as deep as the cold of the poles; and above all simplicity in everything from the way shoes and leggings were fastened to the putting up of tents and the cooking of food, because at such altitudes the brain was numbed by lack of oxygen, and the hands were like fingerless clubs.

Kit, looking at her mother neat and handsome in her morning dress and at Gail always the smart young matron, admired them.

"I don't see how you can think of these things," she said.

"We Tallants are not so far from the wagon trail," Mrs. Tallant answered. "I can remember my grandmother telling me how she had to put everything she owned into a wagon and be ready for hot weather or cold."

Kit felt the same solid heredity in herself. It compelled her to buy books on mountain climbing and Himalayan expeditions and study them and compare them with what Bert could tell. He could not read a book. Print brought no image to his mind, but a photograph made him break into eager explanations. His blunt forefinger tracing the lines of a photograph guided her up the slope of Mount Everest.

"That's the trail they took, Kit. Up that north ridge, a col, they call it. They tried three times, but they couldn't get up those slabs of rock that were covered with snow. And they died a thousand feet from the top. I'd have found a way, I bet! I wish it'd been Everest instead of Therat! That'd been something, wouldn't it, Kit?" His blue eyes were illuminated. "What'll you bet I do Everest some day?"

"Why do you want to do it, Bert?" she asked. At such moments he seemed ready to come out of that shell of inarticulateness.

Something trembled in his look, as if his soul were about to awake, but if it were, he always pushed it back with a short laugh.

"Oh, I dunno," he said. "Maybe it's just that I like to get ahead of everybody else."

"It must be more than that," she persisted gently.

"Honest, I don't know," he said. "It's no fun, I know that. I kicked myself all the way up Therat. What the heck, I said. Here I am frozen and pantin', my eyes poppin' out of my head. I was so short on oxygen, and—say—oxygen makes me think. We ought to have some tanks of it, just to be on hand. Fessaday was nutty on that. He thought it wasn't being a good sport to carry oxygen. But I can't see it. If it's the top you want, get it anyway you can is the way I look at it."

"Oxygen," she wrote down. "Ask Baker," she added.

"Ask Baker" was now the postscript to most of her notes. John Baker told her the names of firms and of men to see and went with her to dusty wholesale offices where they looked at samples and catalogues. He argued prices in his flat toneless voice and talked about the special sleeping bags made to order and tents with flaps long enough to provide even for an anchorage of heavy stones.

"You have to think of the wind," he said to Kit. "There's wind enough up there on those heights to carry a house away."

Out of khaki-colored samples he chose linings and coverings and felt and rubber pads for floors. "Rocks don't make a good mattress. They work up into you about three o'clock in the morning," he said.

Downstairs in the huge basement of the Tallant house the cargo accumulated in ticketed piles. Bert looked at it.

"Got to keep it down," he said.

Together, Kit and Bert and Baker and Mrs. Tallant and Gail went over everything and took away the doubtful and the experimental. Baker was better than any of them at this, and he alone could end Gail's sharp arguments. He would not look at her while she talked, and pique made her talk the more. She had never met a man who did not look at her. But Baker examined alcohol stoves or the battery of a flashlight or the lid of a thermos bottle she had brought and when she finished said, "We don't need it," and put it aside. Thus one day were put aside a fireless cooker, a new brand of compressed soup tablets, electric body pads, and several things which he suspected of gadgetry. Gail was very angry.

"Light my cigarette, please," she commanded him imperiously. And when he was near, his hand holding the lighter a few inches from her pretty lips, she raised her lashes and looked up at him. No one knew better than Gail the value of a flame burning under her uplifted eyelashes. But he was not looking at her.

"Wait, it's not lit yet," she said and put her fingers upon his hand as though to steady it.

He did not pull away. Instead, his hand completely steady, he gazed down into Gail's eyes, and under that scornful look the fox in her took to its hole again. And after a moment he put into words what Kit had felt like a mist rising, a mist of doubt, a question and a curiosity half eager, half unwilling. He turned from Gail to Kit and said clearly, "Why don't you come with us, Mrs. Holm? We could do with a woman like you."

He was looking at her, though he would not look at Gail, and she accepted his sad, sexless gaze, a gaze as distant, as clear, as gratefully impersonal as evening light upon the mountains.

"I think I'd like to come," she said and knew as she spoke that it was true. She wanted above all things to go to the Himalayas where there were no people and nothing but mountains, though until this moment of expression she had not known it. Besides, since there was no need for her anywhere else, since she must not be where Norman was, why not go with Bert?

She held to that compelling impersonality in the clamor when it became known that Bert Holm's wife had decided to accompany him to the Himalayas. The clamor began at home.

Her mother completely disapproved. "You aren't strong enough, Kit," she declared.

"What's the matter with her?" Mr. Tallant demanded. "She's never sick." Though he himself did not approve any more than Dottie did it was for no such reason. He simply did not want his daughter to suffer hardship however healthy she was.

"No, but, Robert!" Mrs. Tallant exclaimed, "mountain climbing like that's terrible. It wears men out."

"Men wear out a lot more easily than women do," Mr. Tallant observed.

"Why don't you just go to Darjeeling?" Gail suggested. "I've always wanted to go to Darjeeling myself. People seem to have a lot of fun there."

Harvey Crane, sitting on the edge of family conclave, said nothing. He would be glad to have the expedition go as soon as possible. Men, all on the brink of adventure, were wearing Gail thin. She knew the whole expedition, and with all of them, as far as he could see, maintained a mocking flirtation. They were constantly under foot at his house. He kept watching to see if one were more at home than the others, but could discover no difference in her treatment of them.

"Poor fellows, maybe they'll never come back," she said when he complained. "It's like sending them off to war." She smiled at him. "All's fair?" she inquired.

He had grunted. "I give you too much leeway."

"Only to the end of my rope," she had said and laughed.

He tried now to imagine Bert and Kit upon the Himalayas. But he could not imagine the Himalayas or why anyone should go there. Certainly he could not see Kit's slight figure toiling upward. What did they do—rope themselves together, didn't they? Kit roped to Bert, her life depending upon his! The solemnity of this symbolism held him a moment. Things were very unfair for women. How would he feel if it were Gail? But Gail was married to a safe man. He decided to speak after all, though he made it his business never to interfere in Tallant affairs.

"In my opinion, Kit had better wait at the foot of the mountain," he said. Inwardly he thought that there was always the possibility of an avalanche sweeping Bert off the map.

Kit in a low green satin chair sat listening. At such conclaves she had always sat in silence until she was sure how her life was going. If it went as she wished, there was no need to speak. If it did not, she would simply wait until later and then announce quietly what she was going to do. Thus she had decided that she must go to France for a year with her mother to perfect her French and again that she was to go to college instead of to a finishing school as Gail had, and in her sophomore year that she was to make her quiet little debut during Christmas holidays and the year after her graduation that she was to go to China with her parents. Now she must speak.

"I think I'll just go as far as I can," she said peaceably. She looked around at them apologetically and smiled. None of them believed much in her when it came to doing something difficult, she could see, for nothing could change her slight stature and smooth dark childlike face. She did not blame anyone for thinking she was incapable of any greatness. She probably was, but then she had no desire for it and she was not going for that. Behind their affectionate tolerance she could go on living in herself as she liked.

"You needn't worry about me," she added vaguely. "I won't do anything dangerous." They laughed at her with sudden delight, as they probably had laughed at her when she took her first step, not expecting it then or now.

"Kit, you look like a baby! Come here and kiss me," her mother commanded her. She went over to her mother obediently, and on the way over met Harvey's cool gray eyes. They were filled with distrust.

She did not foresee what this decision to go to the Himalayas would do in that strange great presence in which she lived with Bert, the presence of all the millions of people who concerned themselves with the details of Bert's life. She was one of those details, she now discovered, and as a detail diverted to herself letters and telegrams and newspaper reports. Mr. Brame on one of his regular daily visits laughed soundlessly and showed her a swelling file in his briefcase. "Mrs. Bert Holm," it was marked. Without replying, she handed to him that day's unopened mail.

He counted the letters. "Fifty-seven more today than yesterday," he said and fumbling in his case he brought out a neatly typed sheet. "I thought it might amuse you," he said, "just to see what sort of thing they write to you about. They're nearly all women, but there are a few men. This is a week's resumé."

She took it, glanced timidly at the items. One hundred and twenty six men had "expressed admiration," the stenographer's cool report said, and many more women had sent recipes and good advice and were knitting sweaters and wanted to know the size of Bert's foot for socks and wanted her to know they would pray for her when they prayed for Bert and were jealous of her and hoped she knew how wonderful Bert Holm was and some wanted to know if he believed in God. She saw their faces rising behind the page, wistful, unknown, shy and bold. But even the shy ones could be bold when they thought no one would know. She handed the sheet back to Mr. Brame.

"I thought you would be amused," he said.

But she shook her head. "I am happier if I don't know about them," she answered. "I'm glad I'm going away from them," she added.

That night when she was going through her desk she found in a drawer the seal she had bought in Peking. She had used it for a while and then had put it away and forgotten it. The smooth dull white ivory was polished until it seemed light and warm in her hands. She set it upon the top of her desk and there it took on all the old illusion of perfect proportion. The tiny mountain looked infinitely high and upon its surface the atom man toiled upward. She had felt when she bought it that it would mean something to her. But it had not. Here in New York she had put it away and forgotten it. Perhaps now it would mean something. She decided suddenly to take it with her.

They were very nearly off at last. The ship was ready to move from the dock. Kit, looking down from the deck on the spread of upturned white faces, saw Mr. Brame wandering happily among the crowd. All morning he had been taking its emotional pulse as the people waited for Bert and as they waved and cheered Bert when he arrived and went aboard, handsomer than ever this spring day in his white flannels. Bert's illness had improved him. He looked thinner and becomingly older, and he had learned how to accept cheers without becoming sullen with shyness. Now he stood by the rail, very straight and bold, the sea wind ruffling his shining hair. Sometimes a voice shouted from the crowd, "That's Bert! There he is. Hi, there, Bert!" Then he raised his arm and waved and smiled, his white teeth glittering. Beside him, close-mouthed and gruff with strangeness, was Jackie Rexall, and and clustered loosely about him were the young men who made up the expedition.

Nearer to him than Kit was stood Gail, very handsome in brown and dull gold, a little gold hat with a dark veil pulled down on one side of her head. But Harvey was there, too, and wherever Gail's picture would appear tomorrow, Harvey's solid figure would appear near her. Mr. and Mrs. Tallant stood carefully beyond camera range, and Kit was with them except when a man came up and said:

"Please, Mrs. Holm, would you just for a moment stand beside Bert? The public's interested to see you, too."

She always stepped obediently to Bert's side and smiled until she heard the camera click. Mr. Brame had taught her that. "I suggest you smile, Mrs. Holm, in your photographs. Your face in gravity is not good publicity." She might as well smile because it was over more quickly. The photographers would urge her, "Give us a smile—a nice smile," and wait until she forced the unwilling smile to her lips. "Look happy!" That was what they said. "People want you to look happy!"

Only John Baker was not there with the others. Kit saw him saunter along the deck once or twice, his lips cynical and his eyes averted. To reporters who searched him out as second in importance only to Bert Holm on the expedition, he shook his head. "Haven't a thing to say," he declared. "I hope to find some rare rhododendrons and a couple of new orchids, that's all."

"What will you do with them?" someone inquired eagerly.

"Nothing, just find them," he declared.

Bert made far better copy. He was picturesque and frank, and he did not need Kit to speak for him any more because he knew now there was no reason for him to be afraid. People liked him the way he was and they liked the way he talked.

"Sure, I'm going for fun," he said, laughing. "Climbing mountains is always fun for me. Only, of course"—he remembered Mr. Brame—"I hope a lot of good scientific stuff will come out of it. I'm looking to Baker for that, and the others. What's that? Oh, sure, yes, I'll do some stuff myself, measuring altitudes and getting weather records and all that. . . . Well, we'll land at Bombay and then we'll push on up across North India to the mountains. . . . Yeah, we're gonna have a second honeymoon, Kit and I. Yeah, sure, I believe in preparedness for war! I'd be the first to fight if anyone stepped on old Uncle Sam!"

He had spent March and April at Glen Barry, living in the sun, and he was browned and well and his eyes were bluer than ever and he had never photographed better.

Gail, admiring him, whispered to her mother, "He's really wonderful, you know. Somehow he manages to be himself in the midst of all this."

226

"I suppose so," Mrs. Tallant agreed, "if that's anything."

"Mother!" Gail cried, laughter showing under her eyelids.

Mrs. Tallant did not speak. Just as soon as she could, she was going away to the sanatorium and get her blood pressure down. Mr. Tallant leaned toward her and said in a low voice, "I've a good mind to double Brame's fee on this. He's pulled it off very well."

"He certainly deserves it," she agreed.

Harvey Crane, standing faithfully beside his wife, was inwardly seething, to his own surprise. Why did a fellow like Bert Holm have to look as every man, in his own secret heart behind the threshold of outward scoffing, longed to look? Bert Holm was any woman's dream—no use pretending that even Gail would not have been better pleased if with all else he could have looked like Bert. Life was inscrutable. For Gail had told him that the fellow's forebears were nothing but ordinary farm folk, and yet all the generations of his own New England ancestry had only served to give him his dun-colored thinning hair and somewhat narrow shoulders and an endless battle with a pot-belly, small it was true, but always there. It almost made one doubt the precepts which formed his mother's creed. Blood—there was no trusting it, if out of the crudest, most commonplace blood transplanted to a rocky American farm from none knew where in Europe, it produced this narrow-hipped, broad-shouldered creature of beauty. Who appreciated brains and ancestry today? Not this mob!

The last gong rang. "It's time to go," he told Gail. He was so silly as to dislike it that she held up her cool lips to Bert's enthusiastic kiss. He heard a camera click and grew angrier than he would have thought possible. But it was not a thing he would care to mention to Gail.

"Good-by," he said formally to Bert. He was glad once again that the Himalayas were on the other side of the world.

"Kit, darling," her mother murmured, "don't go about alone in foreign streets. I never did like it."

"Good-by, Kit," Mr. Tallant said. "Do as you like and have a good time." He gave her one of his dry pursed-lip kisses.

"Good-by—good luck!" Mr. Brame said with unusual excitement. "Don't you worry, Mrs. Holm, about anything. As soon as Mr. Holm is gone, I shall begin at once on the plans for his return."

Kit felt an amused compunction as she gave him her hand. "Thank you for all you've done," she said.

"I haven't done anything, dear lady," he assured her, touched by her kindness. People so often forgot to thank him.

"You've made him," she said quietly.

"Well—only perhaps—" he coughed modestly. He looked at Bert with appreciation. Bert was fending off the last reporters laughingly. "Of course he's very good material," Mr. Brame said. "With his looks," he added, "people will always believe in him. And that's the first essential—to get people to believe."

She examined him to see if there were irony anywhere in him. But there was not. He was looking at Bert with the honest admiration of a potter whose hand is full of fine clay.

He still wasn't a hundred per cent all right, Bert decided. Rest was what he needed, after all the racket.

"Guess I'll find me a steamer chair and lie down, Kit," he said. The ship was getting out to sea now. It was only mid-afternoon, and a long time to go before supper. "I'll lie down and maybe get the steward to get me some soup or something," he said.

"I'll go and find the deck steward," Kit said.

He let her, because he felt tired and then waited for her, leaning over the rail, staring at the misty skyline. The deck was almost empty. Everybody must be downstairs unpacking. A good sleep was what he needed. He put his hand in his pocket and took it out again. Connie's letter was there. He'd read it when he was alone, just to see how silly the poor fool was. No, he'd tear it up now and throw it overboard. There were plenty of letters from silly dames in his mail every day, but he never could get excited over letters from women he'd never seen. He wasn't excited over Connie either. But she wrote a wonderful letter. He read it quickly, tore it to bits, and watched the wind toss them into the sunlight. He'd never seen her again—didn't want to. But she worshiped him, poor girl. Not that it was any good—he was faithful to Kit and going to stay so. Mr. Brame had said something funny yesterday when he came for his last talk. When Kit was out of the room he had said in his queer scolding sort of way, "I must warn you once and for all, Mr. Holm, against any entanglement with women on this trip. It will be fatal to your reputation and to the build-up I am preparing. The one thing the American people will not tolerate is open immorality."

He'd spoken right up to Mr. Brame. "Brame, I want you to know I'm faithful to my wife."

It was the truth, but Mr. Brame had looked at him as if he had something on him and he wasn't going to tell. It might be Lily. But he could hardly remember Lily any more, she was so long ago. He guessed that old business was done with—if it hadn't come out by now, it never would. Poor Mom, wanting to come down to see him off and Pop getting sick so she couldn't! He had gone to see them alone for a day and she had groaned about Pop's taking now of all times—and her even with the cows to milk! He'd told them to hire a man and he'd pay for it. Nothing was too good for his Mom. He thought warmly of her enormous soft embrace.

"I don't see you hardly any more, Mom," he had complained. It felt like old days when he was a kid.

"That's what I say," she mourned. "But I can't budge Pop from the place."

"I ain't goin' nowhere," Pop had said from his bed.

"You ought to, Pop," he had scolded the old man. "I could take you places now."

But the old man had shaken his head.

He saw Kit coming down the deck in her white coat. She was carrying her hat in her hand and the wet wind was already making drops on her curly hair. She was so pretty, his heart went out to her and he held out his arms. He hadn't done that for a long time. She smiled but she did not run into them as she used to. He felt hurt for a minute until he saw two women staring out of a window at them. He dropped his arms then. "Damn," he began. But Kit came up to him.

"I have your chair all ready," she said, "on the other side out of the wind. And your rug is there, too. And I told the steward to bring you tea with sandwiches and cake."

It sounded so good he forgot everything else. After all, he ought to take care of himself. . . .

Down in their suite Kit surveyed the mass of mail and flowers. Her mother had wanted her to bring a maid, at least until they reached India, but she had not wanted the nuisance of a maid. Now for one instant she wished for old Sarah or Rose to clean away the heaps. Then she set herself to it. She would sort the letters and telegrams into preliminary piles, and then turn everything except family letters over to Harden Coombes, the young man who was to be Bert's official secretary.

She worked quietly for nearly an hour, and then at the bottom of the pile she saw a long white envelope she knew instantly. It was from Norman. She had waited for that envelope hundreds of times in many parts of the world. Sometimes it had come, often it had not. But today she had not waited for it nor expected it. She had not even seen Norman again or heard his voice since that night on the telephone, because everything was to be as it was until after the expedition; it must in fairness to Bert be as it was. She loathed married women who dallied with other men. She and Gail could never agree on that.

"What does it matter?" Gail had said. "Harvey knows I don't care about anyone else."

"Then why go about with anyone else?" she had inquired.

"For fun, you little Puritan," Gail had said, making a face at her. "I do lots of things only for fun."

It was quite true. Gail was incurably flighty on the surface and infinitely sound at bottom. But she, Kit, was not Gail. Better, perhaps, if she could be more like Gail, and not as she was, so that things either meant too much or else nothing at all and so were worth nothing!

She tore open the envelope, and there in a square block of small writing in the middle of the page Norman said:

"Kit, I see you're off to the ends of the world. Why I care about everything you do, God knows. Here's hoping you have a good time and find your heart's desire, if it's in the Himalayas. I don't believe I ever thought to ask you what it is. Remind me next time we meet—I'd like to know. Meanwhile, here's looking at you! P. S.—My play is postponed. I thought of more stuff to put in and took it back. It's going to be a knockout now."

That was what he always did—dragged his plays back and put more stuff in them. Producers frowned and roared, but if he saw something he had to put in he brushed them aside. "Biggest gamble in the world," she had heard one of them snarl, "play's likely to be a flop, anyway. He's always trying to get in too much. People don't miss it when it isn't there, don't want it when it is. Damn him, I'd turn him down cold if I wasn't afraid he'd run off with it to somebody else and then it would turn out a hit. It would be just his crazy luck."

She sat reading the few lines over and over. He was perilously near loving her again. Perhaps he did love her and would not let himself see it. She realized it, but without exultation. If she were more like Gail she could touch a match to tinder and find out. But she never could—not unless she were ready to throw her own life into the blaze thus begun. She held the letter a moment longer. She would not tear it up. Yes, she would. She did not want any letters over which again to dream since of one thing only was she now sure. Dreams were not to be trusted.

The days on the ship took on their regularity. Bert was taking this expedition very seriously. Whatever Mr. Brame had planned it to be, to Bert it was also the most important thing he had ever done. He began gravely to train himself in food and drink. Liquor, indeed, he refused completely.

"I don't want my heart to go back on me," he declared, "maybe at a minute when I'm hanging on to a rock and need all I've got to go on to the top."

He ate voraciously but carefully and went to bed early and walked miles every day in a close routine which he wrote upon a piece of paper and pinned on the back of the bathroom door. And every morning at eleven he gathered his men together for what he called a "fight talk."

"Where Fessaday fell down with his men," he told Kit, "was he never gave them any enthusiasm for him. Gosh, we didn't care if the old geezer got there or not! He used to give everybody their orders and then he'd never look at any of us again. Well, naturally, we didn't feel loyal. Now I handle my men different. I'm going to tell 'em my plans and ideas and get their co-operation. 'Course I'm the leader, but every man will get what he deserves. When the publicity goes out, their names will be in it. I'll tell Frisk to put it in."

Frisk was the young newspaper reporter whom at the last moment Mr. Brame had decided to send along. "I want the publicity to be centralized in one man," he had told Bert. "I'd like it understood, Mr. Holm, that nobody can send out any publicity except Jimmie Frisk. He's a good man, one of the best young chaps on the *News,* and he'll send all his stuff to me and I'll look it over to see if it is right for the build-up."

James Frisk, when he appeared at Bert's morning conferences, was a slender pale young man with alert, greenish eyes beneath heavy sand-colored hair. He said nothing and kept to himself a good deal. Each evening he handed Bert a sheaf of typed pages to be read.

"That what you want?" he inquired when Bert handed them back.

"Swell," he said heartily, "perfectly swell, Jim!"

For at the very first morning talk Bert had insisted that they all call each other by their first names.

"You certainly can call me Bert," he said to them heartily and laughed as he added. "I guess everybody does, anyway."

They had all smiled at him the responding smiles which he had now come to expect from everyone around him. Baker was the only one who didn't smile. He sat at the far end of the table hanging on to the crooked pipe that he smoked all day.

"Okay?" he had called over to Baker, just to show he wanted to be pleasant.

"I prefer last names, Holm, since you ask me," Baker had answered, and then had gone on to explain, "On an expedition like this where we shall be thrown upon each other's company until we sicken of the way we talk and walk and behave, less intimacy rather than more is the safer thing."

Bert did not understand what Baker was talking about. The fellow was as cold as a fish. He didn't let you like him. But he had only said, "Okay, Baker. Remember that, fellows—I want everybody to have their own way on my expedition so long as it don't hold up anything important."

To Kit when he came upstairs on deck he said, "I'm going to have trouble with Baker."

"Oh no, Bert!" she cried. "Not already!"

"Nothing yet, don't worry," he said, "but I wish I had followed my hunch. I never knew one of my hunches to go wrong."

"What did Baker do?" she asked.

"Nothing," Bert insisted. "He just don't want to co-operate. I can feel he's that way."

He was suddenly secretive and she would not press him. When he withdrew into that stubborn secretiveness which was also a part of his nature, she now knew, even though it were about a small thing, she stopped.

For not yet could she forget, when he turned secretive, that he had never told her about Lily. She wondered now and again whether he ever would, thinking sometimes that he would not and again believing that he must. The fact of Lily no longer mattered to her. She knew it and had adjusted herself to the reality. She could even remember that morning in the drugstore and feel that Lily was honest though her soul was scarcely more complex than an amœba. But there were times still when she was alone with Bert that she wanted him to tell her, if merely that she might not feel so hopelessly far from him. At this moment when her mind flew to his secret, she felt obsessed with her knowledge only because he would not speak, nor could she tell him she knew, until he spoke first, for that would be to force him to a place to which he had not come of his own will. She had long reasoned thus thoroughly in her own brain, that she must not speak if he did not because she could not bear the sight of his eyes growing furtive with resentment at being forced to break open his instinctive secrecy.

But something new occurred to her now as she lay in her deck chair beside Bert's and watched the water rise toward the ship and then foam away again. She had never told him about Norman. Now in this moment she was aware of being unjust in not having told him about Norman. There was not much to tell, not any use in telling, was there? In going back to—no, except that she was demanding of Bert that he go back, and there had been no difference between marriage and the sort of love she had once given Norman, no real difference. She had wanted and planned to marry. She suddenly saw she had been monstrously unjust in not doing herself what she demanded of Bert, but she

234

had not so seen it before. She sat up and rushed to instant amends.

"Bert," she began impulsively, "there's something I haven't told you—about myself, I mean."

Now that she had begun she felt foolish and awkward, but she had to go on—no climbing back. He did not change his look, and she was not sure whether he heard her as he lay stretched out in his own chair where he had thrown himself, his eyes closed.

"There was someone—Norman Linlay—he writes plays. I was terribly in love with him, Bert, before I ever met you."

He looked up, startled.

"Were you engaged?" he asked, solemnly, after a moment.

"Yes," she said.

She saw him taking this into his thought slowly. Yes, he minded it. She went on quickly, "He decided—not to—" No, that was evading it. "I mean he—found he didn't care—" Go on, she told herself fiercely, say the real word! "He didn't love me enough," she said.

There, she had made the cut clean into herself! Humiliation was silly, anyway, but one got over it last of everything. Bert was staring at her with pity plain on his face—nothing but pity.

"Aw, Kit, that's too bad—" He put out his hand and seized hers.

She could not bear his pity. It was repulsive.

"Oh, I don't mind—now," she said quickly. It was necessary to laugh, to speak lightly and quickly, that she might not be tortured. She drew her hand away.

"That's right," he said and turned over to face her. "Don't you care. Besides, Kit, if it hadn't happened like that, look what would have happened to us—we'd never have got married!"

This was all his consolation! She could not answer. She sat there in the bright sunlight of a June morning at sea, so suddenly overcome with misery and a sense of all gone wrong with her that she was compelled toward the whole purpose for which

235

she had spoken. She said, her eyes fixed on the farthest edge of the blue water, "Bert, sometimes you shut yourself against me. Do you know you do? I wish you'd feel you could tell me everything—or even just anything!"

She brought her gaze back from the meeting of sky and sea to bear fully upon him. But what she saw after all was the childish furtive look that she dreaded creep over the blueness of his eyes.

"You mean Baker?" he asked. "I tell you, he just isn't going to co-operate." And then he added with his old sullenness, "I don't know what you're talking about anyway, Kit."

She did not answer. She need not have spoken at all. They were only where they began. They would never be further than that. She longed to have her words back again, but they had gone from her and now were lost and never to be repeated.

And yet if she accepted a fundamental wrong with life, it was amazing how much remained to be right. She found she could separate herself into two persons, one being Mrs. Bert Holm and the other the old Kit Tallant who she had always been, and Kit Tallant need not always be disturbed over the difficulties of Mrs. Bert Holm.

She had been one of those children who had a dream companion, a child, whether girl or boy she never knew so exquisite and evanescent had the child been. As she had grown older the child had vanished, not suddenly but gradually, appearing less and less often as living people crowded in, and at last coming no more. She felt the memory of her still, rather than remembered her. The child had not grown older as she grew, so from looking up to the child and worshiping her as she had when she was little, she came to look on the child as her equal, and at last as she herself grew older and more adequate for her own days the child seemed to her to be quite frail and shrinking, dependent upon her, indeed, for all its being. And at last she had let the child die, not suddenly or consciously, but merely by forgetting her, knowing all the while, too, that the child had somehow once been a part of her own self.

Now Kit found herself looking upon Mrs. Bert Holm very much as once that child had looked upon her. The child seemed to come into being again, but as Kit Tallant and not as Mrs. Bert Holm. And as the little Kit had often been disturbed by what people said or did and had poured out everything to the child, who listened, withdrawn but understanding, so now Bert Holm's troubled wife turned to Kit Tallant.

These two divided time between them. In the morning Kit woke early and bathed herself in the sea water bath and went up on deck alone while Bert slept. She tramped up and down, moving from one deck to the other as they were left wet and clean behind the line of sailors on their hands and knees, scrubbing the white boards. Sky and wind and sea in a trinity of impetuous movement and simple color—they were always the same and never quite the same. The advantage of sea over earth was in the movement of its color. The earth was stolid under its imposed seasons but the sea became its own mood, hourly changed.

She looked up to find someone staring at the young woman who was Bert Holm's wife, and instantly Kit Tallant withdrew as that child had been used to withdraw in the presence of other people, and Bert Holm's wife thought quickly, "People are getting up. I must go downstairs to Bert."

She went downstairs and opened the door upon Bert, sitting up in bed and eating toast and tea.

"Hello," he remarked, "I didn't hear you. Gosh, how I sleep!"

She bent and kissed his cheek and sat down on the couch to listen to him.

"Say, Kit, did you see that old woman yesterday, the one with the white hair? You ought to have seen her! First she comes up and asks me for my autograph. Well, I give it to her. Then she tells me how I remind her of her dear dead boy. He was brave like me, she says—ha, ha!—only he got killed in the World War, and the first time she sees my picture she thinks it's him, come back again. And when she read in the papers that I'm going to be on this boat, she decides she'll come, too. She's got diamonds as big as pullet eggs nearly. She must be well off!"

"What did you say to her?" she asked.

"I was polite to her, of course," he replied, "but if I had to be a son to all these old women who think I look like their babies, I'd have a heck of a life, wouldn't I? What makes women the way they are, Kit? The young ones want you to kid 'em along, and the old ones want to be your mother." He laughed and bit his teeth hugely into toast. "I like you, Kit! You leave me alone. Take this tray, will you? That'll hold me till I get a real meal."

She took the tray and set it on the table by the bed and then felt his arms pulling her down.

"Don't you carry this leaving me alone too far, though, Kit!"

She felt his long arms folding her against him and smelled the clean smell of his skin. It was one of his graces that his skin was fresh and sweet. It was impossible to feel repulsion toward his flesh. Even Kit Tallant, shadowy and aloof, understood how this could be. His body was as clean as the morning at sea and so it was impossible to dislike it and it was impossible, too, to separate him from his body. His mind was mingled with his flesh, or was, perhaps, his flesh, so that all he said and did and was seemed to come as an expression of his beautiful body rather than of a separate mind. The same simple union of movement and color which made the being of the sea was also Bert Holm's being. He was never more complex than his own body and its impulses of food and energy. . . .

"There!" he said, and set her on her feet, "That'll do to start the day."

He leaped up and threw off his clothes and ran in to his bath. Not for a fortune would she have let her mother know that she

238

had had to persuade him to daily bathing and shaving and getting his hair cut often enough and keeping his fingernails clean.

"You're worse than Mom," he had once grumbled. "Saturdays was enough for her, and in summer I went swimming." But he had learned after his fashion, and now if he forgot, she could not keep from laughing at his enormous guilt and his haste to make amends. He did sincerely want most of the time to please his wife, and she never quite forgot this. He came out wrapped in an enormous white towel and looking a large and beautiful boy, and she watched him while he discussed one suit against another and pondered over the color of his tie.

"Bert, you're getting to be a dandy," she said. "Remember at Glen Barry, how you used to go without a tie at all, and groan about changing your clothes for dinner?"

He grinned at her. "Mustn't disappoint the old dames," he replied.

"Then wear this," she said, and threw him a bright blue tie. "That's for your eyes," she added.

He stared at himself with pleasure, whistling out of tune before the mirror. "Think I'm good-looking?" he inquired of her face behind his in the mirror.

"Don't you think so?" she countered, keeping her lips grave.

"Kind of," he confessed, and in her laughter they clasped hands and sauntered in to breakfast.

Mrs. Bert Holm, entering the dining saloon, looked the image of a happy young woman, as indeed she should be, married to that handsome young man. Old Mrs. Townsend, gazing at them over her grapefruit, felt her eyes mist.

"I don't believe one word of those stories about him," she told her sister Emily. "He couldn't be bad and look like that—the very image of my own Phil," she added.

"Except Phil wasn't really blond," Emily suggested. In her own heart she was thinking he looked much, much more like someone else.

239

"Phil's skin was perfect!" Mrs. Townsend said sharply. "Exactly like that boy's!"

She watched Bert Holm with sad yearning eyes. If Phil had lived to come out of the horrible war, he might have married a pretty girl like that and then she would not have been a lonely old woman, taking trips to Europe every year with Emily. She was tired to death of Europe and of Emily, too, but then she was tired of everything. Her dreams, wistful with what could never be, hung rainbow-hued about Bert's bright head. He was laughing again. How she liked to see him laugh!

And Bert, finishing wheat cakes and syrup, was saying, "I got the best of Baker, there, Kit. And he had to own up I did! You ain't going to get people excited over a couple of yards of Latin names! I said, 'I guess I don't climb the stiffest mountain in the world for that,' I said. So what I say is, why shouldn't we take notes on the climate and all that and maybe even find a place for a t.b. sanatorium—you know, where sick people could get into pure air. I heard a fellow say once who'd been to the Antarctic that it would be the best place in the world for a sanatorium. I bet I could raise a million for it, maybe call it the Bert Holm Sanatorium, and get everybody to give a dollar to it if they couldn't do better, little envelopes, maybe——"

"I'm afraid—it would work,—beautifully," she said. She could see her mother's surprised horror at America showered with Bert Holm envelopes.

"What makes you say afraid?" Bert retorted. "The air on those mountains where there's never anything but snow is just great. You feel like a million dollars. You sleep and eat like nobody's business. 'Course we wouldn't want to go too high, only high enough to get good air. Jack Rexall thinks it's a swell idea. I could make him business manager and Frisk could write it all up for me. It might be a big job, building the road up and all, but it could be done. Those coolies they got there work awful cheap, too."

She watched him as he talked. Did he mean what he said, or had Jack Rexall talked him into some money-raising scheme? She did not trust that small weasel-faced friend of Bert's, who, she suspected, knew him better than anyone. Rexall never spoke to her beyond a cool nod, but that she knew was the accepted form of masculine greeting in Misty Falls upon seeing a married and respectable woman. Bert rose.

"Come on, Kit—you finished? Let's go up and walk a coupla miles."

She followed him out of the dining saloon, aware of half a hundred heads turned to watch them. But she looked at none of them until she passed the table where the two old white-haired ladies sat. Then she smiled down into a pair of misty blue eyes.

It was Mrs. Townsend who first made her perceive that the public, which Mr. Brame threw so casually into one great willful tyrannical whole, was not really a whole at all. She was lying in her deck chair dreaming over a little book of newly published poems by an unknown young poet, when she heard a voice, a gentle cultivated old voice, and looking up she saw the old lady at whom she had smiled.

"I wonder if I may—?" Mrs. Townsend breathed. Her eyes finished for her—"sit down just a moment?"

"Do, please," Kit said. She brushed away the heap of maps on Bert's chair.

The old lady sat down on the edge of it.

"I shan't stay," she declared, "but I have so longed to speak to you. Your dear young husband—he so reminds me of my own dear dead son." Her lips trembled.

"He told me," Kit murmured. Her heart moved toward this delicate old creature and then retreated.

"It's not that, of course, about which I want to speak," the old lady said. "I couldn't be so rude as to intrude a private sorrow.

No, it just came to me; the wonderful thing is that there's something about him—your husband, I mean—that seems to fit into each life. Emily—that's my sister—told me a few minutes ago that he made her think of—of the young man to whom she was engaged, who died of typhus, many years ago, in the South. He was a Northerner. I don't know that Emily could ever have married him, because our family was Southern and still so opposed to . . . But they met on a visit Emily made to Washington once, to our aunt who was married to a gentleman in government there. I was amazed when she spoke of the resemblance, for I could see none, but then it came to me; it's because he—your husband—is such an ideal young man, isn't he? And he reminds everybody of the one most loved."

Her lips quivered and she patted Kit's head. "It must be hard for you sometimes, dear, having to share him with the world, in a manner of speaking. But what a privilege, too! And he's devoted to you; one can see it. He's lovely to you, isn't he?"

Her face grew pink at Kit's smile. "I'm just chattering on and on. But I'm so glad I have this chance to be on the same ship with him, and to know, from my own personal observation how good he is, so if I ever hear any more nasty stories I shall just contradict them. I want you to know that. I'm so glad he takes a public stand on so many things that are right. I recall what he said somewhere about thinking people ought to go to church. So few young people feel that now-a-days. Now don't think, dear, that I shall presume on this as an acquaintance. You must have so many people pushing to know you and I would be so sorry to seem one of them."

"I am glad you stopped by," Kit said brightly. This sweet old child! Not if she could would she have stripped a star from the halo upon Bert's unconscious head.

"Good-by then and if you care to know, I am Mrs. Harris Townsend of Richmond, Virginia." She trotted away, waving her black gloved hand.

A ray of light was let into the blank solidity of all the blur of people who made up the curious public. This particle of it became a human being. And what the old lady had said was true. When a little later Bert, flushed with the importance of his morning conference, came back to her, she saw at a distance behind him a pretty girl, not alone, indeed. There was a young man with her, an ordinary-looking young man of middle height and muddy coloring. The girl stopped when Bert stopped to sit down. Leaning her elbows upon the railing, her back to the sea, she stood laughing and talking with the young man, the wind fluttering the ends of the red scarf tied about her brown hair and catching the flying ends of her brown coat. Kit, a half hour ago, would have looked beyond her to the sky and waves. But now she watched her. The girl was not talking to that young man at all, she decided. She did not like him enough.

From the corners of her bright brown eyes as she laughed with the young man the girl was seeing only Bert.

"That poor young man," Kit thought, watching his delight. "He doesn't know she's really talking and being pretty for Bert. She's imagining he is Bert."

But Bert in the chair beside her was thinking about no one at this moment but himself.

"Say, Kit," he said, "they want me to make a speech about the expedition tonight after the concert."

"Oh, no," she said in distaste, "not now, not until afterwards when the expedition is successfully over and there is something to show them." His disappointed look forced her to add, "I'm sure Mr. Brame would say so, Bert."

"Well, maybe—" he agreed, doubtfully.

"Oh, he would!" she said definitely. But while she spoke she thought of that little old Mrs. Townsend and of this pretty girl, and of all the others like them, and of the steward who had stopped her yesterday to ask her if she thought Mr. Holm would mind if he took a picture of him with his little pocket camera and the young man from the radio room who wanted to know if he might send out news about Bert Holm or would he rather not be talked about? She shrank from letting them see a naive Bert, talking in his halting fashion as he always did unless he could use his one familiar speech. Philip Townsend, the son of that silvery sweet old lady, would repudiate from the grave his likeness. And the brown-eyed girl over there against the blue background of the sea would turn back to her young man half bewildered. "I didn't think Bert Holm was like that!" she could hear voices saying it, one voice catching the words from another.

"No, Bert," she said quickly, "I'm sure it would be better not. Besides. you're far too busy to work up a good speech in these few hours. And you can't talk about the old expedition now."

He sat for a moment without answer, and then jumped up restlessly. "Guess I'll go down to the gym awhile and punch the bag before I eat," he said.

He strode off, his hands in his pockets, looking strong and beautiful enough to climb the highest mountain in the world. The girl's eyes following him grew restless, and her voice carried by the wind was bitter with sudden impatience.

"No, I won't!" she said to the young man.

"But, Sally, why not? A minute ago you were all for it."

"Well, I'm not, any more," she answered, and then the wind bore the sound of a sob. "I wish you'd leave me alone!"

She ran down the deck, her scarf flying behind her, and the young man stood looking after her. He turned when she was gone to stare in despond at the sea and Kit holding back her impulse to speak to him got up and went downstairs.

"Say, Mrs. Holm!" a voice called.

There was an urgent tap on her door. She had come to her room to brush her hair and wash the stickiness of the salt wind from her face and hands. She opened the door, and there stood Jimmie Frisk, his spectacled young face full of consternation.

244

"Say, Mrs. Holm, I don't know how to tell you," he began "but something has happened in the gymnasium."

"To Bert?" she asked sharply.

"Not exactly—that is, to both of them," he faltered.

"What——"

"Bert and Baker," he said quickly. "We were all down there and we thought they were just fooling. Bert had been playing some of his tricks the way he does, and we were laughing. He must have done something to Baker. Anyway when we thought they were pretending to fight, they were really fighting—like hell, too," he added.

"Oh!" she exclaimed and brushed past him. This was too childish of Bert! She hurried down the corridor, Jimmie Frisk behind her.

"Of course I know it mustn't get out," he was saying. "It would make a grand story——"

"Don't you dare to tell it!" she ordered him. A grand story indeed! She could see temptation wriggling in his newspaperman's soul.

"No—no," he promised her.

"I trust your loyalty," she threw at him over her shoulder as she went down the stairs.

The door of the gymnasium was closed. Frisk had to shout before it was opened by Jack Rexall. Bert was lying unconscious upon the floor, a frightened attendant pouring water over his forehead, and Baker leaning against a well, his hand to his blackening eye. Two or three men stood about, all, she saw thankfully, Bert's own men.

"What happened?" she demanded.

"We thought Bert was fooling," Rexall explained dryly. "He's always been a teaser—used to be that way in school, but he'd fight fair enough." He looked at Baker.

"If you mean to say I didn't fight fairly," Baker said instantly, "come along and have it out for yourself."

"I ain't sayin'," Rexall answered. "I only said Bert loves monkey tricks but he fights fair. We didn't see how he got knocked out, Mrs. Holm. We was each of us doing something else, and the first thing we knew was Bert's fallin' down like a ton o' brick."

But Bert was coming to consciousness. He groaned faintly, his face greenish, and then opened his eyes.

"Kit," he murmured.

Baker, putting on his coat, laughed suddenly.

"You'd better go to bed, Holm," he said. "Come on fellows." He stooped and lifted Bert's shoulders.

"I can stand," Bert said suddenly. He struggled to his feet and stood swaying until Jack Rexall ran to his side and put his arm about him.

"Come, Bert," Kit said. And then she turned to Baker. "No one must hear of this," she said.

"Why should they?" he asked so calmly that she could not answer.

The gong for luncheon had rung long ago. The corridors were empty and they reached their suite with no one to see them except a busy stewardess hurrying past with a tray. Together she and Jack Rexall helped Bert to the couch. He still looked pale and dazed.

"Got any whisky?" Rexall inquired.

She opened a cupboard and gave him a bottle and he poured a little into a glass and gave it to Bert.

Bert swallowed obediently, and felt better at once. Light returned to his eyes and he drew a great breath and looked at them.

"Did I get him, Rexie?" he asked.

"In the eye," Rexall said.

A great grin spread over Bert's face.

"Damn him!" he said, "he sure can fight."

Kit could have taken him by the shoulders and shaken him

until his teeth rattled, she thought, except that suddenly she was laughing, too. At what? Perhaps at his astounding luck more than anything. There was not a scratch to be seen on him. Poor John Baker, whose solemn ugly square face was marred by his purpling eye—and Bert, though vanquished, without a scratch on him! She had reproof on her tongue's end, ready to pour upon him the moment Rexall was gone. Silly childishness, two men fighting, like naughty boys! She was ready to begin, and then Bert stood up, with scarcely a tremor. "Let's eat," he exclaimed. "I'm always starved after a fight!"

She let reproof remain unspoken. What was the use of scolding a boy for something he did not even know he had done?

"See you in ten minutes, Rexie," Bert said.

"Sure you're all right?" Rexall inquired.

"Sure!" Bert replied.

But when Rexall was gone she said quietly, "Tell me about it, Bert."

"About what?" he asked, his blue eyes bluer than she had ever seen them.

"The fight," she said shortly.

"Oh, that," he replied. "There wasn't much to it. He certainly did knock me cold, though!" He grinned at her. "I think a lot more of that feller than I did!"

She looked back at him helplessly and then laughed with him. It was impossible not to like him. Of course everybody liked him. And so would she—if only she were not his wife!

Kit, stealing upon deck because of the moon, whose light fell in bands of gold across her bed, leaned upon the rail. Everybody was asleep, surely, except the men who watched the ship's course through the night. She and Bert, since it was their last night, had joined in the dancing and everyone had danced until the band, exhausted, had put away their instruments and gone below. Bert had still not wanted to go and people came up to them who had not spoken to them before. "Since this is the last night," they said pleasantly, "perhaps you won't mind—" Only a few had even asked for his autograph. Most of them wanted merely to shake his hand and wish him luck, they said. Kit saw the same eagerness in each face turned to him as he stood in the moonlight. He was always his handsomest in his black and white dinner clothes and now he was fantastic with romance.

Then at last they, too, went below. But Kit could not sleep, and after a while she got up quietly and put on her coat over her pajamas and went above. There was no one in sight, not even a belated couple. She stood alone, gazing at the perfect moon. The moon, she thought idly, needed the simplicity of the sea against which to rise and shine for the sea held no shadows to distract from this pure mellow light, no hills and valleys or sharp horizon lines. The moon hung complete in fullest power over the sea. There was not even the distraction of a star. And then suddenly some one stood beside her. She turned. It was John Baker.

"I beg your pardon," he said. "I hope I don't disturb you. But I wanted all afternoon to see you and tell you I'm sorry."

"How is your eye?" she asked.

"At its worst," he said cheerfully. "What a wallop he has in his right! I hadn't any idea he was serious—until he hit me! He'd been up to one of his tricks—you know how he loves practical jokes—and I let out at him, in fun. Well, nearly in fun. I happen to hate practical jokes." He hesitated and she saw a twinkle in his enormous, shadowy left eye. "Then my eye felt like a pulp, and I was astonished—and angry, all of a sudden. I'm afraid I let go."

"I don't blame you," she said quietly. Bert's teasing mood she knew very well. When something was refused him, he fell into it. In a way she was responsible for this black eye. Perhaps he had really wanted to talk about the expedition and when she had stopped him he had gone to the gymnasium in his willful mood and had begun to tease Baker.

"I haven't done such a childish thing in years," Baker said abruptly.

He turned his face away from her. A man could not tell a woman her husband was a fool. Probably she worshiped him. That was the way with women—the more fools men were, the more they liked them, if only they were handsome. He stopped himself with horror. He was not envying Holm his silly good looks, was he?

"I don't know what he told you," he began.

"Nothing at all," she answered.

"No?" he murmured dryly.

"It really isn't his way to complain," she said proudly. Bert must be shielded against this cold young man.

"See here," he said. He was looking at her again and she could see his eyes, one sharp and stern and the other ridiculous in its black circle. "I wanted just to tell you I'm not going to let myself get into this sort of nonsense again. I blame myself—I don't fight with fists any more, like a coward or a child."

"I don't think Bert's a—a—coward," she said quickly. "He has plenty of courage—physical courage," she added.

"Do you know what physical courage is?" he demanded.

"I fear I have none," she confessed.

"Don't admire it," he said. "It's only lack of imagination. The mind that cannot imagine anything else also cannot imagine disaster or death, particularly to itself." He laughed and lit a cigarette. "Decorations are given more often to a dull mind than to a glowing deed. Look at the head above the next bosom you see so decorated!"

He had not the slightest vanity or he would not have kept his disfigured eye toward her like this!

"The last thing in the world that I want out of this trip is glory," he said. "I hate glory. I distrust it. It's a mess of sentimentality and crowd stupidity. The crowd never worships the true god. It's always running around lost after a dream, a gaudy

249

dream, surrounded with tin horns and rainbow confetti. The true god is far off——"

"The true god?" She was about to ask where that god was, and did not. The night was half way to dawn. The moon was sinking and soon there would be darkness upon the sea. In the immense stillness she could feel this man's god, sitting silent and clear and cold as unending crystal light in the center of the dark universe. To reach him one must traverse alone that long darkness to where he sat. No wonder that people dared not penetrate that loneliness, or that they made little lesser convenient gods and lit them with their own flickering light!

"The moon is setting!" he exclaimed.

They watched it sink and in its last instant upon the horizon it seemed to drop into the sea. She moved while he gazed steadily into darkness. She could not see his face any more, but she felt his presence beside her, sharp, intrepid, scornful, and instantly she was afraid, not for herself, but for Bert, who would be helpless against this man. Bert would not know that he was being wounded with his words, but the wound would be there, increasing in its soreness. And when they came home again this man's words spoken even without malice might lie in people's minds, seeds of distrust.

"Don't laugh at Bert," she said quickly. "Don't be hard on him."

"You forget," he said ironically, "here's my black eye. Doesn't it make him the victor?"

"No, but you know what I mean," she begged him. "He's so —defenseless."

"Maternal instinct at work." His scorn leaped at her. "That's the trouble with you women—you condemn men to perpetual babyhood."

"I haven't a scrap of maternal instinct in me," she answered as sharply.

He said slowly, after a moment, "As a matter of fact I don't believe you have—so why in hell——"

"He's really as innocent as he looks," she said.

"Innocent!" he repeated. "No—but innocence isn't what you want—not innocence alone. A new-born child has innocence, too——"

She shrank a little. "I mean, he's what he is," she said, "so—why hurt him?"

He touched her arm and his voice altered. "Why indeed?" he said. "Thank you. I am recalled to good behavior." And after a moment he added out of the darkness, "Not for him, but for you. If you'd defended him, I'd have wanted to destroy him—why not? I've always liked shooting clay pigeons. But after all, there are more profitable pursuits."

He was as scornful as ever but he was to be trusted. And then her incurable honesty compelled her to meet his integrity.

"You're right, you know," she said. "I mean, in being what you are."

"Of course I am," he agreed. He turned abruptly. "Well, good night, Mrs. Bert Holm," he said.

"Good night," she answered.

He stalked away. In the faint light of the near darkness to which she was now accustomed, she saw him striding alone through the farther darkness as though marching to that cold and crystal god of his. The name of that god she had not inquired, but she knew what it was. His name was called Truth and the multitude feared him and made for themselves other gods. She went downstairs at last and crept into bed. Bert did not stir out of his sleep.

"Marvelous publicity—emphasis admirable," Mr. Brame cabled. They found his cable among the pile of letters and cablegrams when the ship drew into Southampton. The voyage was over but they were not stopping long anywhere. Mr. Brame had said,

"Straight on is what I suggest. A serious expedition must not seem to loiter. In London perhaps a week or two will do no harm with the purpose of buying special English equipment, known to be the best for expeditions. But less time in Paris would be discreet, and I advise no public appearances until afterwards. Ovations in European capitals will be the more important if no previous ones have been given."

They took the plane to France two weeks after they had reached England, and dined in Paris at the home of the American Ambassador. John Baker spoke a sturdy American-tinged French which M. Delanier, the great French botanist who had been invited to meet him, understood easily, and Kit glanced at them talking endlessly and shamelessly together. Baker, asking incessant questions, drew a small book out of his pocket now and again and wrote in it quickly. His eye had mended quickly. When he met Bert the day after the fight he had said with offhand good humor, "Hello, Holm."

"Hello," Bert had replied, and then had gone on impulsively, "Say, I'm sorry I bunged your eye."

"I'm sorry I knocked you out," Baker had returned.

Bert grinned. "So'm I," he said heartily, "only it don't show on me."

"That's your luck," Baker said.

Tonight at the American Embassy he was determined in the good humor he had kept since the night when he had talked with Kit and watched in the moonlight her too sensitive face; he had known then what she was inside with that quivering look of hers. Besides, he wasn't going to take this stuffed shirt seriously again, not seriously enough for a fight, anyway. Some day he would write up the whole expedition and show what fools public heroes were—or at least became. Human beings could not be made into gods without showing their clay. He turned with relief to Delanier. Here was a man of his own kind—science was what toughened a man's soul and kept his blood cool.

. . . Bert, wandering restlessly about the gilt-walled room, thought unhappily that you would hardly know this ambassador fellow was an American any more—he talked and looked Frenchier than a Frenchman. A nice way to cheat the taxpayers, an American taking good money from his government and turning French on them! If old Smedley were here, he'd just skip out for a bit. He glanced at the French butler bringing in liqueurs—no fun in that big flat face! He caught Kit's inquiring eyes and avoided them. What she didn't know wouldn't hurt her. He yawned and sat down on a small chair and got up again quickly.

"Guess it won't bear my weight," he remarked, but no one heard him. The Ambassador was listening to Baker saying something or other—guess he'd go over there.

"Say, Baker," he called, "did I tell you about my sanatorium scheme?"

"Frisk showed me his piece," Baker said.

"Yeah? Well, I have some new ideas——"

He was about to begin on them when he felt Kit's little hand along his arm and heard her soft voice.

"We have to get up before dawn, Bert. Hadn't we better say an early good night?"

And suddenly they were all saying good night and he and Kit were on their way back to the hotel.

"Gosh, I was bored stiff!" he told her in the taxi.

She smiled without speaking and in the way he liked. It made him want to go on talking, only what was there to talk about to Kit? He looked out of the window. The lights were as bright as Broadway. He didn't feel a bit sleepy.

"Say," he cried, "after all, girl, this is Paris! We don't want to go to bed early in Paris, do we? I'll be goin' to bed early every night for months to come!"

She put out her hand. "You're right," she said. "Where shall we go?"

253

"Follies," he answered promptly. He'd always heard about the Paris Follies.

"Folies Bergère," she said to the driver.

"*Oui, oui, Madame,*" the man said excitedly.

Bert laughed. "Wee, wee!" he echoed. "Think of having to say that every time you mean yes!" He laughed aloud, restored to himself now that they were going to see a swell show.

. . . It was a swell show, too—all it was cracked up to be by fellows he'd known who'd seen it. Pity Rexie wasn't here—though it wouldn't be beyond the old snake to be right here in this crowd looking at these girls with no brassieres on! Well, in America they couldn't get away with it. He was glad of it, too. It wasn't decent. He stared at them steadily and then remembered to wonder whether Kit ought to be here. It was a show for men, not for decent women. They ought to label it for men only. He glanced at her uneasily. It didn't seem to bother her. She was looking at it, calm as anybody. Two men were on the stage now, pretending to make love to each other. That sort of thing made him sick. He glanced again at Kit. But she was looking just the same. She didn't know what it was all about, probably. Women oughtn't to know such things. They ought to be innocent, like Kit. He stared down at his hands, waiting for the girls to come back. They oughtn't to allow men to do like that. It wasn't decent. Girls were different and a fellow expected—the girls came dancing back and he was relieved and looked up again.

Then he heard Kit murmuring at his side.

"Those poor women!"

"Where?" he asked.

"On the stage," she replied.

"What do you mean, Kit?" He turned his head to look at her.

"They look so tired," she whispered, "as if they wished they

254

were home with their husbands and children. I'm sure they're quite decent women with families," she added.

He looked back at them and was repelled. He hadn't looked at their faces until now, but she was right. They weren't girls, they were women. Mothers of families going around like that, naked to the waist—it made him sick!

"It's a damned indecent country, if you ask me," he said indignantly.

She laughed, a sharp sudden laughter that made him for some reason think of Gail.

"What you laughing at?" he demanded. But she only laughed the more.

"Oh, you!" she said at last, wiping her eyes.

He understood less than ever, but he let her laugh. Laughing was good for her and it didn't hurt him any.

"I'd laugh too, if I saw the joke," he told her. "Why don't you tell me instead of keeping it to yourself?"

But she only shook her head and laughed until he felt cross with her and shut up. That made her stop, though still she never told him why she laughed. He didn't tell her, but when he got home he wished he had gone to the show by himself. She had spoilt it for him, somehow, he didn't exactly know how. . . .

Next morning the plane, soaring above Europe, turned towards the East, and Bert sat behind the pilot and drew deep breaths. So far as he knew not one thing had been forgotten. He turned and shouted sharply to Rexall. "Where are the lists, Rexie?" Rexall, without speaking, handed him a notebook and Bert began checking them with the fine gold fountain pen Mrs. Townsend had given him when he said good-by to her at the airport. She had been one in the crowd who was there to see him off. "To write your story with for us, Mr. Holm," she had said.

He scratched his name with it several times across the lists and then he began to check them.

"Those alcohol cans," Rexall remarked, "I got a different brand than you said. It's an American brand, more expensive but a better article, I figured."

"Sure," Bert agreed. "I believe in buying American, anyway."

Not a thing forgotten, he thought triumphantly. None of his men could say he wasn't a good leader of his expedition. This plane, now, was a beauty. He'd even picked that out, the best plane the Dutch had. Everybody said take this plane, so he had. The best wasn't too good for him. He leaned over to whisper to Kit, "I'm glad Baker has decided to be all right."

To his surprise she answered a little crossly, "Oh, don't be silly, Bert—why shouldn't he?"

"I banged him up some," he suggested.

"So did he you, for that matter," she retorted.

"That's right," he admitted. "So I guess we're quits."

"Bert, do behave when we start up the mountain," she said.

"Of course I will," he said with dignity. "Don't I always behave?"

"No, you don't," she told him.

"I don't know what you mean," he answered. "You mean I'm to take it, no matter if I'm right and the other fellow's wrong?"

"But you always think you're right," she complained.

"Sure I do," he said. "Who's going to stick up for me if I don't stick up for myself?"

She didn't answer that. She turned her face away from him and looked out of the window over the fields far below so he didn't know what she thought. Half the time now, it occurred to him, he didn't know what Kit thought—just about half the time she seemed to slip off into herself somewhere like she was somebody else and not his wife at all. Or maybe now it was just because it was hard to talk in the noise of the plane.

. . . Kit, staring at the flattened country beneath her, put him out of mind. It had been a glorious morning and it was impossible not to feel excitement over the rising at dawn to go to the air field and climb into this huge silvery monster, waiting with outspread wings.

They were still flying over France, beautiful as a garden in the sunshine. But clouds lay just ahead. They must begin to rise or they would be swallowed. Even as she thought, the plane inclined and they rose swiftly upward, upward, until above them was only clear blue sky and the clouds beneath them, a silvery floor to a new universe.

All day they kept in clouds. Then at evening they dropped through them, abruptly. Far beneath she saw a dwarfed landscape with dots of trees and specks of houses and small masses of forests and tiny ponds of lakes. The plane drifted downward and the landscape grew softly large and clear as though a telescope were being focused upon it. It was another country, she saw at once, a country she did not know. She gazed at it, excited by the newness of its beauty. What country was it? She was about to ask Bert and then did not. Let it be without a name, as though it were a dream country, the land that never was.

"That's Turkey," Bert said, excitedly, unfolding a map.

She stared into it, seeing clearly as they dropped villages and barren-looking little cities. A train crawled along a sluggish gray river. It wasn't wonderful when one came close to it. The dream went out of it and dreams hung a glamorous atmosphere above anything unknown. She had breathed too much and too long today that rare atmosphere and she must come to the earth. What was it her mother once had said—that Bert must bring her to reality? She looked at Bert, sitting very real and solid just ahead of her. When she thought only of beauty, how beautiful his head was! Even now, if she looked only at the line of his head, his forehead and the way his hair grew—she could almost see only that. He looked up at her suddenly, his eyes brilliantly blue, and she smiled. Instantly his eyes grew warm and shy. He leaned over to her.

"Are you laughing at me, Kit?" he demanded.

"I'm not laughing, silly," she said, half tenderly. Yes, beauty moved to tenderness even her most knowing heart. So why should she scorn the unknowing crowds of his worshipers? She looked away to find John Baker's cool amused eyes upon them, and she stared him down until he looked away again. She could see him faintly shrugging as he turned.

In Bombay the temperature was steadily above one hundred and the streets were filled with dark, half-naked people. Kit in the hotel rooms worked in the thinnest of silk pajamas which stuck to her skin like wet paper, and tried to imagine cold and snow and ice, as she checked over supplies they had left to buy in Bombay. In a few weeks they would be battling against snowy winds, the mist frozen on their eyelashes. She had laughed when Bert told her what a nuisance it was to have mist freeze on his eyelashes.

"Serves you right for having eyelashes half an inch long," she had remarked.

"Want I should cut 'em off?" he had threatened.

"What—and ruin your looks for the ladies?" she had answered with such mischief that he shook her.

"I'm asking what you want!" he said.

"I want them as they are, silly," she answered.

He had kissed her and she had kissed him back, at once warm and cool, cool enough to wonder what it would be if he were not there to be kissed at all. There was an alchemy which marriage could work and quite apart from love, this she knew. Marriage had worked a change in her and in Bert, though what change she did not know except that if it had not destroyed Kit Tallant as it should have done, it had robbed her of enough to make a separate being who was Bert's wife. Had it robbed Bert, too, so that a part of him was her husband? So God did in the Garden of Eden when he laid Adam into sleep and robbed him of his rib. Symbolic sleep of the body in love, when the being divided itself, and the mind, without the wisdom of love, for once not knowing! So she mused as methodically she packed heavy socks ready into heavy oiled boots and tucked shaving soap and tooth paste into odd corners.

"Go easy on the shaving soap," Bert ordered. "We won't shave once we get started."

"Tooth paste, though," she said sternly.

"Oh, sure," he answered. But he had not used it before he knew her.

Down her back ran little rivers of sweat and she pushed back her wet hair, but she worked on until a moment when, without warning Bert came to her and took her in his arms and pressed her hard against his own wet body.

"You've got to stay by me, Kit!" he commanded her irrelevantly.

"Oh, I shall!" she breathed, surprised. Did he, she wondered, feel by an instinct her deep wavering? Her heart woke to pity. No, but he was sweet. Even now, hot as she was, stifling against his wet breast, she smelled his flesh sweet and clean. She pressed herself against him and for the moment felt Kit Tallant grow shadowy as a ghost beside her.

Thus she followed quietly in Bert's wake. The governor of Bombay gave them a great dinner. She sat at his right during the stateliest meal she had ever eaten, and perceived with amusement the astonishment of the big grizzled governor at her minute figure.

"I say, Mrs. Holm," he said at fish and roast and salad, "are you really, you know, going to attempt Pangbat? We have lady mountaineers, of course, and I believe there have even been famous ones."

"I shan't go further than I can." Kit said gently. Not very far, she saw him thinking, but she did not trouble herself with him.

At the end of the table sat his tall, gentle, submissive wife, who had exiled her children one by one to English boarding schools. Upstairs in the huge plastered bedroom where she had taken Kit before dinner, she showed her four blond boys.

"I haven't seen them since they were three and four, and Rudy was sent home at two, because he had a fever," she had said sadly. "But I've always felt I should stay at my post beside my husband, so I quite understand, my dear, your coming with yours. They *need* us, you know, poor dears. They seem so strong, but they're so dependent, really." She smiled her sweet sorrowful smile upon Kit, who smiled back without answer. Why she had come with Bert was not half so clear to her as this.

But there was too much to do to spend time in wonder. Perhaps that was as good a reason as any for her coming. Most of their goods had been sent by sea and with Bert she checked case after case. Rexall was there and John Baker, who would trust to no one his own boxes of equipment, though he paid no heed to anything else. When his things were safe, he stayed in his room all day. Only at night had he gone out into the crowded streets of Bombay. Once hearing a brawl in the moonlight beneath her window Kit had looked down to see him the center of a crowd of half-laughing, half-frightened Hindus. Sharing that center was a sacred cow, a big white beast lumbering upon the sidewalk. It had paused, confronted by John Baker, who stood, the cow's face opposite his.

Kit laughed and he looked up.

"I won't give way to a cow," he called up to her.

"You mustn't touch it," she called back. "Remember it's sacred!"

"I'll stare it down," he shouted back. He stooped and fixed his eyes upon the eyes of the bewildered creature until at last with a grunting moo it turned aside and went on.

"Triumph of mind!" Baker called, and waved his hat to her.

"I hate cows," he told her next day. They had met accidentally

260

in the hotel lobby after she had breakfasted late and alone. "They eat plants. Think of nine stomachs to fill in every cow!"

"Think of worshiping them!" Kit answered.

"Might as well worship them as anything," he retorted. "It's no more ridiculous than what most people worship."

"Must we worship something?" she asked.

"Seems so," he answered half carelessly and then went on, "I don't know if I ever told you I was a Presbyterian minister's son and perhaps that's why I can't worship any more. But I remember some pretty caustic bits out of my father's religion. One of them is that people become like the gods they worship. That's true."

She had taken this in thoughtfully as she watched the people coming and going in the lobby where they stood. The people were nearly all English, but a few Continentals and fewer Indians were among them, and one or two Americans. She recognized at the desk, partly because she had seen her name in the morning paper, a rich young American girl, heiress to the millions her father had made in chain groceries. She was petulantly pretty and a dark young Italian was with her, the husband from whom, the paper said, she was about to be divorced.

"Isn't it better to worship something than nothing?" she asked, looking at the bored impatient girl.

"Only for fools," Baker replied, savagely. He was looking at the girl too. He rose and turned away as though he could not bear the sight. "I must be going," he said. "I am getting some presses made of dry cypress wood and I have to watch the old fellow every minute."

He sauntered into the hot glittering street and Kit turned back to her room. Perhaps it was only by knowing what a man worshiped that one could know him. What did Bert worship? She did not know. But millions of people worshiped him. It *was* worship, wasn't it, when people set up an image and made it mean whatever they wanted most?

She stood in the crowded train while the spider-legged black coolies, chattering like apes, packed the compartment full of their things.

Something had gone wrong and a box was missing. Bert was on the platform shouting to a sweating Hindu in hotel uniform, whose large eyes were tragic with anxiety. Then they discovered a dark Moslem woman sitting on the box as she nursed her baby. The Hindu danced in an apology of joy and the woman rose in horror, words pouring from her in an unintelligible flood. The coolies snatched the box while Bert leaped into the door and fell upon a seat and wiped his face.

"Gosh, it's hot enough when everything goes all right," he gasped. "Lucky the train's late," he added.

The train was half an hour late but still there was no signal of departure. The air in the compartment was thick with dust and heat. Kit went to the open door and looked down upon this crowd, so different from the crowds she knew. To these dark creatures Bert Holm was nothing but a white man like any other. They fell back before him simply because they fell back in fear from all white men. She liked being able to stand here without recognition. And then she felt a touch on her knee. It was the Moslem woman feeling curiously between her thumb and finger the linen of her skirt. When she caught Kit's surprised eyes she smiled, teeth and eyes shining like a child's. She said something in a soft plaintive voice, a question it must have been, because she raised her long curled lashes to look up at Kit. There was nothing for Kit but to shake her head, and like an echo the woman shook her head. Between them a thought passed which each could feel, a wish to understand each other, but they could not.

Everybody ought to speak the same language, Kit thought. But then if language were still not enough?

With no warning at all the train began to move sluggishly and she stepped back. An Indian guard ran along the platform and shut the door and locked it, pushing the Moslem woman out of the way. The crowd fell back as the train went, vendors and water carriers and pilgrims and aimless wandering people of all kinds, their faces upturned in a dark mass. There was something familiar to Kit in that silent gazing of many eyes. Worship! For one moment she recognized it, the marveling worship of a machine they did not understand. Then the train went out of the solid British-built station through suburbs of low square houses, and gathered speed across the still barren fields. The land was desert although the heat was intense. It would remain desert until the rains fell. A few thin cows nuzzled the dry soil, and a village passed, its people dried to skeletons by hot winds and scanty food. And the afternoon sun spared nothing of sad detail.

Bert drew the shades. "Nothing to see, so I'm going to sleep," he said. He stretched himself on one of the leather seats, and put a handkerchief over his face to keep off the flies.

But Kit could not sleep. The heat was so fiery that to sleep would be to fall into its furnace. She wet her linen handkerchief from the ice-filled carafe and put it on her wrists and forehead. She smoothed back her long hair and twisted it around her head and wiped her neck. The handkerchief was already hot. Then she took from her hand bag two air mail letters, her mother's and Gail's. They had come just before they left the hotel, and she had had no time to read them.

Now as the train swayed and found its way over the gritty rails, she read and forgot India and all that lay about her. It was her mother's gift to be able to pull everything back to herself and to the house in which she lived. She pulled Kit back now to Glen Barry. Gail was there with the two little boys. There was some trouble between Gail and Harvey—Gail laughed but Harvey was very stiff. Neither of them had said much about it, really, and she had not wanted to know because what she needed most was a little peace. Her father was playing his usual golf. Mr. Brame was really wonderful in the fine dignified publicity he was putting out. The expedition was sure to be a great success. The spring was so far beautiful, plenty of rain and everything green. How would she and Bert like a little house of their own in New York next winter? The Tyndal house was up for sale, small but so perfect.

These long detailed letters she had always written to her daughters. This one was exactly what Kit had had from her every week in college. There were shells around women like her mother so that they lived and moved and breathed inside them. . . . Below her mother's large even writing, her father had squeezed a dozen tightly knit lines.

"Kit, the European war situation isn't so good. Better come straight home when you're through. This is inside stuff. Don't go traipsing around China, stay on the main lines. Been following Frisk's cables with greatest interest—well-written stuff and he admires Bert, which as Brame says, is important. Take a little holiday and spend something for yourself. With love, Dad."

They encircled her with their atmosphere of care and tenderness and pleasant married dullness. Gail's letter fell out of its envelope with a sharp rustle. She wrote with black ink on a thin silvery onionskin paper. Everything Gail did was like her and she made her consistency perfect so that again as she often had Kit envied her sister for a flying second. Gail knew exactly what she was and what she wanted and now her upright handwriting broke blackly from a gossippy page. "Poor Irene is trying marriage again—this time with a Paul Strevens—you remember that fat solid old banker? She'll never stick it. I said to her, 'Irene, why don't you give up respectability and have a good time and get something out of life, at least?' And she said she wished she could just give up comfortably and be a prostitute and know she couldn't be respectable if she wanted to. She keeps climbing in and out of the pale—so impossible!

"Harvey is doing better than ever, thank God. Everybody is losing money, but he manages not to. The cleverness of that man is beyond belief. He's a step ahead of me all the time, and you know me, Kit.

"Mr. Brame thinks it would be wonderful publicity if you'd have a baby, Kit. Not that he said so, but he implied it—says Bert needs build-up in a family way—public likes that and so forth. I told him he sounded like a midwife, which plunged him into one of his gray-blue blushes. Well, Kit, have a good time. Bert will, you know—so why not?"

There was no hint of trouble with Harvey. Gail's teasing, probably, Kit thought, carried a little too far, that was all. Her mother believed the worst too easily about Gail sometimes, though outwardly she defended her warmly, and always. But she never forgot the girl Gail had been.

Kit tore both letters to bits and dropped them on the floor and lay still. She lay so still that a little lizard, shaking and sliding down the wall of the moving car and clinging tremulously with its fragile feet, crept across the floor and tasted a fragment of Gail's letter and gave it up. The tiny reptile had a bright blue tail and its eyes were of black glass. It sat, quivering with the motion of the train, sliding its small forked tongue in and out while she watched it. It looked, for a beneficent being, extraordinarily wicked, like a little serpent in her strange inadequate Eden. She laughed out loud suddenly and it slid away under a shrunken plank in a flash of blue tail.

It was so hot that she loosened her blouse and lay down not to sleep but merely that she need not make the effort to sit up. The leather of the seat burned through the thin stuff of her dress. She wet her handkerchief again and spread it across her eyes. And then like a mirage she imagined the approaching mountains snow-covered, ice-capped, cold and lonely. If she and Bert were upon those mountains climbing them together, at last her loneliness, long made so acute by many people, might be gone.

VII

NONE of them except John Baker knew exactly why he had come to climb Pangbat. Bert had chosen the mountain by chance, or partly by the chance that it was in the neighborhood of Therat and he knew the roads there. Jim Frisk had come as the link between Bert and the people in their homes who, reading their newspapers at breakfast every morning thousands of miles away, followed him wherever he went with all the excitement of those who are themselves imprisoned. Jackie Rexall was there because he liked Bert and because it was a good job. He did not expect to go higher than the base camp.

"I reckon I'm kind of like the business manager of the football team," he said. He had no curiosity about the ultimate reason for climbing mountains. "Bert always was a climber," he said complacently. "Now he's only climbing higher." His small thin figure with its round head and big ears was everywhere, unnoticed and faithful. But he stipulated always that he would go no further than the base camp. "I'm liable to chilblains. Have 'em most every winter anyway at home," he explained to Kit. Neither of them had spoken of Lily Roos. Rexall watching Kit's proudly carried head spat ruminatingly a few times. Bert had maybe jumped from the frying pan into the fire. Anyway with Lily, a man knew where he was—or wasn't. He chuckled as he remembered her farewell. "I ain't saying, you old tinker—not till you get back. Why should I fix myself so I can't have any fun?" she had cried and then had kissed him.

The eight other men whom Bert had chosen came one by one to separate themselves as individuals. Francis Brewer, the tall sweet-tempered young Virginian who had climbed twice before in the Himalayas she knew simply because he had always to be called three or even four times in the morning. She heard his name roared among the men, "Frank, get up!" "Throw some water on him, somebody!" "Hell, throw something at him!" But when he was up he worked at apologetic silent speed. Dick Blastel she knew because he rose early but in such invariable ill temper that without explanations she set his breakfast a little apart from the others and only glanced at him as he sat, glowering and sallow, over his plate. Harden Coombes was a clerk in an athletic goods store in New York City. He had never climbed mountains except in the Adirondacks and once in the Rockies. He was a bright-faced cheerful young man whom Bert chose because he was a worshiper. He followed Bert, always slavishly close, always talking in his sharp city slang. Bret Calloway was a New England professor. He was in India and soon to be upon the Himalayas, but wherever he was would still be New England. His tall body, stooped at thirty-one and his downward twisted mouth and flattened speech were unchanged, though for half a dozen summers he had scraped together money somehow to climb in the Alps.

Lincoln Mayhew from Kansas had climbed, year in and year out, in the Rocky Mountains, but to Kit he said frankly the first day, "My girl ran off with another man—never even told me. I had to hear it from other folks. The Himalayas seem about right for me after that." He was tall, sand-colored and full of a melancholy good nature.

There were besides these Bob Pierce, the mechanic; Elmer Baum, a fat sturdy Pennsylvanian doctor who had never climbed; and Ronald Brugh, a slender weatherbeaten young Englishman lent by the British government in India. He had climbed twice with Sir Albert Fessaday, though not with Bert. And there was Kit herself, in the expedition and yet not of it, to all these men except John Baker a part of Bert rather than separate in herself.

They had grown used to the swarming little villages and the small cities that were only large villages of North India and with more difficulty they were now growing used to the high Tibetan plateaus. All of them had sore throats from the dry and dusty air except Kit. She had learned to breathe in shallow light breaths and more quickly than was her habit and she felt the air and her throat dryly but without pain. Nevertheless she mixed a throat wash from the pellets that Dr. Baum gave to each of them and said nothing. She was half ashamed to be doing so easily what fatigued half the party of men. Long ago on the night of her debut Gail had said, "Kit, my child, don't ever let yourself be more clever than the man you're with—it's fatal."

"Oh Gail," she had protested, "that's as old as the hills!"

"And as eternal," Gail had retorted.

"I don't care whether men like me or not," Kit had said that night, adjusting the silver flower on her left shoulder.

"Don't be silly and a liar, too," Gail had answered.

So though she found she climbed easily and with little fatigue, she made no boasts and whenever Bert shouted to her that she would be tired, she sat obediently in a little bamboo chair tied with thongs of bamboo to poles and carried upon coolies' shoulders. But she could not enjoy it. Though these thin-legged men seemed as yet something not altogether human, still they were too human for her to enjoy being carried upon their shoulders and the sight of the bamboo cross bars cutting into their dark flesh under her weight, slight though it was, made her sick. She turned her eyes away from it to look over high treeless plateaus that sloped upward to the pass, and as soon as she could she tapped the bamboo pole and they lowered the chair and she felt herself gratefully upon the ground.

"You're spoiling them," Ronald Brugh said, passing her. "There will come far rougher country than this and then they won't be ready to carry you. They must grow accustomed to your weight over the gradually stiffening climb."

"What about me?" she asked. "Shouldn't I be growing used to it, too, and on my own feet?"

He smiled and went on, not wanting to waste breath in talk.

They talked very little in this strange high country, though while they had walked among the hot moss-hung forests of the valleys the men could not keep from constant talk of this strange sight and that. Even Jack Rexall, still chewing a quid of American tobacco, had expectorated in the direction of a great yellow orchid.

"Like to take home some seed," he remarked.

Strangest of all flowers in the valleys through which they had passed to Kit were the great daturas growing upon trees in long white trumpets. By day they were only curious. But at night they shone with a moony phosphorescence and poured out into the hot darkness an unearthly fragrance. John Baker shook his head when she asked him what compounded this scent. Orchids and rhododendrons were his prey, and he would not look at anything else.

"There is enough here to drive a botanist insane," he said. "I must fix my limits."

Within these limits he had collected roots and seeds and shipped them whenever he could to the botanical garden he was making at home. Around his head by day the tropical butterflies had floated, themselves like great flower petals, but he did not see them. His hands were busy packing roots into dry moss. For him the tropics meant orchids. When they had climbed beyond orchids, he thought only of rhododendrons. Silver and mauve and white, orange and red, crimson and yellow, he recognized each.

"Argentium," Kit heard him murmur. *"Falconieri*—and there is *cinnabarium*——"

What she liked best all along the way were neither orchids nor rhododendrons but the little primulas that now squeezed themselves into every space. They were pink and very small, but when she stooped and pulled a cluster it resisted her until she pulled with all her strength. Then the spreading root came up still clutching a bit of rock. Beneath all the delicacy that root was sturdy and determined and it would not have come had not the rock given way.

They had risen slowly into the Chumbi Valley. India lay behind them in mists and rains, and ahead was Tibet, silvery in its eternal sunshine. They had all been oppressed for days in spite of the gigantic flowering beauty of the wet forests. The air of India was thick with too much life. They had been surfeited with it.

But upon the pass clean cool winds came sweeping from Tibetan plateaus and their lungs were washed free of dark scents and smells, and through pine woods and oaks they came upon plains of flowers.

"How do you, as a botanist, bear this?" Kit said to John Baker one morning.

"Hardly," he replied.

Whirls of clematis, fields of deep purple iris, yellow saxifrage, creamwhite roses, anemones, these she recognized, and then he taught her viburnum and herberis and frittilarias and cotoneasters, all she was able to remember of the names scientists had fastened upon innocent wild things. He pronounced their names unfailingly and then he showed her the first blue poppies she had ever seen.

"I collected blue poppies once," he said. "They won't grow anywhere but here, though. They're bred to this air. I don't dig them any more or take their seed from them." He leaned over the soft satin-silver blue flower. "It is worth coming just to see them," he said.

But the day of his great excitement was when he found a small ground orchid of a color he had never seen before. Beside him a river tossed and tumbled and through the forests of larch and spruce, junipers and birch, birds darted, white-capped redstarts and wagtails and sometimes a rare blood pheasant. But he saw only the plain little plant at his feet and he dug for its root. At that same moment Ronald Brugh saw a great Tibetan stag in the forest and shouted. There was a glimpse of an enormous leaping body. Kit cried out to the men behind and Bert led them in a plunge through the undergrowth of mountain ash. The stag escaped. When Kit turned to the road again she saw John Baker, lifting his plant delicately from the soil, his back to them. He had seen and heard nothing.

They scarcely knew when the high plain land began to mount again beneath their feet, except that day by day the rhododendrons shrank in size and the irises were paler and the trees grew sparse until the pines were gone and there were no more birches or willows and junipers. Now the pink and orchid rhododendrons were only a foot high, and then they were gone and there was left only a tiny purple rhododendron, scarcely higher than thick moss.

And then this too was gone, fading away into a delicate purple mist, and then before them was the plateau of Phari and then the peak of Chomulhari, sharp and beautiful, standing jealously to prevent them as they came to the true gates of Tibet.

In India Kit had been too aware of herself. The windless nights and the days too hot and moist had made acute every nerve of sense in her body. She smelled not only the strange new odors of an unfamiliar country but it seemed to her that everyone had an accentuation of his own odor—she, too, perhaps? She distinguished one by one the men, Jack Rexall's faint acid reek, the smell of Baker, clean except for the trace of rotted leaf and dried moss that clung to him, the smell of tobacco that was Ronald Brugh—she had labeled each one privately to Bert one night, half laughingly, when they were in tents outside a village.

"What about me?" he demanded.

"What about me?" she countered. And without answering she went on, "It's as though India brought out the essential of one's body."

"What is mine?" he persisted.

She had sniffed a little.

"Machine oil—and sweat—and sacred cow," she said mischievously.

"What's sacred cow about me?" he demanded.

"I smell sacred cow everywhere in India," she said evasively.

He picked up a map and threw it at her, and then reached for her and tumbled her into his arms.

"Call me names!" he said in mock fierceness. Now close against his flesh the heat made her gasp. "Don't," she said sharply. "I can't bear it——"

He dropped her, suddenly angry.

"Oh all right," he said, "if you mean it. You're damned full of notions for a wife, Kit."

"Yes," she agreed. "I know it—sorry! I'll be better when it's not so hot."

But indeed all through India in that atmosphere everything was too much and too intense and all scents were heavy. She could not endure a presence or a closeness. The very taste of food upon the tongue had been too pungent.

Then as their frontiers rose to the sky, Tibet changed them all and with them she was changed. Her too acute senses subsided in the dry high air. She felt clean and lifted up. Even beyond the pass there was no long descent. Tibet stood high above India, and from the pass it lay before them open to the eternal blue of the sky, and as though the map had become stone and mountain and plateau. The very rains that had worn India into deep and jungled valleys were held back at Chomulhari and the mountains forbade the clouds upon Tibet. And yet when she followed the direction of John Baker's searching eyes, Kit saw the buds of coming flowers, incarvillias, he said, that in summer would blossom purple in the shape of small trumpets, and there were blades of dwarf iris yet to flower. Here and there they found new grass growing in a wind-sheltered spot, and little hares nibbled at the scanty shrubs.

But wind was the atmosphere of Tibet. After the brief calm of sunrise was over the days were swept into wind. They struggled against it as they walked, or, if they rode, their small ponies were blown like little ships. A head wind held them back a third of their day's allotted journey, and a wind from their backs hastened them as much. Kit chose often to walk, but she learned to keep a step behind Bert, where his body gave her shelter. At nightfall, when the wind stopped, it left them all dazed and looking strangely alike, their faces parched and browned and all their sweat dried upon them.

In India the men had been irritable and quarrelsome. She had laughed at one and another of these quarrels, guarding constantly her own irritability. But Tibet healed them. When at night each went to his own tent they went in quietness. And this good humor was not peculiar to them. It was a part, too, of the nature of the people whom they passed upon the rocky wind-scoured roads and in little villages. They were people of good humor. They wore jewels, rough lumps of turquoise held in silver, though dirt encrusted their flesh and made their shapeless garments stiff. But the high earth had lifted them toward the sky, too, and sun and wind had purified them. Water was scarce, but none of them needed to bathe as in the heat and dampness they must bathe to keep themselves from their own putrefactions. Filth did not rot here, it dried and blew away. There was no stink.

A physical exaltation laid hold upon the whole expedition. For the first time Kit felt it knit together. The men began to study their maps and to talk of the approach to Pangbat. Ronald Brugh began to find the porters who were able to climb. They paused four days at Phari, filthiest of little towns, a cluster of houses sheltering beneath a fort, and thence made steady upward marches westward, stopping at sundown to sleep in a tent or if there were a monastery, in empty cells, where dirty cheerful monks stood around the door to watch all that was done.

There would have been no reality in all this dream-like passage of time, Kit thought, except that none of it made any change in Bert. He slept in a monastery cell as though it were his bedroom in the farmhouse where he had been born. He woke and was dissatisfied without coffee and ham and eggs. Kit felt herself changed to the heart by the high air, by the stark snow-capped mountains continually beyond the bare brown glacier-rounded hills, by the complete simplicity of this life she now led. She did not look in a mirror for days together. She rose in the morning when the bell clanged for rising and at the early breakfast stood as silent as the men, eating what the Tibetan cook had prepared. All food was good and they were perpetually hungry. The finicking appetites they had had in India were gone. All through the day's march the change held, whether she walked or rode. The land was full of quiet. The wind made a wall around each of them, and within the wall was quiet. Men's faces turned toward her if she spoke, or went on absorbed if she did not. Sometimes she caught Ronald Brugh's eyes and they smiled without speech. He would be likable, she thought, if there had been time for it. But there was no time in this steady upward march toward a mountain top.

So she lived in her own loneliness and let it withdraw her into solitude. One day when she had stayed behind at camp while the men went out to gather in supplies for the climb now very nearly ahead of them, she sat on a box in the door of her tent and opened her knapsack and took out the small black notebook in which for so many years she had written her close short poems. She had written several pages during these last weeks, shaping them in the silence of days and writing them at night by the light of a candle guttering among the flying moths, or of a Tibetan lamp filled with oily butter.

She read them over, one by one, recalling the mood in which

274

each had been written. What would become of these thoughts and feelings which no one had ever seen? Yes, Norman had seen three of them, this one beginning, "Since now we know—"; this one, beginning, "Today when I awoke to my first dawn—"; this one, "Entreat me as you will, I cannot leave you."

After that long poem there was silence upon the pages before her until the one, unfinished still, which she had been writing that day in Peking when she had first met Bert. And then for a very long time there was only the one written in the library at Glen Barry on the rainy day. And now in these last weeks she had written more than she had ever before. She counted them—a hundred and fifty-seven. There were enough for a book, only she would never want to publish them. Here in the solitude of this enormous landscape she thought of that crowd so avid for anything it could get from Bert Holm. It was still there and waiting, and she could give them nothing of this. They would search out everything that might seem to tell them anything about Bert and the woman he loved, looking for what they called "romance." She had come to despise the word. Its gold was forever tarnished for her, and yet if they found none of it, they would mark that, too.

She snapped the band about the book and rose restlessly and wandered out to the brown hillside which fell sharply down from the tents. In the distance a shepherd herded a few gray sheep, his dark rags flying in the wind. It was late afternoon and the men would soon be coming back. Why did she suddenly feel, as she did so often, that she had only a little while left her until—until when? Until Bert came back—not until she died, of course. She was too healthy. But if it were until she died—silly imagining, when she was as well as possible, and more nearly fat than she had ever been in her life in spite of heat and travel! But suppose she knew she were going to die, what would she do with a last little while? She sent her mind flying out into the space around her and it came back to her with the certainty of a hom-

275

ing dove. All these vagrant weeks she had let time slip by in a solitary stillness that could pass for a content, but underneath the content she knew all through that passing time, that she would write to Norman again some day, somewhere, a long letter. The last necessity had never come but now it was here. She knew why. Tomorrow, Rexall had said only this morning, their last mail would be sent back.

"If I don't write now, I'll never write to him again," she thought with a certainty as unreasoning as the rising wind. If ever it were to be done, it must be now. After Pangbat no one knew what change might come to them all.

She had finished the letter at last. She would not count the pages nor re-read them to see what she had written. She did not know whether she had told him everything or even anything. She had not one or several things to tell him. She wanted simply to communicate with him utterly and completely at the point where she was. It was in no manner a love letter. She did not want to write him a love letter. No, what she had done was this: she had gone back to the moment when he had told her he could not love her enough and step by step she wrote down everything that had happened to her until this present moment. She put down Lily as clearly and justly as she could, and did not dislike her. She saw Lily clearly. She saw everything clearly in this sharp Tibetan sunlight. But all that took only a few pages. What took page upon page were these last weeks when with Bert and yet alone she had been rising upward out of heat and confusion toward the Tibetan sky. That sky reached above her now, blue and always cloudless.

"So here I am, Norman," she said at last. "I don't know what is ahead. Perhaps you will never hear of me again and perhaps you will hear a great deal of me. Mrs. Bert Holm, of course, won't write to you. She hates any sort of double life. She wants to live simply and clearly with nothing to explain or hide in the intolerable way people do hide things. What Gail finds fun would bore her. You remember how Kit Tallant always was—such an everything-or-nothing sort of person. Mrs. Holm is the same way in an even narrower fashion."

She hesitated, and looking up, stared into the white tops of distant mountains. The afternoon was so clear that she might perhaps see Everest. Ronald Brugh had said it was barely possible at this spot. She sat, her inward gaze penetrating the empty sky until she could see across the ocean, homeward to where Norman was—not waiting for her, for he would wait for no one—so, simply to where he was. And instantly she felt him so clearly that he seemed to spring into her presence, alive and himself. She had always half believed in clairvoyance, and now she did believe in it. He sat at his table, writing. "Norman!" she said. He looked up and smiled his unwilling smile. But his dark eyes were warm and she felt him glad to see her, not ordinarily glad but as she had never seen him before, eagerly, passionately glad, relieved even, as though he had been anxious and even a little longing. She thought with a sort of shock, too sudden to be joy or anything but pure surprise, "Why, I believe he could love me—if I tried——"

He was gone again. If Norman were going to love her, did love her, perhaps had loved her all along and had only fought against love and not against her, then what? "When I go home, if I lift my finger the way Gail lifts hers," she thought, laughing suddenly, "I believe he would!"

She wrote hurriedly across the end of her letter, "Dear Norman, I am yours ever, Kit." That was the right end, wasn't it—the true end? It seemed so, in this clear and distant solitude. She folded the letter crookedly because it was so thick, and put it into the envelope and sealed it with a row of Indian stamps. It would be carried back into India and mailed there.

Then she went outdoors and stood facing the western sky. Far below her to the left she could see the figures of the men returning. Bert was ahead. She saw him wave his arms to her, and she took the blue scarf from her throat and let the wind wave it toward him. She was full of peace as though a thing inevitable had been well done.

The wind was dying now for night. She could smell food cooking in the kitchen tent, and the scent of dry sunbaked hillside. Below in the valley lay a small lake, blue all day and now turning coppery as the evening light grew strong. She could see a brown skylark rise above a patch that was a green garden. The bird rose and rose, but not as high as she was standing, and then fell again. She heard a mountain finch and the rustle of a partridge in a clump of grass, though she could not see them. Their feathers were brown, as most birds were brown in this brown country. Color could not live here except in the sky, and except as light searched it out or painted it where it was not. Then suddenly out of the translucence of the sky she saw something rise far above her, distant as a cloud, and as white as cloud. She stared at it, amazed at the cloud, and then she knew it was no cloud. It held its shape immutably in the sky, and she recognized it. It was Everest. She gazed at it and felt swept upward to that spotless snowy crest until twilight covered the sky.

"I saw Mount Everest," she said solemnly to the men returning, and met their varying half-envious, half-doubting comments by insistence. "It couldn't have been any other—it was the highest thing in the world—half way to zenith!"

"I felt it was Everest," she told Bert in their tent that night.

"Yeah?" he said comfortably from his sleeping bag.

"Do you wish still you were climbing Everest instead of Pangbat?" she asked.

"No," he replied and yawned. "I guess Pangbat is about high enough for me. Just so it's higher'n anyone else has gone, I'm satisfied."

"Somebody will climb Everest though, some day," she went on dreamily. "I wish it were I."

"I like climbing, but I don't want to die at it or at anything," Bert said. He was silent while she made sure of the tent flap and put out the small lantern. Then in the darkness she heard him murmur drowsily,

"Come in with me, Kit—I'm cold all by myself."

She hesitated and then, feeling her essential solitude assured, she once more could obey.

Pangbat, as they approached it from the western side of the endless ridge in which it stood, was a mountain built in long simple slopes sweeping upward to clustered crags. They walked now in a straggling line among rough uneven hills. Twenty miles away these hills became low mountains. Ten miles and five miles further away they were mountains upon whose highest surfaces was a sift of snow. Above them, like a gigantic curled wave, was Pangbat.

"Got to find a way through them," Bert said. He was growing more silent day by day as he approached Pangbat. At every mile or two he stopped and through his binoculars surveyed his mountain.

"It isn't as easy as it looks," he announced one morning. "Those slopes aren't smooth." He handed the glasses to Kit, and she gazed through them at the mass that stood against the sky. Pangbat leaped at her and the lens magnified faithfully a surface which, seemingly smooth, was in reality broken by steplike cliffs. Only on one surface did the snow still lie smooth and that surface was attached like a saddle to another peak. Pangbat indeed stood between two lesser peaks from which it seemed to spring, but one rose higher than the other and from it the saddle to Pangbat was less steep.

"That's where we'll put the base camp, in that hollow," Bert decided.

John Baker, walking with his eyes always upon the ground, looked up.

"Too high," he said.

"You mean it's too high up for you," Bert growled.

"That's true, too," John Baker said equably. He had steadily refused to quarrel with Bert again though Bert was daily more irritable as he planned the final climb. "No use for me to go above the snow line," Baker added.

The terrific landscape began to have its effect upon them all. Behind them came a long line of pack animals and porters. Jack Rexall and Ronald Brugh, working together, had rounded them up out of mountains, out of little villages and small fortified cities. Men and beasts seemed strangely alike before this oppressing landscape upon which they struggled together. When Kit grew exhausted at the burden of her own body, she thought of these loaded creatures and kept silent or uncontrollably quarreled with Bert's complaints.

"Gosh, I'm a fool for not staying in a comfortable house in the U. S. A." he said now as they went on together.

"Why didn't you?" she said sharply.

"Because I'm a fool, I said," he retorted.

"If you feel so, you are a fool," she said.

"Not if you say so," he growled. "My feet are all blisters," he added.

"I'm tired of hearing about your feet," she replied. She had a blister on her own heel, but she would not speak of it. "These porters are splendid," she said, "carrying loads as they climb."

"They'd do anything for a few cents," Bert said.

"At least they do it," she replied, and then wondered at the stupidity of quarreling.

As they left the rounded foothills and began the serious ascent of lower Pangbat a strange wretchedness fell upon them all. Ronald Brugh bore it better than any of them. He plodded steadily onward, watching the porters as he walked, but he looked at Kit shrewdly.

"Feeling sad, aren't you?" he inquired one morning.

She nodded. "Why should I?" she asked.

"Everyone does," he replied. "It's a sort of spiritual mountain sickness, a warning, perhaps, that men are not made for high places. The body is afraid of where the spirit may take it and puts out its hands to drag it back by misery."

"Why do you keep watching the porters?" she asked, seeing his eyes upon them.

"Soon they will begin to try to desert," he said. "I know. I've been through this before. White men keep on, but those Sherpas and Bhotians are nearer their beginnings than we are—or farther, I don't know which, depending on whether you think of the race's span as ascent or descent. The Tibetans will go farther than any of them if they have their lama's blessing before they start." He smiled. "I paid the lama to bless them well," he added, "but they don't know that."

That night when they were half way to the saddle of Pangbat, three Bhotians deserted and turned back. Ronald Brugh's anger fell like an avalanche of ice upon those who were left.

"Dare to leave!" he told the ones who were left. "I will bring down the curse of the Snowmen of Pangbat upon you." They stared at him fearfully, and went slowly to their loads.

At the snow line, John Baker stopped and put up his own tent. "This is the end of my world," he said. "I'll have time to put my specimens into shape, and I want to explore just along the snow line and see what I find."

He kept with him a tall Tibetan boy who climbed above the edge of glaciers and explored the ravine bed by the hidden waters. "Anybody else want to stay?" he inquired.

Francis Brewer wavered. He had grown into a deep friendship with Baker. Then he looked up at Pangbat. It was a day so clear and still that Pangbat was crystal set against azure. "I reckon I'll keep going," he drawled, "Pangbat's got me."

The others merely smiled at Baker's question. Each for reasons of his own was determined to try for Pangbat. It was no longer

281

a matter of following Bert, for one by one they had withdrawn from him. Kit had watched an early deference to Bert lose its eagerness and turn to edged politeness. Dick Blastel did not even pretend politeness, and he ignored Bert's presence as he did his share of the work. Whether Tibet had wrapped them all in her own solitude, or whether as Ronald Brugh had said it was inevitable, the pattern of the expedition had changed.

But none of the men changed as Jimmie Frisk had changed. The sandy-haired young reporter grew into a silence almost ferocious. What he was feeling Kit did not know but continuous quarreling had sprung up between him and Bert. Bert had not been satisfied with the last stories Frisk had sent and he could not forget.

"They might have been about anybody," he said. "I wanted them to be about the Bert Holm expedition. People want to hear something personal, not a lot of stuff about scenery."

"I'm sorry," Jimmie Frisk said shortly. "This scenery—gets me." He stared upward at the strong snowy shoulders of Pangbat. "Nothing personal seems worth writing about any more."

"Brame won't be able to make anything out of that stuff," Bert said stubbornly. He was handsomer than ever in his white fur parka. Though they were now thousands of feet up Pangbat's slopes and within a day of the site for the final base camp, the sun was warm and the men were sitting bareheaded before their open tents. An ocean of cloud lay beneath the sunlight through which rose snowy peaks and beyond them were the distant mountains of Nepal. Of all the men only Bert in his white parka, his fair head bare of the hanging hood, was not dwarfed in his own beauty. Kit looking at him pondered the cruelty which made the mere size and color and shape of one body, Bert's body, only more beautiful in the midst of snow and sunshine, and at the same time pinched little Jimmie Frisk, and made him shrink inside his leather windproof coat and reddened his slightly upturned nose, and blistered his too fair skin and dried his straight colorless hair. He was possessed by this landscape which used him so cruelly, and Bert cared nothing for it and suffered nothing from it and yet looked born to stand upon it. And still, though she could enjoy his beauty, at the same time she knew it meant nothing and to her it was worth nothing.

And yet she was sufficiently just, watching Bert calmly here in the presence of the Himalayas, to realize that she must not blame him. Thus had she been changed. So it seemed they all grew indistinguishable each day as they crept a little higher up the side of Pangbat, all except Bert, whom even Pangbat could not change.

Gail had said once in half-envious mockery, "Think of the fun you'll have being the only woman!" But even Gail, had she been here, would have become less than woman. Man and woman ceased to be in the increasing severity of their days. The laws of earth were in abeyance here where earth stood under the sky. She lived and moved among the men as though they were all a race of neutrals, existing upon ice, breathing the rarefied atmosphere which left them no strength for more than the duty of food and sleep after climbing. And had it been otherwise, somehow the mountain would have shamed them. In its presence there could be nothing so trivial as lovemaking between insects.

She understood the look of rage in Jimmie Frisk's eyes when Bert spoke of Roger Brame, a rage silent because it could not speak to Bert and be understood.

"Suppose you write what you want said about yourself," he said to Bert.

"I have my own job," Bert replied shortly. "Besides, you're paid to write."

"Just tell me what to say then," Frisk insisted. "Come on—give me an idea of how you want it laid on." He was growing white about his peeling lips. "The people's hero speaks!" he added, looking around at them.

Bert turned to him calmly and by his beauty and calmness put the gibbering little reporter unjustly into the wrong.

"You know I don't mean that," he said simply. "What I want is just straight stuff about what actually happens. I don't mind a little description on the side, but you could tell, for instance, about the exploring I did yesterday for this trip today——"

"Where a devoted native porter fell into a crevasse and Bert Holm risked his own life and went down at the end of a rope to get him!" Frisk flung out.

Bert did not answer. He turned and went inside his tent. In the circle of idling weary men Kit felt the atmosphere grow tense.

"What's the matter with you, Jim?" Harden Coombes said. Of all the men, Coombes had remained most the man he was, a gentle believer in that in which he had believed about Bert Holm. He had not stood climbing well, being at each new altitude attacked afresh by mountain sickness. Now, within a day of the base-camp site he was terrified least he could follow Bert no farther and so be left behind. "After all, Jim, Bert did go down after the fellow, didn't he? It was just like him, too."

"That's why I say, 'Damn him!'" Frisk retorted.

"But—it was a noble thing to do!" Coombes protested. Under the shining clear light of the setting sun his snow-strained eyes were running and bleared and he wiped them with the end of his scarf.

"Too damned noble!" Frisk growled.

Coombes began again, sniffling a little. "I can't understand——"

"Then damn you too!" Frisk broke in. He jumped up and slipping and stamping upon the crunching snow he went off to his own tent.

In the midst of this quarreling one night the others sat in an apathy and watched the tremendous sun fling its colors against gigantic palettes of snow. The mountains grew rose and purple and the valleys were ice green in their hollows. It was too huge for them. A little beneath them the porters began to chant one

284

of their dirgelike prayers. And one by one the men rose and went away.

Kit sat a moment alone. The only human sound was the faint intermittent tapping of a typewriter from Frisk's tent. It had no importance and yet it broke the enormous silence into fragments of its own size and she rose and went into the tent she and Bert had for their own. He was lying in his sleeping bag staring up into the tent top. When she came in he turned bewildered eyes upon her.

"Not that it matters," he said, "but have you any idea why in hell Jim was so mad at me?"

His eyes were as innocent as blue water in a lake. She was dismayed by such innocence. What could one do with it or how escape from it? Nothing and never, she thought. She smoothed out her own sleeping bag.

"Perhaps the mountains make him queer," she said. "They do us all maybe except you, Bert. You don't seem to mind."

"Why should I?" he asked. "I'm only doing a job. I don't see what that has to do with it——"

"Nothing," she hastened to say. "Nothing at all."

He accepted this and lay, she thought wickedly, looking as noble as a recumbent Greek statue.

"Come and kiss me," he commanded.

"My cold's no better," she warned him.

"Come on over here, I tell you," he said.

She went over to him to receive his kiss. But then Bert never had colds. Not even that small ailment ever marred the perfection of his looks. She let him press her against him and felt for that moment as helpless as an insect upon a mountain cliff.

Here in the presence of endless time and of space stretching from earth to heaven in these mountains it was no longer of importance that between Bert and herself there could be no companionship. She watched herself shrink into a tiny being the size of the little man upon her Chinese seal. That ivory mountain was

285

in her knapsack, and sometimes when she was alone she looked at it and came in the presence of Pangbat to understand what it meant. The man had no face. He was too small for any distinguishing mark except his human shape.

Two days of slow climbing had brought them to this narrow plateau upon the right saddle of Pangbat. This was as far as she was to go, Bert told her. While they were climbing the slope the height had looked as distant and difficult as the crest and that crest indeed seemed only a little further than the saddle. But now above their small pitched tents Pangbat had again withdrawn itself and stood remote. She said nothing as Bert removed it still further. It was not necessary for her to climb higher. Roger Brame's last cable, brought to them in the foothills by a Sherpa runner, had made that clear——

"Everybody following stories of expedition with utmost excitement," the cable had said. She could imagine Brame in his little office in New York dictating calmly, "Extremely important Bert to reach Pangbat top to avoid public disappointment." They were all here upon this icy saddle of a Himalayan mountain in order that a public thousands of miles away, in comfortable farm houses, in warm suburban houses, in city apartments, might be freshly excited and above all, not disappointed. It was necessary only for Bert to climb as high as they expected.

The plateau was not so good a camping place as it had looked from below. It sloped too sharply downward, so that inside the tents the ground was too slanting for good sleep and there was no wind shelter. This first morning there was already a hint of the coming monsoon storms. The wind was bitter and it tore at the tents and whistled through the guy ropes. The porters looked frightened and miserable and they received apathetically the extra food and clothing which Rexall handed out to them and they turned their backs upon Pangbat and stared hopelessly toward the valley from which they had come.

And yet after rest and food and a noon sun which shone warm against the wind, through them all crept the quickening of the rush for the top. The wind had hurried Bert's determination. Monsoons would make the ascent impossible.

"I'm going to make my first stab at it tomorrow," he told them.

Coombes was ill. He lay in his sleeping bag, breathing heavily, his round face green with nausea. They were all weary with altitude. The very weight of a hand lifted was three times what it should be. But Bert was not weary. Now that Pangbat rose before him every petty habit of complaint fell from him and some strange strength upheld him. He ignored discomfort and cold and the difficulty of breathing which troubled them when they moved too quickly, even after a day of rest, and he sat in his tent, planning with pencil and paper, and lifting his eyes to Pangbat, white against the deep blue sky of afternoon.

"Tomorrow at dawn, Kit," he ordered her. "We want breakfast over by five, me and Brugh, Brewer and Blastel and Calloway and Mayhew. Rexie won't go. Baum better stay ready for anybody that gets hurt and to look after Coombes. I'll take the lead. None of them can work with ice the way I can." He was boasting, but it did not seem boasting now, and they allowed him anything because of what he had to do. "I'll take porters for three camps. Brugh will handle them."

Upon a photographed map of Pangbat's side were three carefully drawn little tents to mark the camps. Three days and they would be sleeping in the last and highest one and from there at the fourth dawn they would make the last dash for the top. He would have with him those who were able to follow so far.

Hundreds of feet below at this base camp Jimmy Frisk would have his long range camera trained upon Pangbat, as it stood hanging against the sky. He would photograph Bert climbing step by step up that final crag, surmounting somehow the cornice of snow which the telescope showed them was there, standing at the top, looking down on the world. It never occurred to Kit that anyone would be there with him. She always saw Bert there alone.

The base camp had indeed been badly chosen. There was not only the sloping icy surface, deceptively gentle and so smooth beneath powdery snow that a piece of icy rock dropped slid for miles, but the wind continued to tear at them. It swept the snow from the ice and blew it in bright whirls through the sunshine and whisked it into their tents until it was sifted everywhere like sand. The porters groaned and Coombes lay patiently entombed by drifts. Too ill to struggle after Bert he lay suffering with disappointment.

"Of course I know Bert couldn't wait a day or two for me," he kept saying, "I oughtn't to think of myself, except I've come a pretty long way for this."

"Bert is so afraid of the monsoons coming," Kit murmured. "Every day counts now."

"Oh, he's right," Coombes agreed sorrowfully. " 'Tisn't that."

But it was that. For Bert was thinking now of no one but himself. The day and the night was absorbed in the preparation for his great solitary effort for the peak. He made meticulous examination of ropes and ice axes, of *pitons* and boots, and spent half his last evening arguing with Elmer Baum as to whether or not he would take a small supply of oxygen with him. He decided first against it.

"By the time I take the extra load of it to the point where I need it," he told Kit, "I'd have spent enough energy to carry me on to the top." Then suddenly he changed his mind. "Nope, maybe it would be just what I needed at the end."

She agreed quietly to anything he said and went on packing into a small flat box the concentrated rations he would take for the last. They all agreed to anything he said now. There was no more complaining even from the porters, though the wind did not cease and there was a shortage of water. At this altitude snow and ice evaporated without melting and there was no trickle of water anywhere even at the edge of a glacier. The dry snow had to be melted and fire was sluggish.

But everything was endured in preparation for the moment for which they had come. For this moment all individual life was in abeyance. Beneath the high Himalayan peak the world was waiting. Though they were thrust too near the sky to hear or see the earth, they knew that beneath the clouds which spread around them like a silver floor, radios caught from the air the news that Bert Holm was preparing for his last quick ascent. Ships carried the photographs over seas, scientists made their guesses upon his failure or success and in America men's Rotaries and women's clubs prepared programs of celebration and newspapers saw to it that all the facts were ready for Bert Holm's obituary, in case . . .

The wind died suddenly that night. In the morning Bert led out the five men he had chosen, and there in front of the little huddle of tents the others gathered to see him off, all except Coombes, who was too ill to leave his sleeping bag. It was just after dawn. Kit had crept out of her bag an hour before and seen to breakfast herself. She was growing used already to the altitude and was able to breathe without too much effort, and she had planned to make a little fete of this breakfast but when the moment came the men were in no mood for it. They stood about the flat rock which served as a table and ate quickly. Bert was almost totally silent. She saw his eyes checking sharply each piece of equipment. Eight porters were to go with them as far as they could. Brugh had chosen them carefully, Sherpa men, accustomed to carrying loads over the mountain passes into Tibet. They stood in a semicircle waiting and silent. Early in the morning while it was still dark, they had risen and turning their faces toward Pangbat had prayed one of their wild chanting prayers. It was hard to believe now that that strange passionate cry to the gods had come from these stolid silent men. "Without it," Ronald

Brugh had said, "you can't get them to undertake danger. They have to have their gods, these fellows."

For a moment she thought Bert was going to go away without kissing her good-by. Actually he had shouted before he thought of her, "All right, fellows! On your way!" She felt a twist of laughter in her breast. How shocked Roger Brame would be if he knew!

"Aren't you going to kiss your wife good-by, Bert?" Jimmie Frisk yelled. He was standing with his camera ready.

Now she could not keep from laughing. The breath of her bitter laughter blew from her lips in a mist, silver and cold. Bert halted, turned and came stamping toward her through the snow.

"Hell," he said frankly, "I almost forgot, Kit."

"God, what a chance you nearly lost!" said Frisk sourly.

It was suddenly completely ridiculous. Still laughing, she threw her arms about him and clasped him and kissed him heartily on the lips. The Tibetan porters stared, struck with amazement, and even horror, and the men, seeing the Tibetan faces, laughed one after the other until in the silence the echoes of their laughter were thrown mockingly back to them from Pangbat.

Bert turned and raged at them all.

"What the hell are you fellows laughing at?" he shouted.

"Not at you," Ronald Brugh said in his smooth voice. "It's the Tibetans. You've shocked them. Kissing your wife before you climb Pangbat is reckless defiance of the mountain gods. You ought to deny yourself, old chap. It means bad luck for one of us."

Bert's sun-reddened face grew redder. "I never know what you're talking about, Brugh," he said shortly. "Come on, let's get going." His harshness snuffed out their laughter, and they filed behind him, Brugh alone, and then Brewer and Blastel, and Calloway and Mayhew in pairs, and in the midst of it, Jimmie Frisk ground at his clicking motion-picture camera.

Watching Bert's figure at the head of the scattered line moving slowly upward, Kit tried to think that it was possible she would never see him again. If Bert should not come back, this would be their last moment. A strange last moment then, belonging not to her but to the whole world, for over and over she could see it spread upon Sunday supplements and picture magazines and newsreels. "Bert Holm Bids Wife Good-by." The crowds would spell out the words and then sit staring and absorbed, to share as they were able by the imagination that romantic kiss, given in the midst of the peaks of mountains high enough to be the dwelling place of gods. She turned to Jimmie Frisk.

"Did you get all the men laughing?" she inquired.

"If I did, I'll cut 'em off," he replied. "It'll spoil the romance."

His lips were so cracked and swollen that she could not discern a smile, and his eyes, which might be full of his peculiar mischief, were hidden behind the camera which he still focused upon Bert leading his men upward.

She stood watching the diminishing figures. Once she thought Bert turned and waved. She was not sure but she snatched the red scarf from her throat and waved it back. Then while she waved she had the sense of being watched, and turning, saw that Frisk had swung the camera on her.

"Swell!" he cried. "Go on, go on!"

"I won't," she said violently. "Stop it! You haven't the right to—to take me. I'm not Bert Holm."

He lowered the camera astonished until he saw that she was hurt.

"See here, I'm sorry. I didn't dream you minded."

"I do mind," she replied shortly and without another word went into her tent and closed the flaps tightly and sat down on the hummock of ice under a fur which served as a chair. It was absurd that here in such remoteness she had suddenly reached the point of last endurance of that invisible crowd before whom she and Bert must play out their lives eternally.

"I can't even wave to my husband," she muttered alone childishly, "without everybody's seeing me do it——"

It was perfectly possible that Bert would never come back. What he was doing was foolishly dangerous, and he would shirk nothing because of danger when his mountain mood was on him. She had already seen him in that mood, when no advice, no criticism, no fatigue swerved him from his determination. The higher he went the more completely possessed he would be. At a certain point the porters would go no further. The other men would stop one by one. But as long as Pangbat's crest reached higher than he had climbed, Bert would put forth all the energy he never used for any other effort, to reach this one goal. Why, she would never understand so long as she lived. What magic was there in a mountain top? What satisfaction in the mere physical achievement of its height? It must symbolize in some way a need of Bert's soul that in no other way he could achieve.

"Bert, he always wanted to be on the top of things," his mother had once said. "He wasn't satisfied when he could crawl without he climb on top of a table if it was in the room, and as soon as he got outside he was on top of the barn, and then always on top of the highest hill. Afraid of nothin'—that's Bert."

It was not true, of course. He was not fearless. It was only that he saw nothing to achieve except, physically, the tops of mountains. Nothing else waked imagination in him. She sighed and shivered. She must go out in the sun. Now that the wind had gone down, it would be warmer outside. Then she must go and see how Coombes was. Three days of this must pass somehow before Bert could come back.

She went out and looked up at Pangbat as it reared itself in the sunshine. The north face was almost sheer ice. She had studied it with Bert through the telescope again and again. Precipice rose upon precipice of old ice, greenish blue, centuries deep. Bert had given up the north face, but the southwest side rose by white folds and slowly rising slopes. He had chosen that way, though what lay between those curves and angles of snow none could guess. They hid him now; she could see nothing upon the whiteness of the snow. The telescope stood swinging upon its standard. She went to it and lifting it to her eyes gazed through it and again Pangbat leaped at her. She saw the seeming smoothness of its surface broken by rocks and by black gaps which must be crevasses. To the south a great glacier hung, seeming ready to move at a sound. But search as she did, already she could find nothing of Bert. She saw, or imagined she saw, tiny marks in a steep face of ice which might be steps cut by an ax, then she decided that at this distance she could not see such steps. Besides, it was too soon. Pangbat had taken Bert into itself, and whatever he was, he was alone with Pangbat. Perhaps he was another man when he was thus alone with a mountain, but if he were, she would never know. He had forbidden it.

That night, unexpectedly, Harden Coombes died. The camp had been very quiet all day. The silence after the wind, the sense of release from effort until Bert's return, the unusually warm sunshine had spread quiet everywhere. Rexall had gone again and again to the telescope as long as daylight held, and Jimmie Frisk had disappeared into his tent with his typewriter. Kit herself had written letters to Gail and to her father and mother. "It is so unreal here upon this mountain," she had begun each letter, "that I am sure this letter will never reach you." Nevertheless she had written, and then feeling somehow free and pleasantly idle, she had played with a poem. She was curled into her sleeping bag for warmth but the flap of her tent was open to the sun and she was very comfortable. When she thought of Bert it was still without fear, because the weather was perfect. Tonight she knew exactly where he was to encamp. The porters would be left there tomorrow, except for the two strongest, trained by an expedition upon Everest. In this ease and unusual warmth she had fallen asleep at mid-afternoon, still in the sun.

When she woke it was from cold. It was twilight, the sun was gone, and though there was still no wind the profound cold of the darkness was welling into the tent like a chilly flood. She was about to spring up when she heard her name called. She recognized Elmer Baum's voice.

"Yes?" she answered.

"Could you come to Coombes's tent? I'm worried about him."

"Yes, certainly."

She struggled out of the bag and stood up, stiff with cold. He had a flashlight and in its glow she saw the circle of his face, as crudely cut as a cartoon, in the enveloping hood of his parka.

"He's had a heart attack. I think he's out of it. But a woman's help would be handy. The men mean well, but I need a delicate hand on his pulse while I give an injection——"

"I'll come at once——" She followed him across the rough snow asking anxious questions. "When did it come on? Why didn't you call me? Poor fellow!"

"Only about an hour ago. I had no idea; I thought he was pulling up all right. He oughtn't to be up here, of course, at all. He shouldn't have got by the doctor in New York. His heart isn't made for high altitudes, and that dysentery in India didn't help him."

"I didn't know he had dysentery," she exclaimed.

"No? I told Holm about it. I said then I didn't think his heart would stand climbing."

"Bert didn't tell me," she said. "I wish I had known."

"He said Coombes didn't need to go any higher than he wanted to," Elmer Baum replied. "And in fairness to Bert I must say Coombes put up a stiff fight to come. He worships Bert. Curious, but I believe that's what's taken the fight out of him, Bert's going on without him. Too bad, besides, that Bert forgot to come in and tell him good-by. Coombes had been counting on it."

She did not answer, suddenly too angry with Bert to speak.

They were at Coombes's tent now and she went in quietly. He lay in his sleeping bag, his face blue and pinched. A common little face, it looked now, though when he was himself it had a certain pleasantness of expression that made one forget small features and a dingy skin. Now he looked a little clerk who should have stayed behind his city counter. Kit knelt beside him.

"Mr. Coombes?" she said softly. A torchlight lit the tent. He opened his eyes slowly—"Hello, Mrs. Holm," he said.

"I ought to have come in before," she said quietly. "But I've been lazy and sleeping. Bert left a message for you—he heard you were asleep when he went and he didn't want to wake you."

"I wasn't—asleep," Coombes muttered with a tongue too thick. "I was waiting; maybe my eyes shut."

"Oh, I'm so sorry," she said. "He wanted to see you. He wanted you to wish him luck. He said, "Tell Coombes I'm taking him with me in my thoughts.'"

"I thought—he must have said—something," Coombes said faintly. "I thought it wasn't like him just to—go off like that."

"No, indeed," she said clearly. She did not look at Elmer Baum.

"I'm cold," Coombes whispered.

"I'm just giving you something to warm you up," Baum said. He pushed up Coombes's sleeve a little way and nodded and she took the wrist between her fingers. It was piteously thin. She could feel the pulse fluttering faintly just beneath the skin's surface.

"Tell me if it changes," Baum said softly. He was injecting very slowly. Coombes's eyes were closing again and they could not hear him breathe. She clasped the wrist a little more tightly, counting its irregularity. Then in a moment it steadied.

"Stronger," she whispered.

It settled into something like a beat.

"More regular," she whispered.

The doctor pulled down the sleeve and took the wrist from

her and crouched down to hold it himself. Coombes had slipped into sleep. They could hear him breathing now, deepening breaths as though he had not for a long time really had breath.

"I'm sending him down tomorrow if he can be moved," Elmer Baum said in a low voice, and went on, "It's a strange thing, this attack. He began to feel worse as soon as Bert went this morning. I thought it was imagination from his disappointment. We kidded him and he shut up. Then an hour ago he seemed just to collapse. He'd been trying to hold up all day, evidently. I blame myself. He's got to get to a lower altitude."

"I'll stay with him tonight," she said.

"No need," he replied. "I shan't leave. I'll call you. You'd better get something to eat and crawl into your bag and stay warm. He'll sleep now."

So, unwillingly, she rose to return to her tent. When she stepped outdoors the moon was shining. By some chance she had not seen the moon since they had left India. Night after night there had been mists or the wind had been too bitter to encounter for any cause. But tonight there was still no wind. The clouds were suspended half way to the valleys, and their peaks of mountains rose in their unearthly white around her. They stood as gods might stand, in immense silent watchfulness, to gaze upon a human they had never seen before. For a moment she was frightened into a loneliness that had no human quality, she was a being in a universe not hers. It belonged to those huge watchful gods. Against Pangbat Bert contended—she could not at this moment imagine why—and it was as fantastic as a crazy dream that she should have followed Bert here.

She heard footsteps on the snow. Someone passed her. It was a porter, a young Tibetan whom she remembered because he wore gold earrings and was always laughing, but he was not laughing now. She watched him as he went to the slippery edge of the plateau. Then he turned his face toward Pangbat, and opening his rough fur coat, he bared his breast and beat it with

296

his fists, he raised his hands above his head, and then stooping, knocked his head upon the ice upon which he stood. Then out of his bosom he took three sticks of incense and lighting them he set them in the snow. He was chanting something under his breath, but she did not quite hear it. She listened and caught Bert's name twisted and Tibetan upon a Tibetan's tongue— "Bertu Hollem—Bertu Hollem—" He was praying to the mountain god for Bert.

She went on, feeling somehow conscience-stricken. She had not prayed for Bert. But then, she had no gods. And if she had, perhaps she would not pray for Bert, at least not until she had first prayed for poor Harden Coombes, who needed it the more . . .

It must have been a little after midnight that she felt a light upon her face and woke and saw Elmer Baum flashing his light at her through the flaps of her tent.

"Yes?" she called. He put in his head.

"It's no use calling you," he said gravely, "but I thought I ought. Poor Coombes has died." She sat up and opened the fastening of her bag so she could breathe more easily. "He was sleeping," Baum went on. "I'd been watching him and I thought he was all right when I left him for one moment to fetch something from my own tent. When I came back he had struggled half out of his bag and then—died."

"It's horrible," she said, "that none of us knew how ill he was."

"I don't believe he was so ill," Baum insisted. "I didn't expect this myself. Under ordinary circumstances he would have been all right. It's just that he let his expectations mount up until his disappointment took him off. Sounds crazy unless you're a doctor. But the truth is a man can die almost any time just by feeling he wants to stop living. It takes longer, of course, when the heart holds out; Coombes's didn't. It was ready to give up at this altitude, when the will did."

She did not answer. Of course Bert was not responsible. He had made no promises nor pretense. He had been simply himself. It was natural that this morning he should have thought only of himself and that when the mountain was to be conquered, he had no though for a little clerk from a store that sold him his equipment.

"I don't suppose there is anything to do," she said.

"Nothing," the doctor replied gently. "There was a weakness in his constitution. He tried to do more than he could. He'd probably have lived his life out if he'd stayed at his level. Go back to sleep. I'll see to things until morning."

He closed the flap securely and she lay down again. It was not Bert's fault that a little clerk had followed him too far to live or that Coombes had been too small for his own dreams, and so had died.

But she could not sleep that night or the next, and the day between was restless. By his death Coombes had made himself an individual, someone separate from the group she thought of as Bert's men, who thought of her as something belonging to Bert. Even John Baker since his quarrel with Bert had withdrawn from her because she was part of Bert. They gave her plenty of deference, instant aid if she so much as moved, but she was no more real to them than they were to her. Gail, of course, would have made herself real to them. She would have seen to it by a score of little tricks she had that each man would have felt he had a secret understanding of her, peculiar only to him, as yet innocent, always innocent but always with the tantalizing possibility that innocence might be suddenly swept away. Gail as Bert's wife would have made them all feel that in her loyalty to Bert there was something heroic. She would at once have destroyed the expedition for Bert and held it together for herself. After it had scattered the men would never forget her, and when they met again they would say privately to one another, "The fact of the matter is—between ourselves, of course——"

Kit laughed a little at her imagining of Gail. Then she remembered that Coombes was dead and was ashamed of herself. Well, Gail was Gail and she would never have been perched on this ice slab. She would have come with Bert comfortably and with plenty of publicity, so far as Darjeeling, and then in a superb climate, escorted by English officers on leave, she would have made her gay pretenses of waiting and anxiety and Bert climbing Pangbat would somehow have added only to her own glory.

But Kit herself had come for no glory of her own or indeed of Bert's. She had come because she wanted to see Bert upon the mountains. She must find some strength in him for herself if she were to go on with him. She could not despise him and stay with him. She had come near to despising him in her father's house, and in his own father's house. There had been no heroic necessities in ordinary life and he was not heroic, however people like Harden Coombes had adored his heroism. But Pangbat was full of heroic necessity, cruel with ice and wind and precipice. Bert had to measure himself against the tremendous repellent cruelty of the mountain. If he could endure that measure, she would never forget.

She lay listening in the second dawn. Outside her tent she heard the wind beginning again in deep distant roars out of the valleys. She could hear it begin, created at the point where the heat of Nepal rose and struck the cold that Pangbat poured down and the wind born of that eternal conflict rushed upward with a snarl and the guy ropes whistled. She curled down into her bag and braced herself against a rock that had been put to correct the slope of the tent site. This wind would go rushing up the mountainside to the col where Bert had planned to spend the second night. It was cold here, but by the time it had swept over the glacier to that point, it would be a thrust of ice. Surely it was a sort of heroism that led a man up Pangbat! Poor Coombes, who had come for Bert, was no hero for coming, nor John Baker, who had come for his own reasons, nor any of them, perhaps, who came because Bert came. But Bert came of his own compulsion toward a mountain top. "When I set my feet upon the top of a mountain, I know I've got it down," he had told her, "and then I feel like a king."

To feel like a king! Men pursued women and overcame them for that kingly triumph. Men drank themselves toward death for the moment when before insensibility darkened their world there was the moment of triumph, when they felt as strong as kings. Men trod upon their fellow beings and crushed them and trampled upon them for the moment that they could feel like kings.

She lay, her whole being for the instant sharp with lucidity and understanding of Bert. The scanty air drained her of physical feeling. She was all brain, thinking, perceiving from this height and in this darkness what she had not perceived before. She had learned very well now how to breathe in this air, not deeply and slowly, but with quick shallow breaths that fed her brain but not her body. She did not move her body unless it was necessary, because there was not enough air for body and brain, and she chose brain. She felt half hallucinated, perched so high above ordinary people in this air too thin for them.

"A little lower than the angels," she thought.

The whole world lay in the valleys about Pangbat, millions of people waiting to worship. For them, though he did not know it, Bert forced his way upward step by step. She did not doubt that he would reach the crest alone. One by one he would leave the others behind. He had not told her so, but Rexall had, ten minutes after Bert had gone.

"Bert's smart," Rexall said yesterday, "he ain't going to have any competition when he gets to the top. He'll fix it," he replied. She had been so repelled at the sight of Rexall's blue, half-frozen, mean little face that she did not answer.

But now she saw that it was necessary that Bert reach the top alone, necessary for him, but more necessary for those who waited to worship. Moses had gone up Nebo alone. But Moses had stayed too long talking to God and the people had grown tired of waiting, and having to worship something they had made a golden calf, which had served. Bert would not linger. It would not occur to him to look about for a god on Pangbat or anywhere. He would struggle to the uppermost crag, stand upon it for his own moment of kingship, and then come down to make his claim.

She fell into a chilly sleep where the gusts of howling wind were transformed into the rise and fall of human voices and the floor of clouds upon which they had gazed day after day, into thousands of white upturned faces. Far above them all, above her watching self, suspended somewhere in vague space, she dreamed she saw Bert, indistinct in distance, but resplendent, a crown of gold upon his head.

The photographs were not satisfactory. Jimmie Frisk, spending hours in his tent developing them, was haggard with worry and disgust, and did not appear except at meals. Then he fretted, "This damned wind—blows the snow into everything like dust, and my solutions freeze solid before I can get them mixed."

For two days he could not understand the greatest difficulty he had and at twilight of the third day he called Kit into his tent to show her his pictures. They were all blurred. She saw herself kissing Bert good-by in a mist of blurred edges, and Pangbat seemed to dance.

"Just the ones I wanted to have right, too," Frisk complained. "I can't think what I've done wrong. Machine's in perfect order." He turned the crank of his motion picture camera as he spoke, and in the semi-darkness they saw sparks fly from it.

"What the deuce!" Frisk cried. He turned it again with a flash of tiny sparks.

"Like my hair," Kit said, "and like the silk and down lining to my sleeping bag. It's the electricity."

"You're right!" Frisk said. "I never thought of it. That's what makes the blur. The air's too dry and cold."

He sat down and looked up at her helplessly, his cold cracked acid-stained hands upon his furred knees. "I don't mind telling you, it was the mountain I really came for, Mrs. Holm. I thought I'd get a mountain in pictures the way nobody ever had seen it before—stills and movies." He whistled sadly under his breath, his eyes on Pangbat and then he stood at attention and saluted Pangbat smartly.

"Looks like Pangbat gets us all where we feel it most! Killed Coombes off so he couldn't climb at all, and it sure has got me. I surrender!" he said, shrugged his shoulders and began putting his stuff away. "No use," he said. "I'll have to wait until Bert comes back."

In his tent Harden Coombes waited, too, his sleeping bag his coffin. Elmer Baum had fastened the hood over his face and the snow blew in and packed about him in a close protecting shroud. They thought of him without missing him. Alive he had been a little man whom somehow they did not notice. Dead they felt death with him, but not the absence of Coombes alive.

Kit waiting through the days and nights thought of John Baker below the clouds, wandering happily in search of flowers. How wise a man to set his heart on what grew below the line of the snow and make Pangbat's floor his sky!

The mountain covered itself with fresh snow. By the fourth morning, the day on which Bert should return if all his plans went well, they could not see a hundred feet beyond the camp. Behind the curtain of the blizzard the struggle between man and mountain went on. Kit, looking out from her tent between the flaps, talked with Rexall and Frisk as they stood before her, clouded with snow. Rescue was out of the question from here. Besides, Bert had planned that the men he took with him would proceed two by two, he and Brugh always ahead, and Brewer and Blastel, Calloway and Mayhew alternating in their advance

302

behind them, so that there would always be two who were fresh enough for a rescue if it were needed, and he had left his command that none at the base camp were to imagine themselves able to climb Pangbat for any reason.

"What are we to do if you don't come back in four days, Bert?" Kit had asked.

"I'm taking food enough for eight days. Rexie has food here for twenty. Wait fifteen, and then go home." His voice was careless and she looked to see if it were not bravado. He was at that moment rubbing oil into a leather boot. "I'll be back, though, sure," he added without looking up.

She had believed this easily enough. That day Pangbat had looked as gentle as a white sheep in the sunshine.

Now the frozen mists curled in spindrift around her. The young Tibetan came out of the cook tent and spat and looked upwards, scowling. He shook his head and spoke to Frisk and went in again. Frisk had learned a little more than the others of the border dialect which was the language of the porters.

"He says Pangbat wants to kill," Frisk translated. "He says Pangbat will never allow anyone to reach the top without a death to pay for it."

"Poor Coombes is dead already," Kit said. "That's enough, I think."

Frisk did not answer. "Guess I'll get back to my stuff if there's nothing to do," he said. "I can write a swell piece about what it's like to sit halfway up Pangbat, at ten below, waiting for the return of the hero."

He went into his tent and Kit stood a moment longer with Rexall. She disliked him as much as ever and yet when they talked of Bert she trusted him altogether.

"Are you afraid?" she asked quietly.

He spat a black blob upon the snow. Somehow he managed even here to have tobacco to chew.

"I ain't goin' to worry yet awhile," he answered. "Fellow like

Bert's awful hard to kill. He carries his luck with him." He hesitated and then went on, his little shrewd face in a knot. "Bert's got no imagination, ma'am. That's a great thing in a man. He don't get into danger because he don't see it, and he don't see it because he can't imagine it. Now I'm all imagination, myself. That's why I said to Bert, 'I'll go this fur and no further.' Why, I lie here in the night sweatin' drops of ice thinking about avalanches and crevasses and slippin' down this danged mountain in front of the wind. I'll never get anywhere because of my imagination. Bert don't see nothin' except what he's agoin' to do. So he goes on to do it and is took by surprise if somethin' happens to him." He laughed without opening his mouth. "Once when Bert took a dare and climbed the church steeple he slipped and fell into the belfry. Wasn't hurt, but mad as hell because he hadn't thought of slippin', even. He'll go climbin' on to the top of Pangbat like it was the house roof, not seein' what could happen to him. That kind's always safe, I say."

He spat three times in diminishing amounts and went into his tent.

By noon the wind had died again and the mists did not move. Perhaps cloud was better than a clear sky, because with sunshine the wind mounted. For herself she was grateful for cloud. It shut out the world around them which was growing strangely oppressive. She had come to realize in the few days upon this sloping plateau hung among the tops of lesser Himalayan peaks, that the spirit cannot live so high. For the first day she had been excited by the magnificence. Thirteen major peaks rose about them and a score of lesser ones. At this distance, green valleys were like pools of jade sunk in the crystal white upper landscape. And then she had felt herself beginning to grow quiet before the magnificence. She had sat until she could no longer bear the cold, gazing out over the distance of earth and sky, until she felt dulled and silent before it. Now she could understand the stupid look of people who lived among mountains. Anywhere in the world they looked the same. The porters they had taken from the last Tibetan village had the same eyes she had seen among dwellers in the Alps. Men were not made for mountains.

She was grateful, then, that this morning the misty snow made a wall, so that she could not see the edge of the plateau and so that the sky had come down to her own level. She had not been able to sleep well. Now suddenly she felt she could sleep and she was eager for it. Time went of itself when one slept. Perhaps they were all sleeping. There was no sound of the typewriter from Frisk's tent, nor any smoke rising from the funnel that was the chimney for the portable oil stove in the kitchen tent. The little collection of tents was as still, enveloped in mist, as though nothing living were there. She crept into her own tent and into her sleeping bag and drew it warmly about her. The cloud-wrapped, snow-filled silence, now that the wind was gone, was the sweetest she had ever known.

. . . Upon the cloud under which the base camp slept, Bert looked down as on a floor. His luck held. Just when he was thinking he had to take his choice of wind with clear sky, or snow every time the wind fell, this floor of white cloud came up around the mountain, shutting off the wind and the warmth which made it. The temperature rose nearly ten degrees that morning in the last camp where he and Brugh had spent the night before, together. It had been a bad night. He knew now why he didn't like Brugh. It wasn't only because he was an Englishman, but because he did not trust him. It occurred to him in the middle of the night that Brugh might pull the same trick on him now that he had pulled on old Fessaday, get up while he was still asleep and make the dash up the last thousand feet alone. The peak was definitely between the two of them now. Blastel and Brewer had given up at the end of the second day. The wind had sent the thermometer down until Brewer had to be slapped to keep him awake. Finally Blastel had said he'd take him back to the camp they had made the night before. And before night of the next day Calloway had begun to see double for some reason or other, and Mayhew complained of snow blindness. He'd told them to stay at the camp yesterday morning and left them most of the oxygen. Mayhew saw more clearly after a little oxygen. But there was no use dragging him on. Fessaday used to say every man had his own height, and you couldn't make him go higher and have him any use.

What his own height was he did not know. Certainly it was higher than Therat. Up there he had felt the air thin enough to make him careful about breathing, but he didn't feel stupid with it. He could still feel that last great lift when he stepped to the topmost rock. It was like nothing on earth. He panted to feel it again. Every step upward brought him nearer to it.

But Brugh was as good at climbing as he was. Brugh showed no sign of being tired. He could bear the cold as no one he had ever seen could bear it; last night before they turned in they went outside their tent for a moment, and Brugh had stood looking at the stars as though he were at home. The air was solid ice. When you breathed it you felt like you were drawing chunks of it into your lungs and it cut. But Brugh stood as though he were made of ice and did not mind breathing it.

"One does not become acquainted with the heavenly bodies," he said, "until one climbs mountains." Brugh could not open his mouth without long words coming out of it. "I used to think I was familiar with the stars," he said. "Now I know I was merely presumptuous."

He did not know what to answer Brugh and so he said nothing. He was always safe if he said nothing.

The stars were hanging there big as pumpkins around them and near enough to pick. Kit would like them. He looked in the direction of the base camp but the edge of a col hid the right saddle of the mountain. He'd like her to know he was all right. But then he had told her he would be. It was swell of her to come along so far. But why shouldn't she when she was his wife? And when he came down tomorrow she could be proud of him all over again.

"Difficult to imagine human beings down there," Brugh was saying. "Difficult to believe in all that little life stirring about as it does, generation after generation, never getting out of its own mud!"

Brugh was putting on airs again, Bert thought. People didn't talk like that unless they were putting on airs.

"Guess I'll turn in," he said. No use standing out in such cold just to hear Brugh talk!

He went inside and then wondered if Brugh had gone crazy. He heard him out there still talking—no, singing, in a big clear voice, loud enough to start an avalanche. The words were some foreign language. He could hear them coming back in echoes.

"Here you!" he shouted. "I don't know about so much noise up here. We don't know the lay of things—might start vibrations or something and peel down an avalanche!"

Brugh shut up instantly. "Right," he said and came into the tent.

They did not speak again. But it had been queer enough to make him feel Brugh was a little off and could do a thing like getting up and going on by himself. It was a bad night anyway, and the wind forced snow into every crack of the tent. Then suddenly it dropped. When Bert woke in the morning the floor of cloud was not five hundred feet below them and there was no wind.

Brugh was still asleep. Bert looked down into that long thin English face and was suddenly burning with temptation. Suppose he just slipped out and went on?

The moment he thought of it he knew he had to do it. Now that he looked at him, it seemed to him he had never liked Brugh. Why should Brugh be the one to get to the top with him?

Brugh did not move. His pale long face looked frozen, but it was not. He was breathing evenly in slow breaths. When he got up, Bert thought scornfully, he would have to have tea to drink before he could start, even though they couldn't get water to boil up here, and tea was nothing but brown tepid water. That one delay was reason enough why he should go on.

It took only a minute to make up his mind and get things together and he knew how to be perfectly quiet when he wanted to be. So now, slipping into his extra garments, picking up his crampons to put on outside, stuffing his pockets with food, he was outside the tent in ten minutes wrapped in his fur parka, with three sweaters underneath and three pairs of trousers, and under his hood two caps, ready to begin the long steady climb which Pangbat spread before him. What he was doing now that he had begun it seemed the only thing he could do, and he remembered, besides, that he and Brugh had already half-decided yesterday that this last day they would climb independently and without a rope to tie them together. He chuckled. He was only being a little more independent. . . .

There had been a light snowfall during the night. That must have been after the wind died. Upon the old ice of now more sharply increasing slopes, the new snow was three inches deep, and right for crampons to stick into and hold. Luck was still following him. By a miracle the wind had not begun again and yet the sky was clear. After noon the sky would cloud, and by mid-afternoon there might be snow. But he would be at the top by noon, if his luck held. . . .

He could see nothing of Brugh coming after him. For a long time the tent had been visible, a dark inverted cone upon the snow. Then he had lost it behind a bergschrund and going between that and the mountain he saw that the easiest way was not up the face he had been climbing, but around its base and up the irregularities of the side at right angles with it. The smooth face, he now saw was deceptive. It ended in that sharp cornice at the top which might prove impossible for him just when he needed his utmost strength. Or, if the day went on as quietly as it now was under the sun, the weight of the cornice, pressing upon the sheet of snow upon the blue ice beneath, might cause the sheet to peel off the ice into an avalanche. It was better to get to rough ground, even if it meant slower going. It occurred to him that yesterday he and Brugh, planning this last dash for the top, had decided that the smooth north face which he was now climbing was the best way up and that now he had no way to tell Brugh that he had changed his mind. But Brugh was an older climber and he would see for himself the threat of the cornice.

"At least he ought to see it, and it's not my fault if he don't," he told himself.

By mid-morning he was beginning to feel dull with the altitude. He had heard men talk about that dullness, though he had never had it before. But he was already higher than he had ever been in his life. Dull and heavy-footed, his breath difficult to draw, and the weight of his ice ax trebling, he stopped a moment to take in oxygen, and for the first time it occurred to him that Brugh had no oxygen! He had not thought of that when he lifted the tank this morning. He thought about it now for an instant and then was comforted. Brugh wouldn't get near the top, so why would he need oxygen? He felt better and went steadily upward.

He had forgotten Brugh by eleven o'clock. He had forgotten everything except his wonderful luck in the weather and this push within him to go on up and up. Imperceptibly as a poison gas the dullness grew upon him, and oxygen, though it relieved his lungs, did not clear his mind. He could not remember things. He tried to remember Kit's face and could not see her. He entirely forgot Brugh, and he tried for a long time to remember why he was here. And all the time he worried himself over these things, he kept on climbing, step by step. Just before noon he was delayed by a steep face of blue ice from which the snow had slipped into a heap at its bottom. He had to cut steps in the ice, hard as rock with depth and age. His arms seemed anchored to his thighs when he lifted them, and he had to cling to the wall gasping between every step. Still he could think, "That snow—soft to fall on—if I fall—luck!"

But he did not fall. He crawled over the edge of the highest cliff and lay panting for a few moments, remembering always to breathe through his mouth. Then he looked ahead and his heart gave a thick jump. Pangbat had given up. From where he lay the rise to the flattened knob of the crest was as gentle as a sloping meadow. He had only to gather himself together, leave his ice ax, because it was so heavy, leave his camera—the oxygen tank—leave everything, and walk across that hundred feet or so, to the top. He would feel no worse than he felt now. The crest was scarcely higher.

He rose slowly and plodded forward, step by step. Weights were upon his feet and against his knees and his blood had stopped running, though he was not cold, but the engine in him drove him on. He went to the end of the rise, stepped up twice, and Pangbat was beneath him.

He stood, dizzy and panting, and then his head began to clear. She was under his feet, this mountain! He was on her where nobody had ever been. He was doing something nobody had done before—maybe would never do again, because nobody might have just his luck again of sun and no wind. It was not all luck, though. It was partly him, a big part of it him and his push that always made him want to get to the top. He was at the top and Pangbat was his mountain. He felt like a king.

He stood looking around. Then he saw the cornice of snow was in his way. It was like a frozen wave springing up against the top of the mountain and curling away again and it kept him from being able to see everything. It was only a small cornice of snow. If he gave it a push it might crash down and let him see over the edge of the top. He wanted to see the whole world lying beneath him.

He struggled to it and looked down and saw a fissure a foot wide where the cornice clung to the ice crag on which he stood. If he gave the stiffly frozen snow even a touch, it might drop and he could see over. He put out his hand against the wall of snow which was just higher than his eyes. It was safe enough. There was plenty of room where he stood, and from it the sides of Pangbat's crest sloped gently to the supporting cliffs. He pushed, and heard a creak of parting snow surfaces and a slight crash. The top of the cornice had fallen and was beginning to slide downward. He could see over now. The noonday sun was shining upon the vast spreading snowy skirts of Pangbat.

And then, upon that whiteness he saw, a hundred feet, two hundred feet, beneath him a slowly moving speck of black. Brugh! It must be Brugh! He had forgotten Brugh.

"Brugh!" he yelled. "Brugh! Look out there!" The thickness of his head cleared completely. He was as much himself as he would have been at sea level.

"Look out!" he screamed.

For, in an instant so short he could not grasp it, the whole cornice began slowly to peel itself from the rocklike ice beneath it. The thing he had dreaded for himself was about to happen to Brugh. He could not stop it. He saw the harmless edge of the wave pull after it the whole frozen wall, and that weight of snow crashed downward and suddenly it seemed to him the whole side of Pangbat began to move in deep wrinkles and then in waves and then in torrents.

He kept on looking, not able to imagine what it would do when it struck Brugh. It struck him. He saw the crinkled, slipping edge of the moving mass catch him at the knees. He saw Brugh fling up his hands, and his ice ax flew away and then the roaring grinding mass of snow overwhelmed him in a tide and swept downward, on and on, to be caught and held at last by the bergschrund they had rounded last night. The small valley where their tent had stood filled like a bowl, and snow brimmed to the top and frothed over it in a coomb of white.

He stood motionless and dazed, and, as though that downward rush had released some demon locked in Pangbat, he heard the familiar growl of a rising wind. If he reached the safety of the second camp before night fell, he must hold his luck very fast indeed. . . .

In the long twilight of the mountaintops Calloway was cooking a soupy stew over a small portable oil stove. He and Mayhew had followed exactly the instructions which had brought them to this point, their only change being that they had had to come without the two Sherpa porters who had started with them. In the middle of the morning one of them had fallen into a hidden crevasse. His load saved him. He hung, caught by its breadth, in the narrowing fissure of the chasm below him and waited without moving through the hour and a half that it took the others to devise a means of lifting him out. Safe upon his feet, his calm cracked and he wept and shivered and could not be prevailed upon to go higher. There was nothing to do but to send him back with the other Sherpa, giving them to take back to the first camp what Calloway and Mayhew could not carry.

All day as Calloway and Mayhew traveled over the path that Bert Holm and Brugh had traveled the day before they examined the higher slopes with their glasses. They saw at two different times the small ascending dark spots. The first they lost. And then inexplicably, a little after noon, they lost the second one. They discussed this scantily, sparing breath.

"Fools to separate," Calloway said.

"Men get ornery at this altitude," Mayhew agreed.

This Calloway did not answer. His throat was aching, and he longed to breathe through his nostrils, but if he did, the pain in his head became intense. He plodded on, thankful for steps in a face of ice which yesterday Brugh's ax must have cut. He recognized the Englishman's finished technique, trained in mountain-craft. Bert could beat him in endurance and in individual dash, but they all liked Brugh, though they made fun of his differences, such as wanting tea instead of coffee and needing always a fork and knife for his food.

They reached the spot they found marked for them and set up their small portable tent, and prepared, after they had rested, to heat the canned combination of soup and stew. It was not too windy, for the tent was in the shelter of a hummock of ice, and once they stopped climbing they could breathe. Mayhew watched Calloway's lean figure and wondered at its resilience. Seemingly fragile, always acid, he was somehow unbeatable. Before Mayhew could bring himself to move, Calloway had the stove going and was working at the tin can. Mayhew stirred himself finally out of shame, though he was still weary with exhaustion. He went outside to see if by the waning light there were any sign of Bert and Brugh. He stood a moment, searching through glasses the mountainside. The mountain had never been more beautiful. The afterglow of the setting sun above the clouds poured a soft streaming light upon the snow. For an instant Pangbat looked warm. His eyes moved to the crest, for this last moment of the day clear against the sky. Its shape was different! Through the glasses he could see that the ruff of snow about the final crag was gone. The top looked squared.

"Hey, Calloway!" he called. Calloway came out and he handed him the glasses. "Just take a look at the top."

"Looks like there might have been an avalanche," Calloway said gravely. They looked at one another. "Anyway we can't go on tonight," Mayhew said.

"Nope," Calloway agreed.

They waited, hesitating each in his own sober mind. Could they or could they not go on? They could not until dawn.

Calloway went back into the tent to the stew and Mayhew followed. Among the mountaintops this small insecure spot, this lit-

313

tle pot of food, seemed their one safety. They tried, each in his own silence, not to think of this.

"Flashlights working?" Calloway inquired.

"I'll see," Mayhew replied.

It was at this moment when light was ebbing out of the sky like a swiftly receding tide, that they heard Bert's shout. When they went out he was picking himself up out of the snow. "Here I am," he said; then he snarled. "What you leave a big hunk of ice there for?"

"Hello, Bert," Calloway said gently. He knew how Bert felt, so tired he could only quarrel with everything.

"We were just fixing to come out and find you," Mayhew said.

"I got to the top," Bert panted. "I made it—by myself."

"Great," Calloway said.

"Swell!" Mayhew cried.

They took Bert's elbows and guided him into the tent. Calloway poured out a tin cup of tepid stew for him. Then he poured out two more cups for himself and Mayhew. They ate, waiting for the moment when Bert lifted his head. It came, and Bert drew a gust of breath.

"That's good," he said.

"Where's Brugh?" Calloway asked instantly.

"Dead," Bert said simply. And then he told them what had happened. "I went ahead. Brugh didn't pull with me yesterday anyway and so we agreed to go our own ways today. I kept ahead and reached the top about noon. I didn't go up this slope. When I got half to the top, I decided to go around half way to the other side, where it wasn't so icy smooth. But Brugh came along the slope. Well, I was standin' there——"

Bert stopped and gulped.

. . . It wasn't going to look good, he suddenly realized for the first time. It hadn't come to him before, but it certainly wasn't going to look good, though he had not seen Brugh or thought of

314

Brugh even, and nothing was his fault. It wasn't even his fault that he had taken the oxygen, because he hadn't thought about that until he was too far to go back. But he was glad he'd left the tank far up there where no one would ever find it. He hadn't felt able to think of anything up there, that was the truth. And anyway the cornice would have fallen maybe anyway. There had been an awful big crack.

. . . He chewed a mouthful slowly, swallowed it and went on. "It was terrible, boys," he said. He looked from one face to the other. "But that cornice just peeled away while I was lookin' at it. A little piece fell. Well, I didn't think nothing of that, except that the snow began to pucker up and start down. Then I saw a black speck way down that I knew must be Brugh. I yelled and hollered, but he didn't hear me. And I couldn't do a thing but stand and watch that snow gather up and rush down and cover him. I came down as fast as I could but what could I do? The snow had filled in the valley where our tent was last night. I couldn't find a trace of him——"

They had to believe him, for what he said was all true. They did believe him, he saw with relief. Their grave faces gazed back at him.

"Poor Brugh," Mayhew said. He put down his cup. He could not eat any more. "Queer," Calloway said. "The porters told Brugh that somebody would have to die if you got to the top, Bert. They said Pangbat would kill somebody for it." His narrow melancholy face looked like a withered yellow pumpkin.

"That's just their notion," Bert said quickly. "It hadn't anything to do with me."

"Of course not. I don't mean that," Calloway said.

They made ready to climb into their sleeping bags, Calloway and Mayhew together.

"We ought to go tomorrow and dig around some, oughtn't we?" Mayhew suggested. "Blastel and Brewer will catch up to

315

us and if they have rations we could all go on. Somebody ought to go back to base, though, and tell 'em."

"I'll go back," Bert said. It was no use their looking for Brugh, he knew. But let them if they wanted to.

They lay silent, body against body in the small tent. It was impossible to sleep. The wind rose suddenly to ferocious speed, and tore at the tiny cover under which they lay. They had to get up a dozen times to tighten guy ropes and hunt for stones to pile against the stakes. The sky was utterly clear. The stars upon which Brugh had gazed the night before hung in the sky as lively and as intense as they had been when he looked at them, but he lay at the bottom of the snows hurled at him from Pangbat's crest.

"I'm a fool for luck," Bert said suddenly. "It might have been me, instead of Brugh." He waited for an answer from the two men. But they made none.

At the base camp Frisk had his camera focused upon Bert as he came glissading down the final slope. Brugh had taught him how to glissade. He ended up with a flourish right before the camera. "Here I am. I got to the top!" he yelled.

"Good!" Kit cried. And then with a quick glance, "Why, where is everybody? Did you come down alone?"

He had then to tell it all over again. He told it very well, simply and clearly, exactly as he had told it before. Then he added, "There's no hope, I know, but I sent them up, just to look. They had plenty of rations. I saw to that. And they were pretty fresh."

Kit was the first to speak. She spoke quickly, as though she wanted to say it first. She did indeed. It must be she, she decided instantly, who put into words what Jimmie Frisk and Elmer Baum were thinking, what even Rexall might be thinking behind his wizened chewing mask of a face.

"Why didn't you go with them, Bert?" she demanded.

He stood before them in his white parka seemingly himself.

Then before their very eyes he began to shiver and tremble and his eyes glazed. Rexall ran to him.

"Whatsa matter, Bert?" he shouted. He slipped his arm around Bert's waist and Bert collapsed on him suddenly.

"Lay me down," he gasped. "I'm done for——"

Kit, working over him with hot-water bottles and pouring hot broth and whisky down his throat, felt his body strong beneath her hands. She could not quite understand his collapse. There was frostbite on his hands and cheeks, and one of his feet was frozen, Baum told her, and would take attention. Of course there had been a great strain on his heart, but Baum, examining him minutely, could find no damage and no excuse indeed for the extreme weakness in which Bert lay for twenty-four hours.

At the end of that time Calloway and Mayhew, Brewer and Blastel came back with the Sherpas. No sign of Brugh had been found, they reported. The avalanche had filled the valley full and there was nothing to do but come down.

They heard of Coombes's death in silence, except that Calloway remarked, "I always wondered why he came."

"He hadn't much constitution, that's right," said Rexall. He had told Bert about Coombes ten minutes before and Bert had said, "No guts, that fellow."

"It don't look so good for you to criticize, Bert," he had told him.

"Poor Harden Coombes died, Bert," Kit said gently. It was the third day at the base camp, and their last day before going down the mountain and Bert was better.

"Rexie told me," Bert said. "It's a shame, I didn't think he was that bad."

"He minded your leaving him without good-by, and I told him you sent him a message before you went."

"I'm glad you did that," Bert said heartily. "I ought to have thought myself. But I had a lot on me."

He evaded her with his smile and his self-blame. She was uneasy as she had been uneasy ever since he came back. He was too conciliatory, too quick to meet her eyes with his smile. She felt a shrewd distrust of him. Bert cold and tired was normally bad-tempered. Bert ill was sure to be cross with her. She was frightened by this smooth good temper.

"I'm going to look up his family," she heard him tell Frisk an hour later. "I'm going to see that they get all they want."

Frisk was pressing Bert carefully for the story of the last climb. He was dismayed by Bert's having no photographs, because he had himself filled a small camera with films and put it in his pocket. "All you had to do was to snap the button," he told Bert scornfully.

Bert, sitting in the sunshine pouring into his tent, his lower half in his sleeping bag, looked abashed.

"I'm the dangdest fool," he agreed. "But that high altitude kind of makes you crazy, Jim. I remember putting down my ice ax just at the last, because it was heavy. And I remember looking at the camera and being kind of dazed and thinkin', 'What in hell is this I'm carryin'?' Must of left it there, too, for I didn't bring it down."

"Well, then, tell me how you felt, anyway," Jim insisted. "Think hard, Bert! You'd been climbing all morning. You were just ahead of Brugh. You wanted to get there first, all America watching you. You climb desperately up the last crag and stand on top. Beneath you are the mountains; nothing but Everest looking higher, and any other mountain like flattened lumps of dough. You are standing on Pangbat, where no human foot has ever stood." Frisk leaned over Bert, his thick little forefinger prodding before his face. "How did you feel, Bert?"

Bert's beautiful white smile lit up his being. . . .

"Like a king, Jim," he replied instantly.

318

It was this prodding forefinger of Frisk's that first pointed out to Kit, though Frisk himself did not know it, the glimmering of that in Bert which she had felt was there. Day by day she had become convinced, by an instinct she felt and could not comprehend, that Bert was hiding something in himself.

"When did you last see Brugh?" Frisk's forefinger demanded.

"I was standin' on the top," Bert said patiently, "and I saw him comin' up the slope. I yelled to him—no"—he corrected himself—"I didn't yell to him until after the cornice fell. I knew it isn't safe to yell around frozen snow. Sometimes avalanches begin that way. I saw the cornice fall, and then I saw what was happening and I yelled——"

The utmost clarity of blue in Bert's eyes did not waver but doubt shot up out of Kit's mind.

"He did shout first!" she thought. That was it, then!

She sat, in the full explosion of the thought—this was what Bert was hiding! But she could not speak to him of it, not only because there was no time in the confusion of moving camp, but also because she was not sure of the necessity of speech.

If he had shouted to Brugh, as he might naturally have done, could he be blamed? If he had forgotten to take pictures, might he not reasonably have forgotten the danger of a shout, vibrating upon frozen snow pinnacles delicately balanced? If he were dazed by cold and altitude, could he be blamed, and if not, why speak? To which her inexorable conscience, inherited entire from her father, made answer that if he had shouted, or if for any reason he had touched the frozen cornice and the snow, trembling with its own overweight, had fallen and gathering snow as it slid, had caught Brugh in an avalanche, Bert should know what he had done and tell it.

This burden grew in her like a spiritual tumor until she could not forget it day or night. It came between her and the men like an obligation unfulfilled. She imagined it known to them all, though unspoken.

She felt it between her and John Baker, waiting for them at the snowline. She went a little ahead of them, having planned it so, and found him outside his tent smoking his pipe after lunch. He rose, his plain face full of pleasure.

"You first!" he cried and in his joy put his arm about her shoulder and gave her a slight hug.

"Ronald Brugh is lost," she said immediately, and she told him in twenty words, and then about Coombes. Before she could finish, the others were there and behind them came the Sherpas carrying the blanketed figure that was Coombes.

John Baker clasped the men's hands one after the other and went and stood for a few moments beside the load the porters put down and then came back to her.

"I was growing very fond of Brugh," he said.

"We all were," she replied.

That was all, and in a little while they went on down the mountain to make camp nearer to the valley. That was all, and yet she felt the burden of Bert's silence between herself and Baker when she saw him carefully avoiding Bert. She felt it in Calloway's reticence, in Mayhew's politeness, in Blastel's curtness, and in Brewer's quiet occupation with the daily details of their continued travel. Brewer took upon himself especially and unasked the care of Coombes's body now in its Chinese coffin, sealed against decay, and heavy as a mahogany log. Brewer, understanding the necessity, had taken that frozen body and with Baum's help had embalmed it and made it ready to return to the village in Connecticut where his parents waited for their son. The coffin he had found in a Tibetan village. It had belonged once to a Chinese mandarin traveling home from India who had been lost in the spring flood of a swift Himalayan river, and the coffin he had as part of his necessary baggage had floated down the stream and been salvaged and sold.

Only Jack Rexall, it seemed to Kit, behaved toward her exactly as he always had, as though knowing Bert from childhood, he was surprised by nothing. And then she wondered if it was only the increasing discomfort of the downward journey that made them all different again. The expedition was pulling apart. The end was near and each man was thinking of himself and of what he would do next. At Bombay the expedition would officially end. Bert had decided to avoid Calcutta. In Bombay was waiting the welcome of the America-in-India Club for the first American to lead a successful expedition to Pangbat. Looking ahead to this she saw a moment inevitable as a day of judgment. It was when reporters, pencils poised, would ask, "Tell us about Ronald Brugh's death, please, Mr. Holm."

And she would have to listen to Bert telling how Ronald Brugh died, and she would have to see John Baker's small piercing dark eyes, fixed upon Bert as he spoke, doubting, weighing, envisaging shrewdly every step of that perilous hour of Bert's triumph.

She made up her mind that before that moment she would have made Bert tell her the truth.

In the deep night that surrounds a little hotel outside a town on the inner edge of India truth trembles in the air. Life is close. The villages are near, those collections of huts of clay scraped from the soil. There is no pretense of anything in those huts, little furniture, no luxury, nothing to keep man from his primary life of food and sleep and work and these are truth. In the hotel built by white men for white men, Kit and Bert were alone. One by one the men had scattered. Blastel and Brewer had gone north through Tibet; Calloway and Mayhew to Calcutta to take sail for China. Frisk had hurried ahead to Bombay to mail his pictures. And Rexall was behind them, ending the expedition, dismissing porters, and shipping boxes to Calcutta, thence to go by freight train and ship. He had sent the Indian cook with them. The man served them with an intense devoted silence, hanging over them as they ate, watching them like an anxious dog if they moved. But at night he, too, was gone to some unknown spot of his own choosing, and then they were left alone.

In one of these nights she had arranged with herself that she would say out of the quivering darkness, "Bert, tell me exactly how it happened." And then she would compel him here in India, where they were completely unknown and alone, and she would know the real material of his being as she had not yet been able to discover it. Soon he would be covered by the glorification that many people would wrap about him and perhaps never again would he be quite without that golden mantle. But here there was no one to care who he was or what he had done. Whatever waited for him beyond, here he was only a common white man to be looked at with averted eyes. They were walled into the immense isolation of the white among black and she felt she had never been alone with Bert until now.

And thus alone with him she felt the moment she had imagined approaching her in reality. How she knew it when it came she could not say, but expecting it, questioning its presence, it came upon her one sleepless night.

"Why not now?" she thought. "Why isn't this it? I shall never be more alone with him than I am now."

And as though this were a presage, her mind told her coldly, "If you think this is the moment, it is the moment."

And immediately she said aloud in the darkness, "Bert, did you push the cornice of snow?"

He had been flinging himself about on the other side of the wide bed under the mosquito net, groaning because it was so hot. For the same reason she on her side had lain motionless. He stopped. For a moment she heard nothing except in the black stillness the little frequent rush and plop of a lizard sliding off the wall to the floor.

"What do you mean, did I push the cornice?" he evaded.

She repeated her question patiently. "Did you, when you were standing on the crest, shout or move or do anything to start the avalanche—that killed Brugh?"

They were completely alone in all the world. From the infinite distance she heard wailing music but it had nothing to do with them. Miles unknown lay between them and anything they knew. He could not escape her by any evasion.

But she had not counted on the one gate of escape over which she had no control. It was the gate into himself. He could go through this and close it against her and however she beat upon it he would not open it unless he chose. So now he did not answer.

"Tell me, Bert," she said gently.

If he blustered or protested she would know what to do. She could destroy any small pretense, but what if he were silent? His silence was impenetrable. He could build it about himself and shelter himself fathoms deep in it. He did not speak. She waited.

"You aren't asleep, I know," she said at last.

"So what?" he asked insolently, as if he had been waiting for her to speak again.

She replied, "I shall just wait, Bert."

"Wait, then," he answered. He beat his pillow and turned it over and lay down again, and drew his silence over him.

"But if you are silent," she said, "it will mean you did do it." Cruel, but she must use weapons!

"Nothing of the kind. It only means I don't choose to talk," he retorted.

"If you don't choose to talk, it will mean you don't dare to talk," she said.

"So you say," he grunted.

"So I mean," she replied.

He did not answer this. And after waiting a long time, she knew that he still would not speak. Like a perverse child he was enjoying the power over her of his refusal.

But if he could escape her thus, so could she escape him. There

323

was no compulsion upon her, she thought suddenly, to endure this. She was quite free. She had lived before he came and she could go back to herself. There was always herself. She did not need to think of Norman or of any return except to herself.

"I am very tired of your silence," she said calmly into the darkness. "You think you can refuse me by silence. But silence is positive; it means you did something you won't tell me, exactly as though you said it. And when you keep saying you won't tell me, you shut me out of yourself. And if I have no place in your real self, there is no meaning to my living with you or being in the same house with you. You are like any other ordinary person whom I don't know. And if that is so, I will leave you as I would leave anyone when there is nothing more to be said between us."

She could feel him lie still for a moment. He was digesting this and weighing its importance.

"I don't know what you're talking about," he grunted.

"Yes, you do," she said. "But I'll repeat it. If you don't answer what I have asked you, I shall leave you at Bombay and go home alone, and you shall never see me again if I can help it."

He seized her arm in the darkness. "Kit, you're crazy! You can't talk like that—you're my wife!"

"I'm not your wife if you refuse to speak to me."

"You're my wife no matter what I do."

"Oh no, I'm not, Bert," she insisted.

There was another long silence. She thought against her will of Lily.

"Damn women, anyway," Bert burst out in a loud voice. "They're all the same, nagging and nagging and butting into what's none of their business and then holding a fellow up!"

He was thinking of Lily too. She was very near to decision against him. His next word would crystallize all wavering. Repulsion, weariness, the full comprehension of his eternal childhood, were closing about her mind like a mold. Then his voice came to her full of trouble and pleading.

"What do you want me to tell you, Kit?"

Decision stayed for a moment. "Only the truth," she replied. She could wait one moment more. At the end of it his voice came again, still hesitant and humble.

"I didn't do what you seem to think I did, Kit. I swear to God—well, the truth was I forgot about Brugh. I'd left him asleep——"

"Why did you leave him?"

"Well, we'd been climbing alone the day before. I told you that. He said he could do better by himself and so could I. So I left when I wanted to. We'd mapped out the road the day before, anyway."

"But you went another way."

"He could see that when he got to it."

"Did he get to it?" she pressed.

"No." The words came out of him half angrily. "But I couldn't help it, could I?" He paused again and then rushed on.

"I couldn't see over the cornice, so I gave the top of it one little touch, that was all. I didn't mean a thing but that. Then I saw him. I yelled to him, but he didn't hear me. And that damned snow started to wrinkle like a blanket and began to go down. It was too quick for me to do anything."

This might be the truth, she thought sadly. It sounded true. Truth was nearly always like this, no more clear, after all, than anything else. He had pushed the cornice but he had not killed Brugh.

It was not in him to do the thing she had feared. It was in him simply to be like a child and when he found before his eyes a wall of snow that he wanted to see over to push that wall away. That he had killed Brugh was an accident, the accident, actually, of his own stupidity, and he was not to be blamed for stupidity any more than a child could be blamed for the lack of

325

a limb when it was born. "You didn't go down then to find out whether you could help Brugh?" she asked. He answered her eagerly, like a child wanting to be good after a discovered fault.

"Kit, honest, it wouldn't have been any use. I was half-dead myself. When you're high up as I was you can't think, you can't hardly move, you're smothered. I just had sense enough and strength enough to get myself down to the camp. And anyway one man wasn't any good. As soon as I could think, I sent all four of them back. But you know even then they couldn't find anything."

She had unwillingly to recognize this, too, as truth.

"Is that all you want to know, Kit?" he asked.

"I suppose so," she replied after a second.

"You understand how it was, don't you, Kit?" he pleaded.

"I suppose so," she said again.

Decision had retreated once more to its old lair in her being. How decide against a child, even when it was not one's own?

He laughed with relief. "Gee, Kit, it don't seem so hot as it did; I guess you raised my temperature a good deal for a minute." He rolled to her side and curled his big body about her as she lay straightly upon the matting-covered mattress. "I think I can go to sleep now," he murmured in her neck.

And like a child he was asleep almost at once. When she moved his arm away from her it was heavy with unconsciousness and with rest. But she lay enclosed by the night, facing the lair and that beast which had retreated into it. She looked at the beast steadily hour after hour, but she did not go nearer toward it nor did she encourage it to come toward her. She could decide nothing yet. Decision indeed had become infinitely more huge and more difficult. It was no longer now whether she would or would not leave Bert. It had become this: Could one, or could one not, honorably, leave a child?

The next morning was like every morning. Night never lasted

with Bert. Every day was itself, new and without memory. She could see him look at her to know that she was what he called "all right"—that is, that she had no queries in her of him. They ate breakfast in the barren little dining room. From somewhere in the village the Indian cook had found eggs and shriveled fruits, and he had coffee and bacon from his stores and he had made muffins. There was even a can of marmalade that some Englishman had left with the hotel caretaker and which he had thriftily sold again.

Bert ate enormously, refreshed with sleep, and Kit ate, half listening to his talk—plenty of talk, this morning!

"Say, Kit, what say we take a little vacation in Europe? I have a kind of hunch I'd like to see—" Beneath its surfaces her mind was working steadily upon its problem, delving for material long since stored away, dragging it up to serve this present. Innocent or guilty, what ought she to do with Bert?

All men were children, her mother said. Women had to recognize that. Fortunately, her mother went on, women were naturally maternal and could realize it, and even enjoy it. "He's just like a boy," women said as they adored and in saying it brought the men they loved down to the size they loved and understood best—the size of children!

But long ago Kit had known she was not maternal. She had neither the longing nor the desire for a child. Gail's children she liked, especially the elder boy, not because they were children but rather in spite of it. She liked them as persons, and she would like them better when they were grown than she did now. If she had children of her own it would be the same; she would like or dislike them as persons. What held her still to Norman, if she were held, was the fact that he was as adult as she was herself. His power over her, half physical as it was, was because he never approached her as a child. He did not want or seek her caresses as Bert did. The repulsion for Bert which she had frankly now to accept was never stronger than when, as he had last night, he became pleading and troubled and came to her to put his head on her breast and to curl his body against hers. There was some spiritual incest here which she loathed with her entire being. It was wicked to live with a child as with a man. If Bert, then, were a child . . . ? The beast made a lunge from its lair——

"Wait," she said to it, "I am not ready to decide."

She heard Bert still talking. "I'd kinda like to go to Italy and Germany, Kit. I don't know why. But I've got a hankering to see those two big fellows over there that are running the show. I'd like to know how they got on top the way they have."

"Dictators," she murmured.

"Yeah—how do they do it?" Bert asked with wonder. "They've got people just eating out of their hands."

"What do you care about that?" she asked.

"Nothing," he replied with a laugh. "I'd just like to know the trick, that's all."

"You don't want people eating out of your hand, do you, Bert?" she asked.

"Well, it might be fun at that," he replied.

But before she had time to think he was through and eager to be on their way.

"Come on, Kit. Let's get going. I'm getting anxious to get back to civilization," he said.

In less than an hour they were on their way again in the wheezing, squeaking automobile which they had hired to take them to Bombay. She had plenty of time to go on thinking as they drove over the country roads. The green of North India was dying to grayness as they went south. The rains were delayed this year. But the grayness suited the mood in which she was approaching what was called civilization, that is, white men and women and a hotel in Bombay, and then ships and Europe and home. When she thought of all that waited for her as Mrs. Bert Holm, decision fled in retreat again. It was impossible to decide anything as Kit Tallant. There was always Mrs. Bert Holm to consider.

VIII

"M RS. BERT HOLM?" "Is that her?" "Is that Bert Holm's wife?"

She fled, her name echoing after her in the hotel lobby.

"Mrs. Bert Holm! Mrs. Bert Holm!"

She turned into a side corridor and into another, all but running, and found a narrow back stair and ran up it until she recognized the corridor of her own room and went in and locked the door.

Even so, though she knew she was perfectly safe, it was at least five minutes until she got her breath. Silly to run so—they were only people! But they had suddenly seemed dreadful to her, fresh from the mountains. Panic had rushed at her and she could not keep herself from escape. She ought to have stopped and smiled and accepted greetings. Gail would have done it perfectly. But being still at bottom only Kit she had run away. She was trembling as though she were very cold. She hated them, she thought passionately. She was born to be alone—at least, never to be the game of this hungry crowd—and never, never, she knew now, to be Bert's wife!

She did not turn at the sound of the door. She felt as she stood that not Bert but an excited stranger had burst into her room. The people had made him a stranger again. From behind she felt herself seized in his great arms and clutched to him, her face pulled back to his lips. She drew away from the strangeness, repelled beyond control. A stranger was what he would always be to her.

"What's the matter?" he demanded.

"It's just that I'm not used to all these people again," she replied. He laughed and drew her palm down his cheek. "If that's all—" he exclaimed, and put his hands on her shoulders.

He was intolerably near, he was horrible to her. She could not help this rush of something in her against him, not hatred, something far deeper than simply hating. He was abhorrent to her, and she was terrified of her abhorrence.

"No, don't!" she whispered. "I don't want you to—" She kept swallowing over and over, staring at him.

"What the heck?" he said slowly. "See here, there is something funny about you. Why didn't you stay there with me?"

"I was going to," she said quickly. How could she explain that she had to escape from him? "But I—the crowd was frightful; it was, wasn't it?"

"It was just a crowd," he said. He was still staring at her. "Kit, you're pulling some funny business on me—why don't you kiss me?"

Now he was getting angry. She could see red creeping up his neck.

"Wait!" she begged. "Give me a minute!"

"A nice thing to say to a man!"

She could not speak. Her throat was dry.

"I might as well have died instead of Brugh!" he shouted suddenly. "You make me feel as if you wish I were the one!" He stood before her, his hands hanging at his side, staring at her. Then she saw his eyes cloud with tears. His anger never lasted but a moment. She wished it would. Anger was much easier to bear in him than tears.

"Don't!" she said. "Wait!"

She turned to the window and stood looking out. What had come up out of her to sweep her along, to make her dizzy, to

330

make her say things she had not planned or thought or even known she felt? But in a minute she would be all right—a minute for control.

"You don't love me any more," he said. "I've known it ever since that night in the hotel."

"Hush!" she replied. "Wait!"

"I don't care for anything if you don't love me any more," he said. She could not answer, and he kept on. "When I was standing there on top of the mountain—the only one to make it—standing freezing in that cold like swords going through me, and half dead and my eyes sore and hurting so I couldn't hardly see—what I was thinking of was me telling you I made the top—" His lips were trembling. It seemed to him now that was all he had thought about on Pangbat.

She turned her back to the window and faced him. Every fiber in her body was quivering and shrinking. Where did the blood go when it left the flesh like this?

"But I do—I didn't stay downstairs with you because all the people——"

"Yeah, but, Kit"—his voice took on aggrievement—"people like to see us together!"

She was hateful to herself, even. Little things she had learned not to notice long ago, she kept seeing: the thickness of his hands, the way his lips scarcely moved when he spoke, the clumsy farm speech which he could never change so long as he lived, because it was grown into him. And she who loved particularly the pure music of words rightly articulated! Why were love and hatred entangled with small senseless things? Her uncontrollable irritation flamed out of her.

"I wish you wouldn't say 'Yeah'!" she cried. Oh, how stupid of her to say that now!

"What?" he asked, dazed.

"Nothing," she said.

331

He stared at her a moment, and the dazed look began to pass from his eyes.

"What we been fighting about, Kit?"

"Nothing," she said quickly. "Nothing, nothing——"

The telephone was ringing and she snatched the receiver.

"Is Bert Holm there?" an excited voice demanded.

"Just a minute." She handed him the receiver and blessed the interruption. While he was talking she could turn away and powder her hot cheeks and smooth her hair and quiet her heart.

"Yeah," he was saying, "yeah, sure, only I haven't got to my mail and stuff yet— Yeah, sure we can make it. How far is it? Well, if the car's here in half an hour, we'll be ready, I guess. Yeah, all right." He hung up the receiver and turned to her importantly. "The Governor," he said, "wants we should eat at his place in half an hour. Think you can do it?"

"I should think so," she said calmly. Whatever she did must not be decided now. Nothing must be decided until she had tried it all again, being Mrs. Bert Holm——

He was laughing suddenly. "Gosh, Kit you had me scared stiff!" he cried. "Why, you looked so queer, I didn't know who you were for a minute. I guess you have been away from civilization too long."

"Perhaps I have," she agreed.

From that day in Bombay to this first day in New York there had been but a triumphal procession. They had not gone to Germany or Italy or anywhere but straight home. Mr. Brame had advised against Germany and Italy.

"Proposed trip unfortunate for publicity," he cabled. "Any interest in that quarter derogatory to popularity in present temper U.S.A."

So the nearest they had come to Germany was a stout little German army doctor on the ship that brought them across the

332

Red Sea. He was being recalled from a private practice in Bombay to report for army duty. He told this to Kit.

"Why, I do not ask," he said. "It is not my place. When I am called, I come. It is enough for me."

He puffed out his little chest. "I am told it is for my special knowledge of Oriental diseases," he said.

"Is your country planning something in the Orient?" Kit asked.

"I do not know," he replied. "I do not ask."

"Don't you ever wonder?" Kit asked with malice.

"No, never," he replied with dignity. "With my countrymen I follow our beloved leader."

"Asking no questions," she said with a slight smile.

"It is not for us," he agreed.

Millions of people, she thought, with a curious familiar distaste, loving one man, following one man, making of one man hero and god! Was the inevitable consequence of the destruction of the gods by man merely this, that people then fell to worshiping a man? But the old gods were wiser and safer, for, being unseen, those who must worship could endow them with all the goodness and truth for which they longed, and power and wisdom could be given them without danger, as one could put a sword into the hand of an image and not fear its use. But when people worshiped a man they put a sword into a living hand and by that sword they could die.

Millions of people were waiting for the return of Bert Holm. Mr. Brame, having met them, was almost tearful with pleasure.

"Absolutely perfect," he kept murmuring to Kit. "He is simply to the manner born, I may say, Mrs. Holm. It's instinct in him. He says exactly the right thing in exactly the right homespun way. He's American and Americans love him. They're saying everywhere that success hasn't spoiled Bert Holm. They're saying he's the same honest farm boy he was born, and he is, of course, that's the beauty of it, he really is! The trip did him good—he looks like a king." Mr. Brame's pale eyes rested with affection on

333

Bert laughing and waving his arms to the crowd. "People have to have a king or something like it," he added calmly.

"A figurehead?" she murmured, half-smiling.

"Say a symbol," he amended, and added courteously, "and a very fine-looking one Bert is. You can't imagine how important that is, Mrs. Holm."

"Yes, I can," she replied.

They had flown across the Atlantic because Mr. Brame said there was such a clamor for Bert. Only when they were in the air had there been relief from people pressing and pressing by letter and telegraph and cable and again the simple roar of mere machinery was rest in comparison to articulated demands. Yet she and Bert were falling into constant little bickering quarrels. For she hated more and more this sacrifice of everything she had to the insatiable public, the public who demanded every last detail of what Bert ate and drank and how he looked and what he wore and what he said, and of her because she was Bert's wife. There was nothing left private to her—nothing!

But the quarrels came because Bert, who had no such inward private needs as hers, had so completely changed that he was liking the very things she hated. It was as though having conquered Pangbat he felt himself all that people made him by their adulation. His food, his habits, his clothes, had always been important to him. They grew more important to him now that other people found them so as well. Not for anything would he wear a hat when he heard that it had become a legend that he never wore a hat, and that everywhere over the United States young men went carefully hatless because Bert Holm went so. Somewhere he heard a woman say, "I'll bet he smokes a pipe—I like a man who smokes a pipe, don't you?" He began to smoke a pipe, though for a long time it made him a little sick and so he only smoked in public. Kit might have laughed at him for that trifle had he not given her his careless grin.

"I don't care for the damn thing, but it gives 'em more to talk about, and they might say something worse," he said cheerfully.

At the airport near New York he had leaped from the plane, his body full of grace, and all his charm made easy now with usage, and people pushed and shouted and laughed themselves hoarse because he was so exactly what they thought he was. They hugged the very image of him to their hearts because he was so exactly what they thought, no better, not more learned than any of them, a regular fellow, they told each other, just like anybody, and so, Kit thought bitterly, worthy doubtless of their worship.

There was no denying her growing inward bitterness. It made her look somehow more like Gail than she had ever looked in her life. It made her voice take on an edge of sharpness that was like Gail's. She held herself more erect, her head higher, her face closed.

Gail, coming to meet her with Harvey and her parents, stood separated by the struggling crowds between and stared across the massed heads at Kit. Each of the family looked at her, trying to find answer to their common question, "What has she decided to do?" But if Kit knew her own answer, nothing about her revealed it to anyone else.

"She looks five years older," Gail said to her mother.

She said it complacently because she herself, as she very well knew, was looking unusually young and pretty. That was what the bitch did for her, so that something under a half an hour ago a young man holding her hand in both his had said, "Gail, you are twice as beautiful as you were the day we met, and then I thought I had never seen any woman so beautiful!" He had drawn her to him by the hand he held and had kissed her for a long moment. She had let it be long because it was sweet. Then his lips murmured upon hers, "I didn't know whether you would let me do this or not."

"I didn't either, Jerry," she said.

"Adorable!" he had whispered. . . .

She turned her eyes, made clear and innocent, upon her mother as she accused Kit of aging.

"Well, Kit always looked too young," Mrs. Tallant replied and after a moment added, "It's becoming, I think." And a quarter of an hour later, having felt Kit's composed kiss upon her cheek, Mrs. Tallant murmured to her husband, "I believe she's settled herself. I knew she would. After all, she's a Tallant."

"We'll see," Mr. Tallant returned. He wasn't going to commit himself on Kit, not but what he would be glad, of course, if things were settled. He hated a family scandal. And Bert, it must be said, stood this sort of thing pretty well. Look at that silly girl now, hanging on his shoulder! He would not know what to do in Bert's shoes, with all this adulation. The crowd was pretty much of a fool and he was glad he did not have to come into it in his job. All the same, probably no one in the country just now had the influence this blond-haired boy had. Brame said so. If Bert wanted to head a cause he could storm the nation. Thank God, Bert had not an idea in his head and so was not dangerous. It was safer for the crowd to worship a fellow like that than someone like some of those dictators—a golden calf, instead of Moses, leading them out to God knows what——

"Well, sir!" Bert's hard big hand was grasping his painfully. "It's good to see you!"

"Welcome home, my boy!" Mr. Tallant said. No use pretending there was not something very likable here! But Kit's mouth looked tight and queer. Her lips had always been full and soft. They were no longer so.

"I think I'll go home," he told his wife after an hour. "I'm getting tired."

"We'd all better go," she said. "There's such a crowd."

They had all gone home then except Bert and Mr. Brame, who had stayed. There was no use trying to get Bert yet. After the family handshakes, photographed in flashes of light, he was swept away again and they went home without him. They would not see him again until the mayor's dinner. Mr. Tallant hated great dinners, but of course they all had to go because the mayor had invited them. This morning there would be the procession up Broadway. Thousands of telephone books would be torn to bits again, tons of paper fragments would fly through the streets and have to be swept up tomorrow. It would cost the city a mint of money, Bert riding in an open car up Broadway, his hair shining in the sun. But people did not think of that.

In her own room at mid-afternoon, Kit was unpacking quietly. The maids had hung up her clothes but she had told them to leave the small bag for her. There were a few things in it, gifts for her family, a Tibetan turquoise bracelet she had liked, some wild flowers she had found in India and had pressed, her book of poems, and the little old Chinese seal that had gone with her everywhere. They had stood on a balcony and watched the procession while it passed, then because they could stand no longer they had come home, she and her parents and Gail and Harvey, and had tea together in the drawing room. But one of the maids had served it because Smedley had asked for the afternoon off so that he could see the procession.

It had seemed so cosy there together that the tightness in her which she had felt since the day at Bombay loosened suddenly and she felt shut in and secure. Bert had drawn the crowd away with him. These were her own family.

"I don't see myself how you stand it," her father said, and drew a great sigh. "Another piece of toast, please, Kit. People in the aggregate are oppressive, to say the least."

"It's awfully amusing, really," Gail put in. She couldn't keep from looking at Kit. She was dying to find out, she had whispered to Harvey, what was behind Kit's eyes. That look had always meant something. Gail was very affectionate with Harvey today. He felt it and watched her, but each time he caught her eyes they were clear upon him. He needn't worry, those eyes said. He was the eternal rock. He was, he knew—but he must keep Gail from being a public fool with that young Jerry Todd, who was in love with her. She did not pretend he was not.

"Can I help it?" she had inquired when he asked, still with those amber clear eyes. . . .

"I suppose I stand it because it's Bert they're after," Kit was saying.

Now she can't be jealous of Bert! Gail's mind flying about like a bright dragonfly darted at this and dismissed it. Harvey had said, "Maybe she's jealous—women are." But Kit had never been jealous.

"By the way, Kit," Harvey said suddenly, "your old boy friend, what's-his-name, has made a tremendous hit with his play."

Ah, there was something! The dragonfly hung poised and glittering upon Kit's joyful eyes, suddenly upturned.

"Norman?" she cried.

"The same," Gail replied.

"And the play—is it *Freedom*?"

"It is," Gail said. "We haven't seen it, but we must, mustn't we, Harvey? Such reviews, Kit, as never were—even the old crabs of critics who never like anything are saying great, magnificent, real theater, and all that." She laughed suddenly. "But I don't know about the box office." She looked at Harvey, her eyes glittering with laughter. "We heard that girl, didn't we?"

"Last night?" Harvey inquired. "You did—I didn't." He never paid any attention to what people said on the streets, but Gail was always picking up things.

"We had to walk to find the car," Gail explained, "after we'd been seeing that new revue thing, *A Penny For Your Thoughts*. We passed by the Booth, where *Freedom*'s playing, and a gumchewing, platinum blonde, swinging along between her two men, said, 'That's a play I don't give a damn to see—*Freedom*—sounds like too much poetry and too profound.' "

They laughed. Gail told things well enough to have been an

338

actress herself, Harvey thought. Only he would never have married an actress.

"No, but tell me—" Kit was beginning eagerly.

The door opened suddenly and the maid stood there.

"Oh, ma'am," she cried, her face all open like a child's, "he's on the radio now! Mr. Holm, ma-am—it's five o'clock."

"Then the procession's over at last," Mr. Tallant said.

Mr. and Mrs. Tallant looked at each other uncertainly. Did they have to go into the other room and hear Bert? The maid, waiting and excited, compelled them. They were ashamed of their own coldness. "Oh, we must go," Gail cried. They rose, Harvey last, and went in and sat down, and Bert's voice, full and young and clear, came half-laughing into the room.

"Well, folks, here I am again—same old bad penny! And I haven't a thing new to tell you, except I set out to climb Pangbat and I did. But I wouldn't be fair to my fine men if I didn't say they stood by me, all of them, and made the expedition a success. Jack Rexall will be home soon with the stuff. I left everything to him, except the records which I have. Well, nothing will be too good for old Rexie when he gets home. He may lose a finger with frostbite. And one of the other men had snowblindness." His voice grew solemn. "Two of the men lost their lives—brave fellows. I'll never forget them. To me they'll always be alive. Well," he paused and his voice grew lighter, "but those things happen. Maybe you'll ask why do we have to climb a mountain anyway? Well, maybe I didn't have to do it. But I thought I did. And I hope our records will be some use to the scientists, and I found a wonderful place for a t.b. sanatorium, if anybody wants to have it, a level valley, full of flowers, on the edge of snow, with the bluest sky and best air in the world——"

Gail whispered, "You didn't say anything about a sanatorium, Kit!"

"I thought he'd forgotten about it," Kit whispered back.

Bert paused again, and mischief crept into his voice. His eyes,

Kit knew, would be lighting now, and the slow grin creeping over his face.

"But folks, I'd be fooling you if I let you think I went there for anything but a good time. Heck, I am what I am, that's all. I went there for a good time and I had it. I went to climb higher than anybody ever had before, and I did it!"

Such roars and handclapping and laughter burst out of the radio that the room was suddenly crowded with noise.

Mr. Tallant turned the button sharply. In the silence he said drily, "Bert certainly has improved in his public speaking."

"He seems to have learned the touch," Harvey agreed, unwillingly.

"In other words, my dears," Gail said briskly, "he's done it again!" They all turned to look at her, and she looked back at them and smiled cruelly, and said no more because at that moment an idea had come to her. All day an idea had been growing bigger and more possible as she thought of it. Why shouldn't Jerry do something and be a public hero? Why not the next? Why not steal the heart of the great public away from Bert? Jerry was better looking than Bert, as tall and even more blond, Swedish, out of Minnesota, and American to the core! What a pity he could not fly a plane! But what about the war coming in Europe—something in the next war? What excitement heroism would add to her affair with Jerry! She rose slowly and went over to Harvey compelled by some contradictory instinct. He looked up in surprise from his cigar.

"What now?" he inquired.

"Nothing. I just want to sit by you." She pulled a footstool to his side, and sitting down leaned against his knee, a picture of a wife. They looked at her one by one, uneasy, without knowing why Gail, devoted and demure, always alarmed them.

"How's Dickie's knee?" Mrs. Tallant said abruptly.

"Better, thank you," Gail said, and explained to Kit, "He fell while he was roller skating, and it got infected."

It was at this moment that Bert burst in upon them, "Here I am!" he cried. He had escaped, he explained, laughing, and in the bright success of his presence Gail was forgotten. Her family, Kit decided, watching them, were being all they should be to Bert, tolerant, amused, and appreciative. If Gail led him on to talk too much of himself, it was simply that she might be amused the more, and that was only Gail, and if her father was a little more ironical than usual, it was an irony not unkind. Underneath even Harvey's silence and her mother's bright, practical questions, Kit felt that somehow or other, worthily or not, inexplicable though it assuredly was to them, they too had come to accept Bert as a hero.

Two days later on the schedule which Mr. Brame had made for him, Bert went home to see his parents, and Kit on the morning after found John Baker's letter at her place when she came down to breakfast with her father.

She had not gone with Bert. She knew that she would never go to Misty Falls again, not having decided consciously that she would not, but merely becoming aware of it as a fact that she could not go because nothing in her belonged there. So she had said to him quite easily, "Do you mind if I stay at home while you go? After all, I haven't seen my parents either for a long time."

"I want you should do what you want to, Kit," he answered.

So he had gone off to Misty Falls, and newspaper men went with him and millions read of Bert Holm's return to the home of his childhood, and of how the whole village was at the train to meet him and how the railway station was decorated with lights and how the band played and how his parents were there in new clothes, their honest faces lit with joy and their toil-worn hands outstretched to grasp Bert's hands. And Bert's mother, interviewed, said over and over again, "No, I'm not surprised at anything Bert does. He was a wonderful baby. I got pictures showing him walking at nine months, and he chewed meat as good as I could."

The old man would not talk, it seemed. But that made a good story, too, the taciturn silence, the strong reserve of this weather-beaten old farmer who had given Bert his immense physical energy. The same vigor that had gone to a half a century's plowing and sowing and reaping of the land had been given to Bert to conquer mountains.

At breakfast in the large quietly furnished dining room Mr. Tallant put down his paper at the same instant that Kit put down hers, and their eyes met. He smiled slightly.

"They seem pretty fond of him, don't they?" he murmured.

"It's a sickening word, but that's what they are," she answered. "More coffee, Dad?"

"Thanks," he said. He appreciated Kit's still coming down like this whenever she was home. They did not speak for a moment, needing silence after the raucous fulsomeness of the newspapers.

"Sometimes I am sure restraint is the loveliest thing in life," she said after a while.

"If it's not carried too far," he said. "Well, it can be at that. But for a steady diet I'd rather have it."

"So would I," she said, "More toast, Dad?"

"No, thanks," he replied.

It was then she saw John Baker's letter. She had glanced at the letters by her plate and beneath them there was a square white envelope. Mr. Tallant was folding his napkin.

"Wait a minute, Dad," she said.

She tore open the letter and read it aloud. "Dear Mrs. Holm: It seems in accord with my promise to you that I see you in regard to some data put into my hands by certain members of the Expedition. If you will appoint a time, I shall be glad to call upon you. Yours faithfully, John Baker."

"Short and to the point," Mr. Tallant murmured, and wiped

his mouth. "Sounds as though he had something up his sleeve."

"I suppose I must see him," Kit said.

"Only thing to do," he replied. "Brame know anything about it?"

"I haven't had time to see him," she replied. "Shall I have him come, too?"

Mr. Tallant shook his head. "Better not," he said. "Better see the fellow alone and get whatever it is straight for yourself. Do you want me?"

"Would you?" she begged, instantly relieved.

"If you think he'll talk before me, of course."

"He will, I'm sure. You'd like each other."

"All right—my office, then, why not? Day after tomorrow, at two. I'm tied up until then."

"The best possible place," she said gratefully.

He came over to her and kissed her hair. It was as fragrant as it had been when she was a young girl.

"Good-by," he said.

"'By, Dad." She smiled up at him. Her face looked a little fuller again than it had, just for the moment anyway, he thought to himself, as he rolled down the avenue toward Wall Street behind the chauffeur. It was a changeful face, Kit's—no telling what it really was because it was never static. He had never been satisfied with any pictures of her. Gail, now, always looked exactly like her pictures, always pretty—dangerously pretty he'd thought for some reason the other day when she had sat with her head against Harvey's knee. But Kit could be pretty or plain, by the moment. He had always thought if things were just right in her life some time she would be actually beautiful. He'd like to do something to make her so—mustn't forget to tell Miss Hopkins to cancel everything for day after tomorrow at two o'clock.

At the breakfast table Kit, left alone, searched all her instincts and discovered among them the most sensitive. It stirred at the remembrance of the name of Ronald Brugh.

Two days later, coming into her father's enormous, darkly furnished office at two o'clock sharp, she found John Baker already there at the great window overlooking the harbor. Mr. Tallant was standing beside him.

She put out her hand to John Baker. He was exactly the same as he had been when she saw him last on the foothills of the Himalayas.

"I'm glad to see you," she said.

"Thank you," he said. "I wasn't sure."

"But why not?" she asked.

"I thought perhaps Mr. Holm——"

She shook her head. "He hasn't mentioned you," she said quickly, and thought, her heart dropping, "Bert's kept something secret again."

They sat down, she in a deep chair of fragrant old leather, her father at his desk, and John Baker at a table. He began unpacking a stuffed briefcase.

"That makes it rather hard," he said. "I wish he had. I don't want to present both sides—only my own."

"I suppose Bert can tell his side of it himself, anyway, whatever it is," Mr. Tallant put in.

Kit did not speak. She knew as well as though John Baker had read aloud the papers before him what they were.

"I have here," Baker said steadily, looking down at them, "a series of statements from the four men who went up Pangbat with Mr. Holm. They wrote them separately, each giving his opinion upon a certain important matter. Then they brought them to me as one impartial because I was not even present at the final climb. Shall I read them?"

"If you please," Kit said.

Mr. Tallant picked up a small silver paper weight in the shape of a crouched watchful dog on guard, and sat twisting it and polishing it with his long thumb as he listened. Baker read, one after the other, the four sheets of paper he held. He mentioned no names but Kit did not need to be told who had written each. Francis Brewer's good-natured southern courtesy, beginning in a large negligent script, "It is with the greatest reluctance that I commit to paper such nebulous material as my own doubt and fear that—" And Bert Calloway's clear, hard statement, "On the thirtieth of July of this year, I, as a member of the Bert Holm Expedition, was stationed at Camp III upon the northeast slope of Pangbat. It was my duty, assigned by Mr. Holm, to remain in readiness for possible rescue in case—" And Lincoln Mayhew's disturbance as he began, "I certainly hate this necessity to write down something which may bring trouble. Disappointment is always hard. But it is more than personal disappointment in a man which leads me now to express a certain point of view. Justice demands it—" Dick Blastel began in belligerence. "Ronald Brugh was my friend. He is dead, and maybe he does not need anything more from me. But I would like to ask a few questions about how he died, if only for my own satisfaction. First, Mr. Holm, did you or did you not quarrel with my friend Ronald Brugh before you set out alone on the morning of the thirtieth of July? If not, why did you make the start alone? Second, why did you deviate from the route you had told us all would be the one we were to follow in case of any trouble? Third, did you or did you not leave any message or signal for Brugh at the point at which you turned? Fourth, did you take the oxygen tank with you?"

On and on the questions went. John Baker read them steadily and turned the page Blastel had covered on both sides with his remorseless questions. When he had finished, Mr. Tallant put down the silver dog.

"Has Bert seen these?" he asked.

"No," John Baker answered. "But he knows the way the men feel. I thought it only fair to speak to him before I brought them to Mrs. Holm."

That was what Bert had hidden again from her! The fresh silence started all Kit's old distrusts, but she did not speak.

"What did Bert say?" Mr. Tallant inquired.

"He did not seem to take it seriously—said that men in an expedition usually turned against their leader and were jealous if he succeeded and despised him if he didn't. But perhaps we should not blame him for taking nothing very seriously just now in the way of blame. It would be difficult for any man in Mr. Holm's position to judge himself for what he was."

What he was! She saw again through Baker's cold unprejudiced contempt what Bert was. He put Bert aside as unimportant and went on talking. The whole question, he said, was one of moral right and of justice to Ronald Brugh, whom they had all respected.

"The important thing now is," he said at last, "what shall I do?"

"What you feel you should do, I should like you to do, please," Kit said with swift authority. She had not once spoken to interrupt him. "Indeed, I should never be content if you did not."

John Baker's small gray eyes were as clear as points of steel. "It will be very serious for Mr. Holm."

"Bert has told me about this. He will stand up for himself," she said, and rising, she put out her hand for good-by. She must get out and away, out of this grave room, away from everything, into the outdoor air.

"Thank you," she said.

"Thank you," he said. "You're pretty swell, Mrs. Holm."

"Oh no," she replied soberly, "just fair—I hope—to Ronald Brugh, as well as to Bert! Good-by, Dad—see you a little later, won't I?"

"I may be home early," he said.

She nodded again and slipped out of the heavy mahogany door and flew down the halls to the elevator. When she got out she would jump into a taxi and drive up the highway to the park and walk and walk—and think what to do. She would have to talk to Bert, of course. But she had not a moment's doubt that John Baker would be right in whatever he did. One could not look at him or listen to his steady voice without knowing his complete cold integrity. She could not imagine what he would have done if she had begged him not to tell, for Bert's sake. But she could never have asked him for such hateful silence. . . . If Bert were criminal it would be easy. But with deepest certainty she still knew he was not criminal. He was simply without the conscious sensitive integrity of a good intelligence, that was all. But conscious integrity was everything—the vessel which held all beauty. If there were no containing vessel, then there was nothing.

By the time she reached the park she was completely angry. No, but this time she would make Bert speak for himself. When he came back she would tell him straightly what John Baker had told her, and ask him what he proposed to do. She would force him to face himself as he was and not as that figure that Mr. Brame had made.

She stopped, aware that she was muttering half aloud between her teeth as though she were insane. She sighed and slowed her steps. Silly to let herself be burned up for Bert, who would never know it! It was a glorious afternoon in late August, but she had seen nothing of summer since they came home. Every day had been filled with this ridiculous rush. Ah, what would she do with her own life? That was the real question—not Bert, really. She was no good to anyone living this way. She sat down on an empty bench. And instantly the engines in her that had been going so powerfully stopped.

The stillness was intense—the stillness of a summer's afternoon when everything was waiting for the evening coolness. Life paused. The very children passing her on their way to the zoo seemed dreamy with stillness. Near her an old man slept, and a woman, motionless, stared at nothing. The park this afternoon was a heart of stillness in the city. The sunlight poured into it, warm and strong. She wanted to stop, too, to be silent and unthinking at least for a moment. The moment stretched and lengthened into an hour and then very nearly into another before she moved. When she did she was half drowsy with rest. The sun had done it, perhaps, or the trees and a playful squirrel, a flash and flutter of pigeons, or children calling faintly in the distance at the edge of a pool where they sailed their ships. The old man waked and wiped his mouth and stretched himself and went away, and the woman rose at last, her eyes full of peace, and walked past without seeing her.

And Kit, too, rose and went toward the east where the nearest street was, and called a taxi and went homeward. She had always loved the park from the days when it had stood as the nearest best to Glen Barry, from which each winter she must be taken. But today it had become something more. It had become the maintaining of this principle of life, that in the heart of the world's greatest confusion there was stillness and only out of stillness could there come the final clarity.

She met her father hovering near the library door, watching for her coming.

"I was a little worried," he confessed. "Nobody seemed to know where you were."

"Only in the park," she answered. Then she smiled at him. "I needed air," she added.

"I don't blame you," he returned.

She followed him into the library and sitting down, took off her hat and gloves and put them in her lap. He stood before the empty fireplace, tall and thin and a little brooding.

"Kit," he began, "I've been thinking. We must see Brame and get him ready for this attack. Bert is going to be ruined by this unless it's very carefully handled. People will hate him the more for having worshiped him as they have."

He gazed sadly across the room at nothing. "We're a strange people, we Americans," he mused. "We are doomed to hate

348

whatever we love. The seeds of that hatred are in us from the beginning because what we really hate is having given ourselves away so much as to worship anyone. Those old fellows, our grandfathers, planted pretty deep in us the Commandment—'Thou shalt have no other gods before Me,' but of course we do make other gods as the other heathen do; only after a while we hate them because there's the old conscience in us still."

"Meaning Bert is a false god?" she inquired.

"Any man is a false god to a people born of Puritans and Calvinists as we are, and nurtured on the Constitution," he replied. "And that's why if we love him, we are doomed to hate him . . . I feel sorry for Bert."

She did not answer this. His brooding deepened as he looked at her and he pulled his short gray mustache and coughed. Her eyes were so dark and full of something, he didn't know what except that they always made him ache a little—always had. When she was little her eyes always made him want to buy her things, but what she wanted now was beyond any buying.

"Kit," he said, clearing his throat, "I want to tell you—if you decide on—a—on a divorce or anything like that, just let me know what you want."

"I would, Dad, anyway," she said quietly. He thought, relieved, that she was very sensible. All the same——

"Your mother has a good deal of family pride," he made himself go on, "and very proper of course. All the same, if it's your happiness that's concerned the family will have to stand the publicity."

"Thanks, Dad, I know that." Her little face was quite serene.

"I just wanted you to know," he murmured.

"I do, but I haven't made up my mind," she said, and added, "I will, of course, when I know everything."

It was time to get out of this. "Well," he said in his usual voice, "the thing is to see Brame and get his advice. And I suppose you'd better talk to Bert. You want me to?" he asked anxiously. But what would he say to the fellow? They didn't have much speech in common.

"Oh no," she said quickly, and actually laughed. She jumped to her feet and came over to him and kissed him and squeezed his arm a little. "Don't worry," she said. "I'm used to Bert now. And he's so awfully lucky. He'll come out of this, too."

"That's right," he said heartily. He was suddenly relieved. She sounded just like her mother, sensible and matter-of-fact. It was the thing he liked best about Dottie. Whenever he felt himself getting emotional in the way he hated and yet somehow could not stop once he began, she helped him by just such a calm, everyday voice. It brought him back to himself. He hated softness and feared it in himself because he knew it was there, deep in his core.

"That's my good girl," he said, and gave her a diffident kiss on her forehead, which just then he found conveniently opposite his lips.

When she was gone he sighed loudly. He felt tired and rang the bell and Smedley came in.

"Is there some of that special Scotch left?" he inquired.

"Yes sir," Smedley said, "one bottle."

Smedley had secretly put away that bottle on the day Bert Holm reached the top.

"Bring it," Mr. Tallant said. He made a point, when there was only a single bottle left of some fine old stuff of drinking it quietly by himself, bit by bit. Why not? He doubted all other palates except his own, the only palate he could trust.

"Yes sir," Smedley said, dolefully.

Kit, wandering restlessly about the house, wished that Bert were here so that she could have it over. But Bert would not be back until tomorrow.

She picked up a newspaper from the table in the hall where

350

she happened to be passing. There was the headline, "Bert Holm Visits Home Town." She turned the page quickly.

If she knew Bert had been actually dishonest with her that night in the little Indian hotel then she simply could not go on with him—though, she thought mournfully, what difference in truth was there between dishonesty and her uncertainty concerning it? If she could not be sure of his honesty, was that not in itself the one unendurable thing? Certainly she had not been able to cry out for him to John Baker, "Bert could never do such a thing!" The real trouble was that, whether he had done it or not she knew he could have done it.

As she thus feverishly reasoned her own case, she went on turning the pages until now suddenly she came upon a small square of advertisement wherein was lettered boldly the one word, *Freedom*. She stopped and stared at it as though it were a message to her.

"Norman's play!" she thought.

It was actually as though he had spoken to her. She had thought of him since she came home and not incidentally but as one to whom she might still go when, or perhaps if, it ever became necessary for her to go anywhere. Now with his peculiar dramatic power over her he had simply stepped into her indecision with this favorite word of his. Immediately he gave her direction. Being compelled to postpone talk with Bert, she would go and see the play and she would go quite alone and tell no one. She had been going to dine at Gail's with the children, since there was a bankers' dinner to which her parents and Gail and Harvey were going, and her mother, arranging her family's smallest destinies, had said briskly, "Why don't you go and have a nice cosy dinner with Gail's children? You haven't had a visit with them since you came back." She had not, indeed, and they had grown so that she was shy of them. She had never been intimate with the children, and yet they had had some sort of relation with her, too, a tenuous fairy-tale relation, out of which in their small boyhood she spun rhymes and stories which fascinated them and shamed them at the same time. Gail did not believe in fairy tales, especially for boys, and they knew it. And the truth was they liked Bert's hearty roughness with them better than Kit's sensitive courtesy, and she knew this. When she came home and found them now definitely boys and no longer babies, she both dreaded and longed for renewed acquaintance with them. . . . It would be easy enough to ring up at the last minute and say she could not come because she had decided to go to a play.

Norman had designed everything, of course. He always did for his own plays. She was much too early so that she had plenty of time to gaze at the heavy black curtain with the huge red letters flung across it, *FREEDOM*. Here from where she sat too close to the stage, the word looked enormous and out of all focus. But this was the only seat she could get and even this was luck, for someone had turned it back. The house was full. When she reached the theater over half an hour ago, there was already a sign up, "Standing Room Only." Down the aisle two rows behind her she heard an indignant discussion over seats, the disturbed usher helpless. She had had no idea that the play was going like this, though Gail had said it was a hit. She did not look around, wanting to see no one she knew.

Besides, the curtain was going up at last. . . .

All Norman's plays were somehow about himself. She had flung that at him once and he had granted it immediately.

"That is why they are real," he said calmly. "I know myself, at least."

Thus *The Plough* had been the recoil of his brain when he had been sick of his own intellectualism and while he had been working on it he had found healing in the yokels he created. When it was finished he was healed and he forgot them. All his plays had been like fragments of himself, each some momentary

352

crisis magnified into an hour's plot, though it was a trick of his, too, to catch into the seeming slightness of a play's immediate tangle the portent of life. Critics granted him what they called the quality of being universal. That was because he himself was of that quality. He was a fragment of the universe rather than in himself an individual. Else how could he have so cruelly understood his own love of her?

But this play, this *Freedom,* she saw as the scenes unfolded, was more Norman than anything he had ever written before. He had taken a young man, again himself, and had shown him stripping away one need after another, but always finally having the need for a great single love. That he struggled against as he would against his own death. It was the play of which he had told her, and without any shame she saw he had taken her to symbolize love. He had even taken her looks, her nature, her ways and tricks of speech, her poetry writing, and fastened them on a slight dark girl. Now more than ever she was glad no engagement had ever been announced between them. Gail alone would guess, perhaps, but Gail would never say anything about her sister.

She waited for the end she knew—Norman, of course, in triumph, free and alone. She was touched as the play unfolded in the midst of her being half angry and half hurt, because he had created the woman with a sort of delicate sympathy and understanding of her suffering. Andrew in the play, casting off Helen, did so without ruthlessness and with actual sorrow, bewildered as much as she by his compulsion toward freedom. Kit listened, tears in her eyes, to his halting, sweating explanation of why he could not marry her, because if he did he would somehow be lost. He could not explain, he could only feel. And watching the girl she watched herself. She was prepared then, when the curtain fell, for Norman in triumph and freedom.

But the curtain did not so fall. He had, she now remembered, withdrawn the play and rewritten it while she had been away.

This was what he had written while she was gone, this new end. There was no triumph. This was not Norman free. It was Norman, who, having sent away from him everyone, even her, could not send away himself. He was subject still to everything in himself, to his own despondency, to his own weariness, but above all to that great bondage, the longing for the love he feared and would not have, and so at last to eternal discontent with the very cause for whose sake he had put everything away. He who had wanted freedom above everything was still not free, and so the curtain fell upon him alone, still in bondage but to himself.

She rose while the theater was full of applause, compelled by the necessity to see him again and talk to him. He would not be here, she knew, because he never saw a play of his own after it opened. "I've given it away, then," he always declared.

She went, therefore, to a drugstore across the street and shut herself up in the little public booth and rang his rooms. He might be away. She had heard nothing from him since she came back, but she remembered because she had never forgotten that he was usually there at the hours when his play was on. She heard after a moment his voice, impatient as ever, at her ear.

"Yes—who is it?" he demanded.

"Kit," she replied.

"Kit!" he cried. "I was just trying to write you a letter—been trying every night for weeks."

"I've seen your play," she said.

"When?" he asked.

"Tonight," she answered.

He paused the fraction of a moment. "Like it?" he asked.

"I didn't like it or dislike it," she answered quietly. "How could I? I knew it was true—except the end. I don't know anything about the end, Norman."

"The end's the truest of all," he said.

"Is it, Norman?" Then if it were true, she thought, anything could come out of it.

"Where are you?" he demanded.

"At the drugstore opposite the theater."

"Go to the counter and order something and wait until I get there."

The receiver clanged in her ear. She turned away. She had been nothing but Mrs. Bert Holm for days upon days, but now she slipped out of the shell of Bert's wife as a moth out of a chrysalis and went to the counter feeling suddenly free of all Bert's troubles. Let Mrs. Bert Holm look after herself!

"A strawberry ice cream soda," she told the clerk. Over by the telephone booth she seemed to see a staid little brown thing she had left there, watching her in consternation. What would Bert do if this—came to anything? She began her soda resolutely. It might happen, she thought. Anything might happen to her, depending on Norman. She drank slowly, glad for the coldness in her mouth. Her cheeks were hot and her eyes burning under the lids. Perhaps the time had come as it had when she was a little girl afraid to dive, when everything had at once seemed to compel her to a leap she had always refused. Perhaps tonight when she walked out of that door she would have decided, and for freedom.

He came in at that moment. She saw the shape of him upon the mirror behind the counter and knew it was his. She knew the set of his shoulders and the tilt of his hat. Then he was swinging to the stool beside her, smiling at her.

"Hello, Kit."

"Hello," she said. She looked up over her straw and went on. "What is it?" he asked.

"Strawberry," she replied indistinctly.

"I'll have the same," he told the clerk.

They did not speak for a few minutes. Then he snatched her out of her dreamlike silence.

"The first end was the one I wanted," he remarked. "It was the original end I'd planned. The second end was the rewrite."

"Why did you rewrite?" she asked him.

"Because that was the way it turned out to be," he said, and then added with emphasis, "and still is."

"I know it," she said.

"Don't think you win," he rejoined.

"Don't think you do, either," she said, glancing up at him. She wanted to laugh and did not. It was such pure pleasure simply to talk with him. They flung their sentences at each other like balls, sure of the other's catch.

"It's a sort of draw," he agreed.

It was a draw, and yet she knew more certainly than ever that if she put out her hand, if she showed him a need, she could make any ending now that she chose.

"I expected the end to be Norman the Magnificent, marching alone into the sunrise," she remarked.

"Shut up," he told her.

The sleepy clerk, swabbing his wet rag within inches of their glasses, stared. He could make nothing out of this. But "shut up" was nothing for a man to say to a nice girl. He glared at Norman.

"Want anything else?" he demanded coldly.

"No," Norman replied and flung down small coins. "Come along," he told Kit.

She got down from her high stool and followed him out. Behind them the clerk still stared; then shrugged. Some dames would take anything from a fellow, he thought. He moved their glasses and swabbed rapidly the places where they had been. He saw queer ones at a job like this.

Outside in the darkened street, Norman took Kit's hand firmly and put it upon his arm.

"There!" he said. "Hang on, will you?"

"Where to?" she asked.

"I don't know," he answered. "Along o' me, that's all."

She went along with him, then, into the huge staring crowds

who pace the streets of Broadway all night long. The crowds were strangely silent. She had often noticed that, though crowds in other countries were gay and chattering and noisy, these Broadway crowds were always grave and absent-minded and staring and they pushed each other as though they were long since due at some place still far away. But then perhaps she and Norman looked so, too. She glanced up at his profile to see, and at that instant he turned and looked down at her.

"Aren't you ever going to change?" he asked. His voice was hoarse. "Damn you, Kit, won't you please change a little? I thought marriage was supposed to do something to a woman— make her fat or old or something. How can you square it with your conscience to keep right on being just the way you used to be?"

His arm tightened on her hand and in the blue light from a neon sign she saw his face looking ferociously down upon her.

"Another moment," he said, his voice desperately light, "and I'll be asking you to run away from home and duty—with me."

"Will you?" she replied.

"Only if you drive me to it," he replied.

"I might not go," she said. And then, hating coquetry, added, "Though if I wanted to, I would."

"See here," he said, "we're up against something, aren't we?"

She nodded, and saw his face set and deciding.

"Well then, let's get somewhere and have it out," he said. "Only where?" He frowned a moment, without slowing his long stride. "Damnedest town, if you want to take a woman somewhere at night—wait, let's get on the ferry—the Staten Island ferry, that's it. It's as private as a theater after the show. I've gone back and forth on it half the night when I wanted to get off by myself."

They stepped into a taxi and he put her into a corner and sat far off in the other. "Sword between," he muttered. "I want a clear head and you can muddle me up more than anyone in the world. Talk about something, will you, Kit—not you and me."

She did not laugh, because he meant what he said. Besides, she wanted a clear head, too. Something might come of this night—something must come. Lives might be changed, tossed together, separated, not only her own and Norman's and Bert's, but all those other lives of people she did not know so inexplicably linked to them.

"All this success of yours," she said abruptly, "I suppose it's inconvenient if you want freedom, Norman."

"Damned inconvenient," he agreed, and then said honestly. "But it's queer, Kit. I like it, too. That's the queer part. I'd have said that I didn't care—I, of all people. But I do. It touches me when somebody writes that my play's done something for him. Then I curse and swear at myself for being like any other fool, and I tear up the letter. I don't write to be helpful, like a damned evangelist or something. If I write for anything except myself it's to make people mad, maybe."

"Don't you ever answer them?" she asked.

"No," he said harshly. "I don't want to get mixed up with people!"

She sat thinking about that. If she were with Norman, he would be ruthless with her and they would be free through his ruthlessness in any marriage they might choose. She would have to learn how to bear ruthlessness, if not to use it. But ruthlessness was the price of freedom. If she told Bert, for instance, that she wanted her freedom from him, she would have to get ruthlessness from somewhere—perhaps from Norman—to do it, though if she did it quickly—tomorrow, say—she might hold her present ruthlessness in her long enough for that.

"Here we are," Norman said. He paid the fare and they went onto the ferry. There was no one else near, except a small old man with his head wrapped up in a gray muffler, in spite of summer, and with his hat on top. He scurried ahead of them.

"Come over here," Norman said. "There's a nook I know." He led her forward. "Say, what about your home?"

"Bert's away—" she began.

"I saw that," he broke in. "The fellow's face is everywhere!"

She overlooked this. "Mother and Dad are out to dinner. If they are home they will think I'm safely in my bed."

They sat down in the shelter of a stairway and the ferry began to move. They could feel nothing, but the lights quietly retreated. She watched them, as she sat very erect and a little apart. Norman had turned up his collar and put his hands in his pockets. That was still keeping his head clear, she thought. And then he spoke suddenly.

"Now then—what about your marrying me, Kit Tallant?"

She was so startled that she began to stammer, as she had when she was little.

"I—I—" she stammered. Her heart began to pound.

"Stop and count ten," he commanded, and waited. "Then, begin again."

"What I wanted to say was—" she said laughing, "was that I didn't expect you to say that at once. I thought we were going to talk about it."

"I put the question," he said.

"And the arguments for and against?" she inquired.

"I have it by heart," he answered promptly. "It is mostly against, too. In fact, it's all against. I hate marrying another man's wife. I hate like hell the noise and publicity of marrying Bert Holm's wife. I don't want to marry anybody. I have a home and I don't want any children. The one damned argument for is that I seem to keep on loving you."

Her heart surged back over years to another moment when he had cut her life to pieces.

"How shall I know now that it is enough?" she asked. "How shall I know that perhaps some time you won't say again that you don't love me enough to go on?"

"I don't know," he said in a low voice. "I'll probably say it sometime, at that. I'll probably feel sometimes that I wish I weren't married, and you know when I feel it I'll say it. I can't hide anything."

No, he would never hide anything, she thought. If she and Norman were married, everything would be lived out between them. There would be no silences.

"You know what I mean, Kit." Norman's voice, speaking now out of the darkness, was quiet. But she could still hear it clearly in the soft splash of the water against the side of the ferry. "You know I'll change from one thing to another. But if you'll just not take it seriously, if you'll remember that maybe tomorrow I'll be back to the way I feel now——"

"How do you feel now?" she interrupted him.

"Exactly like that fellow you saw when the curtain went down on him," he answered.

They sat for a long time. The scattered lights were growing nearer on the shore. She was a little cold, but she did not want to move, lest the swiftness of her thinking be disturbed. For she was thinking in long clear definite strokes. One did not suddenly decide upon a life, did one? Not she, at least. What her mother called "considerations" were still waiting for her. However hotly she might throw them now to this night wind they would return. She was not one to throw things off and never think of them again. Yes, she could throw away, but then she might remember. If she could be sure, for instance, that she would never think of Bert again—no, put it thus, if she could be sure that she would never think of anything again except Norman—him only! But she was not so single a woman. There was Mrs. Bert Holm, who, though she were a ghost outgrown and left behind, might still be waiting where she was.

"Lord, I want to kiss you," he muttered. "I've got to kiss you."

She felt confusion mounting in her head, and ebbing away again before one desire, to turn to Norman and give him kiss for kiss. It was the primary need. And yet, hesitating, she heard faint echoes of all the things she knew. If she kissed Norman and took his kiss it would be no mere caress. Gail might count a kiss as small coin interchanged here and there, but she, Kit, never, in any circumstance. And in this one circumstance, she very well knew, and so did Norman, that it was no caress at all. If their lips met it would be the torch set at last to the tinder, and the tinder set to that illimitable fire waiting to blaze between them and envelop them both and with them millions of people.

"Kit!" he said hoarsely. She could feel his eyes burning on her in the darkness.

"Norman," she said faintly, "it's not just a kiss——"

"I don't care what it is—" he muttered. "Kit!"

He put out his hand. She was afraid and, longing, she trembled and her hands fluttered beneath his. And then when she had all but leaned to him, suddenly someone stopped beside them, and a high voice said weakly, "Excuse me, but would you give me the price of a cup of coffee?"

It was the small man with his head in a muffler under his hat and at the same moment the boat jammed against the dock and shivered and stopped.

"No," Norman said to him in fury.

"Oh dear," the man said faintly.

Norman took out money and gave it to him.

"Here—get yourself a real drink," he said angrily.

The small man clutched the coin and hurried by them to the dock. The lights were shining on them clearly now, much, much too clearly. They could not go on.

"Damn!" Norman said loudly. She did not answer. She rose restlessly and walked to the railing. No one came aboard and in a few moments the ferry backed out again and turned its nose to the farther lights.

But she did not return to him in the darkness and at last he rose and came to her.

"We're going back to where we came from," she said.

"Looks that way," he said.

Strange how a living moment, seeming inevitably ahead and about to be, could slip out of being for so foolish a cause and never come to life! But behind the little man had been a million shadows.

She walked awhile up and down the deck and Norman walked beside her. They even spoke once or twice, he to ask if she were cold and she to answer no, and to speak of how near the lights loomed now. And all the time the lost moment was not found again.

Only at the very last, when the taxi stopped in front of her own door, did he touch its fringe.

"Kit—what I said, I meant."

"I know it."

"What are you going to do about me, Kit?"

"When I know I'll tell you."

"Good night, little Kit."

"Good night, Norman."

Their hands touched and clung and parted.

There was no use in trying to sleep. She had turned often enough in her bed trying to find a spot whereon she could rest. But it was not possible to rest when within herself debate was furious. She thought, her mind glancing aside for a moment, how wonderful were the days when people decided such debate by a moral stand. If she had only been taught, for instance, as her grandmother had been taught, that divorce was wrong, any divorce for any cause, how simple all would be! It was this modern business of having to decide for one's self that was so terrific.

But she had, in the course of the hours since she left Norman, come a long way from somewhere to somewhere else. She had examined that luggage of the soul which her mother called considerations, and one by one she threw them overboard. Family, for instance, which her mother put so high, yes and Gail did, too, and Harvey with her, she would not suffer anything for family's sake. If the Tallants were so honorable and distinguished, then they could stand anything. The brunt would fall on her, anyway, not on Bert nor on the Tallants. She, Kit, must take it, and she would be compelled to take it. All over the nation women at least would cry out that she had deserted Bert. They would never understand it. Well, let them misunderstand. She threw them away. For what was a public, this public which Mr. Brame served so abjectly, what but an insatiable monster, pleased with nothing? If you bowed to it, it wearied of you; if you would not bow, it hated you and tore you to pieces. Besides, though she gave up her life for its idolatrous dream, what could the public do for her in return? It could not give her the one companionship she lacked. It could not give her the sort of love that made a home for closeness and warmth and daily intimate joy.

"If I marry Norman, I shall want a child!" The thought burst upon her like light. Mere birth was meaningless. A child must come as fruit after flower or there was no use in adding only another being to this too stupid world. She had been right to have no children. Her aversion to children had been sound instinct. Bert's children would simply have been more hostages to the public and they could never have been her own. Besides, children had to be made out of more than mere flesh and blood.

She got up at last, though the dawn was only just begun, and bathed herself and brushed her hair a long time to ease her head. In such confusion the thing to do was to plan her steps. She had seen Norman. Now she would see him no more until the confusion had become clear. To see him again would be to overweight her heart against Bert. No, the next step must be to see Bert. And in all her confusion she realized what she had not before, that not until the moment Bert came back, not until the moment he stepped before her eyes, would he be real again. When he was gone she could never remember him. There was nothing in him to lay hold upon, nothing he said and did gathered together to make a definite person, and even though she had been married to him now so long, he was still not clear to her at this moment. Tall, handsome, a ringing voice, bright blue eyes, his hair fair and straight and thick—what more? No more, until she saw him there before her and let these things appear again for him.

She wrapped herself in her old blue velvet robe and sat by the window. She must wait for Bert if decision were to be just and she would never be content with anything to come if she did less than that justice. He must bring himself before her, and in his presence she must decide her course. Norman she need not meet, because she could not forget him. She saw him as clearly, she felt him as sharply, as though he were in this room. Nothing could drive away his image. And her mind, wandering aside again, asked, "If I see him so clear and feel him so present, is that not proof enough? Why do I still hold back from him?"

For she did still hold back. Whether it was the remembrance of the hurt she had once suffered, or whether it was that she knew she might be hurt again because Norman would always be capable of hurting her, she did not know. And after a little while she perceived that these had nothing to do with her holding back. To be hurt was not important if the end were right. No, not family, not that cold and hateful public, not her own hurt delayed her. Nor, to be truthful, was it Bert—or was it? She could not tell. At this hour he was phantom.

After a long while she felt weary enough to give up thinking and perhaps to sleep. She drew down the shade and flung off her robe and went to bed and pulled the covers about her. There was indeed nothing more to think. Her mind had run its round, over and over, and stopped each time before the dead end of waiting for Bert to come.

She slept so heavily that she could barely drag herself up out of sleep to discover what was waking her. Something was waking her. She felt her hair pulled, her cheeks pinched, her palms slapped, her shoulders shaken. At last, out of desperate effort, she heard Bert's voice.

"Kit, you're not dead, are you?"

"No—no—I think not," she muttered indistinctly.

"Then wake up, Kit! I'm back!"

Bert back! Then it must be nearly noon. She had slept all morning. And now, struggling against lassitude, she opened her eyes. Yes, there he was.

"Tall—handsome—blue eyes—" she murmured.

"What you say, Kit?" he demanded, astonished.

"Out of a book—" she murmured again. Never mind if he didn't understand! She couldn't be bothered to explain.

"Kit, what's the matter with you?" he shouted.

"Nothing," she said suddenly, and sat up. But she felt a little dizzy and lay back again. "I couldn't sleep for a long time, and so I overslept at last, that's all," she said.

He was staring at her. "You weren't out on a wild party or something?"

She shook her head. "I went to a play, all by myself, and afterwards I talked awhile with the playwright!"

"Who?"

"Norman Linlay."

"Him!" he said. He looked suddenly very grave. "I should think you'd be ashamed, Kit."

She did not answer. She wished she had never told him about Norman, but she was too tired to think even about that. If she got up and took a cold shower and dressed and had lunch, then, perhaps, fortified—she got up and put on her robe.

"Mom sent you her love," Bert, watching her, lay back on her pillows. She resisted her dislike of that.

365

"Did she? Thanks." She began brushing her hair. "Everything the same?"

"Yeah, only you should of come along, Kit. They certainly were glad to see me. The town went on a real bust."

She had said she would not speak until she had dressed herself and eaten. And yet suddenly now she turned on Bert, her hairbrush poised in her hand.

"Lily, too?"

It was not in the least what she had planned to say. She had not even thought of Lily for weeks until this moment. She clapped her hand to her mouth like a child and stared at him.

He got up. "What the heck to you mean?" he demanded, and reached out as he spoke and pulled her hand away and crushed it in his. But in her astonishment she did not feel pain.

"I don't know," she said honestly. "I haven't the faintest idea why I said that; I haven't really cared about her—for a long time. I'd almost forgotten her Bert—truly."

"You mean to tell me—" he said thickly.

"That I know? Oh yes, Bert. I've known for a long time."

"And you let me think——"

"Why not?" she broke in. "Why shouldn't I let you think if you let me think?"

"You didn't tell me—" he stammered.

"You didn't tell me," she said sharply. "Besides, Bert, I did tell you all I had to tell. I told you about Norman that day, and I waited for you to tell me about Lily, and you said nothing at all. That's what I mind—and I'll always mind—that you never say anything."

"It was all over," he muttered, "long before I saw you."

"Then all the more why didn't you tell me?" she demanded fiercely and was astonished at her own anger. This was not her quarrel with Bert!

He looked at her. No, but he was amazing—his face was only complete and innocent bewilderment.

"I don't know," he said slowly. "I just don't know why, Kit. I didn't plan it that way. At first I didn't want reporters nosing in, and then after I said one thing it would have seemed funny to say another."

"But to me!" she pressed him.

"I guess," he faltered, "I guess I just sort of thought—what you didn't know wouldn't hurt you."

"But it did, you see," she said gravely.

He did not answer her. Instead he sat down on the foot of the bed and laid his arms on the footboard and hid his face in his arms. She stood looking at him. What was going through his brain? She had not the faintest knowledge. He lifted his head suddenly to ask:

"Does anybody else know?"

"My father and mother, Mr. Brame, me—that's all," she answered. "Some newspaper men, perhaps. But they never heard anything from us. We've kept it."

He stood up, turned away from her, straightened his tie, smoothed back his hair and looked at his fingernails. She could see his stubborn stupid instinct for secrecy justifying itself, though he would not look at her.

"It was a regular divorce," he said defensively.

"I knew everything," she said quietly. "Lily told me—nearly everything."

"Lily told you?" He turned to stare at her and she saw he could not believe her.

"I went to see her when you were ill, Bert," she said in the same quiet voice.

He was looking at her now hotly enough.

"Of all the damned nasty things for a wife to do—" he began.

"Why? I'd heard the rumors. And you didn't tell me anything," she reminded him again. He had to be told the same thing over and over, she knew, or he escaped it as he always escaped.

"How could I if I was sick?" he demanded.

"There were months before that," she retorted. "Weren't there?" she persisted, keeping her voice gentle.

Still he did not speak.

"Bert!" she said again.

And then she saw that once more he had made up his mind not to answer. She felt suddenly giddy with anger.

"If you don't answer me," she said, "I really will not stay with you. This time decides me."

For a moment she thought he would fly at her, strike her, shake her, and she held herself ready. But instead he burst out.

"What do you want me to say? I'll say anything—goddammit, I'm just about sick of women——"

"Very well, Bert," she said. "Let's not talk about women. I don't know why I began, anyway. She's not the real trouble. Let's talk about men. Why didn't you tell me what the men had told John Baker—what they hold against you?"

He broke in, "Kit, if I don't let on all I know sometimes, that's not telling a lie. You always act like I was lying to you just because I don't tell you something."

She was cornered by his astonished eyes and outraged voice. She could not possibly say, "Yes, I think you are, Bert," though she did think so. But if he didn't mean it so? Now he was beginning to shake her again—pity he had forever to have those clear blue eyes!

"If the men are right—" she began uncertainly.

He broke in eagerly. "Kit, if the men are right I'll say so, of course—it's the only decent thing."

"It will ruin you," she said. She looked at him, measuring him. Would he really confess himself?

She did not believe he could.

"Brame would have to get to work on it," he said shrewdly.

And then his face changed again with some sort of feeling she had never seen in him before.

"Kit, you probably won't understand me when I say what I'm going to say. But it's the truth. I'm not the same fellow I used to be before all this happened to me. I mean, the way all these people feel about me has made me different."

He hesitated and threw her an embarrassed glance.

"Yes, Bert?" Though she did not love him she felt herself wanting to help him to self-defense if she could. What magic had he, even over her? He stood, tall and beautiful as ever and she could see his beauty, even now, and his voice was charming and shy before her.

"What I mean is, I used to think only about myself, Kit, whether I was getting what I wanted everywhere and if I was having a good time and getting what I liked to eat. Now I'm different. I feel I'm responsible for myself."

She had not the least idea of his meaning. She sat down on the bed and stared at him. Was something going on in Bert that had entirely escaped her?

He looked at her solemnly. "You don't see how changed I am, Kit, but I tell you I am changed. I don't hardly drink nothing at all any more, and I don't look at a girl—I mean, even the way married men do when it doesn't mean anything, because now I don't feel I ought to behave like just anybody. All the time I was climbing that mountain I kept saying to myself, 'Bert Holm, thousands of people are thinking of you, thousands of fine Americans are saying, "Here's hoping, Bert!" They're all wanting you to get there.' And when I was dizzy with the cold wind and the snow was flying in my eyes and even my blood seemed to be aching and frozen in my veins, I kept myself going—because that's what they'd all be expecting me to do."

He came over to her and put his arms about her and said, "That was the way I am now, Kit."

She stood, letting him hold her, and put decision away again. She would not say, "But in the hotel that night you said you were thinking of me!" He believed whatever he said himself and she

369

knew it and knew that he could not help it. No, all she could do was not to decide in pity or in understanding or whatever it was that so compelled her, that childlike magic he held by some gift of nature as freakish as a poet's birth in a miller's house, or as a great musician's in a peasant's hut. She would not think of herself now. She would postpone herself again through whatever trouble lay ahead for him and after that, perhaps, she would feel free.

"I'm hungry," he remarked, letting her go.

"So am I," she said and was suddenly starved for mere food.

There was no time to be wasted before seeing Mr. Brame. All the time she was eating and listening to Bert, her inner mind was planning what she would say to Mr. Brame. He must see John Baker at once before he went to Mr. Canty. For Baker had said Mr. Canty must be told first, as the man who had invested thousands of dollars in the expedition.

"Why on earth do I care?" she inquired of herself again, watching Bert across the table. Now that he felt all was well between them again he was laughing at everything. She watched him with eyes as detached as Gail's might have been.

"You're really hatefully good-looking, Bert," she said, smiling.

"That's what Gail's always telling me," he retorted without a particle of conceit.

The amazing thing was that it was quite true; he was not conceited. He had a vast unconscious vanity, a colossal self-centeredness that was nevertheless completely amiable and free from petty conceit, and honestly enough he did not care even about his own beauty. He accepted the fact of it with enormous imperturbable complacence, but an innocent complacence. And it was true that he was different. What she had once not been able to change in him, his sullenness, his laziness, his carelessness in dress and even in cleanliness, millions of other people had been able to do simply by worshiping him. But what had finally changed him was his own desire, awaking sluggishly and slowly but steadily at last, to be as far as he could what they thought he was. In a measure he had become what their worship had made him—or at least to seem to be, her watchful irony added. She would never know whether he was or only seemed to be what he was. Simplicity so extreme was in its way as bewildering as complexity. One doubted it could be. She felt, a little grimly, that she did not like the public more for succeeding where she had failed.

Smedley was bringing in hot English muffins and, having served her, had gone to Bert and was bending beside him, his red face full of devotion.

"More butter, Smeddy," Bert said.

"Yes, sir, at once." Smedley rushed for the butter.

Smedley simply panted to give Bert all he wanted, she thought. There was no use pretending not to know he would have died for Bert. And again, why? No answering—because she herself was postponing everything for him. Well, it was only for justice, wasn't it? She was so made that she had to see justice done.

Bert's voice broke across her thoughts. He was saying cheerfully, "Get out, Smeddy. And shut the door, will you? I want to kiss my wife."

She glanced at Smedley; he would be in a misery of embarrassment. His face was nearly purple. But it was not embarrassment. He wanted to laugh!

"Yes, sir!" The words burst out of him and he rushed for the door.

"Oh, Bert!" she cried laughing too, though against her will.

He was on his feet and coming toward her. No, she would not have more of this sort of thing.

"No, Bert, please—not now," she begged him.

"Can't I kiss you again?" he demanded.

"No, please, not now," she repeated. She ought to prepare him a little. It was indecent to yield to him now only perhaps to refuse him later—everything. He should at least know her indecision, and why she postponed its end.

"Why not? I love you, don't I?" he demanded.

Characteristic—"I love you"—never, "Don't you love me?"

"I don't feel like being kissed," she said.

"Not mad at me again?" he asked.

She shook her head, and saw laughter bright again in his eyes.

"Because you don't need to be, Kit. I wasn't going to tell you, but I will, after all. You don't need to mind about Lily. She's going to get married." His great grin broke over her. "She's marrying Rexie!" he said.

She stared at him and burst into laughter she could not avoid, not laughter at what Bert had said, but at everything, herself, most of all, for thinking about Bert.

"No, Bert! Not really!" she cried, her eyes full of tears.

"Yep. I wasn't goin' to tell you—just to punish you a little, Kit —but heck, why not? Don't it make a horse laugh? She went right after him even before he got home and everybody was makin' a fuss over him. And he fell, by cable. They're going to have a bungalow all furnished modern, Kit—nice as can be."

Why was she still laughing? How absurd everything was! He was laughing too, enjoying his success with her.

"So you don't have to be jealous any more, Kit!" he roared.

Useless, impossible to attempt the task of telling him she had never for one moment been jealous of anyone! He would never understand that she had suffered not because of Lily, but because of himself.

She checked her laughter at last, half sobbing, sighed and wiped her eyes. "I must stop this nonsense and go to see Mr. Brame, Bert."

Only why? Everything would turn out lucky in the end for Bert whatever she did. Justice had nothing to do with him.

"I don't know why I bother myself, though, even for that," she said aloud. "It'll probably be all right."

"Aw, Kit, you better go," he urged her. "I'd go myself, only you'll do it better."

He was smiling down at her.

"All right then," she agreed.

"Now will you kiss me?" he demanded. And without waiting for her consent he bent over her, and again she felt the familiar freshness of his lips. She was, for the moment, helpless against him. Then she beat herself back into self awareness. At least she would not respond to his kiss! He stood up.

"Guess I'll go out for a while," he said.

He had not noticed at all that she drew herself away.

She was alone in Mr. Brame's quiet little office before she had herself back again completely. He had not yet come in from his luncheon. The gray-haired stenographer, drawing a sandwich out of a paper bag, had let her in and given her a seat in the inner office, and had gone back to the paper bag. In the silence Kit could hear mouselike rustlings and small quick gulps.

She looked about the room. Above his desk Mr. Brame had hung Bert's photograph framed and autographed. It was the largest and most conspicuous of all the photographs and Bert still looked exactly like it. How many years must pass before any change came upon that eternally young face?

The door opened and Mr. Brame came in, wiping his mustache in agitation.

"Really, Mrs. Holm, I don't know how to apologize for my delay. I seldom loiter over a meal, particularly in the middle of the day. I assure you the telegram came not an hour ago."

"I haven't come about a telegram," she said.

Mr. Brame's pallid face beamed with pleasure. "Ah, then, I am the bearer of the good news!" He took a telegram out of his vest pocket.

"Dear Mrs. Holm," he said with such unusual warmth that she was startled by the change warmth made in his small pale

373

eyes. "Dear Mrs. Holm, here is your reward. I had heard rumors of this but I had said nothing, not wanting to raise hopes only to dash them. One never knows; as a matter of fact, I believe the vote was very close between you and the President's wife. Allow me to congratulate you on a richly deserved honor, Mrs. Holm!"

She took a telegram from his excited hand and read, wondering,

"You have been unanimously chosen to receive our gold medal as most successful American woman of the year, in recognition of your outstanding qualities as a wife and homemaker for our beloved national hero Bert Holm. League of American Homemakers."

She looked at Mr. Brame, stunned by the malevolence, the absurdity, the ridiculously-timed accurate irony of what she held in her hand.

"It is a joke?" she whispered.

"Indeed it is not," he said heartily. "It's completely sincere and a wonderful tribute."

"I don't want it. I can't take it," she said. She put the telegram on his desk. "I should have telephoned you why I came but I had something urgent and I came straight on. Please let's put the telegram aside. I must talk about something important, Mr. Brame."

"Yes, certainly, if you wish." Mr. Brame coughed and patted his lips with his handkerchief and sat down, smelling faintly, she perceived, of lamb chops. He was trying as quickly as he could to put aside the matter of the telegram.

"I don't know if you know," she began quietly, "that John Baker has in his possession a serious charge against my husband." She stumbled slightly over "my husband" and then she went on. "It concerns the death of Ronald Brugh."

Mr. Brame's pale eyes bulged a little at her. He forgot the telegram completely.

"Will you explain, Mrs. Holm? I'm afraid I don't take it in exactly," he said.

She explained as quickly as she could the four letters John Baker had read aloud in her father's office. She concealed, though with a sense of guilt her own distrust in the hotel and remembering this morning, she said, "Of course he was innocent of intention to harm Ronald Brugh——"

Mr. Brame interrupted her.

"Why, it's horrible!" He sat in complete dejection, staring at her. "It's perfectly awful! I've built all the new publicity on Bert Holm's fineness to his men. Unfortunately, I don't suppose there is a more reliable man in the country than Baker. Anything he said would have to be accepted. I've never had such a thing happen before. Why, it's even worse than what happened to poor Charley Bigge!"

"I'm afraid I don't know what you mean," she said. Mr. Brame looked near to weeping.

"Why, my whole build-up—everything—it would all go like a skyscraper in an earthquake! You don't know how peculiar the public is about its heroes; they don't allow the least failure, Mrs. Holm. If in one little thing the hero isn't what they thought he was——"

"But the truth—" she began. He cut her off.

"Truth can be too disastrous to be believed, Mrs. Holm. Besides, there are all kinds of truth. Take Bert Holm, for instance. He exists, doesn't he? I don't mean your husband, Mrs. Holm, I mean the real Bert Holm, the hero, the man everybody knows and admires. He exists, just because people think he does."

He had no idea of what he had just said—not her husband, but the real Bert Holm.

"Why, he stands for the very image of truth to millions of people. You do not know—no one does except me, because I've seen him grow from that fair-haired boy who burst upon the crowd, to this public figure he now is, a man everybody believes in. Bert Holm could run for President if he wanted to on any ticket he chose. He'd be sure fire. The people would choose him because—here, look at these letters, Mrs. Holm. They'll show you what I mean. He's an actual part of all these lives."

Mr. Brame began in a frenzy to pull out one file folder after another.

"I've filed all of them by states, Mrs. Holm, Alabama, California, Connecticut—not many from there—Delaware, Georgia, Kansas, Kentucky—well, you'll find the whole country here and some from Americans abroad. It was a great question how to classify them." He stopped to give her a pale glimmer of a twinkle. "Once I thought I would do it by qualities or virtues, all alphabetically, of course, the great things we love to think we have more than other people—Ambition, Amiability, and so on— B for Bravery—Courage, you see, and Candor, Chastity—that would be very important—and after that, Daring and Drive and— skip E—and Frankness and Goodness and Honor—Home Life, you know—there would be a lot in that after your own medal— and a lot on R—Romance—that would have been mostly about you and Mr. Holm and your perfect marriage—and so forth. I've even got letters I could have put into Z—Zest, you know. But I gave up the idea as being perhaps a little romantic for a business office."

She laughed a little sadly with him and then forgot laughter. "Mr. Brame, if John Baker is right——"

Mr. Brame grew still more excited. "I'm going this instant to find John Baker. Mrs. Holm, right or wrong has nothing at all to do with this. Now John Baker could be absolutely right in one thing and absolutely wrong in a big national thing like Bert Holm."

She was bewildered.

"If you please—Mr. Brame——"

But he was pouring letters out of the files recklessly.

"Please, Mrs. Holm—if you'll just see for yourself what I mean.

You aren't in too much of a hurry, are you? Just read these letters and see what they say—letters from all sorts of people; there's even one from the President of the United States. If you'll just read them, Mrs. Holm, and I'll leave you a little time while I talk to Mr. Baker. I am beginning already to think of a possible program of action. If you'll forgive me for insisting, Mrs. Holm, I do want you to read these letters so that you will understand my peculiar responsibility to all these people and to thousands of others who shape their beliefs about anything by what Bert Holm says. They'd be lost without him, anyway until some one else comes to take his place. You can't build something up as I have, and then just destroy it. Excuse me, Mrs. Holm, I'll be back as soon as I can."

He shut the door of the office softly and she was alone. . . . No, not alone. The desk was piled high with the letters. For a moment she did not touch them. She had not for a long time read any of Bert's enormous mail. It was only another intrusion into their life, an intrusion not so easily repelled as photographers and reporters and sight-seers and all the visible forms of persons at the door. Letters, she had often thought, passing the great daily stack of them on the mail tray in the hall, were worse than any of them, for by virtue of three cents apiece people forced their way beyond the door into the house and made their demands. She had been glad enough when Mr. Brame wanted the letters and it had become Smedley's business to see them taken away as soon as they came.

But they had been here, after all, lying in wait for her. She reached out an unwilling hand and picked one up—a small cheap white sheet of paper, a girl's probably, a servant girl's.

But it was not. It was a letter written by a young boy, a cripple, a boy who dreamed of airplanes and flying and spent his days in a chair with his legs in steel braces. He had written this not long ago—she glanced at the date—when Bert was climbing Pangbat.

"Every day I read in the newspapers about how you are fighting your way up the mountain. I got my mother to find me a book in the library about mountain climbing. I wish I could buy the book to keep it to help me remember. But we are poor so I can't. But I would like you to know that you help me to keep on fighting, too, and trying to walk. Every day I say, 'Bert Holm's fighting his way, step by step. I can, too.' So I get up and take one step and then the next, and I pretend I am climbing beside you. And when I sweat I think about how the going is hard for you, and when it hurts I pretend it's frostbite, and I got to rub my legs like you do when you start freezing."

She put the letter down. She could hear the boy's voice. "I'm sentimental," she thought scornfully. But she took up another letter and another.

"Dear Bert, you are so wise, so wonderful, tell me what to do. The man I love doesn't love me."

"Bert, do you believe a man has to stay by his mother just because she won't learn to like the girl he wants to marry?"

"Bert, I have lost my job and have three children——"

"Bert, do you believe there's going to be war——"

Voice upon voice upon voice of the people crying to Him!

This was that public she had so hated and feared. She saw them and heard them at last and knew them for what they were —only people, separately feeling and longing and searching for that which they could worship, since worship they must, being helpless in themselves. If she tore down by her desertion the image they had made to worship, how could she escape what she did?

She sat swept into a comprehension suddenly as vast as the universe. She leaned her head on her hands and trembled with comprehension and would have wept and could not. Tears were too small, herself even too small, before this immense pathetic need of helpless beings to worship and to dream. And upon her like a judgment came certainty, inexorable and huge. She could not break the image. She was no iconoclast. She could not break into the temple and smash down the god. She dared not. For then there would be only emptiness—the awful emptiness of the dream lost. No, not when she herself had gone through that once upon a time could she bring it to pass upon the least of these. She saw something else. She saw now the real reason why she had not gone to Norman at once, even for love. Norman could not put back himself, whom he had torn down from that high place where once she had worshiped him—never, never! He could never be again to her what once he had been—a god, a dream. She could not, in the pitiless clarity out of what she had herself known and suffered destroy the dream of all these to whom Bert Holm meant Achievement—Ambition—Bravery—Courage—Chastity—Daring—Frankness—Generosity— Her mind rushed over the big beautiful words that held, like golden grails, the highest that millions of people together can imagine in a god.

She could not do it. As quietly as the sun sets upon the day, she gave up her separate secret hope of the end which she had thought might be. No, she was so made that she could not do it. The dream must be kept, whole and undimmed, in all the glory of its untruth. For it did not matter what Bert Holm really was. It mattered less what she was and whether or not she was happy. Besides, she could never be happy anyway, not if she betrayed these voices. She knew herself.

She picked up the telegram she had thrown down and read it again, "You have been unanimously chosen——"

The door burst open and Mr. Brame came in. He was looking cheerful again.

"Ah, Mrs. Holm!" he said. "I do hope you have reconsidered that!"

"How can I accept it?" she asked. Indeed how could she?

Mr. Brame saw her distress and entirely misunderstood it.

"Dear lady," he said soothingly, and sat down. "It is natural, with your modesty, that you should feel overwhelmed, but believe me when I tell you that millions of people will rejoice in this recognition of Bert Holm's wife. Now just leave it all to me. I will frame a suitable acceptance and arrange the occasion for the presentation of the medal. Don't give it a thought; just remember how much pleasure you will be giving many faithful women, working obscurely in their homes, who in you fulfill themselves."

She woke enough in her stunned silence, the yellow paper in her hand, to think, "He's preparing the publicity already." But Mr. Brame was going on. "Perhaps I had better say to be accurate, their dreams——"

That one familiar word brought back her senses. She put the yellow paper down on the pile of letters. Dreams!

"Whatever you say, Mr. Brame," she said quietly. Sometime she was going to laugh and laugh, sometime when she was quite alone and dared to begin laughter that would inevitably end in weeping. But this was not the time for anything except going on as she was. "Shall we go on?" she asked.

"Indeed, yes," Mr. Brame said gladly. "I've been gone unforgivably long, but Baker wanted to see me at once. We had a talk. I put it up to him. There is too much at stake. I feel responsible, I told him. I don't know if I make my point of view clear, Mrs. Holm. I am, perhaps, too sensitive about the public. But they believe in Bert Holm. In a sense, Mrs. Holm"—he sat down and looked at her shyly over the heap of letters—"I can't—let them down—not just on someone's say-so, that is. Besides, nothing will bring the man to life again."

"No, nothing will bring back what is dead," she agreed.

"Exactly," Mr. Brame said. "I put it to Baker, and at last he saw that he had no real proof. He said something about a promise to you that seemed to settle his own decision. I was relieved. Now even if it should leak out after a while that there was—ah —something more than—an unfortunate accident up there, if the thing is handled right——"

380

She interrupted him.

"I am sure it was purely an accident, Mr. Brame."

"You are?" he exclaimed.

"Absolutely," she said firmly. Yes, she was sure. Bert was only a fool.

"Then," Mr. Brame said briskly, "I can fight it through." He leaned back, sighed and smiled. "I don't mind telling you," he remarked, "I was more scared an hour ago than the day you came in here and talked about a divorce. Well, that passed, and you've received your reward in this telegram. If the American Homemakers knew, I am sure they would only appreciate you the more. But for a moment what Baker said was a horrible possibility. I saw Bert Holm accused of—of murder, even."

"He is as innocent as a child," she said.

"Yes, of course he is," Mr. Brame said. "Well, his men may talk, but a nation full of people won't believe a handful of men. This will pass too."

"Yes," she agreed, "it will all pass—" She looked across the desk at this peculiar man, and suddenly she saw that he at least would understand her. "After all, dreams are all that most people have to live by," she said. "Out of mere duty, one can't—destroy them."

He looked back at her with a startled pleasure.

"Exactly," he said. "You see it."

But what she really saw in his pale appreciative eyes was his own soul, as wistful as any other. As little as any other could it have endured the destruction threatened to the image he had made. Then he coughed and covered his soul.

"Now," he said briskly, "now for the build-up——"